STAR
WARS
LEGACY OF THE FORCE

EXILE

By Aaron Allston

Galatea in 2-D

Bard's Tale Series (with Holly Lisle)
Thunder of the Captains
Wrath of the Princes

Car Warriors Series
Double Jeopardy

Doc Sidhe Series
Doc Sidhe
Sidhe-Devil

Terminator 3 Series
Terminator Dream
Terminator Hunt

Star Wars: X-Wing Series
Wraith Squadron
Iron Fist
Solo Command
Starfighters of Adumar

Star Wars: New Jedi Order
Enemy Lines I: *Rebel Dream*
Enemy Lines II: *Rebel Stand*

Star Wars: Legacy of the Force
Betrayal
Exile

EXILE

AARON ALLSTON

BALLANTINE BOOKS • NEW YORK

Star Wars: Legacy of the Force: Exile is a work of fiction. Names, places, and incidents either are products of the author's imagination or are used fictitiously.

A Del Rey Books Mass Market Original

Published in the United States by Del Rey Books, an imprint of The Random House Publishing Group, a division of Random House, Inc., New York.

DEL REY is a registered trademark and the Del Rey colophon is a trademark of Random House, Inc.

This book contains an excerpt from the forthcoming book *Star Wars: Legacy of the Force: Sacrifice* by Karen Traviss. This excerpt has been set for this edition only and may not reflect the final content of the forthcoming edition.

ISBN 978-0-345-47753-8

Printed in the United States of America

www.starwars.com
www.legacyoftheforce.com
www.delreybooks.com

OPM 9 8 7 6 5 4 3 2 1

acknowledgments

Thanks go to my editor, Shelly Shapiro; to Keith Clayton of Del Rey; to Sue Rostoni and Leland Chee of Lucas Licensing, for tieing off loose ends and untieing knotted plot problems; to my agent, Russell Galen; and to my Eagle-Eyes (Chris Cassidy, Kelly Frieders, Helen Keier, Bob Quinlan, Roxanne Quinlan, and Luray Richmond).

THE STAR WARS NOVELS TIMELINE

1020 YEARS BEFORE STAR WARS: *A New Hope*

Darth Bane: Path of Destruction

33 YEARS BEFORE STAR WARS: *A New Hope*

Darth Maul: Saboteur*

32.5 *YEARS BEFORE STAR WARS: A New Hope*

Cloak of Deception
Darth Maul: Shadow Hunter

32 *YEARS BEFORE STAR WARS: A New Hope*

STAR WARS: EPISODE I
THE PHANTOM MENACE

29 *YEARS BEFORE STAR WARS: A New Hope*

Rogue Planet

27 *YEARS BEFORE STAR WARS: A New Hope*

Outbound Flight

22.5 *YEARS BEFORE STAR WARS: A New Hope*

The Approaching Storm

22 *YEARS BEFORE STAR WARS: A New Hope*

STAR WARS: EPISODE II
ATTACK OF THE CLONES

Republic Commando: Hard Contact

21.5 *YEARS BEFORE STAR WARS: A New Hope*

Shatterpoint

21 *YEARS BEFORE STAR WARS: A New Hope*

The Cestus Deception
The Hive*

Republic Commando: Triple Zero

20 *YEARS BEFORE STAR WARS: A New Hope*

MedStar I: Battle Surgeons
MedStar II: Jedi Healer

19.5 *YEARS BEFORE STAR WARS: A New Hope*

Jedi Trial
Yoda: Dark Rendezvous

19 *YEARS BEFORE STAR WARS: A New Hope*

Labyrinth of Evil

STAR WARS: EPISODE III
REVENGE OF THE SITH

Dark Lord: The Rise of Darth Vader

10-0 *YEARS BEFORE STAR WARS: A New Hope*

The Han Solo Trilogy:
The Paradise Snare
The Hutt Gambit
Rebel Dawn

5-2 *YEARS BEFORE STAR WARS: A New Hope*

The Adventures of Lando Calrissian

The Han Solo Adventures

STAR WARS: *A New Hope* YEAR 0

STAR WARS: EPISODE IV
A NEW HOPE

0-3 *YEARS AFTER STAR WARS: A New Hope*

Tales from the Mos Eisley Cantina
Galaxies: The Ruins of Dantooine
Splinter of the Mind's Eye

3 *YEARS AFTER STAR WARS: A New Hope*

STAR WARS: EPISODE V
THE EMPIRE STRIKES BACK

Tales of the Bounty Hunters

3.5 *YEARS AFTER STAR WARS: A New Hope*

Shadows of the Empire

4 *YEARS AFTER STAR WARS: A New Hope*

STAR WARS: EPISODE VI
RETURN OF THE JEDI

Tales from Jabba's Palace
Tales from the Empire
Tales from the New Republic

The Bounty Hunter Wars:
The Mandalorian Armor
Slave Ship
Hard Merchandise

The Truce at Bakura

6.5-7.5 YEARS AFTER *STAR WARS: A New Hope*

X-Wing:
Rogue Squadron
Wedge's Gamble
The Krytos Trap
The Bacta War
Wraith Squadron
Iron Fist
Solo Command

8 *YEARS AFTER STAR WARS: A New Hope*

The Courtship of Princess Leia
A Forest Apart*
Tatooine Ghost

9 *YEARS AFTER STAR WARS: A New Hope*

The Thrawn Trilogy:
Heir to the Empire
Dark Force Rising
The Last Command

X-Wing: Isard's Revenge

11 *YEARS AFTER STAR WARS: A New Hope*

The Jedi Academy Trilogy:
Jedi Search
Dark Apprentice
Champions of the Force

I, Jedi

12-13 *YEARS AFTER STAR WARS: A New Hope*

Children of the Jedi
Darksaber
Planet of Twilight
X-Wing: Starfighters of Adumar

14 *YEARS AFTER STAR WARS: A New Hope*

The Crystal Star

16-17 *YEARS AFTER STAR WARS: A New Hope*

The Black Fleet Crisis Trilogy:
Before the Storm
Shield of Lies
Tyrant's Test

17 *YEARS AFTER STAR WARS: A New Hope*

The New Rebellion

18 *YEARS AFTER STAR WARS: A New Hope*

The Corellian Trilogy:
Ambush at Corellia
Assault at Selonia

19 *YEARS AFTER STAR WARS: A New Hope*

The Hand of Thrawn Duology:
Specter of the Past
Vision of the Future

Showdown at Centerpoint

22 *YEARS AFTER STAR WARS: A New Hope*

25 YEARS AFTER *STAR WARS: A New Hope*

Boba Fett: A Practical Man*

The New Jedi Order:
Vector Prime
Dark Tide I: Onslaught
Dark Tide II: Ruin
Agents of Chaos I: Hero's Trial
Agents of Chaos II: Jedi Eclipse
Balance Point
Recovery*
Edge of Victory I: Conquest
Edge of Victory II: Rebirth
Star by Star
Dark Journey
Enemy Lines I: Rebel Dream
Enemy Lines II: Rebel Stand
Traitor
Destiny's Way
Ylesia*
Force Heretic I: Remnant
Force Heretic II: Refugee
Force Heretic III: Reunion
The Final Prophecy
The Unifying Force

35 *YEARS AFTER STAR WARS: A New Hope*

The Dark Nest Trilogy:
The Joiner King
The Unseen Queen
The Swarm War

40 YEARS AFTER *STAR WARS: A New Hope*

Legacy of the Force:
Betrayal
Bloodlines
Tempest
Exile
Sacrifice
Inferno

*An ebook novella

dramatis personae

Alema Rar; Dark Jedi (Twi'lek female)
Ben Skywalker; Jedi apprentice (human male)
Booster Terrik; captain, *Errant Venture* (human male)
Cha Niathal; Galactic Alliance admiral (Mon Calamari female)
Corran Horn; Jedi Master (human male)
Han Solo; captain, *Millennium Falcon* (human male)
Iella Antilles; operative (human female)
Jacen Solo; Jedi Knight and commander, Galactic Alliance Guard (human male)
Jagged Fel; operative (human male)
Jaina Solo; Jedi Knight (human female)
Kiara; Chud (human female)
Lando Calrissian; entrepreneur (human male)
Leia Organa Solo; Jedi Knight and co-pilot *Millennium Falcon* (human female)
Luke Skywalker; Jedi Grand Master (human male)
Lumiya; Dark Lady of the Sith (human female)
Mara Jade Skywalker; Jedi Master (human female)
Matric Klauskin; Commenorian admiral (human male)
Mirax Terrik Horn; operative (human female)

Myri Antilles; intelligence operative (human female)
Shaker; R2 astromeck droid
Uran Lavint; smuggling ship captain (human female)
Wedge Antilles; Corellian admiral (human male)
Zekk; Jedi Knight (human male)

chapter one

OUTSIDE CORELLIAN SPACE
STAR DESTROYER **ANAKIN SOLO**

It wasn't exactly guilt that kept Jacen awake night after night. Rather, it was an awareness that he *should* feel guilty, but didn't, quite.

Jacen leaned back in a chair comfortable enough to sleep in, its leather as soft as blue butter, and stared at the stars.

The blast shields were withdrawn from the oversized viewport of his private office, and the chamber itself was dark, giving him an unencumbered view of space.

His office was on the port side, the bow was oriented toward the sun Corell, and the stern was pointed back toward Coruscant, so he'd be looking toward Commenor, Kuat, the Hapes Cluster, the length of the Perlemian Trade Route . . . But he did not try to pick out these stars individually. Astronomy was a lifelong occupation for people who spent their entire existences on only one planet; how much harder must such a study be for someone like Jacen, who traveled from star to star throughout his life?

He let his eyelids sag, but his mind continued to race, as it had every day since he and his task force had rescued Queen Mother Tenel Ka of the Hapes Consortium from an insurrection, instigated by treacherous Hapan nobles aided by a Corellian fleet.

In the midst of all those events, believing that Han and Leia Solo had been part of the plot, Jacen had ordered the *Anakin Solo*'s long-range turbolasers brought to bear against the *Millennium Falcon*. Later, he had heard compelling evidence that his parents had played no part in that plot.

So where was the guilt? Where was the horror he should have felt at an attempted act of patricide and matricide? What sort of father could he be to Allana if he could do this without remorse?

He didn't know. And he was certain that until he did know, sleep would continue to elude him.

Behind his chair, a lightsaber came to life with its characteristic *snap-hiss*, and the office was suddenly bathed in blue light. Jacen was on his feet before the intruder's blade had been fully extended, his own lightsaber in hand, thumbing its blade to life, gesturing with his free hand to direct the Force to sweep his chair out of the way.

When it was clear, he could look upon the intruder—she was small enough that the chair had concealed all but the tip of her glowing weapon.

On the other side of the desk stood his mother, Leia Organa Solo. But she did not carry her own lightsaber. Jacen recognized it by its hilt, its color. It was the lightsaber Mara Jade Skywalker had carried for so many years. Luke Skywalker's first lightsaber. Anakin Skywalker's last lightsaber.

Leia wore brown Jedi robes, and her hair was down, loose. She held her lightsaber in a two-handed grip, point up and hilt back, ready to strike.

"Hello, Mother." This seemed like an appropriate time for the more formal term, rather than *Mom*. "Have you come to kill me?"

She nodded. "I have."

"Before you attack—how did you get aboard? And how did you get into this office?"

She shook her head, her expression sorrowful. "Do you think ordinary defenses can mean anything at a time like this?"

"Perhaps not." He shrugged. "I know you're an experienced Jedi, Mother, but you're not a match for any Jedi Knight who's been fighting and training constantly throughout his career . . . because you haven't."

"And yet I'm going to kill you."

"I don't think so. I'm prepared for any tactic, any ploy you're likely to use."

Now she did smile. It was the smile he'd seen her turn on political enemies when they'd made the final mistakes of their careers, the feral smile of a war-dog toying with its prey. "*Likely* to use. Don't you know that the whole book of tactics changes when the attacker has chosen not to survive the fight?"

Her face twisted into a mask of anger and betrayal. She released her grip on the lightsaber hilt with her left hand and reached out, pushing. Jacen felt the sudden buildup of Force energy within her.

He twisted to one side. Her exertion in the Force would miss him—

And then he realized, too late, that it was *supposed* to.

The Force energy hurtled past him and hit the viewport dead center, buckling it, smashing it out into the void of space.

Jacen leapt away. If he could catch the rim of the doorway into the office, hold on there for the second or two it took for the blast shutters to close, he would not be drawn out through the viewport—

But Leia's own leap intercepted his. She slammed into him, her arms wrapping around him, her lightsaber falling away. Together they flew through the viewport.

Jacen felt coldness cut through his skin and deaden it. He

felt air rush out from his lungs, a death rattle no one could hear. He felt pain in his head, behind his brow ridge, from his eyes, as they swelled and prepared to burst.

And all the while Leia's mouth was working as though she were still speaking. For one improbable moment he wondered if she would talk forever, rebuking her son as they twirled, dead, throughout eternity.

Then, as in those last seconds he knew he must, he awoke, once again seated in his comfortable chair, once again staring at the stars.

A dream. Or a sending? He spoke aloud: "Was that you?" And he waited, half expecting Lumiya to answer, but no response came.

He turned his chair around and found his office to be reassuringly empty. With a desktop control, he closed the blast shutters over his viewport.

Finally, he consulted his chrono.

Fifteen standard minutes had passed since the last time he'd checked it. He'd had at most ten minutes of sleep.

He put his booted feet up on the desktop, leaned back, and tried to slow his racing heart.

And to sleep.

CORUSCANT
GALACTIC ALLIANCE TRANSPORTATION DEPOT, NEAR THE JEDI TEMPLE

The *Beetle Nebula* settled down to a landing on an elevated docking platform adjacent to the blue, mushroom-shaped transportation depot. The maneuver was smooth and gentle for a craft so large—at two hundred meters, the *Freebooter*-class transport was an awkward-looking vessel anywhere but in space. From above, she looked like a crescent moon bisected by a knife blade, the blade point oriented in the same direction as the crescent tips, and her wide, curved stern put observers in mind more of fat-bottomed banthas than of sleek, stylish vessels of war.

But that wide stern could carry large volumes of personnel and matériel, and in the moments after the ship settled onto her landing pylons, a dozen loading ramps came down and began disgorging streams of uniformed soldiers—many on leave, others, riding repulsorlift-based medical gurneys, being guided to hospitals.

From a much smaller platform fifty meters from the *Beetle Nebula*'s starboard bow, Jedi Master Kyp Durron watched the event unfold. At this distance, he could barely see facial features of the new arrivals, but could distinguish enough to see faces light up with happiness as they recognized loved ones in the crowd below.

And through the Force he could feel the emotion of the day. It swelled from the *Beetle Nebula* and her surroundings. Pain radiated from shattered bones and seared stumps that had once been connected to organic limbs. Pain flowed from remembrances of how those injuries were sustained and of how friends had been lost forever to battle.

But more than that, there were sentiments of relief and happiness. People were returning home from battle, here to rest and recover. They were veterans of the extraordinary space battle that had so recently been waged in the Hapan system. Some of the veterans knew pride in their role in that battle, some knew shame or regret, but all were glad it was over. All were glad to be here.

And for a few quiet moments, Kyp relaxed, letting the emotions from the other platform wash over him like a cool, refreshing stream in summertime. The muted nature of the sounds of welcome from that platform, of Coruscant air traffic not too far away, of transport and commerce from the adjacent depot, allowed him to stay comfortable, detached.

Then he felt new presences in the Force, specific presences for whom he had been waiting. He glanced away from the depot and up, toward the origin of that sensation, and saw the *Jade Shadow* on an approach angle straight toward him.

The craft approached the depot at a speed slightly faster than safe, then rapidly decelerated and dropped to a smooth repulsorlift landing atop the platform, mere meters from Kyp. He grinned. Whoever was piloting—probably Mara—had either playfully or maliciously made the approach as intimidating as possible, the better to spook him into sudden retreat. Of course, he hadn't budged. He waved a hand at the shapes within the cockpit, indistinct behind its viewscreens, and waited.

Soon enough the boarding ramp descended and down trotted Luke Skywalker and Mara Jade Skywalker. They were dressed simply, Luke in black, Mara, for once, in the standard two-shades-of-brown Jedi robes.

Kyp offered a smile and extended a hand to Luke. "Grand Master Skywalker."

Luke took it. "Master Durron."

"And Master Skywalker."

Mara gave him a nod of greeting, but Kyp detected a trace of irritation or impatience. "Master Durron."

"That's a new hand, I take it." Kyp released his grip. "I heard about your injuries. How does it compare with the old one?"

Luke held up his right hand and looked at his palm. "The neural matrix is more sophisticated, so it feels even more like flesh and blood. But—you know how a droid whose memory is never wiped tends to become more individual, more idiosyncratic."

Kyp nodded. "You're not suggesting that a prosthetic hand does the same thing. It doesn't have enough memory."

Luke shrugged. "I don't know what I'm suggesting. Maybe through the Force my brain developed a familiarity with the old hand that exceeded what's normal. Regardless, this one doesn't feel right yet."

"Meaning," Mara said, "that he's dropped from being the most accomplished lightsaber artist in the galaxy to, well, still being the most accomplished, just a little less so for the time being."

"Aunt Mara? Oops. Hello, Kyp. Master Durron." The voice was Jaina Solo's, and Kyp looked up to see the diminutive Jedi at the top of the boarding ramp.

"Jaina." Kyp gave her a friendly nod. He steered his thoughts away from the time, years ago, when he had fixated on her, when she was still a teenager, when he was a younger, more self-centered man who hadn't recognized that his interest in her was more about loneliness and self-appreciation than it was about anything else.

Here today, he pretended that she had never meant anything more to him than the daughter of his oldest surviving friend should. She, perhaps, didn't have to pretend. Giving Kyp a brief smile, she returned her attention to Mara. "So can I take Zekk and Ben to the Temple now?"

Mara nodded. "I think so. Kyp, any reason to delay?"

"No." He glanced to the left, where the nearby Jedi Temple was clearly visible just past the *Jade Shadow*'s stern. "Unless you'd like to save your engines—I can just pick you up and set you down over there." He reached out with his hand, palm up, an overly dramatic gesture, and the *Jade Shadow* vibrated for a moment, moving under the pressure he exerted with the Force.

Jaina gave him a reproving look. She turned around, and the boarding ramp lifted into place, concealing her.

"How *is* Zekk?" Kyp asked.

Mara looked unconcerned. "He'll make a full recovery. The surgeons on Hapes were very proficient. But he'll be out of action for a while." Her expression became concerned. "How many people know how it happened?"

"Just me, for the moment." Kyp gestured to the far side

of the platform, adjacent to the depot. "My speeder's over here." Once they were all moving toward his vehicle, he continued, "I was assigned the investigation on this one." All lightsaber accidents that caused any harm to a living being had to be looked into, and any Master on duty at the Temple might be randomly assigned the duty of investigation.

Mara's face set. "Everybody who witnessed it said it was an accident."

Kyp nodded. "Of course, and Luke's report makes it pretty clear what happened. So I should dispense with our customs, not investigate at all, take the day off?" They reached the platform edge and Kyp's airspeeder, a long, narrow yellow vehicle with comfortable seats in front and a backseat that looked as though it were scaled for children. Kyp hopped into the pilot's seat and extended a gallant hand for Mara.

She gave him an admonishing look and leapt past him into the front passenger's seat. "No, of course not." She sat. "I'm just a little touchy about it, I suppose. *My* son has a lightsaber accident. Suddenly I feel the eyes of all the Jedi in the galaxy on me."

Luke stepped into the backseat and settled behind Kyp. "So what is this all about?"

Kyp sank into the pilot's seat, activated the speeder, and pulled straight back in a speedy reverse that put them within meters of the nearest cross-traffic stream. "You don't want to sit right behind me. Trust me." He swerved so he was pointed in the direction of the traffic stream's travel and accelerated, as though he were playing a *Millennium Falcon* simulator, to merge with the stream.

"Why not—oh."

Caught by the wind, Kyp's hair was pulled from where it lay within the hood of his Jedi cloak. Stretched to full length, its tips whipped mere centimeters in front of Luke's eyes and occasionally tickled his nose.

Luke slid sideways to the center of the seat. "You've grown it out."

Kyp reached up to give his hair an indulgent stroke, then grinned at his simulated display of vanity. "I've been seeing a lady who likes it long. And doesn't mind all the gray in it."

"Congratulations. So again, what is this all about?"

"Chief Omas and Admiral Niathal wanted to see you on your return from Hapes. They asked me to bring you. You can opt out if the timing isn't good."

Mara gave him a puzzled frown. "Is this about what happened on Hapes?"

"Sort of." Kyp gave her a broad, trouble-loving smile. "This time, *they* want Luke to make Jacen a Jedi Master."

OUTSIDE THE CORELLIAN SYSTEM
CARGO VESSEL BREATHE MY JETS

Captain Uran Lavint was an heir to the tradition of Han Solo.

That's how she saw herself, at any rate, and she was indeed a smuggler. Nor was she a small-scale smuggler. Her cargo ship, *Breathe My Jets,* had hold space large enough to carry several *Millennium Falcons*. Nor did she always make solitary smuggling trips—some missions, like this one, were small fleet operations.

Still, she was not rich, not even financially comfortable. Creditors—more successful smugglers, members of organized crime—now demanded their due whenever they could contact her, whenever they could catch up to her during *Breathe My Jets*'s brief stays in port. She'd been threatened, she'd taken a beating at a landfall on Tatooine, and rumor had it that one creditor had given up and hired a bounty hunter to eliminate her—to demonstrate the folly of not paying on time.

She needed this mission to go well. If it did, she could

pay everyone off, start over. If it didn't, she might find herself in a position to describe *explosive decompression* in a firsthand account.

Now she looked at the distant star Corell through the bridge's forward viewport as she sat slumped in her captain's chair. She sagged not out of defeat, but from habit and a deliberate attitude of indifference that gave her a reputation for being cool under fire. Though born to well-fed, well-tended middle-manager parents on Bespin, she now had skin like Tatooine leather and a craggy face that might have benefited from a drooping mustache.

Grudgingly, she sat upright. Glancing at the undersized, youthful Hutt in the specially designed copilot's couch beside her, she nodded. "All right, Blatta. Put me on."

Blatta flipped a switch on the control panel before him. A display there lit up and showed Captain Lavint's face, a live holocam feed. He spoke in typically deep, gooey Hutt tones. "Broadcast in five, four, three . . ." He held up two fingers, silently signaling the continuation of the countdown, then one, then closed his fist to indicate they were broadcasting.

Lavint stared into the holocam recorder. "Captain to fleet. In a minute I will broadcast the nav data for our final jump. That jump will bring us as close as the planet Corellia's gravity well will allow, and then one of two things will happen—we'll be jumped by Galactic Alliance forces, or we won't.

"If we're not, congratulations—the armaments and bacta we're carrying will earn us tidy profits. If we are, our instructions are clear: break and run, straight down into Corellia's atmosphere. It's every ship for herself. You see your best friend being assaulted, you wish him well and get down to ground. Don't hang back and fight to free him.

"Good luck." She gave her viewers a brisk nod, and Blatta cut the transmission.

"Nav data?" he asked.

"Send it."

He did. The instant he did so, a one-minute chron timer appeared on both cockpit displays, counting down. It was just enough time for the fleet's captains and navigators to load the data and test it, not enough time for them to waste and increase their jitters.

More or less as a single body, the thirty-odd ships and vehicles of the fleet accelerated, pointing straight for the distant, unseen planet. Those who had defensive shields activated them. And at exactly the same moment, each cockpit crew saw the stars before them lengthen and begin the axial swirling that was the visual characteristic of hyperspace entry.

This jump would take only a few seconds—

It took less than that. They'd been in hyperspace half the time they should have been when the stars stopped spinning and snapped back into distant points of light. Corell was larger, closer, but not as close as the sun should be, and there was no comforting sight of the planet Corellia directly ahead of them. Instead, there was empty space decorated with the occasional fast-moving colored twinkle of light.

Lavint swore, but her invective was drowned out by Blatta's shout: "Enemy ships! Chevron formation. We're toward the point, and the two flanks are falling in on our formation."

"Which one's the Interdictor?" One of the enemy ships had to be some sort of Interdictor, a capital ship carrying gravity-well generators—devices that would project a gravity field of sufficient strength to yank ships right out of hyperspace.

Blatta highlighted a point of light on his display, and it began blinking on Lavint's display as well. It was just at the point of the chevron, directly ahead of Lavint's ship.

Lavint keyed her comm. "Captain Lavint to fleet. Maintain formation, match speed with me. Our only chance—"

On the sensor display, the crisp line of her fleet was blurring as each member craft vectored in a different direction.

"No, no, maintain formation!" She couldn't keep the desperation out of her voice. The original orders to scatter only made sense if every craft was a short distance from the safe haven of Corellia—didn't the idiots see that? "We've got to run this gauntlet at high speed—"

"Belay that," came a voice over the comm. It was female and a bit rough, a close match to Lavint's own. "This is the real Captain Lavint. Follow your orders. Scatter." *This* voice was calm, self-assured.

Blatta nodded as if impressed. "Sounds just like you."

"Shut up." Lavint put her cargo ship on a new course, vectoring downward relative to her current orientation.

Blatta offered up a sigh. It sounded like a bantha passing gas. "At least they can't know which vessel is carrying which cargo. Since we're not the biggest ship in the fleet, they might not pay us special attention—"

Breathe My Jets shuddered so hard that Lavint's teeth clacked together and Blatta shook like a plate full of Corellian spice-jelly. The cockpit lights dimmed for a second.

Frantically, Lavint wrenched the controls around in a new direction, but *Breathe My Jets* was not a small, nimble craft. In the agonizing seconds it took the cargo vessel to take a new bearing, she heard Blatta calmly describing their situation: "The ISD at the port tip of the chevron formation is firing on us. The first hit was against our engines. If it hits again—"

Breathe My Jets shuddered a second time, hard enough that Lavint would have been thrown from her seat if the restraining straps hadn't been buckled in place. The cockpit lights dimmed again, and the displays all showed static for a second.

The lights did not come up this time, and the cargo ship stopped responding to Lavint's handling. The displays cleared of static. Running on emergency power, they began scrolling a list of damage sustained by the ship.

Blatta watched the data roll by. "Engines out."

"Thank you for that holonews update."

Blatta shrugged. "It's been good working with you, Captain. I only wish—"

"Wish what?"

"That you weren't half a year behind in what you owe me." He switched his main display over to follow the progress of the battle now raging all around them.

OUTSIDE THE CORELLIAN SYSTEM
ANAKIN SOLO

In the Command Salon of the Star Destroyer *Anakin Solo,* Jacen Solo stood staring through the forward viewports. He could see the last few twinkles and flashes of laserfire as this abortive space combat drew to a close.

He chose not to follow the events more closely on the readily available computer displays. Instead he reached out through the Force, sampling the ships and vehicles he could see, looking for oddness, discrepancy, tragedy.

He found none. The smugglers, outmaneuvered and outgunned, gave up almost to a ship. A few nimble craft got away, making the jump to lightspeed before the warships of Jacen's task force could cripple them, but most did not; the majority of the smugglers floated, helpless, their engines destroyed by laserfire or their electronics systems rendered inert by ion cannons. Shuttles were now moving from ship to ship, picking up smuggling crews, dropping off the personnel who would bring the captured craft back to GA facilities, directing tractor beams. In another hour or two this section of space would be empty of everything but a few debris clouds that had once been engine housings.

"Our agent would like to speak with you," said Ebbak. A dark-haired human woman with skin the color of desert sand, she was short and unremarkable of appearance but had been of considerable help to him since he had been assigned the *Anakin Solo.* A civilian employee aboard ship, assigned to data analysis, she had demonstrated a knack for knowing what sort of information Jacen would need and when, and for supplying it at useful times. He was considering whether she would be interested in trading her civilian's post for a commission with Galactic Alliance Guard; he could benefit from someone with her skills if she proved as loyal as she was dutiful.

She had not *quite* materialized beside him—he had felt her walk up—but her approach had been silent. Perhaps she would also prove adept at stealth work.

The question annoyed Jacen; his mind was occupied by details of the capture of the smuggler fleet, and he needed to begin thinking about his upcoming meeting with the Corellian representative. "Why would I want to speak with her? And please don't call her our *agent.* She betrayed her comrades for money. She is our temporary hireling. She is their traitor. She is nobody's agent but her own."

Ebbak paused, then evidently decided not to address those last few comments. "She didn't say what she wanted. But since she's already proven that she had one piece of information useful to us—"

"Yes, yes." Jacen nodded. "Where is she?"

"Your office."

Jacen followed her back through the bulkhead doors aft of the Command Salon. Once in the main corridor beyond, they moved through a port-side door into the office that served as Jacen's retreat aboard the *Anakin Solo.*

Waiting there were two people—a large man, dressed in the uniform of ship's security, standing, and a woman, seated . . . though she rose as Jacen and Ebbak entered.

Jacen looked into the weathered face of Captain Uran Lavint. "Yes?"

Lavint paused, apparently put off by his distant, brusque

manner. "I simply wanted to find out if you had any requests or, more to the point, assignments for me before I left."

Jacen repressed a sigh. "First, I'd never prolong a business relationship with someone who sells out her fellows. Second, you're lying."

Lavint flushed, but her expression did not change. "All right. I mostly just wanted to meet you."

"Ah." Jacen paused, and carefully considered his next words. "Lavint, you now have all the time in the galaxy available to you. In betraying thirty-odd fellow smugglers, you have earned enough credits to pay off all your debts and start over, whether as a smuggler or something legitimate. You can cruise, you can frolic, you can relax. I, on the other hand, don't have time to spare. And you have now wasted some of it. I don't appreciate that." He turned to the security officer. "Take her down to Delta Hangar, put her on her ship, and get her off *my* ship."

Lavint cleared her throat. "*Breathe My Jets* is on Gamma Hangar. And the engines won't be repaired for a couple of standard days at least."

"That's right. I'm claiming *Breathe My Jets* for the current military crisis." Jacen pulled his datapad from a pocket and consulted it. "Your ship is now the *Duracrud.*"

"*Duracrud?*" Lavint practically spat the name. "That's a stock why-vee six-six-six older than I am. It's a brick with wings and a hull that leaks gases like a flatulent Hutt. It's a fraction the size of *Breathe My Jets.*"

"And exactly the sort of vessel needed by a smuggler starting a new career."

"Our agreement—"

"Our agreement was that you would receive a sum of credits—Ebbak, you showed her the transfer proof and gave her the data to claim it from the Bespin account? Yes—and that you would be allowed to depart on your ship, minus her cargo. The agreement did not specify which was to be your ship." He fixed Lavint with an impassive stare. "Now would you care to waste any more of my time?"

The glare she turned on him was murderous. He understood why. He'd just taken her ship, her beloved business and home, and given her a hovel in its place. His father, Han Solo, would have felt the same way.

But Uran Lavint was no Han Solo, and Jacen didn't worry that she might someday return to cause him grief. Her record made it clear that she had no goals, no drives other than the acquisition of credits. She was nothing.

Lavint turned away, her body language stiff, and marched to the door, her security man behind her. Then, as the doors slid open, she paused. Not turning back, her voice quiet, she asked, "What's it like to have once been a hero?" Then she left, and the door hissed closed behind her.

Jacen felt himself redden. He forced the anger away. It wouldn't do to let an insect like Lavint bother him. But clearly, additional punishment was in order.

He turned to Ebbak. "My father used to have endless trouble with the *Millennium Falcon*. The hyperdrive would fail all the time, and he'd tell the universe that it wasn't his fault, and then he'd fix it and be about his business." He nodded toward the closed door. "Delay her in transit to the hangar bays. Have *Duracrud*'s hyperdrive adjusted so that it will fail catastrophically after one jump."

"Yes, sir." Ebbak considered. "Since she's a smuggler, she's not going to go anywhere with a single jump. Her first jump will always be to some point far away from planetary systems or traffic lanes. She'll be stranded."

"That's right. And she'll become intimately acquainted with her hyperdrive."

"She might die."

"And if she doesn't, she'll be a better person for the experience. More polite, probably."

"Yes, sir." Ebbak moved to the door. It slid open for her. "Sir, your meeting with Admiral Antilles is in one hour."

Jacen consulted his chrono. "So it is. Thank you."

"And, Colonel, if I can make a personal remark—"

"Go ahead."

"You're not looking well."

He gave her a humorless grin. "Crisis will do that to a man. I'll be fine."

The door slid shut behind her.

chapter two

Exactly an hour later, Ebbak returned, escorting Admiral Wedge Antilles of Corellia. The aging military officer, upright and moving as easily as a man half his age, wore the full-dress uniform of an officer of the Corellian Defense Force and a grave expression that concealed his feelings like a mask. Even through the Force, Jacen could pick up little of what Wedge was experiencing—alertness, confidence that might or might not have been forced, a patience born of self-control.

Jacen rose from behind his desk to shake Wedge's hand. He gestured for Ebbak to leave, and she did so without speaking. Jacen resumed his chair and gestured to its comfortable, high-backed double on the opposite side of the desk, situated there just for this conference. "Have a seat."

"Thank you." Wedge did, his posture perfect, and Jacen felt a tiny trickle of annoyance. Wedge had to know that Corellia was beaten at this point—he could have the decency not to pretend otherwise.

"I know you don't like to waste time," Jacen continued. "So do you have a position statement for me?"

Now, at last, Wedge did look confused, if only faintly. "A position statement?"

"As in, *It's clear the Corellian position is hopeless, so I'm here to talk sense.*"

Wedge chuckled. "I'm here because you suggested a meeting with a top-ranking representative of the Corellian military or government. You're here because, having achieved a military victory on Hapes—one that has been spectacularly covered in the media, and let me add my congratulations on that—you want to press your advantage and conclude a peace with Corellia to give your brilliant political career one more boost."

Jacen felt a flash of anger and instantly clamped down on it. Wedge's words hit close to their target. If Jacen could negotiate a peace here in the next few days, everyone would benefit—Corellia, the Galactic Alliance, and Jacen himself. "You're not in a good position to make accusations about other people's motives and ethics. Not after signing off on the coup attempt at Hapes." He knew the anger in his voice was real.

Wedge was silent for a long, chilling moment. "Because I think you need to know, I'll tell you something that constitutes a Corellian government secret. I didn't know about the plot against Hapes. You already knew I had nothing to do with its planning."

"How would I know that?"

"Because it failed."

Jacen almost asked whether belligerent cockiness was part of the genetic pattern of all Corellians, but he resisted the urge. His own father was the archetypal Corellian, and if belligerent cockiness were credits, the Solos would be the wealthiest family in the galaxy.

Jacen gave Wedge a condescending look. "You don't need to offer a defense yet. War crimes trials haven't even started. And if your negotiation is particularly skillful, they might not happen at all. So let's get back to the subject. Admiral, your position is hopeless. The Corellian system is surrounded, blockaded. Despite the fact that numerous planets made noises of support when Corellia took its stance of defiance, not one has rebelled in support of Corellia; you are friendless. And you're running short of crucial supplies. The smuggler convoy that you expected an hour or so ago is not running late; it is entirely in our hands, with all its bacta, all its munitions now helping the GA cause."

Wedge smiled. "First you say we have no friends, and then you say people were arrested trying to bring us essential goods."

"They were smugglers, not friends."

"Sometimes smugglers become friends. Your father and I were smugglers who joined the Rebel Alliance cause. And now, since you've seized those cargoes rather than paying for them, you can be sure that fewer smugglers will become friends with the Galactic Alliance. Are you saying that the GA doesn't *need* friends? Or just doesn't need friends like me and your father?"

"You're changing the subject again."

"True." Abruptly Wedge looked weary, reflective. "I'll be honest. I'd like to see Corellia reunited with the GA. If it isn't, something very bad will happen."

"Now you're talking."

"If Corellia doesn't rejoin, if war truly erupts . . . I may never get my pension from the GA."

"Wedge—"

"I earned that pension. Decades of service."

"Be serious—"

"All right, I will." All humor gone, Wedge fixed Jacen with a stare. "You're dealing with a coalition government that hasn't settled in place yet. Thrackan Sal-Solo hasn't been dead very long, and the larvae are still wriggling out from under his rock. We need time to stamp them out. You don't need to hurry. You don't need our answer today, tomorrow, or next week, and any answer you provoke in a short time frame is an answer that will make everyone unhappy. Sit back, be patient, negotiate in good faith, and I have every reason to believe that Corellia will rejoin the GA."

"So you'll go back and recommend that Corellia surrender to us."

Wedge shook his head. "Never in a thousand years."

"What are you talking about, then?"

"I'll recommend that Corellia rejoin the GA. Full acceptance of standard GA planetary admission terms, but no reparations. No punitive measures, no extra tariffs, no under-the-table activity against Corellians, and a genuine attempt to undo the effort to undermine the general Corellian reputation that has been taking place in the GA population. Can you negotiate toward that sort of resolution?"

"I . . . could. But if we suffer any more catastrophes like the bombing on Coruscant, all bets could be off."

"Understood." Wedge relented just a bit, some of the stiffness leaving his face, his posture. "So what are you going to do when the excitement's all done? Stay on with your planetary police force, or go back to wandering the galaxy and rescuing cubs from trees? You used to be pretty good at that."

Jacen masked a twitch of annoyance by shrugging. "Some combination of the Galactic Alliance Guard work and resuming my studies, I expect."

"Hmmm. Has the political bug bitten you, then? Or do you just like the way you look in the uniform?"

Jacen sighed, exasperated. "Now you're joking again. And I think we've done all we can with this meeting."

"I think so, too." Serious again, Wedge stood. "Jacen, may I say something to you not as an officer or negotiator, but as an old friend of the family?"

Jacen rose, too. "Something off the record, you mean? Of course."

"No, no. On the record, off the record, it doesn't matter.

As an old friend of the family. Can you listen as an old friend?"

Still a trifle confused, Jacen nodded.

"Another old friend of mine, Wes Janson, the galaxy's least serious man, except when he's killing the enemy or trying to make a point, once said this to me. 'The real sign that someone has become a fanatic,' he said, 'is that he completely loses his sense of humor about some important facet of his life. When humor goes, it means he's lost his perspective.' Jacen, you've lost your sense of humor about, well, *everything,* and you're doing things you never would have done when you were younger. What does it mean?"

Jacen shook his head. "It doesn't mean that I'm suddenly a fanatic. It just means that I've grown up."

"I wonder."

"Ebbak is waiting outside. She'll take you back to your shuttle."

When Wedge was gone, Jacen sat again and stared at the office doors, not seeing them.

Blast Wedge, he thought. *As if losing an adolescent sense of humor has anything to do with fanaticism. As if . . .*

There was a thought circling around the periphery of his awareness. It was something Captain Lavint had sparked into existence, something Wedge had fanned into a live flame. But he couldn't quite bring it into focus.

Well then, he needed to look more closely.

Captain Lavint thought Jacen *used* to be a hero. Clearly, if such things were measured by numbers of admirers, he was now a greater hero than he ever had been, and yet she thought he no longer constituted one. Why? Because he'd passed judgment on her? Perhaps. Maybe it was because the sentence he'd passed on her was one that would have broken his father's heart, or the heart of any smuggler. Perhaps it was because he'd hurt her where she was most vulnerable. *It wasn't necessarily a heroic thing to do,* he conceded, *but it was fair. So let's dismiss that for now.*

Wedge thought the loss of his sense of humor meant that he'd become a fanatic of some sort. Whether it had or not, Jacen had to admit, it did mark a change in him.

Both Lavint and Wedge had addressed changes Jacen had experienced, and that recognition bothered him at some level.

For a moment, he tried to recapture a sense of what he had been as a teenager, before the war against the Yuuzhan Vong: gawky, happy, usually in the company of his twin sister, Jaina, and younger brother, Anakin, all too infrequently in the company of his parents . . . His sense of humor, always present, had usually manifested itself in the form of awful jokes learned in the four corners of the galaxy.

And then there were animals, Wedge's "cubs in trees." Once upon a time he'd been able to charm a sand panther into purring, had been able to coax the cub of any species into his hand. How long had it been since he'd done that? Since he'd *wanted* to do that?

Animals, evil animals, with their razory teeth and their hatred for Jedi . . .

He snapped out of the half doze into which he'd fallen, but didn't sit up. There was an answer for him. At the height of the Yuuzhan Vong war, he, Jaina, Anakin, and an elite unit of young Jedi Knights had mounted a mission to an enemy world, there to destroy the voxyn—creatures bred by the Yuuzhan Vong, creatures that could sense the Force, creatures that had hunted and claimed the lives of numerous Jedi before this mission destroyed them.

But Anakin had been fatally wounded on this mission. Had died.

The children of Han Solo and Leia Organa Solo had suddenly gone from three to two. Had suddenly stopped being invincible, invulnerable, immortal. Suddenly there was no room in his life, no room in his universe for humor.

And from that time on animals had all seemed to wear the faces of voxyn. They were no longer his friends.

Jacen had been captured, ending up in the hands of the Yuuzhan Vong. Ending up under the tutelage of Vergere, who was sometimes Jedi, sometimes Sith, sometimes neither. She had taught him much, including how to separate himself from pain or embrace it, how to survive when drowning within the Force or cut off from it, how to be human or Yuuzhan Vong or neither.

She had taught him to distance himself from everything, should he need to.

And now, more than a decade after those events, after her death, he could see another reason why. *Only separation offers perspective. All learning benefits from perspective. Therefore all learning benefits from separation.*

Which didn't explain why the smuggler's and Wedge's comments had nettled him.

You're doing things you never would have done when you were younger.

Such as firing on the Millennium Falcon.

That thought came to him in a rush, like one of Luke's lightsaber attacks, and Jacen was unable to parry it, to deflect it, to pretend it hadn't happened.

Several days earlier he had ordered the long-range turbolasers of the *Anakin Solo* to fire upon the *Millennium Falcon.*

I wasn't sure it was the Falcon. *Its transponder designation was* Longshot.

"You knew."

The first voice was his. The second voice was a bit like his, but a whisper . . . more like Vergere's, perhaps.

I . . . knew it was the Falcon. *I knew I was firing on my mother and my father. But I thought they had become enemies. I thought they had betrayed me, Tenel Ka, our daughter.*

"So, for that, you decided to kill them?"

No . . . I knew the Falcon *could sustain a turbolaser hit or two. I wasn't trying to kill them.*

"Yes, you were."

Jacen sighed, defeated by the relentlessness of his own analysis. *Yes, I was. I was trying to kill them. Because of what I thought they'd tried to do to Allana.*

"And you were willing to kill Zekk, even Ben, even Jaina to accomplish this."

Jacen frowned over that. *Not kill, precisely,* he thought. *I was willing to sacrifice them, though.*

"For the greater good. For the elimination of two enemies who could have cost you everything. Enemies whom you know to be resourceful, relentless."

Yes.

"Then it was the right decision."

But I was wrong! They turned out not to have been part of the coup attempt.

"Yes. But it was still the correct decision based on what you then knew, or thought you knew."

Jacen nodded.

"And so you would do it again. If you knew, truly knew, that they were your enemies, that they stood between you and galactic peace. Or between you and your daughter."

Yes.

"Good." The tones within his mind were more and more like Vergere's. *"You are still learning."*

And you are still teaching. Even though you're dead.

There was no answer. But Jacen was calm, satisfied.

His decision had been correct, flawed only by the incorrect data upon which it had been based. He could do it again if he needed to, and would.

He was capable of sacrificing a lesser responsibility for a greater one, a lesser good for a greater one, a lesser love for a greater one. Lumiya, his Sith teacher, would be pleased . . . if she was still alive.

And he could finally recognize that the boy he had been,

the optimistic, joke-spinning, animal-loving, kidnap-prone Jedi boy, was dead, slain on the same mission that had claimed his brother, Anakin.

At last, understanding what had happened, Jacen did not miss his younger self.

Finally he slept.

chapter three

CORUSCANT
GALACTIC ALLIANCE SENATE BUILDING,
CHIEF OMAS'S OFFICE

It was a small, private meeting this time—Luke, Mara, Chief Omas, Admiral Niathal, and Kyp. Government security men and women waited outside in the reception room, and, if Luke knew their type as well as he thought, they'd be fidgety, unhappy about not being on hand to protect the government leaders in case the Jedi decided to cause trouble.

Luke grinned at that. The likelihood of Jedi causing trouble in a situation like this was approximately equal to Cal Omas and Admiral Niathal proclaiming themselves the new Emperor and Empress. Then he sobered. Historically, the last time anything like that had happened, it hadn't gone so well for the Jedi.

"I understand the demands on your time," Chief Omas was saying. White-haired, earnest, the deliberate embodiment of governmental sympathy and goodwill, he sat opposite Luke, his hands clasped together on the table between them. "So I'll be brief. I—representing many voices in the

GA government—wanted to give you the opportunity to do a very great favor for that government."

Luke nodded. "By elevating Jacen Solo to the rank of Jedi Master."

Chief Omas hesitated. His expression didn't change, but Luke had the distinct impression that the man was taken aback.

Luke kept himself from looking at Kyp. *So Kyp's comment earlier was either a secret or a guess . . . and since Omas isn't suddenly suspicious of Kyp, Kyp hasn't betrayed a secret. A guess, then. Interesting.*

"Well . . . yes," Chief Omas conceded. "These are unsettled times, Master Skywalker. Colonel Solo is a hero of the people, someone all members of the Galactic Alliance can look toward for leadership. In giving him command of the Galactic Alliance Guard, the government has displayed tremendous faith in his abilities and loyalty, and he has demonstrated that he deserves that faith and will continue to earn it. Jacen could now also serve as a potent example of cooperation between the secular government and the Jedi order . . . if only the Jedi would demonstrate similar faith in him."

Chief Omas's voice was as controlled as ever, his manner as persuasive, but through the Force, Luke could sense that the man had no personal investment in this argument. Clearly, he had to be making this proposal at the request of others, perhaps repaying some favor owed to another politician, to one of Jacen's patrons. Luke took a quick look at Admiral Niathal, the highest-placed Galactic Alliance politician who was also a keen supporter of Jacen, but the Mon Cal was under control, offering no emotions for him to detect.

"Well, there's a problem." Luke glanced at his fellow Jedi. Mara was stone-faced, offering no expression for the politicians to read, though Luke could feel, through the Force-link that helped bind them together, her irritation with Omas. Kyp was slouched back in his chair, smiling faintly, and Luke thought he could detect that Kyp was enjoying himself hugely. "In my estimation, Jacen still lacks the emotional maturity he needs to be a Master."

Chief Omas gave him a doubtful look. "Many Jedi, in both the Old Republic and the modern era, became Masters at his age or younger."

Luke shrugged. "It's not a question of age."

"And," Omas continued, "he has demonstrated that he possesses skills and power that not even most confirmed Masters can match."

Mara sighed and finally leaned in to join the conversation. "It's not a matter of power, either. If power were the criterion you think it is, then any eight-year-old with a thermal detonator would be qualified to teach at the university level. Right?"

Opposite her, Admiral Niathal also leaned in, as if positioning herself like a Mon Cal cruiser to counter the Star Destroyer that Mara represented. She spoke in the gravelly tones common to Mon Calamari. "Perhaps power, age, and wisdom are not the only considerations here." Her bulbous eyes whipped around to focus on Mara and then Luke in turn. "If Jacen is a master of the Guard and a Master among the Jedi, it blurs the lines between those who have sworn to obey the government and those who merely acknowledge a vague duty and responsibility to the government. A distressing loss of personal authority for the Grand Master of the Jedi order. Not so?"

Luke let a little frost creep into his voice. "The duty I've acknowledged for forty years is anything but vague."

Niathal nodded. "Precisely. And so you have nothing to fear."

"And that's not the issue." Luke gave the admiral a small frown—a message that her effort to lead the conversation from the realm of logic into the realm of defensiveness would not succeed. "Jacen is not ready. He's making too many unfortunate choices. He needs guidance and is refusing to seek it."

"From *you*. I find that he is very receptive to *my* guidance."

Luke didn't answer. He let the silence between them stretch into long seconds.

Finally Niathal swiveled to look at Kyp. "Master Durron, I have it on good authority that you advocate elevating Jacen Solo to the rank of Master."

The purpose for Kyp's presence finally clicked for Luke. Months before, at a meeting of the Jedi Council, Kyp had proposed elevating Jacen to their rank. Obviously, word of that had somehow leaked out from those Council Chambers and reached the ears and tympanic membranes of Omas and Niathal, and Kyp had been brought in to reinforce their argument.

Kyp appeared startled, but Luke detected no genuine emotion of surprise from him. "I beg your pardon?"

Niathal stared at him. "You did propose that Jacen Solo be elevated."

Kyp nodded, a little uncertain. "In a manner of speaking."

Suspicion crept into Niathal's voice. "What manner?"

Kyp continued to look uncomfortable. "Well, clearly you're unfamiliar with the role of the taras-chi in Jedi Council debates."

"The taras—"

"—chi. Yes. A sort of ritualized debate opponent." Kyp glanced at Luke and Mara as if for confirmation. "In certain Jedi traditions, any discussion group, or its moderator, elects a taras-chi. The purpose of the taras-chi is to float ideas that run counter to the prevailing wisdom. This is so that all ideas will be tested . . . sometimes to destruction. The idea that the taras-chi promotes is not the one being tested—the idea he promotes tests the idea currently under discussion. It's like a larva that only eats dead flesh. Place it on a wound, and it will only devour that which cannot survive anyway. Live flesh, like a solid idea or valid reasoning, will not be harmed by it." Kyp thought for a moment. "I suppose that the closest equivalents you have in the world of government would be court jesters or the free press."

Chief Omas and Admiral Niathal exchanged a look. Omas appeared mildly confused; Niathal's posture suggested she was irritated.

Omas cleared his throat. "I fail to see—"

"The discussion at that meeting," Kyp continued, "was about Jacen Solo's activities and whether they were appropriate for a Jedi. So in the spirit of the taras-chi, I not only spoke out in uncritical support of them, I proposed giving him the most lavish reward the Jedi can bestow. As a test of the principal item of discussion."

There was now a little chill in Niathal's voice. "So you're saying that you never supported Jacen Solo's elevation."

Kyp gave her a quizzical look. "I support the decisions of the Master of the order, Admiral. And let me give you a little example of how power and skill with the Jedi arts do not correspond to mastery.

"When I was still a teenager, I was able to reach into the gravity well of a gas giant and pull a spacecraft out of it. That's something that not many Masters could accomplish. I could do it because I was strong in the Force . . . and because I had *absolute* faith in my right, my need to use that craft for a specific purpose. But I doubt I could do it today. I'm no weaker in the Force, and I'm a lot more skilled . . . but today I'd know that my intended purpose was not a good one, and this knowledge would deny me the focus I needed then to perform that task. So was I a Master then, or am I a Master now?"

Chief Omas and Niathal exchanged another look. Omas's face was serene, but it was clear from Niathal's body language that this portion of the meeting had not gone the way she'd wanted it to.

Omas tried again, catching Luke's eye. "Master Durron's story just goes to reinforce my point. He lacked the experience he needed—experience that would have compelled him to seek the advice of others. But Colonel Solo doesn't lack that experience. He comes to us for guidance. Please, Master Skywalker, don't mistake any anger you might feel that he hasn't consulted enough with you for suspicion about his wisdom and readiness."

Luke smiled, suddenly cheerful. "All right, I won't." As Niathal straightened, expectant, Luke added, "I'll continue to evaluate Jacen's progress as a Jedi, and the instant I find him to be ready for the rank of Master, you'll be the first one I inform."

"Ah." Omas sat back, but maintained a mask of polite cheer. "Please do."

Luke rose and nodded. "Thank you for seeing us. If there's nothing more, I don't want to take up more of your time."

"No, that was all." There was mock good humor in Omas's voice. "Thank you."

The Jedi were silent on the walk out of the office, on the turbolift down to the building's hangar level, and until Kyp's speeder carried them out of the Senate Building.

Mara broke the silence. "What is a taras-chi?"

Kyp smiled, showing teeth. "A bug in the mines of Kessel," he said. "Six legs under a hard round carapace about three centimeters in diameter. Properly roasted, they only tasted a little awful. When you could catch them, they offered a little nutrition, helped you starve more slowly."

Luke looked thoughtful. "Thanks for supporting me back there. Why'd you do it?"

"Luke—" Kyp stopped, shook his head. "No. Master Skywalker. I do think Jacen should be a Master, or I wouldn't have brought up the point at that meeting. But I'm all for showing solidarity, a united Jedi order, when this sort of thing happens. When cracks open and politicians get their fingers in them, bad things happen. Empires are formed. Also, I'm more than a little annoyed that they brought up my suggestion from that meeting—how did they find out, anyway?" He frowned. "Loose talk between Masters and apprentices around the Temple, probably."

"Probably," Mara said, but Luke could feel a trace of suspicion growing within her—as it was within him. Even if Kyp's opinions had been overheard in the halls of the Temple, someone, some Jedi, had to have passed them on to the government. Perhaps Jacen had done so himself.

Luke steered away from that line of thought, and from the even more distressing possibility that it had been Ben who had leaked the information.

chapter four

CORONET, CORELLIA

A bunker always felt like a bunker, Wedge reflected. No matter that this chamber was decorated for entertainment—with wall-mounted displays showing scenes from the city of Coronet and its surroundings in true-life colors, no matter that it was furnished with tables supplied with dinnerware suited to formal company and trays of refreshments, with elegantly curved handmade chairs and comfortable, immaculate sofas in the most eye pleasing of styles. It was a bunker, deep beneath the ground, and the men and women who were gathered here, politicians of the world of Corellia and the drones who worked for them, all sat a little hunched, as though they could feel the tons of masonry and dirt heaped protectively above their heads. Politicians of the other four occupied worlds of the Corellian system, represented by holograms, must have been in aboveground buildings where they were; their postures were not bent.

Wedge also sat upright, both out of habit and to annoy the others, and accepted a cup of caf from one of the drones, this one a pale, slight young man in a CorSec uniform. Wedge waited until the drone had withdrawn before turning back toward the other man on the couch. "So the conversation didn't accomplish much politically . . . except that I think Colonel Solo will advise in favor of the Galactic Alliance giving us more time."

The man he addressed, Dur Gejjen, the Five Worlds Prime Minister and Corellian Chief of State—handsome, younger than his political acuity might suggest, dark-skinned and dark-haired—set his own cup of caf on a nearby table and frowned. " '*Giving* us more time,' " he echoed. "That sounds a lot like a victor doing a favor to the vanquished."

"Obviously, they're not victors here," Wedge said. "But just as obviously, they're in the stronger position. A few more weeks or months of their blockade, and they'll starve our economy past the point of resistance. Solo was right when he said that we were alone. Unless your communications with the Bothans have had a sudden breakthrough you haven't mentioned."

"You sound defeated, Admiral." The speaker was the hologram of a short, wide-shouldered man. The transmission of his seated form was superimposed onto a chair to Gejjen's right. The speaker had thinning hair and a face ideally suited to belligerence. His name was Sadras Koyan, and he was both Chief of State of the world of Tralus and a member of the Centerpoint Party, the minority force within the Corellian system's new coalition government.

Wedge gave him a neutral look. "Clearly, we're not defeated. But if things continue as they are, we will be. I'm telling you that we can negotiate a non-surrender resolution to this situation, rejoin the Galactic Alliance, and experience minimal repercussions, if we negotiate in good faith, starting now." He felt his mood darken and knew his expression had to be doing so as well. "*Good faith* may be tricky to come by, though, in a political body that uses its secret, reserve fleet to execute a plan to *assassinate* a foreign head of state—"

He was drowned out, shouted down by the voices of the

others. Gejjen was saying, "Now is not the time—" while Koyan roared, "—lack of competence in keeping our access to our own shipyards open—" Denjax Teppler, former Five Worlds Prime Minister, now Minister of Justice, grimaced and spoke inaudible words of calm and caution, motioning with both hands for the others to lower their voices. Rorf Willems, Minister of Defense, was grumbling, "—bit more cooperation is called for here." Minister of Intelligence Gavele Lemora seemed to be evaluating Wedge, as if measuring him for a coffin. The drones kept conspicuously quiet while the ministers and Chiefs of State raged.

Gejjen scowled and spoke again, this time at a full-throated shout: "Shut up!"

The others quieted and stared at the Corellian leader. Gejjen returned his attention to Wedge. "Admiral, are you saying that with the assault fleet, you could have kept the GA forces out of our system, kept us from suffering the blockade the GA has instituted?"

Wedge nodded. "It's very likely."

"Very likely . . . and you're also saying that our best course of action now is to negotiate for a no-fault return to the GA."

"Yes."

"Even though it would inevitably cost us control of Centerpoint Station."

The station, home to an ancient gravitic device that could be used to construct entire solar systems—or destroy them—had been near operational when a Jedi mission had sabotaged it, costing the Corellians their most significant weapon. Ben Skywalker, son of Wedge's old friend Luke, had been the saboteur. Wedge's association with the Skywalkers was one that everyone present knew.

Wedge nodded. "Chief Gejjen, that result is far superior to being starved into submission and then forced back into the GA under terms dictated by Cal Omas and Admiral Niathal."

"So we can't win."

"Not without wealthy, powerful planetary systems joining on our side."

"Which we were within a centimeter of having," Koyan growled, "until Jacen Solo and his parents fouled up our action in the Hapes Consortium."

Wedge bit down on a response. Assassinating a good ruler, such as Queen Mother Tenel Ka, so that a treacherous, deceptive pro-Corellian one could take her place might help win a war, but the peace that followed would be fragile, uncertain, even evil. However, saying such a thing before this body of men and women would do no good.

Gejjen, seeming to read Wedge's reply in his expression, looked over at one of his aides. "Bring Admiral Delpin in." He returned his attention to Wedge. "Admiral Antilles, we have a problem, and the problem is that I don't think you're willing to win at any cost."

"I'm not," Wedge said. "And neither are you."

"I am," Gejjen said.

"If winning meant the Corellian system was the only center of civilization to survive the war?"

Gejjen frowned. "That's a ridiculous and extreme example."

"Exactly." Wedge nodded. "But I'll bet that it constitutes an example of a victory you wouldn't be willing to accept. Meaning that you're not willing to win at *any* cost. We just have to establish, for this ruling body, what is the maximum consequence in victory that we're willing to accept."

Gejjen tried again, demonstrating a level of patience and even respect that Wedge found surprising. "Admiral, you were kept out of the loop on the decision to, eh, adjust Hapan politics because it was clear to the rest of us, based on your history of performance, that you would never sign off on it in its final form."

"You might be right."

"But we're already in agreement that sacrificing the dictator of a distant government is well within the *maximum consequence in victory* that we're willing to bring about."

The door into the chamber hissed open, and a woman in the dress uniform of an admiral of the Corellian Defense Force, the same uniform Wedge wore, entered. She was Wedge's height and was muscular of build, the sort of woman whose hobby time was probably all spent in a gymnasium. Her hair, cut close, was black and picked up blue glints from the glow rods around the room. She was about half Wedge's age and good looking; there was no trace of makeup evident on her features.

There was, however, a trace of sympathy on them as she glanced at Wedge. She came to a stop in front of Gejjen's chair, her cap tucked military-style beneath her left arm. "Admiral Genna Delpin, reporting as ordered."

Wedge knew her. She was a fast-rising star in the Corellian armed forces, and had led the assault fleet in the disastrous coup attempt at the Hapes Consortium. Its defeat had reflected not on her ability but on factors well outside her control, such as the interference of the Jedi and unexpected armed forces.

Gejjen acknowledged her with a nod, then turned again to Wedge. "Admiral, what you accomplished in the liberation of Tralus makes it clear that we couldn't have chosen a better leader for our united armed forces. But times change, and your personal code of conduct is, I believe, going to become a greater impediment in dealing with your government's needs. Admiral Delpin has a clearer understanding of her role and her duties to the government, and has your skill at moving and motivating subordinates. For this reason—and understand, it's nothing personal, we continue to hold you in the highest regard—I'm removing you from the position of Supreme Commander of Corellia's armed forces." He turned his attention to the newcomer. "Admiral Delpin, I'm appointing you to that position."

"Thank you, sir. I accept." Her voice was smooth, controlled.

Wedge stood. He did it slowly and carefully, the better to mask what he was feeling. Regardless of how inevitable this moment might have been, regardless of how inflexibly he might hold on to the ethics that had made it happen, being relieved of command still felt like taking a sledgehammer blow to the gut, and he didn't want anyone in this group to see how he felt. Smoothly, he saluted. "Congratulations, Admiral."

She returned his salute. "Thank you, Admiral. After this meeting breaks up, perhaps we could have a cup of caf and discuss things."

Wedge limited his reaction to a faint smile. He knew what that conversation would consist of: *I'm sorry this had to happen. I hope there won't be any uneasiness between us. We need you . . .*

No, they didn't. But that realization, and what he had to do next, caused Wedge's stomach to turn even further.

Gejjen said, "Admiral Antilles, your tactical and strategic planning abilities continue to make you invaluable to our armed forces. If Admiral Delpin agrees, I want you to join her operations staff."

Delpin gave Gejjen a crisp nod. "I do agree."

Wedge took a deep breath. "I'm sorry, I can't. Admiral, ordinarily I would have no hesitation in accepting, and in working with you, and for you. But circumstances are not ordinary." He fixed Gejjen with a stare. "Sir, I hereby resign my commission in the Corellian Defense Force."

The room fell silent. A moment later, someone behind Wedge said, "Good!"

Gejjen shot an angry look at the speaker, then addressed Wedge. "I won't accept."

Wedge shrugged. "You have no choice. Or rather, your choice is to keep me on as noncommissioned personnel or offer me a full discharge. From this point on, or at least from the point I submit my resignation along official lines, I am no longer a commissioned officer."

Gejjen heaved a sigh and thought for a moment. "You can either stay on as a sergeant—a speeder pilot for our landing forces—or you can make one last public appearance as Admiral Antilles, cheerfully handing off your post and duties to Admiral Delpin, and honorably retire."

Wedge considered it. The public appearance would help convince the majority of the populace that everything was fine with their leadership, that he had every faith in the new Supreme Commander, that he supported the new regime and all its ways. Which was a lie.

But if he didn't do it, members of the armed forces might lose a little faith in their leadership. And that could result in breakdowns in authority, in the deaths of good soldiers.

Wedge's entire deliberation took a quarter second. "I'll make the appearance, of course."

"Of course," Gejjen echoed. "Dismissed."

Wedge saluted and, a little stiff-legged, made his way from the room.

His posture was perfect for the long walk through the doors, down the long corridor beyond, past a guard station, and into the turbolift that would carry him up to ground level. But once the lift doors closed behind him, he sagged against the wall. His legs felt like rubber, and his stomach rebelled like a ground-pounder's upon its first experience with zero gravity.

From admiral in charge of an entire planetary system's armed forces to civilian in two easy steps, he thought, and managed a slightly nauseated smile.

And once again, he might just have signed his own death warrant. A government that was willing to assassinate foreign rulers wouldn't hesitate at ridding itself of someone who could be a potent symbol used against them . . . and who had just proven that he wasn't *with* them.

The instant he finished his public appearance with Admiral Delpin, the chrono would begin ticking down on his life.

The thought, so familiar after a lifetime of warfare, settled his stomach and beat back the nausea he'd felt from the moment he knew he was to be relieved of command. By the time the lift doors opened, he was standing tall again. He walked past the ground-floor security station and flashed its guards a smile suggesting that he was a rancor and they were made of meat.

GYNDINE SYSTEM
TENDRANDO REFUELING AND
REPAIR STATION

The vehicle lining up for an approach on the refueling station's spinward docking bay had once been a Corellian YT-1300 transport—efficiently disk-shaped, with aggressive-looking forward mandibles and a cockpit that protruded from the starboard side of the bow to give the craft an oddly pleasing, asymmetrical profile. Now, however, countless burns of battle damage darkened the hull, and the top and bottom turrets, which had once housed laser cannons, were just *gone.*

As the craft made her last bank before the approach, the man waiting in the docking bay could see that the top-side turret had not been replaced or even covered over; where it had once been installed, there was a hole that gaped into the vehicle's interior.

The waiting man would have recognized the *Millennium Falcon* instantly, even if he hadn't known she would be coming to this place. He had once owned her. He still loved her, and now he winced to see what had become of her.

Still urbane and handsome, and now distinguished looking with age, Lando Calrissian stood in complete contrast with the famous transport. He was dressed in a silken ensemble that would have cost what it took to buy a good speeder but whose components were all chosen for unobtrusive elegance; the dark blue tunic, black trousers, and purple hip cloak were subdued of color and fashion. The silver-tipped black cane he carried was his one outward concession to age.

He watched as the *Falcon* slowly approached. As frail as she looked, he half expected her to bounce off the atmospheric shields that kept the vacuum of space at bay, but she floated gently in through that negligible barrier. Now that the transport was within atmosphere, Lando could hear a rhythmic clanking from within her hull—something gone awry within her engine housings.

The *Falcon* slid gently forward on her repulsorlifts and settled down to a remarkably smooth landing. Lando walked around from beneath the mandibles to look through the cockpit viewport, but the occupants had already left, so he continued around to the boarding ramp.

He had a handful of jokes in mind for the arrival of Han and Leia—*I've seen transports crashed into the sides of World Devastators that looked better; what have you done to the old girl this time; did you buy your pilot's license at the Drunken Mynock School of Instruction*—but then, as the pair descended the boarding ramp, he caught sight of their faces.

There was not one iota of good humor, cheer, even hope in their expressions, just grimness and, under the surface, pain. Han wore his customary pants, tunic, and vest, and had his left arm in a sling. Leia was in brown Jedi robes. Both sets of clothes looked wrinkled and slept-in.

Lando cleared his throat to gain a moment to think and clear away the good-natured, mocking vocal mannerism he had intended to employ. Then he said, "I'm glad to see you. I have caf and food in the lounge."

* * *

While Han and Leia ate—slowly, barely tasting their food—they told Lando what had happened. Jacen was the central figure in almost every element of the story.

Jacen supporting laws to concentrate and imprison Corellians on Coruscant. Jacen interrogating a prisoner until she died—the daughter of Boba Fett. Jacen believing that Han and Leia would conspire against Tenel Ka, and punitively firing on the *Falcon* . . . when his own parents, sister, and cousin were aboard. Cakhmaim and Meewalh, Leia's Noghri bodyguards, killed in that attack—not just killed, but incinerated, instantly obliterated so that there was nothing left to bury.

As their account of the events ran down, Lando shook his head, almost unwilling to believe what he was hearing. "I'm sorry. I've been up on the holonews; I knew about his promotion to head of the Galactic Alliance Guard, but all this . . . I don't know what to say."

Finally Han looked up from his plate. "Can you help us fix the *Falcon*?"

Lando nodded. "Consider it done. This place is an old repair station I—we—picked up in a corporate merger. It's not cost-efficient, so we've transferred most of the personnel to other locations and are going to be closing it down. I'll keep this repair dock open long enough to make the *Falcon* shipshape. Better than new." He winced again. "It'll take some time, though."

Han and Leia exchanged a look, and Leia said, "We'll need a fast transport for the interim, too. Something that can get us through the Corellian exclusion zone if we need to. And something that doesn't scream *The Solos are back* whenever it's noticed."

"I've got you covered."

They were silent for several moments. Then Leia asked, "And how are you doing, Lando?"

"I don't want to tell you."

That got the attention of both Han and Leia. "Why?" Han asked.

"Because it's all good."

Leia managed a little smile. "I appreciate you not wanting to make us feel worse by gloating. We know that's not what you're going to do. We could use some good news. Really."

"Oh. Well, then." Lando heaved a sigh. "I'd have to say that all my wishes from when I was a young man have pretty much come true. I'm rich. I can travel wherever I want and do whatever I want. I'm married to a smart, beautiful woman who doesn't worry about where I am every second of the year. I can visit a gambling den and lose a fortune and not catch any heat; Tendra knows that at some point I'll win another fortune or a patent or a planet and make up the loss. Tendrando Arms isn't as big as it was during and right after the Yuuzhan Vong war, but it's doing very well selling to security forces in the private sector, and we've diversified. We're very healthy."

Leia frowned. "You almost sound . . . sad."

Lando paused, groping for the right words. "No . . . but there's no risk in my life. The years aren't going to make me old, but sitting around being successful, popular, and responsible is." He scowled. "Do you know how long it's been since a bounty hunter came after me?"

Leia offered him a wan smile. "For us, not so long."

Lando heaved himself to his feet. "I'm going to show you to your quarters. You get some rest. I'll arrange for a suitable transport to be brought up here."

CORELLIAN EXCLUSION ZONE
ANAKIN SOLO

Jacen sat cross-legged in his cabin, floating a meter above the floor, tranquil.

For once, he was fully open to the Force, letting it flow

through him, sustain him, support him in the air. He let the Force do as it wished, showing him pictures, flicking little traces of thought and emotion through him . . . and all the while he searched, peering as if the entirety of the Force were an ocean and he wanted to find one distant, familiar face among its waves and currents.

He found it. Very far away, tiny in the distance, but demonstrably still alive . . . Lumiya.

And suddenly she was nearer, much nearer. She appeared in his physical vision as well, no more than two meters before him. She looked as though she were a two-dimensional being who had been at right angles to his line of sight, then suddenly rolled over and into plain view.

As she had in years past, she wore a dark pants-and-tunic ensemble, and on her head she wore a wrapped headdress. One portion of it concealed her nose and mouth, ending in a sharp point oriented down toward her chest, and two other portions radiated from her forehead as if concealing a Devaronian's horns, giving her head an oddly triangular cast.

She lay on her side as if resting on a couch. There was no couch to be seen; she floated in the air as Jacen did. Her head was lifted and her eyes were unfocused. They took a moment to orient on him. "Jacen?" Her voice was distant, echoing as though she were in a large room with hard walls.

For a moment he was nonplussed. He'd known about her ability to project realistic Force phantoms from her home, an asteroid suffused with concentrated Force energy. But he hadn't imagined her using the technique for simple communication. He envied her the technique. Perhaps she would someday show him how she did it. "Lumiya," he said. "I'm happy to know that you've survived."

"Thank you." She laid her head down again, as if on a pillow. Her movements suggested exhaustion, even pain. "I am healing. Here I can summon my strength. Your uncle hurt me."

"Yet you don't sound angry."

She laughed. The noise was faint. "I'm used to it. Whenever we meet, I expect him to hurt me. He will probably do so until I die . . . or until you and I have won and he is forced to understand us."

"I'm in a holding pattern for the moment, Lumiya. Waiting for negotiations with the Corellians to bear fruit. Thinking about where my studies need to lead me."

"Ah." She was silent a long moment. Jacen watched her breathe—it seemed to be an effort for her. "You have been considering your sacrifice. Sacrificing what you love. Loving what you sacrifice."

"Yes. I am becoming . . . more ready."

"Good. And you have been looking for an apprentice?"

"Ben is my apprentice. Though I realized not long ago that I can sacrifice him if I have to."

"Ben is your Jedi apprentice. Not your Sith apprentice."

"I'm not a full Sith yet, and therefore cannot have a Sith apprentice."

Her sigh sounded exasperated. "You're stalling. You don't know whether he *will* be fit to become a Sith apprentice. The time to learn that is now, not when you reveal yourself. You must test him."

"He's back with his parents, and they don't want him to see me."

Lumiya lay there, silent, unhelpful. She watched him and waited.

"So . . ." He considered. "I must separate Ben from Luke and Mara, and test him."

Lumiya nodded. "If you wish, I will coordinate the test. But you must decide what it will be."

"All right."

"And you must decide what to do with him if he fails."

"Yes."

"If he fails, will you love him less?"

Jacen paused over his answer. He had to look deep into his own feelings to imagine how he would feel about Ben if the boy failed. "I think . . . initially it would make little difference. But we would soon grow apart."

"So if he fails, he will not long be suitable as your sacrifice. Keep that in mind."

"I will."

Lumiya rolled over again, away from him, and was gone.

chapter five

CORUSCANT, THE JEDI TEMPLE
QUARTERS OF LUKE AND MARA SKYWALKER

Luke and Mara kept an apartment away from the Jedi Temple, but also quarters in the Temple itself—austere chambers for those times when late-night Council meetings or other duties made it more practical to walk a few dozen meters and fall over, rather than board a speeder and fly kilometers to do the same.

Sometimes those Temple quarters served an additional purpose—such as when the Skywalkers found themselves in command of a surly, defiant, Jedi son who was certain that "unfairness" was a Force power and his parents were its masters.

The silence and chill radiating from the boy's room, one door down a common hallway, were formidable. Luke, pacing, was certain he could feel them like air blowing through a wampa's meat locker. He turned in midpace to look at his wife. "How is it that *I* feel guilty?"

Sitting on the bed, Mara looked up from her datapad. "You're feeling guilty—*we* are—because he's unhappy. And he's going to continue being unhappy until we stop slandering and persecuting Jacen, the perfect Jedi, hero of the people and male model for black uniforms. Or until he grows up enough to revise his thinking about his cousin." She sighed. "Do you think we can brick him into his room until he does grow up?"

"Tempting." Luke resumed his pacing.

"How long did it take you to stop being a headstrong kid who made as many bad decisions as good ones?"

Luke shrugged in midstride. "I don't know. From the time Uncle Owen and Aunt Beru were murdered to the time I started calling myself Master. About four years."

"I'll set the timer, then. It should go off when he's just about to turn eighteen. We can check then and see if he followed your example."

That elicited a dry chuckle. "All right. We need to figure out what to do with him now. We've got him in the Temple, where dozens of Jedi eyes can keep an eye on him when we're not around. Which is bound to make him more paranoid and angry. What do we do to make him *learn*?"

"Give him a project. Something relevant. Such as, write a history and analysis of his grandfather's fall to the dark side."

Luke stopped again to stare at his wife. "That's complex psychology to assign to a thirteen-year-old."

"Almost fourteen. I'm thinking that if he does his homework, he'll recognize a similarity in the decisions made by Anakin Skywalker . . . and Jacen Solo."

Luke moved over to sit beside her. "That could be helpful. But how do we make sure he does his homework? What do we use to motivate him?"

Mara took a deep breath. "We tell him that if we like his work enough to submit it to the Jedi library, we'll let him resume his duties as Jacen's apprentice."

Luke whistled. "Very chancy."

"Yes. But several things might happen by the time Ben has finished his project to *our* satisfaction. We might become convinced that Ben can see Jacen's flaws, his problems. Jacen might recognize his mistakes and become a fit teacher again. Jacen might . . . die."

"I could feel Jacen in the Force a few minutes ago. That's a rare thing these days. He hides from it whenever he wants . . . and just now he was channeling it, very strongly. I wonder what he's up to."

Before Mara could reply, Luke's comlink beeped. He pulled it out and thumbed its switch. "Yes?"

"Grand Master Skywalker, this is Apprentice Seha in the Reception Hall." The voice was female, young, breathlessly enthusiastic. "There is a man here who wishes to see you. He won't see any other Master."

"What's his name and his business with me?"

"He says his name is Twinsins Thlee. He doesn't have any identification to corroborate that. He says his mission concerns a lightsaber with a silver blade."

Luke and Mara exchanged a look. Luke thumbed the comlink microphone off. "Twinsins—Twin Suns Three?"

Mara nodded. "That's what it sounds like."

Twin Suns Squadron was an X-wing unit formed by Luke during the Yuuzhan Vong war more than a dozen years before. He had led it for a while, then turned command over to Jaina. It had been decommissioned after the war had ended, but in the years since, Luke had occasionally given the designation temporarily to ad hoc squadrons he'd commanded.

"Who was Twin Suns Three?" Mara continued.

"At various times, several different people." Luke thought back to a recorded holocam message he'd viewed only a few days before, a message sent by Han describing his and Leia's recent encounter on Telkur Station. "Jag Fel," he said. "Han said he was back. As for a silver lightsaber—" Silver blades were rare on lightsabers, and a woman who had once owned one of them had recently been of serious concern to Luke, though her new lightsaber had a different blade color.

"Alema Rar," Mara said.

"Right." Luke thumbed the comlink back on. "Tell our visitor we'll be right up."

Their visitor was only a little over average height but stood so straight that he seemed much taller. Dressed in a black flight suit and engulfed by a dark gray traveler's cloak, his face shadowed, he looked more like a forbidding figure from a cautionary children's tale than a peaceable visitor. The darkness of the lofty Temple Reception Hall, with most of its glow rods extinguished because of the late hour and shadows gathering in every corner, reinforced his somber manner.

Seha, the receiving apprentice on duty, bowed to Luke and Mara as they entered. She twirled a lock of red hair around nervous fingers. At Luke's gesture, she moved out into the main corridor.

Luke and Mara approached the visitor. Luke could read very little from him—no sense of menace, but also not one of friendliness. Perhaps a trace of anger, deeply buried. "Colonel Fel," Luke said.

Jag bowed and offered a little heel-click. "At your service," he said. He reached up to throw back his cloak hood, revealing the features Luke remembered. His was a lean face with startlingly bright green eyes and a scar leading up from his brow to his hairline. His hair was still dark, a bit longer than the military haircut he had once typically worn, with a mop of it hanging almost into his right eye; where his scar entered his hairline, one stripe of hair was white. The trim, rakish beard and mustache were new, and gave him an even greater resemblance to his father, the famous Soontir Fel.

Luke stepped forward to stretch out a hand. "Why the secrecy? You could have visited us officially, with your credentials."

"There are no credentials." Jag shook Luke's hand, then

Mara's when she offered it. "I'm no longer a colonel, no longer an ambassador. No longer a citizen of the Chiss, no longer even a member of my father's house. Technically, that suggests I'm no longer even Jagged Fel. I'm as much Twin Suns Three as I am anything else."

"Ah." Luke considered. Jag wasn't awash in self-pity, wasn't seeking sympathy with his words; he was just letting Luke in on things the Jedi Master needed to know. "And if I understand correctly, your mission here has something to do with Alema Rar."

"*Everything* to do with her."

"Take a walk with us," Mara said.

They walked through the halls of the Temple, which were mostly dim and little-trafficked at this hour, and Jag told the Jedi Masters, in unemotional tones, of the events of his last few years. How, during the Dark Nest missions, he had guaranteed the parole of Lowbacca, how Lowbacca had violated that parole, how the damage done by Lowbacca and his Jedi friends had become the responsibility of the Fel family . . . how Jag had been exiled from that family, as a matter of consequence and honor. How Jag had been shot down on the world of Tenupe and had survived there, a lean and dangerous existence, for two years. How Alema Rar, mad as a half-crushed bug and carrying within her mind the dual imperatives to re-create the Dark Nest and avenge herself on Luke and Leia, had also survived, also escaped.

"In those two years," Jag concluded, "I gave a lot of thought to Alema Rar, to what she was, what she could do. Afterward, I continued researching her . . . and investigating ways to counter her Killik abilities. She can scrub herself from the short-term memory of people, meaning that you can run into her and, if you survive, moments after the encounter you have no memory of meeting her. It makes her terribly hard to track. Her Killik abilities and remaining Jedi powers make her an extreme danger to you and your sister—and to the galaxy."

"So you've come here to warn me," Luke said. "I appreciate that."

"More than that, I come with gifts." From a tunic inner pocket Jag drew two items. One was the shape and size of a large credcoin, but silvery and featureless; no portrait of a long-dead hero or deserved-to-be-dead tyrant graced its faces, though a blob of some whitish substance adhered to one side. The other item was a common data card.

He handed the card to Mara. "This is a graphical interpreter and communications program," he said. "It operates in concert with most security holocam programs found in government installations, capital ships, any secure building. Basically, it evaluates every humanoid figure the cam sees, comparing them with a database of Alema Rar's unusual physical characteristics, and when it finds a match, it notifies the security department and sends a coded message to any data repository you specify. If you can get this installed on enough systems, we can perhaps plot her movements, find out her whereabouts before she does any more harm."

"That may not be as useful as you think," Luke said. "Alema probably knows the technique of the Force-flash, a method by which a Jedi can cause interference with holocams—even ones she's unaware of—in order to avoid being recorded."

Jag frowned, but he did not seem daunted. "This technique—does it make her invisible?"

Mara shook her head. "No. It creates a little static on the recording. Causes a sort of timing hiccup."

"That's not so bad," Jag said. "Part of the code involves analyzing incidence progression along a sequence of holocams—tracking an identified target. If we extend its analysis to these 'hiccups' and assign a probability that they indicate a single Force-using individual, the code could still plot her movements in observed areas."

"That might be useful in detecting Lumiya, too." Mara pocketed the card. "Thank you."

"Also on that card are complete schematics for this, so you can reproduce it." Jag handed the coin-like object to Luke. "You use the sticky material to affix this to your neck, or to a shaved spot on your skull. You activate it by saying 'Alema.' Deactivate it by tapping it twice with a fingernail." He demonstrated, tapping it as it lay in Luke's open hand. "From the time it's activated until it's deactivated, it sends electric shocks through your nervous system at one-standard-minute intervals."

Luke grinned. "That's helpful. Did you also bring me a brooch that will pinch my skin from time to time?"

"The shock," Jag continued humorlessly, "is very precisely attuned to human nervous systems. I haven't had the resources to determine the exact frequency needed by other species. The specific pain generated helps cause whatever is in your short-term memory to be transferred into long-term memory."

"Ah." Luke looked at the device more closely. "Meaning that Alema—" The disk began vibrating in his palm. Hastily he tapped it twice, and it ceased vibrating. "Meaning that she can't slip back out of your memory again."

"That's right."

Mara frowned. "You know, we ought to be able to duplicate that effect with use of the Force."

Luke nodded. "It's worth researching. I'd prefer a Force technique to going through something like circus-bantha obedience training. I'll put Master Cilghal on it." He tucked the disk into a belt pocket. "Fel, thank you. I mean that. Is there anything we can do for *you*?"

"I . . ." At last Jag sounded uncertain. "I hesitate to ask."

"Don't," Mara said. "I mean, don't hesitate."

"I don't have anything to do," Jag said, and his voice became curiously hollow, empty, "except chase Alema Rar until I run her to ground and make sure she can't do any more harm. But I don't have much in the way of resources. No transportation, little funding." He chuckled. "So odd to be living in the private sector. In the military, they give you a mission and whatever resources they can offer, sometimes too few, sometimes too many . . . repeat until you retire or die. Outside the military, everything is so complicated."

Luke clapped him on the back. "I'll get you resources. Starting with some quarters—"

"No. I have a room. The address, and my comm code and frequency, are on the data card. I'd . . . prefer not to stay here."

"All right."

"I'll go now. I can find my way out." With a final bow to the Jedi Masters, Jag turned—correctly, Luke noted, despite the many twists and turns their walk had taken them through, toward the Temple's main entrance—and strode away, pulling his hood up as he walked.

Mara watched him go and shook her head. "That's a man with not enough to live for."

"He'll bounce back," Luke said. "He's young." He fingered the device Jag had given him. "C'mon. Let's see if Cilghal is still up."

Returning to the Temple from a late errand, Jaina passed the lone Jedi performing guard duty at the building's wide-open main entrance and walked into the main corridor.

Just leaving was a man wrapped up in a dark cloak. He kept to the left side of the corridor, away from her, not even appearing to notice her. She hesitated as they came abreast of each other, his upright posture, military bearing, and the unconscious arrogance of his stride causing bells to sound in her memory.

When he was one step past her she stopped and turned her head to look at him. *"Jag?"*

He stopped, too, but did not turn. His face remained completely hidden within the folds of his hood. But it was Jag Fel's voice that answered: "Yes?"

"Were you just going to walk past? Not even say hello?"

"Yes." And then he was gone, swallowed up by the Coruscant night beyond the doors.

GYNDINE SYSTEM TENDRANDO REFUELING AND REPAIR STATION

Hands on hips, Han stood in the lounge of the vehicle now parked alongside the *Millennium Falcon.* "You have got to be kidding."

"If you'll forgive me, Captain Solo," C-3PO said, "Master Calrissian's vocal mannerisms, though laced with humor, do not suggest that his basic thesis was in jest."

Han glared at the gold-toned protocol droid, then returned his attention to his surroundings.

The lounge was, if not a thing of beauty, a testimonial to obsessive detail. The walls and ceiling were covered by thick velvety material in a dark blue that matched the deep carpet on the floor. Silver glow rod housings, polished to a dazzling level of reflectivity, protruded at tasteful intervals from the walls and ceilings. Furniture included four comfort couches, each with ceiling-mounted, semi-transparent privacy curtains that would glide into position or retract at the touch of a button. Controls for the couches' temperature and vibration settings were mounted on silver panels inset in the velvet walls. Hanging chairs of woven plantstalk, plated in a silvery surface, were suspended from the ceiling, gleaming tables stood nearby to bear the weight of platters of food, and a water fountain reproducing, in miniature form, a famous waterfall from the world of Naboo burbled in the center of the chamber.

Leia, beside Han, nodded. "It's even more crass than the *Lady Luck.*"

Lando, facing them from across the room to view their first reactions to the pleasure pit, smirked. "She's a bit like the *Lady.* An older model, a SoroSuub Twenty-four-hundred yacht. Her owner—her former owner—fell on hard times, and they got harder when he decided to win back his fortunes in a sabacc match I was sitting in on." He shrugged. "We had a lot in common, including taste in luxury yachts, but not including the fact that he drinks while gambling. I won his craft and a year's contract for his services as a salesman. He's marketing my droids in the Outer Rim now—and conveniently, the yacht is still officially registered in his name, since I somehow haven't found time to file the change-of-ownership documentation."

"What's her name?" Leia asked.

Lando modulated his voice to its richest, most seductive tones. "The *Love Commander.*" He stretched out the word *love,* an exercise in mockery.

Leia looked at him as though he could not possibly be telling the truth. At his confirming nod, she put her hands over her mouth, the better to restrain any laughter that might emerge.

Han shook his head. "I don't want to say what I think of her as a vehicle, but as a disguise, she's perfect." He pulled his left arm from its sling and flexed his hand experimentally. Several weeks' worth of medical treatments since he sustained the injury and a good night's sleep had improved his condition somewhat, and his manner suggested he would soon be his old fighting self. "Let's move our gear from the *Falcon* to the master cabin," he told Leia.

Lando shook his head. "No, you're in the biggest of the guest cabins. *I'm* in the master cabin."

They both looked at him. "You're coming along?" Leia asked.

"After due consideration, it seems to me that you'll be a

lot more anonymous as my pilot and navigator—*me* being Bescat Offdurmin, holo-entertainment mogul and pleasure-seeker of the Corporate Sector—rather than the faces the authorities see whenever they establish communications with the *Looooove Commander.* Right?"

"Well . . ." Leia considered. "That's true. But I don't look forward to Tendra tracking us down and killing us if we get you hurt."

"She'll be glad to get me out of the home for a while. She knows how twitchy I've been lately." Lando picked up his cane and twirled it theatrically. "Come on, nameless crew. Let's get to it."

Han clapped C-3PO on his metal shoulder. "Goldenrod, you get the most important mission of all. You stay here and record every single thing they do to the *Falcon* during repairs. And try not to talk to them while you're doing it."

"Oh, dear."

An hour later, personal possessions moved aboard and pre-flight checklists completed, Han, sitting at the navigator's console, was a bit more favorably disposed toward the *Love Commander.*

Despite the yacht's name and pleasure-oriented mission, despite her swirly, mood-altering sky-blue-and-green exterior paint job, the vehicle wasn't a bad choice for their current needs. At fifty meters, she was nearly twice the length of the *Falcon* but didn't mass much more, having a long, sleek design with two outrigger propulsion pods, one on either side, each carrying sublight ion drive and hyperdrive components. The hyperdrives were nothing special, but the ion drives had been rebuilt and overbuilt, giving the yacht considerable speed in sublight situations.

Nor was she unarmed, though at first glance it had appeared she was. A pop-up turret hidden beneath an artfully concealed access plate on the top hull held a turbolaser. At the bow beneath the bridge was a concussion missile port hidden behind a false dish in a sensor array. And the yacht did have shields, though the shield generator, appearing to be an auxiliary hatch, lay folded down against the top hull when not in use and would take a few seconds to raise into position and become active.

Now, with Leia in the pilot's seat—at Lando's insistence, since Han was not yet fully healed—and Lando in the oversized, preposterously comfortable captain's chair at the rear of the command cabin, the *Love Commander* lifted ponderously from her berth, backed on repulsorlifts away from the *Falcon,* and slid stern-first into vacuum.

"Where to, navigator?" Lando asked, activating his chair's massage vibration. "Someplace interesting, I hope."

"Should be interesting enough." Han finished putting their course into the nav computer. "Corellia. We're going to zip through the exclusion zone, laughing at the Alliance picket vehicles trying to blow us up. Then we're going to drop down to the planet's surface, determine whether Prime Minister Dur Gejjen was acting alone when he ordered the hit on Tenel Ka—which probably means beating a confession out of him—and then deciding whether to forgive him or kidnap him and his co-conspirators and bring them to justice."

"Oh," Lando asked. "What do we do on day two?"

Despite himself, Han snorted, amused. "We'll figure something out."

"Well, wake me when we get there, whatever-your-name-is."

EMPTY SPACE
ENGINE COMPARTMENT OF THE DURACRUD

Captain Uran Lavint lay on the grimy durasteel deck, half propped up against an almost equally grimy wall, and waited to die. Her tools lay scattered on the deck, along with the deck plates she had pulled up—plates that gave her access to the various components of *Duracrud*'s hyperdrive.

The only sounds to be heard were her own breathing and the distant, rhythmic noises made by the ship's life-support system. There were no lights on in the ship except here—mechanics' glow rods magnetically clamped to offer light to the hyperdrive compartment—and on the bridge, where status lights should still be winking in their various colors.

Lavint knew it would take her a long time to die. The *Duracrud* would continue to provide breathable air for weeks. The stores of food and water would run out first, in a few days. She'd have plenty of time to record and transmit a few final messages. One would denounce Jacen Solo for his treachery. One would confirm that her will, on file with an advocate's office on remote Tatooine, did accurately record her final wishes. She might even record a final speech, something to put her life into perspective.

Then she'd die of thirst, or, if she chose to end her suffering faster, she could shoot herself or step out an air lock.

But one thing she could be sure of: given the remote, untraveled nature of the spot she'd chosen for her first hyperspace jump, no cargo vessel or fast-moving courier would ever chance upon her . . . and her last transmissions, traveling at the speed of light, would take eight years to reach the nearest star.

She was as alone and doomed as anyone in the universe could be.

"Delicious, isn't it?" The voice was female, and came from outside the meager light provided by Lavint's glow rods.

Lavint jerked upright. She grabbed for her blaster, then remembered it was with her holster belt in her cabin—she'd left it there when collecting her tools. "Who's there?"

"Your suffering, we mean," the voice continued. "You suffer like a child who cries herself to sleep each night, knowing that her parents will never, ever understand. How long has it been since you were that child?"

Lavint rose on shaky legs and began to edge her way back to the door out of this compartment. At the door she could turn on the overhead glow rods and see who was tormenting her.

But she almost didn't want to turn on those lights. What if there was no one in the compartment with her? What if recognition of her fate had driven her crazy, and she was doomed to spend her last few days hearing voices?

As if reading her mind, the voice in the darkness laughed.

Lavint reached the doorway, found the light control by touch, and activated it. The overheads came on, bright, blinding her—

And then, as her eyes adjusted, she saw her visitor. And she knew she was not crazy, because her accumulated experiences and neuroses would never concoct a being like the one she saw.

Her visitor was a blue Twi'lek woman of no unusual size. She was dressed in a dark traveler's robe and black clothes. Her features were pretty, but she had obviously been the victim of catastrophe at some point in her life. Her left shoulder was lower than her right, with her left arm hanging in such a way that Lavint suspected it was nonfunctional, and her right head-tail had been severed at about the halfway point.

And now, as she stepped forward, she limped.

This was no monster in the night or phantom of the imagination. Lavint stared, incredulous. "Who are you?"

"We are Alema."

"Alema. And what are you doing here?"

"We are a stowaway."

Lavint stared at Alema for a few moments more, and then it happened. The laugh came bubbling up out of her like a high-pressure sanispray stream. The laugh became a painful howl. It shook her and it kept coming.

Dizzied, Lavint bent over to rest her hands on her knees and rested her backside against the bulkhead; otherwise she would have fallen. Finally her laughter trailed away, leaving her throat hoarse, her body weary.

Alema's expression did not change, except to become slightly curious. "Why do you laugh?"

"Because you're the worst stowaway in the galaxy, in history." Lavint straightened. "Because you picked the worst *possible* ship to stow away on. The Hero of the Galactic Alliance sabotaged my hyperdrive."

"We know this. We watched his agents do it."

That snapped Lavint out of her manic mood. "You *watched* it?"

"Yes."

"And got on board anyway."

"Yes." Alema smiled. "No, we do not wish to die. We stowed away after making sure of what the agents had done . . . and after acquiring the parts needed to repair the drive."

Lavint took an involuntary step forward. "You can fix it?"

"Yes. Though *we* will only fix it if you are dead. But if you and we come to terms, you will live and *you* will repair the drive."

Lavint had to parse that statement. Alema's use of *we* to refer to herself caused her sentences to jump through flaming hoops like a carnival bantha. "You mean, if we come to terms, I make the repairs and we both get out of here. If we don't come to terms, you presumably kill me and then you make the repairs and *you* get out of here."

Alema's smile broadened. "Good. Yes."

"What are your terms?"

"You help us find the parents of that Hero of the Galactic Empire. You act as a public face for us in that search.

You do not reveal our presence to the authorities. You do not attack or unnecessarily endanger us. You are one of the smugglers, yes? You use your knowledge of smuggling to help in this search." She furrowed her brow for a moment, then relaxed. "You treat us as an esteemed paying passenger."

"And once you've found the Solos?"

"You will have fulfilled your obligation."

Lavint considered her options. She'd always admired Han Solo, and this woman's obvious need to stay out of public sight didn't argue well for what her intentions were when she found him. Lavint could ask, but then she'd have to decide whether she was willing to object, and ruin this deal, if Alema's intentions were hostile.

Well, if they were, she could admire Han Solo as a unique piece of galactic history. "I agree."

"Good. We will find the replacement components where we have hidden them. We will even hand them to you as you effect repairs."

"Much obliged."

chapter six

CORONET, CORELLIA

The crowd seated in the assembly hall, mostly holonews professionals, applauded, but more courteously than enthusiastically.

That was all right, Wedge decided. He wasn't here to be validated. He just wanted brevity.

With a glance at Prime Minister Dur Gejjen to his left and Admiral Delpin to his right, Wedge leaned in over the lectern to conclude his speech. "The reorganization of any military force works best if it synthesizes mature experience with youthful innovation, mature patience with youthful energy. I like to think that in this time of crisis I've been able to provide the experience and patience. And I have every confidence that Admiral Delpin offers the innovation and energy to finish the job. Corellia's armed forces are in good hands."

He stepped back as the questions started.

Gejjen took his place. "Admiral Antilles and I will be taking our leave of you, but Admiral Delpin will be making some introductory remarks and then taking questions. Thank you." He nodded to Wedge, and together the two of them made their way to the end of the stage and the comparative privacy it offered.

The applause increased, and out of the corner of his eye Wedge saw a few of the news professionals rise to their feet for him. Then he and Gejjen were in the darker, cooler backstage area.

Not that Wedge could relax. Not yet.

Gejjen gave him a close look. "You're sweating."

"Hot under those lights."

They passed through the doors leading out of the backstage area. The CorSec guards waiting there—Gejjen's bodyguards, a tiny uniformed woman who moved like a dancer, and a YVH battle droid—fell in step behind them. "So what will you do now that you're a civilian again?" Gejjen asked.

Get assassinated, Wedge thought. *Maybe you personally won't have anything to do with it, even in thought or intent, but someone in your government will.* "Back to my memoirs. Maybe give my daughter some flying lessons."

"That's Myri, correct? Congratulations on her recent graduation. I understand Corellian Intelligence has made her an employment offer."

Wedge nodded. "So has the Galactic Alliance Intelligence Service, a bit more covertly."

Gejjen almost missed a step as he walked. He looked sharply at Wedge. "You're joking."

"Of course I'm not. The Alliance risks an undercover contact in Coronet to try to recruit my daughter as a double agent? I'm a proud father." Gejjen's suspicious look didn't waver, so he added, "Oh, don't worry. She didn't *take* the offer."

"And she reported everything she knew about that recruiter to CorSec, I assume."

"Of course not. Her mother and the institute taught her too well for that. That recruiter now falls into the category of one of her personal set of contacts. Maybe she'll choose to suborn *him*. Or use him for some other purpose."

Gejjen shook his head. "I really prefer to think that you're just kidding me."

Wedge nodded, affable. "You do that." He came to a stop beside a door leading into a refresher. "I need to make a quick stop. I'll catch up with you later."

"Don't forget the dinner three nights from now."

"I won't."

Gejjen and his bodyguards continued on their way. Wedge ducked into the refresher.

That dinner, a testimonial affair arranged to celebrate his retirement, was one piece of evidence pointing to the unlikelihood of an assassination attempt occurring today. Public appearances were the events where it would be easiest to eliminate him, and he had only two scheduled—today's holonews conference and the dinner. Nothing had happened at the conference, so the dinner became the next most likely opportunity.

But as Iella had pointed out, the story was just too good, too fulfilling to the public if he were to die today. *Minutes after stepping down from his position as military Supreme Commander of Corellia, Wedge Antilles was cut down by an Alliance assassin . . .* The viewing audiences would sympathize and say "Of course," and Wedge's life would fall into a neat little pile of perspective for them.

Once in the refresher, Wedge took a quick look around, making sure that no one waited in any of the stalls or the sanisteam unit at the end. He peered out the door again, assuring himself that the only beings in sight were Gejjen and party, now meters away and continuing toward the building's exterior doors.

From under his tunic, Wedge pulled a government-printed sign that read FACILITIES UNDER REPAIR. He pressed it to the front of the door, to which it adhered; then he shut and locked the door.

His package was waiting for him where it was supposed to be, affixed out of sight under the sink. He pulled the anonymous gray bag free and opened it on the sink counter.

Inside were a change of clothing—lightweight black pants, shirt, shoes, cap, belt—and a jacket decorated on its back with a view of Centerpoint Station. The long, lumpy, unlovely space station was now a rallying symbol for Corellians, and there were hundreds of thousands of jackets just like this one being worn on the streets.

Wrapped up in the clothes were a sun visor to conceal his eyes and a DH-17 blaster pistol, scoped, the precise pattern of venting on its barrel indicating that it was not of recent manufacture. But its gleaming black surface suggested that it had been meticulously maintained or recently restored. Wedge didn't care for the DH-17 as much as some other models—the grip angle prevented it from being a natural pointer for him—but it was a good weapon, and Iella was sure to have found one that could not be traced back to the Antilles family.

Hastily he shed his white admiral's uniform, tossing it into the sanisteam stall, and dressed in the garments from the bag. He put the DH-17 into the right-hand jacket pocket and kept his hold-out blaster, a smaller, less powerful weapon, in its little holster at the base of his spine.

Finally he looked at himself in the mirror.

Staring back at him was Wedge Antilles in a Centerpoint jacket and a visor over his eyes.

He sighed. Disguise never had been his strong suit. But at least someone fixated on looking for a man in an admiral's uniform might miss him.

Two minutes later he exited a side door of the government building, well away from the public front exit and the rear access that were the most likely points for his departure, and merged instantly with pedestrian traffic. At the same time he gave his comlink a click.

There was an immediate reply of two clicks, Iella letting him know that she saw him.

He had proceeded about a hundred meters down the walkway—as speeder traffic hurtled by to his left, he'd counted ninety-eight steps—when he heard three clicks on his comlink. Iella reporting that he was being tailed.

Wedge swore. This wasn't going to be a clean departure, then. He put his hands in his jacket pockets, gripping the blaster with his right.

Ahead, one street up, was the speeder hangar building where Iella had left the airspeeder that was to be his departure vehicle. It was, in fact, a vehicle belonging to the Corellian government, to the fleet of speeders used by minor functionaries; the day before, Iella had stolen it and put it in place on the building's fourth floor.

As he approached the street corner, Wedge weighed his options. The obvious one was to continue ahead, down into the depressed, plascrete-lined pedestrian underpass. But that would put him in a straight tunnel about twenty meters long with nowhere to duck if enemies entered behind him and began shooting.

Beside him, speeders occasionally slowed to allow passengers to board or depart. He could jump into one of those vehicles, commandeer it, make a run for it. But that wasn't inconspicuous, and he was likely to be identified.

He could break into a run, see if that flushed out his pursuers so that Iella could deal with them—

His decision was forced on him. His comlink crackled with Iella's voice, her cry of "Down!" He dived for the sidewalk, hit it hard, felt the air above his back heat up. Ahead, a speeder making a right turn onto the cross-street between Wedge and the parking hangar took a blaster bolt, a blaster *rifle* bolt, in the starboard side. That plasteel panel and the transparisteel viewport above it blackened and bowed in, and a moment later the speeder was lost to sight, hidden behind the building Wedge had departed mere moments ago.

Wedge rolled over toward the street to his left, freeing the blaster pistol from his pocket before he was completely on his back. He took quick note of the orange airspeeder now heading his way from a proscribed altitude above the normal traffic flow—realized that, from the angle of the shot meant for him, the speeder couldn't have been its source—and kept rolling, inverting as he did so, leaving him facing back the way he'd come as he rolled out into the traffic lane.

That wasn't as dangerous as it would have been had the traffic included ground vehicles. For the moment, it was all speeders, and the ones headed his way swerved or gained a little altitude as their pilots realized there was a man sprawled in the road.

They didn't swerve or climb particularly well. Three ran over him in the space of a second, but only their repulsorlift pulses hit him, pushing him harder into the roadway duracrete. And in passing over him, they provided a little cover from the oncoming airspeeder, giving him time to look for—

There they were on the sidewalk, two men in traveler's robes—Jedi robes? One carried a blaster rifle; the other, a silvery tube Wedge thought had to be an unlit lightsaber. There were no pedestrians between their position and Wedge's—no shock there, as they had obviously waited for the walkway to clear before firing.

He returned fire, squeezing the trigger as fast as he could, using each bolt's passage through the air to show him how to traverse. He knew the Jedi attacker would ignite his lightsaber and bat the bolts out of the air, but perhaps his wild spray of fire would cause the sniper to panic—

It didn't work out quite that way. Both men dived for the ground. Wedge's shots still hit the Jedi in the groin and then the face; that man twitched and then lay still, scorched and smoking.

The sniper resumed aiming . . . and Wedge resumed rolling, moving farther out into the traffic lanes, banging knees and elbows with every revolution, being hammered by the repulsors of each speeder that passed directly over him. His ears rang from the impacts.

A man dressed in an eye-hurting green jumpsuit fell out of the sky and landed beside the sniper. He was broad-shouldered, not tall, and had a bushy red beard that fell nearly to his waist. Even at this distance, something about him shouted *disguise* to Wedge.

The sniper looked up at the man from the sky, losing his fix on Wedge.

Wedge glanced up for a moment. The airspeeder that had been heading his way was now moving from a position directly over the sniper and back toward the traffic lane—back toward Wedge. The bearded man had to have come from it, and had to have dropped four stories to land beside the sniper.

The red-bearded man kicked the sniper full in the face. The force of the blow snapped the man's head back and sent him skidding for a meter across the sidewalk.

Wedge's comlink crackled again with Iella's voice. "Are you all right?"

"Yes—oof—bumpy." Wedge scrambled farther to his right, ending up in the gap between two traffic lanes moving in opposite directions.

"The awful orange speeder is your new ride. I'll retrieve the one I dropped off."

"Understood. Love you."

"Love you."

The orange speeder did a complete barrel roll as it roared over two lanes of traffic, then dropped precipitously into the gap where Wedge stood. He forced himself not to flinch as it came to a stop, its bow only a meter from him.

The pilot was a woman in her early twenties. Her eyes were hidden behind dark goggles, and her hair was a riot of colors, every lock seemingly a different hue. She pointed a gloved finger at him as if aiming a blaster pistol. "Hi, Dad!"

Wedge scrambled across the speeder's bow and over its windscreen, dropping into the front passenger's seat. "Myri! I thought you were supposed to stay at home, keep it secure."

"Plans change. Are you mad? Spelled, *ungrateful*?"

"No. Let's go."

"Just a second, we're waiting for—"

The speeder rocked and sank almost to ground level from the impact of something landing in the backseat. Wedge spun, saw a flash of awful green jumpsuit and red beard, and kept himself from swinging his pistol fully into line.

Then he caught sight of the eyes behind that preposterous red beard. "Corran!"

Corellia's resident Jedi Master grinned at him.

Myri hit the thrusters, and Wedge was shoved by acceleration into his seat back, toward Corran. He continued, "So Iella's message got to Mirax."

Corran nodded. "And my wife got the message to me, and I got to your quarters in time for Myri to get me here. Everybody got something. Hey, girl, keep it down to fifty meters or lower."

Myri waved at him, cheerfully ignoring his advice as she climbed to near rooftop level, but then her ballistic course reached its apex and she began a stomach-twisting dive toward a traffic lane a few blocks away.

"Sorry it was such a mess," Wedge said. "I really thought the disguise and side-door gambit would throw off pursuit."

"It did," Myri said. "Mom says the main hit teams were

assembled front and back. We missed about three-quarters of the assassins this way."

"Oh. Good. Please tell me that all that stuff will wash out of your hair."

"It will. But the tattoos are permanent."

"Tattoos?"

Myri laughed at him.

CORUSCANT
JEDI TEMPLE VEHICLE HANGAR

It wasn't a large number of starfighters, less than a full squadron's worth—nine X-wings, one E-wing—but they were all beautifully maintained, and Jag Fel felt an unexpected pang as he looked at them. It seemed so long ago that flying craft like these had been his whole life.

He missed that. He missed belonging to a band of comrades, divided by individual needs and peculiarities and prejudices but united in their goals and their support for one another.

He let none of what he was feeling reach his face.

"The Jedi order would like to fund and support your mission," Luke Skywalker was saying.

That snapped Jag's attention back to the present. "To find and destroy Alema Rar," he said.

"To find and *neutralize* Alema Rar," Luke corrected. "Yes, obviously, it might entail killing her. But should an opportunity arise to capture her, transport her back here . . ."

"So that she might be convinced to see the error of her ways?" Jag let just a hint of mockery enter his voice.

"No. So that she might find her own path to redemption."

Jag considered. Dealing with thc Jedi would always be like this, he decided. The military made plans based on objectives—such as *Find and eliminate an enemy force.* The Jedi didn't so much make plans as choose directions—

such as *Make things better.* Back in the days of the Yuuzhan Vong war, the two different approaches had been a bit closer to each other; in these less defined times, the basic incompatibilities were more obvious.

So he would have to adjust his thinking a bit if he was to work with the Jedi. But he was a bit unsettled to realize that he wasn't sure the Jedi approach was the wrong one. Even with Alema Rar . . . Once he, Jag, had known a Jedi girl who had stepped off the right path, gone the wrong way for a while. She had found her own way back soon enough. But what if she hadn't? If she had continued, might she not be a bit like Alema Rar, and would Jag be just as sanguine about hunting her down and killing her?

"I accept," he said.

"Good. I'm actually heading up a similar unit, pursuing leads involving the Sith lady Lumiya. She may be dead now—or maybe not—but what's clear is that she was in alliance with Alema as of a few days ago, when they ambushed me and Mara. Now that it's clear that Lumiya was, or is, employing agents, and who some of them are, we stand an improved chance of finding her trail."

"I don't know much about her. I assume the term *Sith lady* doesn't bode well."

"Not well at all. I'll get you the basic information on her." Luke reached into a pocket and handed items over to Jag. "Identicard. It identifies you as Jagged Fel, a civilian specialist employed by the Jedi order. The second one's a credcard. It gives you access to a drawing account set up for your task force. The third is a security card with what you need to assume control of"—he pointed—"that X-wing. Sorry I can't provide you with a Chiss clawcraft."

"That's all right. I'm fond of X-wings, as well."

"I also want to assign a couple of Jedi to you. You're hunting a Dark Jedi; you'll benefit from having Jedi with you."

"I agree."

Luke glanced toward a door leading into the hangar. "Speaking of which . . ."

He must have been alerted by an impulse in the Force, for when Jag followed his glance, the door was shut. But now it slid up and open, and a woman in brown Jedi robes walked into the hangar. "Uncle Luke, you wanted to see—oh."

Jag refrained from stiffening. It was Jaina Solo. His mind clicked through a number of possibilities and arrived at one inescapable conclusion: that she was going to be—

"I'm putting together a small task force to find Alema Rar," Luke said. "Colonel Fel here is in charge. I'm assigning you to it, and Zekk, when he's fit to fly."

Jaina came to a stop a few meters away, looking between the two men as if still expecting the punch line to a joke that already wasn't funny. "That is not a good idea. I don't think I can operate as this man's subordinate."

Luke gave her a quizzical look. "Back in the Yuuzhan Vong war, though he outranked you, he didn't offer you any grief about being *your* subordinate."

"Things are different now."

Luke nodded. "Yes. You're both older and wiser. And on top of that, the two of you have worked together before, know each other's strengths and weaknesses, and have complementary skills. Consider it settled." He glanced between them. "I'll leave you two to get caught up. Jag, please get me a plan of operation at your earliest opportunity." He turned and headed toward the door.

Jag waited until Luke was out of hearing. "The problem with Jedi Masters," he said, "is that they can't be beaten with impunity."

Jaina looked at him, suspicious. "Jag, did you just make a joke?"

"No." He clamped down on the anger rising within him. "He knows why I wouldn't want to work with you and has decided to disregard my wishes. I'll have to assume that his reasoning is sound, whatever it is, until proven otherwise. All right, let's do some strategic planning."

"Why wouldn't you want to?" Jaina was clearly confused and, so far as Jag could tell, possibly hurt as well. "Because of what happened with the Dark Nest?"

"It doesn't matter. We have planning to do." He gestured toward the door.

She stood her ground, glaring. "It does matter. If I'm going to be working in a hostile environment, I need to know why. If we have a problem, you should have told me about it years ago."

"I couldn't." The words, heated, snapped out of him. "I was stranded on Tenupe for two years. And because of your actions, ignoring the consequences of freeing Lowbacca and what he did subsequently, I am now barred from my family forever. And *that* is the why."

She gaped. The anger didn't leave her face, but something in it changed. Jag supposed that she was offended either by his blaming her or by the fact that he had been punished for the action of others. "Yes," he added, "the Jedi way preaches forgiveness, but that isn't the Chiss approach. To the Chiss and my family, I am an unperson, and that's forever. Don't bother thinking about ways to correct the situation—it would be roughly as useful as worrying about painting out the laser damage your uncle left on the hull of the Death Star. Instead, worry about Alema Rar."

Finally her mouth closed. It took her a few moments, but military discipline reasserted itself. "All right. Strategic planning." At his gesture, she preceded him to the door back into the Temple hallways.

CORELLIAN EXCLUSION ZONE
LOVE COMMANDER

"I feel," Lando announced, "like an idiot." He studied himself in the main display screen serving the captain's chair on the *Love Commander* control cabin. Mounted on a swing-out arm so that it could be positioned directly before him or moved out of the way, it was now beside his chair and switched off. Reflective when not active, it showed him in his new guise, wearing a white beard and mustache, and a white wig with hair so long that the braid swinging from it would reach to his thighs when he stood.

"But you look magnificent," Leia said.

"Oh, I know that. Not even the wig could downgrade me to 'just startlingly handsome.' " Shrugging, Lando swung the display screen completely out of the way. He affixed Han with a stern stare. "Navigator, our heading?"

Han returned his glare. He'd had to go to a greater extreme to disguise himself. Without a beard, he looked like Han Solo; with one, he looked like his cousin, Thrackan Sal-Solo, the late Corellian President. So more significant efforts were called for. He'd sprayed all exposed areas of skin with a cosmetics compound that turned him a yellowish hue, and the spiky black halves of his false mustache, had they continued up to his nose, would have made a perfect chevron. "Same as it was five minutes ago, *Captain,*" he said. "Straight toward Corellia. Straight from Coruscant. Along the most heavily patrolled corridor through the exclusion zone."

"Good, good." Lando nodded benignly. "I'm glad you haven't managed to foul up in five minutes."

Han flexed his shoulder experimentally. He was recovered enough not to need the sling at most times, but still not in shape to handle piloting in extreme situations. "When I'm better, I'm going to throttle you."

"Good, good."

Leia smiled and turned back to her control board. She was the least dramatic looking of the three. Dressed in a dumpy brown jumpsuit padded here and there to make her less visually interesting to male observers, wearing makeup that diminished her beauty rather than enhancing it, her hair in a nondescript style and tucked up into her cap, she was unexceptional in every way.

Then, as her attention fell on the sensor screen, her eyes brightened. "We have an incoming blip. No telemetry yet, except that it's bigger than a starfighter, smaller than a capital ship."

"Good, good."

"Stop *saying* that," Han muttered.

"Here we go." Leia patched the comm board through the overhead speakers.

"Incoming craft, this is *Spinnerfish,* Galactic Alliance Second Fleet. Cut your sublight engines and identify yourself immediately." The voice was male, curt, an alto trying to force itself into the range of a baritone.

At Lando's nod, Leia killed the ion thrusters. Lando swung out his display screen again and activated it.

Before him was the image of a young man, crisply attired in an Alliance Fleet lieutenant's uniform. He was clean-shaven, his face angular, his manner stern, official. Behind him were cockpit chairs arranged in a configuration Lando recognized. *Armed shuttle,* he told himself. *Don't we rate at least a corvette?*

But he put on his friendliest smile and modulated his voice into its richest tones. "Hello! I'm Bescat Offdurmin, master of the private yacht *Looooove Commander.* What's a spinnerfish?"

The lieutenant opened his mouth as if to answer, looked confused for just a fraction of a second, and thought better about responding. "*Love Commander,* you are entering restricted space. You have to turn around and depart the Corellian system."

"Oh, no, son, I'm here for at least a month. I'm here to gamble."

"Gamble—sir, what's your planet of origin?"

"That would be Coruscant."

"Then you have to be aware that the Galactic Alliance and the Corellian system are currently in a state of war."

"You don't say. What has that got to do with gambling?"

"It means you can't visit."

"Son, I don't see that gambling has anything to do with anything. My gambling in Corellia won't alter the course of the war one millimeter. I mean, it's not as though I had a bunch of smuggling compartments filled with bacta or offers of aid from Commenor, is it?"

The lieutenant's mouth worked for a moment. Then he said, "*Love Commander*, prepare to be boarded and inspected."

Lando smiled agreeably. "Now, that's the kind of thing I like to hear. Decisiveness. Crew, activate the top air lock and prepare to be boarded."

The lieutenant and two security officers came aboard. Han took the security men on a tour of the yacht while the lieutenant came to the control cabin, his datapad in hand and questions on his mind. He sat in the navigator's seat while Leia pretended to ignore him.

"Captain Offdurmin, do you know what the penalties are for offering aid and comfort to the enemy in a time of war?"

"I imagine they're pretty harsh," Lando said. "Good thing we're not doing that."

"Good thing we're not doing that," Leia quietly echoed, making a small gesture with two outstretched fingers.

"So it's a good thing you're not doing that," the lieutenant said. He checked an item off on his datapad.

"No," Lando continued, "what we're actually doing is something else. Something vital to the Alliance's war effort."

"Vital," Leia said.

The lieutenant nodded, earnest, interested. "Vital."

"So we have to get to Corellia."

"So we *have* to get to Corellia."

"Well, you obviously have to get to Corellia, then."

Lando shrugged. "But how?"

The lieutenant thought about it. "Well, it's a pity you don't have any of the access codes provided by Intelligence. That would allow you to fly right in."

"Oh, that *would* be handy." Lando fixed the lieutenant with what he hoped was an honest look. "Do you have a lot of those recorded on your shuttle, son?"

The lieutenant laughed. "I can't tell you, sir."

"Of course you can," Leia said.

"Of course I do."

"Why don't you just give us one, then?"

"Why don't you just give us one, then?"

The lieutenant nodded. "That would solve everyone's problem, wouldn't it?"

Lando smiled. "It sure would."

The lieutenant rose. "I can't just transmit that sort of information. I'll go download it from our bridge computer and give you a datachip. How does that sound?"

"Sounds wonderful."

"I'll be right back."

When he was gone, Lando looked at Leia. "That wasn't really fair, was it?"

She shook her head, smiling. "He was even more weak-minded than I'm used to. I don't think he's going to progress far in the service. But I still prefer this sort of thing to cutting people's arms off."

"And what's your plan for when we're past the Alliance blockade and dropping down into Corellia's atmosphere, with starfighters coming up to blast us out of the sky?"

"Well, we can either transmit who we really are and that we want to see Dur Gejjen, which will either get us an audience or get us assassinated. Or we can try the Jedi mind tricks again, but it'll be harder to cover up because lots of planetary sensor sites will have picked up our presence. Or we can orbit until we detect a distraction and try to go to ground near that spot, using it for cover."

Lando dithered for a few seconds. "I say Number Three. And we can resort to Number One if it starts to go bad on us."

Leia smiled. "You always did like to have a skifter in reserve."

chapter seven

STAR SYSTEM MZX32905, NEAR BIMMIEL

Today it was to be makeup—good old-fashioned powders and pigments and pseudo-skin appliances. Lumiya sat before a brightly lit mirror and got to work.

It was painful, of course. Not long ago, Luke Skywalker had shot her five times with a blaster. Two of those shots had hit prosthetic limbs, with simulated pain that could be switched off instantly and damage that could be repaired within minutes. But three of those shots had found meat, and despite the fact that she healed at an unnaturally high rate—both from Force-based healing trances and from the alterations made to her body decades earlier by the science of Emperor Palpatine—she was far from recovered. She *hurt*.

And that was why it was to be makeup today. When trying merely to hide her scarred features, she normally wore an identity-concealing scarf wrapped around her lower face; she could bring up the Force illusion of normal features if obliged to reveal herself. But distracted as she now was by injuries, her control might slip, allowing viewers a glimpse of the real features beneath.

Properly applied pseudo-skin didn't slip.

Paint-on pseudo-skin eliminated the web of age lines at the corners of her eyes and mouth. Little pads affixed to the insides of her cheeks gave her face a rounder appearance. A dot of fluid that caused flesh to contract or even wither convincingly provided her with dimples. Pseudo-skin appliances covered her scars and gave her jaw a softer, less angular line. An application of foundation smoothed out all discrepancies of texture or tone . . . and on top of that she added blush, a striking red lip color, eyeliner. She donned the wig at the end, covering her graying red hair with a tumbling mass of long golden curls.

When she was done, she appeared to be a woman of thirty, roughly half her true age, and to possess the beauty and many of the racial stock characteristics of a woman of the Hapes Consortium.

She drew on the Force to dull her pain while she rose and dressed in a green gown and matching neck scarf, both overlaid with a webwork of gold thread, and altogether too much sapphire jewelry, all appropriate to a wealthy Hapan woman.

It was important to dull the pain. If she hurt too much, she'd perspire, and her makeup would be undone.

Dressed, she looked at herself in the mirror again, ensuring that the makeup had endured. "The decorator is through with my Battle Dragon," she said. A mnemonic, the phrase allowed her to recapture the Hapan accent quickly. "The decorator is through with my Battle Dragon."

Ready and confident, she gave herself a nod and then marched into the next room.

It was a hemispherical holocomm chamber. The central area, essentially a studio-quality stage, was surrounded by a ring of holocams that together would sample a three-dimensional image. Carefully programmed and adjusted for depth of field, they would only record images from that central area; they could not read objects farther away. That meant there was a safe zone around the central area, a ring where observers could stand and not be captured by the holocams. The walls were covered to a height of three meters by the broadcasting equipment, which transmitted via hyperspace, allowing instantaneous communications with targets half a galaxy away.

Lumiya's servant-droids had set up the central area with a chair that plausibly looked like a marble throne—Lumiya knew it to be foamplas covered in a beautiful mottled green-and-white veneer—and a matching side table. On the table was a bowl of peeled oversized grapes.

She sat carefully on the throne and sampled one of the grapes. It was gummy, nasty—not a true grape at all, but a candy-like material produced by an ancient food fabricator that had been new when this station was built. She smiled as though the grape were the best she'd ever tasted, and the pang of pain from her stomach wound would only add to an observer's impression that it was delightful.

The chrono above the main comm board counted down the last few seconds remaining to her. As it neared zero, she said, "Contact three three nine."

Lights above the holocams flared up, bathing her in brightness, and the holocomm unit activated with a surge of noise resembling the engine start-up sound of a well-tuned high-performance speeder.

The disembodied voice of the system computer, male and pleasant, said "Contact." A moment later it added, "The target system is acknowledging. They are receiving." The computer's voice would be electronically scrubbed from the audio signal being sent.

No return hologram appeared before Lumiya. The target was receiving but not yet responding. Lumiya ignored the fact, presenting an appearance of unconcern while devoting herself to the bowl of repulsive grapes.

After nearly thirty seconds, a hologram materialized before her—the image of a Bothan male, his fur mostly black with patches of tan, including one patch surrounding his eyes that gave him the appearance of a mask wearer being broadcast in negative. He wore informal attire: gray pants and a matching loose tunic that bared much of the fur of his chest and neck. "Who are you, and how did you get this frequency and access code?"

Lumiya finished her grape before turning her attention to the hologram. "I am a humble daughter of a noble house, and I obtained these things by paying a fortune to the correct people. And *you* are Tathak K'roylan, deputy intelligence leader for the esteemed world of Bothawui."

Esteemed was perhaps too strong a word, but it was true that there was a certain amount of respect between the Hapans and Bothans. They did not have much contact, but each recognized in the other a mastery of political maneuvering, manipulation, and conspiracy.

K'roylan didn't bother to insist on her name. She hadn't offered it when asked; she wouldn't volunteer it. "So," he said, "you have my attention. Briefly."

Lumiya smiled. "I will say things. You do not have to confirm or deny them. Then I will give you my frequency and access code. After this message ends, I suspect you will speak with your superiors and then, eventually, initiate a return communication."

"Go ahead." K'roylan was professionally civil. Even if he was outraged by this intrusion into his personal time and by the fact that his security had been at least partially compromised, it wasn't smart to insult someone who could reach him this way . . . and it always helped to have very wealthy contacts.

"The Bothans are preparing three fleets for an assault on Galactic Alliance forces," Lumiya said. "A just response to what you have suffered at their hands, including a series of assassinations of key Bothan personnel on Coruscant. But your planners are impeded because it will be impossible to launch the fleets from the Bothawui system and other origin points without being detected, and probably shadowed, by Galactic Alliance forces. This eliminates your ability to perform surprise attacks."

The Bothan shrugged, looking at her as though he hadn't recognized a single term she'd used.

"So," she continued, "I am communicating to inform you that I can blind the GA observers and give you an opportunity of, oh, ten to twenty standard hours in which to deploy your forces without being detected. Of course, to do this, I would have to have information sources planted deep within the GA government, and I do. I shall prove this by providing you with some information. Free, useful information." She modulated her voice, making it lower, more sultry. "Favvio, transmit the package."

The computer's voice responded, "At once, Mistress."

"The files now coming up on your displays," Lumiya continued, "are from the internal records of the Galactic Alliance Guard. They include details on the assassinations I mentioned a moment ago. By details, I mean details that the holonews services never had. Exact times, places, and methods of assassination. Personal items the victims were carrying. What the victims were doing before they were killed, including recordings of their conversations and transmissions. Things that only the killers and their superiors could possess."

The fur rippled on K'roylan's snout, just for a moment. It could have been nothing more than an itch. Lumiya admired his self-control. As cold-blooded as the Bothans could be about such matters, K'roylan could well have lost friends to this spree of assassination, and probably had.

"Irrespective of your earlier statements about imagined Bothan military activity," he said, "if these files turn out to be accurate, you will earn our thanks. They will be most useful when we prosecute the killer or killers."

"You are welcome." Lumiya gave him a nod, pure Hapan condescension. "Now I will go about other duties.

The last file transmitted has information on how and when to reach me . . . should you need to."

The Bothan opened his mouth to reply, but his hologram suddenly disappeared—Lumiya's computer, primed to end the transmission when she made a specific statement, had done so.

Lumiya sagged in her chair. Her upright posture had put pressure on her abdomen, and it had been a drain through the second half of the conversation to keep the pain at bay. Now she could assume a more comfortable pose and concentrate on managing it.

But she didn't have forever. The Bothans would check out her files, which would be verified. After all, she'd killed or arranged for the deaths of most of those Bothans—the details she had about those murders *were* accurate.

And the Bothans would accept her further help. They had to.

Now it was time to offer Jacen a little aid. "Transmit the Syo package to Coruscant and to Jacen," she said.

"At once, Mistress."

ELMAS PRIVATE SPACEPORT,
CORONET, CORELLIA
LOUNGE OF THE **LOVE COMMANDER**

The insertion onto Corellia had not been as difficult a task as Leia and the others had feared.

They'd maintained a high orbit near a cluster of Alliance vessels, nervously waiting for their intelligence authorization to be revealed as a fake, until they had detected a small task force forming up. It consisted of a sensor-heavy shuttle, several starfighters, and a couple of bombers—obviously intended to make one or more reconnaissance passes over the planet's surface. Playing on their intelligence authorization, Han had commed in, requesting permission to accompany the task force down into the atmosphere.

"Sure," had come the mission commander's reply. "But if you get blown up, you can't expect us to come back and pick up the pieces."

So they had flown down at the tail end of the task force, had waited until a squadron of Corellian TIE fighters had fallen on the force, and had broken away, using terrain-following flying—as terrifying with Leia at the controls as it would have been with Han doing the honors—until they were well clear of the engagement zone and pursuit.

Now, hours later, they waited in a hangar that cost a fortune to rent but came with the scant protection offered by one smuggler when renting to another. Han's old contacts continued to pay off—so long as Lando was willing to pay out.

They waited for nightfall and the covering darkness it would bring, as slight as that might be in the heart of the city, and reviewed recent news broadcasts.

One that was often cycled showed Wedge Antilles at his retirement announcement.

"He'd never retire at a time like this," Leia said, "so he's being forced out."

Lando smoothed his false beard. "But is he being forced out because he didn't approve of the attack on Tenel Ka, or because it was his plan and it failed?"

Han snorted. "He put his career on the line to retake Tralus with a minimum of casualties. That whole mess at Hapes couldn't have been his plan. It didn't work the way he thinks."

"But he'll know who was responsible," Lando said. "I think we should ask him."

Han and Leia exchanged a glance. "It may not be as easy as that," Leia said. "We've already tried to reach him by comlink. All we got was a recorded message saying that he and his family were celebrating his retirement by going on vacation. Not where, not for how long, no information on how to reach him."

"Who would know?"

"Their best friends are on the other side," Leia said. "Tycho and Winter Celchu."

Han frowned. "He's leaving Corellia."

Leia and Lando both looked at him. Lando looked confused, as if Han had been using stepping-stones to cross a stream and Lando couldn't spot the stones to follow him. "How do you figure that?" Lando asked. "His home is here."

Han irritably waved that notion away. "His home is the military. For him, Corellia's just a good place to retire. He didn't even grow up onplanet. He grew up on a refueling station that doesn't exist anymore. No, he's got to get offworld. He's in disgrace with his former bosses, bosses who assassinate, and he's not going to leave his family vulnerable to them." He considered for a moment. "He'll be in hiding now. What we'd have to do is figure out how he's going to get offworld—assuming he hasn't already—and meet up with him. And that would be a lot of work."

Leia nodded. "We may want to forget about him and go straight for Dur Gejjen or Denjax Teppler instead."

As it had on previous cycles, the Coronet news feed reached the Jedi assassins story: "In related events, mystery surrounds the savage street attack by Galactic Alliance Jedi on unnamed Coronet citizens shortly after Admiral Antilles's retirement announcement." The holocam view switched to show a tall, strongly built young man, dressed in sweat-stained agricultural coveralls, a big, panicky grin partially concealing his bantha-in-searchlights look. "First rodder just shot first Jedi," he said, his voice marked by the distinctive twang of agrarian townships surrounding Coronet. "Second rodder kicked second Jedi, put him right out. Whole thing took two seconds." The grin suddenly went from nervous to genuinely pleased. "Jedi aren't so tough. Later, bunch of us are gonna go on a Jedi hunt."

Leia grimaced. "Fake Jedi? Or is the whole story fake?"

"Not our problem," Han said. "Dur Gejjen is a reptile, and I don't intend to walk into his nest. Denjax Teppler may have no power, but he's been friendly before and may know something. Let's see if we can get to him."

CORONET, CORELLIA

In the quietest hours of the morning, the three of them huddled around a small table in the most private sort of cantina.

The privacy didn't come from remoteness. Situated on a major thoroughfare near the city's main spaceport, it was well trafficked during daylight and evening hours. Because it catered so much to offworlders and business traffic, its clientele was not chiefly made up of local regulars. Strangers elicited no curiosity. Bartenders with access to a modified spray-pattern blaster discouraged trouble and the official attention trouble might bring, while a commercially minded bar owner who paid all the correct under-the-table bills discouraged other official or criminal inspection.

The table Han, Leia, and Lando sat at was toward the back of the main room, where the thousand colorful rays of light from above-the-bar decorations and along-the-wall glow rods fell only dimly. They had a good angle on the door, and looked up every time someone entered the cantina.

And this time they didn't instantly dismiss the new customer as a prospect; the glow rods above the door showed him to be wrapped in a cloak, its hood casting his face into deep shadow. He stood there as the door swung shut behind him and scanned the bar's interior.

Not sure whether this was Teppler's intermediary, Han straightened, made a *look-at-me* motion, and caught the new customer's attention. The man walked over and, without invitation, sat on the table's fourth chair. He didn't lower his hood, but at this distance Han recognized Denjax Teppler. His were handsome, if bland, features, the sort that belonged to a drinking buddy employed as a statistician or sales manager.

Han cocked an eyebrow at him. "Isn't it risky for you to travel alone? I thought for sure you'd send a Rodian with a scar and a limp to escort us to a secret hideaway."

Teppler snorted. "All my hideaways are being monitored. As I am. But awhile back I hired a look-alike, and my surveillance follows him home. Meaning I can sometimes walk around freely."

"With no bodyguards," Leia said.

Teppler nodded. "Yeah." He looked up as a waiter droid, a cylinder on wheels with eight arms, rolled up. "Whiskey and water," he said, making his voice hoarse. "Prewar."

The droid rolled away, and Teppler returned his attention to the others, particularly Lando. "I don't know you."

Lando extended his hand. "Lando Calrissian."

Teppler shook it. "Nice to meet you. Though I think you picked a bad time to come out of retirement."

"Just as you picked a bad time to go into politics."

"True." Teppler turned back to Han and Leia. "So why am I here?"

"The attack on Queen Mother Tenel Ka," Leia said.

"Ah."

"First," Han said, "did you have anything to do with it?"

Teppler shook his head.

"Or know anything about it?"

"Not until it was under way."

"Han and I were at the site of the assassination attempt," Leia said. "Because of that and for some other reasons, the GA suspects us of being involved, and because we transmitted a warning to Tenel Ka, the Corellians blame us for spoiling the plan. So we're interested in clearing our names."

"And in beating the responsible parties until they're skin sacks full of stew," Han added.

Leia glanced at her husband, her *that-wasn't-entirely-helpful* look. She returned her attention to Teppler. "Now, I know that doing what we ask puts you in a quandary. If you accept, technically you're betraying the secrecy acts of your government, a treasonable offense. But I also know you're opposed to a lot of what goes on. Thrackan Sal-Solo is dead, but his spirit lives on in portions of the new government. And whoever ordered the attack on Tenel Ka has become our enemy. Our enemies don't tend to fare very well, and we will do whatever we can to bring him or her down. So I put it to you that if you don't tell us who ordered that mission, it's only because it was someone you want to remain in power."

Teppler was silent a long moment, not looking at any of them. The waiter rolled up during his pause and set down his drink. Teppler handed the droid a pair of credcoins, then sipped at the whiskey until the droid was out of earshot.

Finally, he said, "There's no such thing as treason anymore, you know that?"

Han and Leia exchanged a confused glance. "How do you figure that, kid?" Han asked.

"Everything you do helps someone. Everything you do hurts someone. Everything you do violates a law while supporting an ethic, or vice versa. The only differentiation is whether you do things out of selfishness or altruism—and altruism just means, *I'm doing this to create a better world, as I define* better. And if there's no such thing as treason anymore, there's also no such thing as loyalty. You know what I mean?" He raised his glass again, and when he put it down it was empty.

Looking at him, Han felt a little pang of sympathy. Teppler's eyes seemed devoid of life. "I think," Han said, "when we leave Corellia, you ought to come with us."

Teppler laughed. "I can't leave."

"We can get you offworld, no problem," Han said. "We have a good transport."

"I know. It's at the Elmas port, correct?"

Han's hand fell automatically onto the butt of his holstered blaster. He took a quick look around, but no one other than the waiter droid seemed to be paying them any attention. He kept his voice low, under control. "How did you know?"

"Where else would you be? You're smugglers. Organized crime—of the syndicate kind, I mean—controls Port Pevaria, and Galactic Alliance Intelligence has its tentacles all through that place. If you were more upright GA citizens, you'd have had contacts there to berth with. And it's there that CorSec is doing most of its looking for that mystery transport that made landfall earlier today. But smugglers, of the old-fashioned, freelance kind, they have most of their contacts over at Elmas, as they have for generations. If CorSec had any idea that it was Han Solo who made landfall, that's where they'd be right now, in force."

"Oh." Han sat back and forced himself to relax . . . a little. "But that supports my point. We can get you offworld."

"I'm no good with a blaster," Teppler said.

Lando frowned. "You know, you're more than commonly confusing to talk to, even for a politician."

"I'm not a hand-to-hand combatant," Teppler went on, "and I'm an indifferent pilot. I don't have an affinity for technical gear. But listening to people, sorting out truth from lies, guessing at motivations, manipulating people, encouraging them, maneuvering them—that's where I'm strong. You know, politics."

"I still don't get it," Han said.

Leia spoke up. "He's saying that politics is his battlefield, and you're encouraging him to run away from the battle."

"Oh." Han thought about it. "Yeah, I am."

Teppler turned a sad but scornful expression onto him.

"Do you also encourage all your friends to run away from their fights?"

Han shook his head. "Not for a long time. Not since I got to know them and realized that they had a chance to win. You, kid, don't have that chance. If you stay here, you're going to die."

"Yeah, probably." Teppler stared into the depths of his whiskey tumbler. "My ex-wife went on her last diplomatic mission knowing she might die. And she did. Am I so much less than she is?"

The others looked among themselves, for once at a loss for words, but Teppler was the first to speak. "Dur Gejjen," he said.

"Complete sentences, please," Lando said.

"Dur Gejjen was the chief planner for, and signed off on, the mission to kill the Queen Mother, Tenel Ka."

Leia nodded. "And it was an assassination mission? Not a kidnapping attempt?"

"If they had grabbed her, they would have killed her."

Leia pressed on. "Wedge Antilles?"

"He didn't know about it. He was ordered to step down because he didn't support waging a war that dirty." Teppler held up his glass, a signal to the waiter droid to refill it.

Leia felt a little trickle of alarm, but it seemed remote, not directed at her. Closing her eyes, she extended her awareness through the Force to areas beyond her immediate surroundings—through the ceiling and floors, walls on all sides . . .

Outside the front door and wall, she found outrage. Someone wanting to come in, but being prevented. More than one someone. A gradual massing of bodies . . .

She opened her eyes. The waiter droid was just rolling up. She asked the droid, "What's immediately beneath us?"

"That would be the storage and distillery rooms, my lady," the waiter said, its voice cultured like C-3PO's but not as singsong. "We no longer do tours of our microdistillery, but the floor is available for rent for private parties, holodrama recordings—"

"Quiet," Leia said. "Han, Lando, door."

The front door slammed open and two CorSec agents, in battle armor, carrying blaster rifles, were the first ones through it.

Han's blaster cleared its holster and Lando tipped the table over toward the intruders, providing cover.

Han shot the first intruder in his chest armor. The blast didn't penetrate, but the impact knocked the man backward into a new wave of CorSec enforcers trying to get through the door.

Teppler dived behind the table, switching his tumbler to his left hand, drawing his own hold-out blaster with his right. He fired over the table edge. His shot hit the glowing STREET sign over the door, incinerating it, raining sparks down on the intruders jammed there.

Leia ignited her lightsaber. She spun to crouch behind the table, then plunged the glowing blade into the floor. She began to drag it around in a wide circle.

The second intruder fired at the only upright figure in the vicinity. His blaster rifle shot hit the waiter droid at about knee level and neatly severed the cylinder there. With a somewhat inconvenienced-sounding cry of "I say," the droid toppled sideways; the tray of drinks and empty glasses it had been carrying crashed to the floor. A wave of shattered glass, half-melted ice, and unbreakable transparisteel containers washed across table, chair, and patron legs.

Lando extracted his blaster from beneath the folds of his hip cloak. He brought it up parallel with Han's and fired, catching the faceplate of the intruder who had shot the droid. That man, too, staggered back and down, adding to the congestion at the doorway.

Leia finished her sweep with the lightsaber and a rough

circle of flooring a meter and a half in diameter dropped away into darkness, rattling against a hard surface a moment later. "Let's go," she said, making it sound like a suggestion, and dropped through. Her lightsaber lit her new surroundings; she was in a darkened, narrow corridor.

Lando looked at Han. "You first." He took another shot at the doorway, catching a CorSec trooper in the second rank right on the kneecap.

Han gestured for Lando to go. "Age before beauty."

"Idiots." Teppler dropped through, blaster in one hand and tumbler in the other, landing awkwardly behind Leia.

Rear ranks of invaders shoved the plug of stunned or injured troopers out of the doorway; four spilled into the bar, more jamming up at the door. Han fired again and caught one in his armored gut, sending him spinning to the floor. The others returned fire and Han, braced behind the tabletop, stared in alarm as whole chunks of its artificial wood surface were torn away, not impeding the blaster bolts in the least.

Beside him, Lando slid through the hole. He kept his cane from colliding with anything, but his hip cloak caught on one edge of the hole and was yanked free of his shoulders. He landed gracefully and glared up at his traitorous garment. Then he trotted after Leia.

Han grabbed one table leg and fell through the hole, hauling the leg with him. All four table legs dropped into the hole, leaving the tabletop flush against the floor. The awkwardness of his descent caused him to hit the corridor floor hard and go to his knees, but he rose unhurt and sprinted after the others, guided by the glow-rod-like qualities of Leia's lightsaber.

Han rounded a corner and caught up with the others. This chamber was as large as the taproom above but stacked high with plasteel crates and falsewood kegs.

Leia stood at the top of a short permacrete ramp. A metal door barred her way. She slashed at the top hinge of three, cutting through it. Teppler stood behind her, calm, blaster and tumbler at the ready. Lando, like a catalog holo of elegant indifference, leaned against the wall, twirling his cane.

Han gestured toward Teppler's tumbler. "Get rid of that."

"Can't," Teppler said. "It has my fingerprints on it."

Han grabbed the tumbler from him, tossed it into a corner, and pumped three blaster shots into it. When the smoke cleared, it was a melted, charred mass of transparisteel.

There were more blaster shots from back the way they'd come. Han heard pieces of wood raining down into the corridor.

Leia finished the second hinge and got to work on the third. Teppler stepped forward and raised his arm to catch the top of the door when it toppled.

The door fell. Teppler wrenched it out of the way, and it clattered to the permacrete floor. On the other side, the ramp continued up; several meters beyond it, Han could see speeders roaring past what had to be the end of the alley behind the cantina. He, Leia, and Teppler ran toward the escape the street represented. Lando remained behind—to delay pursuit, Han assumed.

Leia extinguished her lightsaber as they reached the alley mouth. A narrow sidewalk gave them an avenue for escape, and cross-traffic just a few centimeters away roared past, the speeders' running lights leaving colorful horizontal streaks in the air.

Han looked at the situation. This was going to turn into either a running blaster battle or a blaster battle performed on stolen speeders. "Ready to go, sweetheart?"

"Garbage loader," Leia said.

"You always know the right thing to say." Han followed her gaze. Lumbering up the flyway toward them, low toward the ground, was a repulsorlift-based garbage loader, a story and a half tall, wider than a standard traffic lane, with droid arms along its upper rim to seize garbage receptacles, lift them into the air, and dump their contents into the vessel's payload bay.

Leia led them from the alley and along the sidewalk in the direction of traffic, but she walked backward, concentrating on the pilot of that garbage loader. "Nice time for a nap," she whispered. "Good place for a nap."

Lando ran from the alley mouth, neither leg apparently causing him distress; he carried his cane tucked under his left arm, military-academy-style. "We have maybe fifteen seconds," he said. Then he gave Leia a curious look and turned to stare at the object of her interest.

The trash loader pulled over until it was mostly in the traffic lane but also fully covering the sidewalk, and came down to a landing directly in front of the alley mouth. The pilot, illuminated by blue cockpit lighting, was a jowly middle-aged man; he leaned back in his seat and closed his eyes.

"Kill the engines," Leia said, and sagged just a bit; the effort to impose her will on someone at range, without benefit of the target being able to see her eyes or hear her voice, had taken a toll on her.

Han and Lando obliged by aiming their blasters at the front face of the garbage loader's underside and firing four or five times each into it. The blasterfire immediately awoke the pilot, and Han saw the man seize the controls and try to lift off, but it was too late: the multiton vehicle was dead, firmly situated flush with the alley mouth. Now Han could hear curses and hammering from where the loader blocked the alley—the CorSec agents had reached the obstacle.

"Time to grab a speeder and run for it," Lando said.

Teppler shook his head. "I'll be less conspicuous on foot and on my own. Good luck." He turned and dashed away along the sidewalk.

chapter eight

ELMAS PRIVATE SPACEPORT,
CORONET, CORELLIA
RENTAL BAY 601208

"Dad, something's happening outside."

Instantly awake, still dressed in a jumpsuit not much improved by having been worked in for a day, Wedge rolled out of his cot and joined his daughter at the hangar's side viewport. The viewport was mostly covered in black sheeting, in which Myri and Iella had cut strategic holes for viewing.

The interior of the hangar was in darkness, so it took his eyes no time to adjust. Across the access way between rows of rental hangars, three people were making a hurried approach. They stopped well short of Wedge's hangar and clustered around a personnel door two hangars down.

"Not our problem," Wedge said, rubbing his eyes. He'd gotten to sleep only an hour or two earlier, after a long session of performing vehicle repairs and maintenance. Myri had been right to awaken him, but he was anxious to get back to sleep.

"I think it is." The voice was Corran's, from just behind Wedge, and Wedge started.

He turned to offer Corran a mock glare. "Ex-CorSec *and* Jedi. Makes you twice as sneaky. What makes you think it's a problem? You can't even see out there."

"But I can feel." Corran gestured toward the distant arrivals. "One of them is Leia Solo."

Wedge whipped around and put his eye to the peephole again. The three people had disappeared, presumably having gone through the door. "You're sure."

"I'm sure."

"What's all the noise?" Stumbling down the boarding ramp of the *Pulsar Skate,* her *Baudo*-class yacht, covering a yawn and half smothering her words with one hand, was Mirax Horn, Corran's wife and Myri's namesake. Wedge had known her for decades; she was the daughter of Booster Terrik, Wedge's mentor in the smuggling trade back in the days before Wedge joined the Rebel Alliance. Round-faced, with black hair cut in a short, practical style, she retained much of the fresh-faced, blue-eyed beauty that had characterized her when she and Wedge were both teenagers.

"Leia's two doors down, with two strange men," Wedge said.

"How do you know they're two strange men?" Mirax asked. "It might be Han and Luke."

"Han and Luke are two strange men." Wedge looked around the people assembled before him. Only Iella was still horizontal; on her cot beneath the S-foil of Wedge's X-wing, she had pulled her pillow over her head to muffle all the conversational noise. "In a couple of minutes, when they've had time to relax, we'll send someone over."

"Me," Myri said. "I'm the only one of us whose face isn't all over CorSec's or assassins' shoot-on-sight guides."

Corran gave her a melancholy little smile. "It's not going to happen, girl."

"Uncle Corran, if you're going to give me the same old you're-too-young argument—"

Corran cut her off with a gesture and a shake of his head. "Listen."

Everyone did. They could all hear the rush of thrusters and repulsorlifts. Wedge found it curious that he couldn't identify the speeder from its engine noise.

Then he realized why. He wasn't listening to one speeder close by, but to several farther away, their engine and thruster noises blending together and echoing off hangar walls. And the noise was getting louder, closer . . .

"Iella!" Wedge called.

His wife pulled the pillow from her face and looked at him, cross but alert.

"Everyone, set up for immediate evacuation."

Iella rolled up out of her cot and began struggling into her boots. She caught Wedge's attention, then glanced in the direction of his cot and boots.

Up the access way, from the direction Leia and her companions had come, a stream of CorSec speeders, orange-and-blue lights blinking to signal their official status, roared toward them, each coming to a stop in front of a different hangar. CorSec officers poured out of the vehicles and immediately began moving to hangar entryways. One began banging on the door into Wedge's shelter.

Corran sighed. "Thanks, Leia."

CORELLIA
CONTROL CABIN OF THE *LOVE COMMANDER*

"Power coming online in two minutes," Leia announced.

Lando tried to keep his dissatisfaction from his face. "I hate transports with slow start-up times," he grumbled. "If that idiot had had any sense, he'd have installed a ten-second starter."

"If he'd had any sense, he wouldn't have lost his yacht to you," Han said. "Relax. We have plenty of time."

Through the front viewports, they could all see the line

of sparks appear at the hangar door as a laser cutting tool outside sheared through the locking mechanism. The door rolled open, and half a dozen CorSec agents charged in.

Just outside, making the final turn to aim at the *Love Commander,* was an old, though doubtless still deadly, TIE crawler. The ball-shaped cockpit, familiar from TIE fighters, was mounted between two low, rectangular sets of tank treads, and Lando could see the machine's twin blaster cannon barrels trained squarely on *Love Commander*'s control cabin.

A CorSec officer with an oversized comlink held up before his face entered with his men. His words came across *Love Commander*'s comm board and, magnified, could even be heard through the yacht's hull: "This is Corellian Security. Power down and exit your craft immediately for identification."

"Leia, stall them," Lando ordered. "We can get our shields online in just over a minute—"

Leia shook her head. "No, they're serious. They'll open fire before then. We can surrender now and escape while we're being transported . . ."

Han's lip had twitched when the word *surrender* was uttered, and now he shook his head. "Princess, we—"

There was an engine roar from outside. All the CorSec agents still outside looked to their right. Some of them ran—into the hangar and toward *Love Commander,* or out of sight on the access way, anywhere that wasn't toward the TIE crawler.

A flash of red light hit the crawler's starboard treads—low, almost at the level of the permacrete. The shot flipped the crawler and it rolled, coming down resting on one of its treads. A starfighter flashed by outside.

"That was an X-wing, wasn't it?" Lando asked.

Leia nodded. "Wedge?"

Han shook his head. "Emerald green, with a checkerboard pattern."

Leia smiled. "Corran!"

Then an X-wing in standard gray with red piping flashed by.

"Power?" Lando asked.

Leia checked her status board. "Coming online in three, two, one . . . now."

"Shields up," Lando ordered. "Get us out of here."

Leia lifted *Love Commander* up on her repulsors and glided forward. CorSec agents scattered out of her way. At the door into the hangar, she delicately nudged the TIE crawler aside—"delicately" in the sense that neither vehicle was damaged by the impact, though Lando shuddered at the sound of metal shrieking and scraping as they passed—then turned in the wake of the two X-wings.

Immediately the sensor screens lit up and began chiming. Lando activated his display screen and got a night-sight image, all in shades of green, of the holocam view from the front of *Love Commander;* he saw little but a line of CorSec speeders parked on the access way.

"I read one vehicle, size suited to a personal yacht, emerging from a hangar behind us," Han said. "Hey, I think it's the *Pulsar Skate.*"

Lando switched his display over to a rear holocam view. Emerging from a hangar door only two buildings away was a long, low yacht, shaped something like a example of gliding undersea life from the aquatic world of Mon Calamari. Essentially a flying wing with twin thruster pods at the back, it had graceful lines that swept back organically from the bow.

Han continued, "We have one vertical takeoff from the port's main launch area, I think it's a ballistic transport, outbound. And—fierfek. Looks like a small vessel, corvette class at least, heading our way."

"Go to battle stations," Lando said, unnecessarily. The shields were already up, and he'd seen Han power up the yacht's weapons without authorization a moment earlier.

"Yes, *Captain.*"

"Try to open a channel to our escorts."

"Yes, *Captain.*" Han scowled at Lando then returned his attention to his boards.

Leia lifted *Love Commander* off in the wake of the X-wings. Lando felt himself being pressed back into his seat as the yacht's inertial compensators failed to keep up completely with the demands of vehicular acceleration.

"*Love Commander* to X-wing escort, come in."

"*Love Commander,* this is *Pulsar Skate.*" It was a female voice, and one Lando didn't recognize. "Stand by to receive line-of-sight transmission of encryption code. Three, two, one, sending. Got it?"

"Got it," Han said. "Implementing . . . now."

There was a burst of static, then the woman's voice returned. "Encryption activated. Can you still read me?"

"We hear you just fine," Han said. "I'm going to switch you over to our captain. I'm going to have to shoot things pretty soon, and he doesn't have anything to do." He pressed a button.

The holocam view faded from Lando's display and was replaced with the face of a girl—young, pretty, with blue hair highlighted by yellow streaks. She looked familiar. "Myri Antilles here," she said. "Impromptu comm officer for *Pulsar Skate.*"

Suddenly Lando felt ten thousand years old. The last time he'd seen Myri, she'd been a little girl. He forced a smile. "Myri! It's your uncle Lando."

"Lando! Hey! The white hair and beard look really good on you. Are they real?"

"No, of course not. It's a wig and makeup."

"Awww. You've lost all your hair?"

"No! My hair is black. Well, gray-black. This just isn't it. *I still have all my own hair.*"

"Sure, you do," Han whispered.

Lando gritted his teeth. "Myri, sweetheart, does your daddy have an exit vector?"

"Sure. First, we go shoot at the corvette—"

"No, no, no, we need to go *away* from the corvette—"

"The corvette's all alone over the ocean, and every other direction has multiple starfighters and attack craft coming toward us. And assuming we can cripple the corvette, we should make orbit with no problem. But then we run into the Alliance blockade ships. That's where the problem comes in."

Suddenly Lando felt young and useful again. "Ah, that's no problem."

"No?"

"No. A kind young blockade lieutenant gave me a passcode the other day."

"Oh, good. Oops—we're at extreme firing range in ten seconds, nine . . ."

As Myri counted down, Lando switched his display view to a sensor screen.

Their miniature task force was now away from Coronet, out over the water, still gaining altitude. There were numerous blips back over the city, small units of attack craft headed their way; mercifully, Han was screening their comm traffic and keeping it from coming over the control cabin's speakers.

Love Commander and *Pulsar Skate* were now side by side, only a couple of hundred meters separating them, and the two X-wings were a few kilometers out in advance. In the distance was the blip of a small capital ship, and as the distance closed a designation popped up for it on the screen: CEC CORVETTE 1177 SILABAN.

Lando winced out of sympathy for Leia. When she was just a teenage Senator for the planet of Alderaan, her chief transport had been a Corellian corvette, the *Tantive IV*. Long and narrow, with a bow like a sledgehammer head turned sideways and a rectangular stern that was little more than stacked banks of thrusters, the *Tantive IV* had held a special place in her affections, and it had to be upsetting to have a near-identical vessel trying to shoot her down now.

Myri's countdown reached one. Lando opened his mouth to order Han to open fire, but Han opened up before he could speak. Lando saw the yacht's lasers lance in on a distant target, joined by the *Pulsar Skate*'s, and saw the glow as the *Silaban*'s shields soaked up the laser barrage.

The two X-wings climbed relative to the plane of battle, performing evasive maneuvering in unison, so close that they registered as a single blip on the sensors.

Lando frowned over that. "What do they think they're doing? They're going to bump and then it'll be all over for them."

He'd forgotten his comm channel was still open. "Bump?" The voice was that of Mirax Horn. "Come over here, Lando, and I'll bump *you*."

"Calm down, calm down." That was Iella. "This is why men should only be put in command of single-pilot fighters. On bigger craft, they have too much time on their hands, so they talk too much."

"Hey," Lando protested.

Love Commander rocked as beams from the corvette's twin turbolaser cannons grazed her shields. Lando started to say something about more evasive maneuvering, but Leia abruptly put the yacht into such torturous dives and turns that Lando's stomach flip-flopped. He clamped his mouth shut and concentrated on not losing his dinner.

Through the viewport, he could see the corvette's bottom turbolasers firing on the *Love Commander* and *Pulsar Skate*, and the craft's top-side turbolasers trying to target the X-wings. As they neared the corvette, the X-wings abruptly separated, both staying above the relative plane of battle but one arcing to port and the other to starboard.

Both sets of turbolasers initially followed the same X-wing—Wedge's, according to the sensor screen—then both switched to open up on Corran's.

By this time both X-wings were past the stern of the corvette. Lando could see some bright spots at the stern of the Corellian ship, points where fire from the X-wings' turbolasers had struck. Now both X-wings looped around to orient in on the engines, and the corvette commander, belatedly recognizing that the two snubfighters packed more firepower than the yachts still headed their way, tried to turn toward them and protect his engines.

But the X-wings came in firing, their angry red laserfire chipping away at the stern shields, concentrating on the same area of engines, and then penetrating. Lando saw red light suffuse the corvette's stern, and an explosion lit the ocean below.

No, the corvette hadn't exploded—only a portion of its engine compartment had been lost. But the vessel began to lose altitude and turned away from the conflict area. The X-wings turned back toward the space yachts.

And finally, because he had the ticket off this world and out of this system, Lando could take charge again. "*Pulsar Skate,*" he said, "and X-wing escorts, form up on *Looooove Commander.* We're headed for orbit."

"And then where?" Han asked.

Finally Wedge's voice crackled over the comlink. "To a gathering of old friends," he said.

CORUSCANT
JEDI TEMPLE

Ben's opponent wasn't particularly impressive. The droid had a scrawny body, its four spindly legs just sturdy enough to allow it to walk around. Its two arms ended not in hands but in tubes about eight centimeters in diameter. And its head was huge, the size of an entire R2 unit, with two green glowing optical sensors where eyes would be and a set of speaker vents in the position of a human mouth.

In the mirror that ran the full length of the chamber on one wall, they seemed unlikely combatants—a droid with a ludicrously large head and a friendly-looking teenage boy with bright red hair in a buzz-style haircut.

"Last series," it announced, its voice surprisingly human considering its alien appearance. "Ready."

To better test himself, Ben left his lightsaber off for the moment . . . and turned his back on the droid. He extended his feelings through the Force and tried to find the droid, and was mildly distressed, once again, to find that he could not. He concealed his worry. "Ready."

There was a *ponk* noise as the first foamsteel ball left one of the droid's arm tubes. And that Ben felt, as a displacement of air; as a little tickle of worry. He could sense the direction of the ball's travel, straight toward the back of his head . . .

He swung around, sidestepping the ball's path, igniting the lightsaber as second, third, and fourth balls shot out toward him. He swung at the first one, but his blade was only half extended and his strike was half a meter short of its target. The second ball shot harmlessly past him, but he connected with the third and fourth, sending them ricocheting away from him. Their glossy exteriors took the momentary contact with the coherent light blade without melting or deforming.

Then more balls came pouring from the droid's arms, *ponk ponk ponk ponk ponk* . . . The droid varied its aim, firing at Ben's feet, chest, head, arms, aiming at positions bracketing Ben in case his dodging moved him into their path.

He didn't deflect all of them. One cracked painfully into his left knee. Another grazed his cheek. But his success ratio was pretty high.

He could feel the balls moving around behind him along the gleaming apocia hardwood floor. They separated into two streams, circling around him back toward the droid, controlled by the magnetic impulses it was sending. As Ben watched and deflected two more balls, the first ones that had been sent against him reached the base of the droid, flew up to hover above the droid's head, and dropped into the slot there. Back in the hopper, they could be fired at him again.

On impulse, Ben chose one of the balls now approaching the droid and reached out to it through the Force. He stomped with his foot, physicalizing the way he wanted to direct his attack, and lashed out with Force energy.

The ball flattened, becoming a disk wider than but about half as tall as it had been before. It still flew up to hover above the droid's head . . . and when it dropped toward the slot, Ben gave it some extra energy. It hit the slot and half folded, jamming into place.

Swatting away at the next four balls, Ben watched as half a dozen more dropped onto the droid's head, bounced off the ruined ball, fell to the floor, and rolled around to get to the backs of the two lines of balls awaiting retrieval.

No more balls emerged from the droid. Ben waited, watching, as expended balls from the two lines flew up over the droid, bounced off, fell to the ground, and got back in line again.

Then that action, too, ceased. Released from magnetic control, most of the balls now stayed where they lay; a few rolled a hand span in one direction or another before coming to a stop.

Ben felt the tiniest of tugs against his lightsaber. He gripped it hard just before it tried to yank itself out of his hand. It struggled with him, attempting to fly to the droid, but he got his left hand on it as well and held firm. He deactivated it and grinned at the practice droid.

Finally the lightsaber, too, stopped trying to move on its own.

The droid said, "Have you sabotaged me?"

"Yes," Ben said. "In the, uh, spirit of defeating an enemy."

"I shall file your action under 'tactics,' then. I designate this exercise complete. Last series success ratio ninety-four percent, last series ended at twenty-two percent of balls expended due to tactical sabotage. Learner weapon retention successful." The droid rolled toward the door out of the Training Hall, and the balls, now returning to their straight-line formations, rolled out after it.

Leaving, the droid passed another Jedi learner waiting beside the door. She must have entered while Ben was in the midst of the last exercise, and he recognized with a little flash of embarrassment that he hadn't detected her—he had been too focused on his task.

She was several centimeters taller than he was, three or four years older, and redheaded, her long hair a shade more coppery than his mother's. She came forward as the balls continued to roll out of the hall. "Hello."

"Hello." Ben returned his lightsaber to its belt hook.

She extended a hand. "I'm Seha. Seha Dorvald."

"I know." He took her hand to shake it. "I've—"

There was something in her hand, something small and rectangular, a card of some sort. But her expression didn't change; she didn't acknowledge that she'd just handed him anything.

A little thrill shot through Ben. He knew why. First, she was really good looking, and she was talking to him. Second, she'd just done something covert. He wondered what was on the card—instructions to meet her somewhere? A communication from the government of Corellia, begging his help to resolve the military crisis? An offer of a bribe? He'd just been kicked out of a practice session straight into a holodrama, and he keenly felt the transition.

"I've seen you around," he finished, trying not to stammer. "I'm Ben Skywalker."

"I know." She retrieved her hand, leaving the card in his grip. "I just wanted to say—"

Pocket the card now? No, if anyone is watching, that might call attention to the fact that she gave me something. And if she's giving me something this way, she thinks somebody is watching. Ben let his hand drop to his side and hoped his posture was natural looking.

"—I thought the thing with flattening the ball was very imaginative, and I was wondering—"

He had to get to his quarters and find out what was on the card. Though he'd also like to just stay here and look at her for a couple of days. It was very hard for him to concentrate on Seha's words.

"—if you'd mind if I, you know, sort of stole your technique for my next session."

About forty different answers roared in to clog up Ben's brain. *Sure. You're really cute. If you're still doing these exercises, are you a late starter like me? Your accent is very undercity, but you talk like you've been educated.*

How would Jacen answer her question?

That last thought allowed Ben to clear his mind. He'd analyze her question, instantly figure out the consequences, and be very cool about it.

"I'd be, um—" What was the word? "—flattered." But before the last word left his lips, a possible consequence occurred to me. "But you probably don't want to do that."

"Why not?" She didn't seem offended, just curious.

Ben gestured at the doorway. "The droid has a learning program. He'll be coming up with or requesting new programming to counteract a ball-flattening tactic. So if you do that, you also need to figure out what he'll do then, and be prepared for *that,* too."

"Good point. I'll do that. You're smart, too."

Too? In addition to what?

"I was wondering about your braid." She pointed to the narrow braid of hair that dangled from his scalp, especially obvious when contrasted with his buzz cut. It was now draped across his shoulder. "That's kind of old-fashioned, isn't it? Does the order still do that somewhere?"

Ben shook his head. "No, just me." He wasn't even sure why he'd grown it out—just to have something that was his alone, perhaps, something to set him apart from his famous parents. He wasn't sure how to say that in a way that wouldn't sound juvenile or egotistical. "It's my custom."

"I think it's astral. Anyway, I need to get to my next lesson. It was nice meeting you."

"Nice meeting you." He watched her leave, feeling as though he had to be flushing as red as her hair, and finally tucked the card she'd given him into his belt, hoping that the action would not be obvious to unseen eyes.

In addition to what?

On the walk back to his quarters, he thought about what to do.

The fact that Seha seemed to think she, or he, or both of them, would be under observation bothered him. *Are Dad and Mom having me watched?* That question left a sour taste in his mind. *Or is someone watching Seha? But if I'm the one being watched, how do I find out what's on the card?*

Not a Temple computer. That could be monitored. Come to think of it, so could any datapad capable of transmitting and receiving. But a datapad without a comlink would be safe, if he could find one.

Or make one.

He stopped in at a playroom set aside for Rontos, students three to five years younger than Ben. There were no children or adults present, but there were games and toys scattered here and there among the cushiony chairs and other brightly colored items of furniture.

As he knew there must be, there were datapads, most of them with larger controls suited to smaller, clumsier fingers, and one of them had a privacy headset. He took it.

He stepped into a closet used to hold cleaning supplies. Standing in the narrow gap between shelves holding pungent-smelling bottles and plasteel containers, he opened the datapad and quickly stripped out its communications chip. He felt nervous doing this anywhere in the Temple, but didn't think that, even if he was under near-constant observation, they could have put holocams *everywhere*. Not in a cleaning supply closet. Surely not.

In his quarters he moved his chair so that he could sit with his back to a corner. He made a slightly exaggerated show of selecting a game card from his small collection of entertainments; as he was sitting down, he palmed the game card and inserted Seha's instead. Then he donned the headset and accessed the card.

The Galactic Alliance Guard logo came up with a brief message: SPECIAL AGENT BEN SKYWALKER, ENTER ACCESS CODE.

Ben typed in the password he used in the GAG offices to access messages and orders.

The message changed to say, SOUND MODE FOR SECURE SURROUNDINGS OR TEXT MODE FOR PUBLIC AREAS?

He chose sound.

The screen flickered, and Jacen's image came up. "Ben," Jacen said, his voice a little thin over the headset speakers, "this is important. Memorize the information on this card. Replay it if necessary. Once you're sure you have it memorized, destroy the chip. Don't just break it, destroy it irretrievably." He paused as if to give Ben time to absorb the gravity of his words.

Ben felt that thrill again. *This is real, this is important. And . . . this means Seha is working with Jacen! She's an ally!*

"I need to send you on a mission," Jacen continued.

"You, specifically, because it has to be someone with the GAG's interests, *my* interests, at heart, someone who is Force-sensitive, and someone who has proven that he can operate alone. That's you or me, and I can't leave my duties at this time. I'm sorry about interrupting your training and sorrier still that this may cause friction between you and your parents, but I'll make them understand that this was all my doing.

"Here's the essential core of the mission. Remember it, so that if anything goes wrong with the operational details I give you, you'll remember what's most important. You're to acquire the Amulet of Kalara and secretly bring it to me."

The image switched to a standard planetary data screen with the name ALMANIA at the top. Jacen's voice continued, "The Amulet is on the planet of Almania, in the planetary offices of Tendrando Arms. It resides in a display case on the two hundred fifteenth floor of their office building. Security in the building is nothing special, since it's shared by hundreds of different firms, and security on the display case is also poor, because the owner doesn't know what he possesses."

The image changed to a close-up view of a jewel hanging from a silver chain. The jewel was a gray oval, its surface knobby and textured rather than smooth. In the center of the face was a vertical bar of some ruby-like gem, flanked by lustrous black semiprecious stone. The effect was rather like looking at a silvery feline eye with a red, slitted pupil.

"This is the Amulet of Kalara," Jacen continued. "Now the important thing. Ben, if this gets into the hands of a Force-sensitive who knows the secrets of its activation, we're all in trouble. Because while such a person has it activated, *he will be invisible in the Force.* Even his *use* of the Force is invisible to other Force-users.

"Think about what that means. He'll be like one of the Yuuzhan Vong warriors, but can be a normal person—

human, Rodian, Bith, whatever. He would be a tremendous danger to your parents, the order, me, everyone and everything.

"If you find the amulet in its display case, wonderful. We're going to give you a replacement to leave for the real thing. Mission accomplished.

"But if anyone gets his hands on it . . ." The image switched back to Jacen, and he was even more grave than before. "You have to assume that he knows its secret, that he's a powerful Dark Jedi or other Force-sensitive, and that he can activate it at any moment. Ben, you have to eliminate him before he eliminates you. I'm sorry, but it's true."

A weight settled in Ben's stomach. What Jacen was suggesting sounded like, under the right circumstances, it could be murder. But if the amulet was what Jacen said, it had to be put in the right hands. *Had* to be.

"So. At any point in the next two nights, you need to visit the Temple's fourth-level exercise changing room. Open the leftmost locker, combination six-eight-six, and retrieve the packet of clothes and items there . . ."

chapter nine

Clad in nondescript rust-colored garments and a hooded green traveler's rain drape that would remind no one of Jedi robes, Ben shut the locker, hit the button to lock it again, and dropped his lightsaber into a belt pouch. He forced his shoulders down. He'd been edgy since entering the chamber, worried that someone would walk in on him as he changed, but it hadn't happened. He'd chosen the quietest hour of the night, and had chosen correctly.

He moved to the loading slot for the laundry chute. It was large enough to accommodate the cloth bags full of dirty clothes, labeled with the names of their owners, that were delivered to the laundry facilities. That meant that it was large enough for children, too. Rumor had it that children couldn't get through the chutes into the automated laundry facilities, but just exactly how they were prevented from descending was a mystery; apprentices who'd tried it told mutually contradictory stories of greased chutes, robot defenders with electrocuting or tickling attachments on their arms, barrel-shaped chambers that whirled offenders until they were sick, stern talkings-to, and extra chores.

Ben pulled the lever, opening the drum into which bags were to be placed, and crawled in. It was a tight fit. At thirteen, almost fourteen, he was physically just a little large for such a stunt. He used his body weight to roll the drum closed, which opened the chute access immediately beneath him. Bracing himself with arms and legs so as not to fall, he pulled out a glow rod and peered into the depths.

"That's a chute, all right," he said. It was a square plasteel hole leading into the depths of the Temple.

He maneuvered himself to enter the chute feetfirst and braced them against the walls. Then he focused his attention on what he was doing, calling on the Force to allow him to dictate the exact amount of friction his feet would experience against the chute sides.

And he dropped.

He did not so much fall as descend in a controlled skid. As he descended, he could see the edges of the individual plasteel panels that made up the chute.

He passed a sensor. What would it be sensing? he wondered. Nothing right now—Seha or some other ally of Jacen's would have disabled it.

Below him, he saw discolored patches along the chute sides. He increased the friction to slow down and descended past them at the pace of a crawling insect.

On one side was a panel with a hinge at the bottom. He poked it as he passed, and it swung freely open, then shut again.

Directly opposite it was inset a small but ordinary repulsor unit, the sort one might find on the bottom of a hoverchair or hovergurney.

He nodded. That made sense. The sensor had to detect density or mass. If something dropped by that was too dense—boys and girls being made of denser materials than bags full of laundry—then the repulsor would kick on, shoving the child into a side chute, probably sending him or her to a holding cell and notifying the appropriate Masters in charge of punishment, lectures, and chores.

Ben slid on past and picked up the pace.

Below was a small square of light, and it was getting

larger. The end of the chute. Ben skidded to a silent stop when he was still two meters above it.

Warm air rose past him, and he heard the hum and clank of machinery. Three meters below the end of the chute was a smooth, wear-darkened permacrete floor with several gray laundry bags lying in a pile.

As Ben watched, a wheeled wagon rolled into view, pushed by a nondescript silver-white droid. The droid picked up the bags, tossed them in the wagon, and then pushed the conveyance out of sight.

Extending his senses through the Force, Ben could detect the droid's movement, but he could feel nothing else moving in the immediate vicinity. He dropped the remaining five meters, rolled as he hit the permacrete, and came silently up on his feet.

In one direction, the droid's retreating back; in the other, no observers. Either way, he was looking at an undecorated access corridor, machinery or storage crates piled here and there against a wall; often there was nothing concealing the drab grayness of the surfaces. The glow rods mounted in the ceiling, widely separated and offering only low light, created an even more dismal appearance.

Per Jacen's instructions, Ben turned right and dashed silently in that direction. Soon enough, the main corridor made a ninety-degree turn to the left, but there was a door in the wall there; heavy metal with an imposing-looking durasteel rim, it was labeled EMERGENCY EVACUATION ACCESS. USE ONLY IN TIMES OF EMERGENCY. TEMPLE SECURITY WILL BE ALERTED.

Only in times of emergency. Well, the whole galaxy was facing a time of emergency. Ben shoved at the metal panel that constituted the mechanical opener, to be used in times of power failure, and he felt his shoulders hunch up again as he unconsciously anticipated an activated alarm.

But none came. Seha had done her job well. The door

swung smoothly into a very short permacrete corridor, unlit, and there was an identical door at the far end, five meters away.

Ben responsibly shut the first door behind him, making sure that it latched into place. He might be disobeying the wishes of his father, but that was no excuse for exposing the Jedi Temple to possible intrusion by an enemy. The order *had* enemies, like the woman his father kept mentioning, Lumiya.

The second door also opened without activating an alarm, but sound washed over Ben anyway, and warm, heavy air—it was raining, individual drops pinging off a surface over his head. In the moments before his eyes adjusted he could see the lights of traffic streams to his right, but they were broken up, somehow disconnected. He doused his glow rod and shut this door, too.

When his eyes did adjust, he found that he was in a strange durasteel framework, long and narrow like a corridor. The floor and ceiling were metal sheeting, but the sides were mostly vertical metal bars with very narrow gaps between them. Through the gaps to the left, he could see only dressed stone, probably the Temple exterior; to the right was darkness and Coruscant cityscape.

Quietly, he moved toward the end of this pseudo-corridor and could feel it sway slightly under his feet. And at the end, its purpose became evident. There he found a stand-up-set of mechanical controls—several sets of wheels to spin. It took him only a few moments to work out their functions.

This was a telescoping access. One wheel would cause it to stretch out to its maximum length, and as it extended, the metal bars all along its length would thin out. Other wheels allowed the controller to change the angle at which it was attached to the Temple—up, down, right, left. Thoughtful use of the controls would allow its operator to place the end at some lower level on the Temple building or stretch out toward a traffic lane, enabling rescue speeders to pick up those fleeing the building in time of fire or invasion.

Ben spun the wheel that opened the end door. He stood out on the exit ramp and looked down. Below was the exterior wall of the Temple, nearly featureless at this point, sloping slightly downward into the depths of Galactic City.

All he had to do was descend, find transportation to a minor spaceport four hundred kilometers away, present the false documentation that had waited with his new clothes in the locker, and board a run-down excursion transport bound for Almania.

Easy.

KUAT SYSTEM
LOVE COMMANDER

"Establish communications," Lando said.

"I really think," Leia said, "you're letting this whole 'captain' thing go to your head."

Lando gave her a long, thoughtful look. "You're right. Dearest Leia, friend of decades, noble Jedi Knight, please do one more favor for this old, old man before his vital spirit leaves his faltering body—"

She gave him a long-suffering look. "Forget I said anything. Ready to broadcast—"

"No, not that. I meant, come live with me. Tendra would understand, I'm sure of it."

She sighed. "Yes, Han, you can shoot him."

"Wouldn't think of it," her husband said. "If I shot him now, I'd never learn just how deep into trouble he could talk himself."

"Ready to broadcast . . . now," Leia said, and pressed a switch on the comm board.

"This is Bescat Offdurmin, master of the *Looooove Commander,*" Lando said. "Approaching the *Errant Venture.* Do you read, *Venture*? Over."

"*Errant Venture* flight coordination here, *Love Commander.* We read you." On Lando's display, the distant view of the *Errant Venture,* the galaxy's sole Star Destroyer to bear a lurid red paint job, faded and was replaced by the face of a young red Twi'lek woman. Narrow orange and yellow piping had been artfully applied to her *lekku,* and the top portion of her clothing, visible at the bottom of the screen, suggested she was wearing a black evening dress rather than a ship's uniform.

"We have a reservation and landing authorization. *Looooove Commander* and the All-Clown Squadron of Fun."

The woman glanced down, presumably at a data screen. "So you do. You're cleared for landing . . ." Her voice trailed off and she looked again, obviously not prepared for what she'd seen. "In the Flag Hangar. I'm sending a guidance beacon on your frequency, now."

"Thank you."

The Twi'lek smiled and the screen went dark.

"What's a flag hangar?" Lando asked.

"The *Venture*'s an old Imperial Star Destroyer," Han said, shrugging. "Commissioned as the *Virulence.*"

"I know that," Lando said. "Well, except I forgot its original name."

"Whenever an ISD served as the flagship for a task force or fleet," Han went on, "the commanding admiral would be aboard, with his own quarters and his own private hangar. Which was called the flag hangar."

"Ah." Lando nodded wisely. "So, Han, old buddy, how long has it been since your Academy education has come in useful?"

"Now," Han said, "I'm going to shoot him."

CORELLIAN EXCLUSION ZONE
ANAKIN SOLO, COMMAND SALON

In the holocomm transmission Luke looked as serene as usual, but even so Jacen could sense that the Grand Master was impatient, distressed.

Mara, beside him, didn't bother to hide it. Her expression was a mix of worry and anger.

Without preamble Luke said, "Jacen, where's Ben?"

Jacen gave him a confused look. "I take it from the question that he's not where he's supposed to be."

Luke nodded. "That's correct. I notice you didn't answer my question directly."

Jacen felt a flash of anger—how *dare* Luke assume he was hiding something? The fact that he *was* did not enter into things. Luke needed to treat him with more respect. It was a lesson he had to make sure Luke learned. That would be soon, he hoped. "Do you see conversational ploys in every discussion, *Luke*?" The way he spoke the Grand Master's familiar name was just short of insulting. "All right, then, let me be absolutely clear. I don't know where Ben is." That was the truth; Lumiya was monitoring Ben's mission, not Jacen.

Even if Jacen had been lying, he was sure Luke would not have been able to detect it. Jacen had been proficient at concealing his true feelings and emotions for a long, long time. He'd grown even better at it under Lumiya's tutelage.

Luke was silent for long moments. Finally he said, "I'm sorry. But we're worried. He disappeared from the Temple and we can't find any sign of where he's gone."

"Can you feel him in the Force?"

"Yes. But that doesn't mean he's safe. Just that he's alive. Somewhere. And not close."

Jacen sighed. "He's too old to be running away from home like this. My guess is he resents the fact that you took him away from me. And you know, that suggests you were right. If he's going to be doing things like this, he may not be mature enough to be my apprentice—at least not yet."

Luke and Mara exchanged a quick look. It seemed like a neutral exchange, but Jacen could read it as though it were a large-text news feed: they were thrown off by his admission that they might have been right all along. He exulted in his power to position their emotions.

Mara said, "Has he communicated in the last couple of days?"

Jacen shook his head. "I received a text message from him explaining some ways he planned to make Luke 'move his feet' in sparring. That was the last I heard from him. Of course," he added, "if he's run away from home and can find a way to get offplanet, he'll probably come here. To me. If that happens, I assume you want me to send him straight back."

"That's correct," Mara said. "And even if he doesn't show up there, if you find out anything about where he might be—"

"I'll transmit it to you instantly," Jacen promised.

"Thanks, Jacen." Luke waved to something outside the range of the holocam view, and he and Mara disappeared.

Jacen smiled. Causing people to think and feel what he wanted them to, even without resorting to the Force, was becoming easier and easier . . . even with difficult subjects like the almighty Luke Skywalker.

KUAT SYSTEM
ERRANT VENTURE

Love Commander followed the *Pulsar Skate* into the Flag Hangar, with the two X-wings bringing up the rear. Waiting at the doors leading out of the hangar was Booster Terrik.

The old man certainly wasn't diminished by age, Han decided. Burly and gray-bearded, he floated around on a hoverchair as massive as the front end of an airspeeder. But he stood up out of the chair as the *Skate*'s boarding ramp came down and Mirax dashed down it. He might be too old to walk long distances, but he was certainly not going to be caught sitting down for a reunion with his daughter.

Lando, Han, and Leia were toward the back of the greeting line. Wedge, Iella, and Myri also embraced the old man. Han and Leia shook his hand. Corran, Booster's son-in-law, was last to approach and did the same, his rueful expression suggesting he still hadn't quite forgiven himself for coming to like Booster.

Booster finally sat again and fixed a glare on Corran. "But you didn't bring my grandchildren."

Corran folded his arms. "They're scattered to the four corners of the galaxy on Jedi business. Not my fault."

"Humpf." The old man fixed his stare on Mirax. "Your husband still can't do simple math. You can't scatter two children to four corners."

Mirax's grin grew broader. "Jedi think that everybody can be divided into fractions. Come on, Father. We really need to talk."

They settled into a private conference room only a few paces from the Flag Hangar. The black gleaming sideboard had been set out with finger foods, alcoholic and nonalcoholic drinks, and sealed sabacc decks with holographic images of the *Errant Venture* on the backs of the cards. Most people present settled for the food and alcohol-free beverages, but Myri took a sabacc deck and practiced shuffling, stacking the deck, and palming cards. Leia watched the sophisticated card sharp's techniques for a few moments before turning her attention to the others.

"So," Booster said, and pointed at Han and Leia. "Everybody in the galaxy wants to arrest you two. Except the Hapans, some of whom want to investigate you and some of whom just want to kill you. Are you going to get the *Venture* blown up?"

"What's the matter?" Han asked, his voice taunting. "No sympathy for someone everybody is chasing?"

Booster snorted. "Good answer." Leia knew that he'd been a smuggler before she had been born, and had been sought for his crimes by both Corellian Security and the Empire. Corran's father, CorSec agent Hal Horn, had arrested him, and the man had spent years on the mining prison of Kessel. These days he was reformed, legitimate . . . about as much as Han Solo. "All right," Booster continued. "What is this all about?"

"I'm sure you know all the public facts about the Corellia–GA war," Wedge said. "I'm equally sure you're running odds."

Booster nodded. "When your retirement ceremony was broadcast, odds went to thirty-seven to one for total conquest of Corellia, unless the Bothans come in, at which point it goes to fourteen to one for a negotiated conclusion, with the Bothans selling the Corellians out and getting the rancor's share of the deal."

Wedge's face twitched. "Right. Anyway, the public records don't talk about the fact that there are odd, unexplained variables at work here. The pressures that have brought this war into being are unambiguous, easy to identify. But there's additional string-pulling going on that is harder to bring into focus."

"Such as," Lando said, "efforts by different groups that would take Han and Leia out of the equation. Take the assassinations of the Bothan politicians on Coruscant. If they were done by Corellians to bring the Bothans in, why haven't those agents also targeted major figures like Cha Niathal to deprive the GA of some of its strategic strengths, or Jacen Solo as revenge for all the Corellian prisoner-taking? Things aren't adding up."

Wedge said, "My instincts tell me that if you bet on all

the forces lining up to keep the Bothans out of the war failing, you'll make a good return on your bet."

"Hold on," Booster said. He spoke to the right arm of his chair. "Log that tip."

"Logged," the chair said, its voice that of a female protocol droid.

"And then there's the whole thing with ghosts appearing and persuading previously rational people to do very bad things," Leia said. "That strongly suggests a Force-user. A dark sider, in all likelihood, if the goal is to help war happen."

"If there *is* somebody pulling strings," Han said, "that rodder is probably on Corellia or Coruscant. That's where most of the puppets are dancing. And I'm talking about people like Cal Omas and Dur Gejjen being puppets."

"We sort of stowed away on the Antilles-Horn rendezvous with you, Booster," Leia said. "But on the flight out here"—she glanced at Han—"we came to the conclusion that the *Errant Venture* would be an incredible resource for gathering information. Park it in the Corellian system, where there are thousands of restless military personnel, provide gambling and entertainments . . . people get drunk, talk more freely . . ."

Han added, "And it's not as though there'd be a big financial loss. Thousands of restless military personnel, like Leia says."

Booster snorted. "You think I'm so old I don't notice financial opportunities anymore? Princess, I applied for access to the Corellian exclusion zone the day it was established. The GA has been sitting on my application ever since."

Leia resisted the urge to take offense. Somehow, when Booster used the word *Princess,* he made it a comment about a spoiled little girl rather than an acknowledgment of her former title. But she refused to rise to the bait. She simply nodded. "I'm glad you have no objection. So now all I have to do is get your application approved."

Booster gave her a dubious look. "Because you and Captain Bloodstripes there are so well loved by the government now."

Leia matched him stare for stare. "No. Because Jacen Solo swings a big lightsaber with the blockade forces. And if Luke Skywalker tells him that letting the *Errant Venture* set up there is a terrible, terrible idea, Jacen will probably accelerate its approval so fast you'd think he slapped a hyperspace engine on it." It hurt to speak dismissively of her own son's powers of critical thought, but it had for some time been obvious that Jacen was not entirely logical when it came to his relationship with Luke. Jacen resented his uncle and balked at Luke's advice. Painful as it was, Leia now found it useful to exploit the fact.

"Huh." Booster thought about it for a second, and then was distracted by more of Myri's prestidigitation. "All right, girl, you can stop it. You're hired."

Myri froze in midshuffle and looked at him, wide-eyed. "Huh?"

"You *were* applying for a job. Right?"

She shook her head, bewildered. "I was practicing. Mom says it's an area where I'm weak."

Booster turned his glare on Iella. "Meaning you're better at it than your daughter?"

Both women nodded.

"All right, then," Booster said. "Iella, you're hired, too."

Iella smiled. "Only if we get the approval for Corellia. But if we do, Myri and I will work for free."

"Hey," Myri protested.

"Well, for tips."

"Done," Booster said. He turned back to Leia. "And done. Drop the word to your brother. And while we're waiting for the approval you're so confident about, slap some paint or fake fur on those too-famous faces of yours and enjoy yourselves aboard *Errant Venture*." He smiled almost benignly. "Spend lavishly. Tip your hosts and hostesses."

CORUSCANT
ZORP HOUSE APARTMENT TOWER

"You're sure," Mara said.

The Neimoidian male gave her a half bow, appropriate to an acknowledgment on Coruscant but insultingly deficient on worlds where the precise angles of such gestures spoke volumes about one's intent and attitude. "I am absolutely sure," he said, his speech flavored with the musicality of his native tongue. "As ever, I cooperate fully with the Jedi order, with the Galactic Alliance Guard, with—"

"With anyone who pays," Luke said. "And you have been well paid."

"I have been well *promised*," the Neimoidian answered. "Not so much paid yet."

"Then show us," Mara said.

The Neimoidian pressed a sequence of buttons on the control panel of the turbolift. Its status display switched from HOLD to 1; then the numbers began climbing as the turbolift did. Mara felt the car accelerate, but turbolifts in habitation buildings as lavish as this one had small inertial compensators to make rapid ascents and descents comfortable.

"When you contacted me," the Neimoidian said, "you asked for comm records from the quarters of your suspect, and for other anomalies in the security recordings."

Mara nodded. Weeks earlier, meticulous police work tracking from the site of the murder of Jedi Master Tresina Lobi had led to this building and the realization that the Sith lady Lumiya was one of the murderers. Even more unwelcome was the fact, gained from examination of the quarters, that Lumiya had strong ties to the Galactic Alliance Guard. That revelation had thrown more suspicion on Jacen, the Guard's operational commander.

"The investigators and the GAG took everything from her quarters," the Neimoidian said. The turbolift came to a halt at the 288th floor. Its doors opened onto a broad hallway lined with walls that gleamed like crushed gemstone. The Neimoidian stepped out, and the Jedi followed. "They also took records from the security office—records, privately owned datapads, legally registered blasters and restraining devices, a servitor droid, half-eaten food—"

"Yes, yes." Luke didn't sound impatient, but he wouldn't have interrupted if he weren't. "But you found something anyway."

"Of course. We had backups on all the security recordings. And I found that the suspect's most frequent communication through the building's comm system was to herself, from one installed unit to a second installed unit."

Mara shrugged. "A common practice in intelligence circles. She would have sensors attached to her comm, measuring noise, resistance, and so forth, to determine whether the unit or the comm lines were tapped."

"Ah." Into that one word, the Neimoidian squeezed a tremendous amount of self-appreciation. "Not so." He led the way along the glittery corridor, past two sets of residential double doors, and stopped at a smaller unmarked door. He held up a datapad and keyed in a number. The door popped open with a quiet *whoosh* indicating that a seal had broken, and warmer air washed over the Jedi.

The Neimoidian pulled the door open. The room beyond was dark until glow rods above blinked on, illuminating a narrow chamber lined with stored goods—cleaning solutions, deactivated mouse droids, bins of replacement electronic parts. "You see, three hours ago, I plugged new comms into her comm jacks and sent a message from one to the other. It never arrived. Yet sending a message from the second to the first, that one did arrive."

"Ah." Mara offered him a slight smile, the first sign of approval she'd given him. "And here is where the interception was taking place."

"I did not touch it," he said. "I remember your words about traps. Bombs. Poisons." He offered a shudder. "I have left it for you."

"Where is it?"

"Before I tell you, I wish to leave. To have a head start in case you trigger an unfortunate event. And before I leave, I wish to be paid. For if you are dead, I can never be rewarded for my efforts."

Mara exchanged a glance with Luke. He nodded, confirming that he, too, had detected no sign of deception in the Neimoidian's story.

Luke pulled a credcard from his pouch and handed it over. "Thirty seconds," he said.

The Neimoidan half bowed again. "In anticipation of close timing, I left the turbolift on standby." He gestured upward, to the top of the shelving directly above Luke's head, and then he turned and ran.

Luke snorted, amused.

Mara leapt up and, with a little propulsion boost through the Force, landed, seated, on the top shelf.

What the Neimoidian had found was obvious. In his search, he had removed a ceiling panel that provided access to a series of data cables and water pipes. Spliced into one of those cables was a commercially available datapad. Mara brought out her electronics tools and got to work on it.

Luke remained at floor level. "Is it a trap?"

"Of course." With gloves, tongs, and tools, she already had the exterior panels off the datapad. "The battery com partment has a smaller-than-standard battery, plus an explosives charge, just enough to destroy the datapad and blow your hand off." Belatedly, she felt a little twinge of sympathy and looked down at her husband. "Oops, sorry, farmboy."

Luke glanced at his new hand. "That sounds like a small charge from someone as dedicated to overkill as she seems to be."

"It is." She returned her attention to the device. "That's because it's backed up by poison. Trihexalon beneath a very thin layer of spray-on sealant. How nice that I didn't touch it. I'd be dead, the bomb would go off, the rest of the poison would go gaseous, the explosion would breach the air duct, the duct would draw the gas in . . ."

"Economical."

"Got it. Defused. Now . . ." She set the poison and explosives package aside, then swiftly cabled in her own datapad. After a brief analysis she said, "A simple intercept-and-redirect. Communications from three hundred seven-twelve alpha to three hundred seven-twelve beta are intercepted and redirected—to neg three four-thirteen."

"Basement level three? Is that bedrock level?"

"Yes, or close to it." Mara disconnected her datapad, restored the panel over Lumiya's 'pad, and placed the explosives and poison package into a self-sealing container. Then, tools and container in hand, she dropped to the floor. "I think we need to see another set of quarters."

chapter ten

The bedrock-level quarters were far less impressive than those on upper stories. The hallway walls were plascrete painted a neutral blue and otherwise undecorated; the ceilings were low; the doors were flimsy-looking metal with large package delivery slots beside them. There was a smell to this level, an inescapable odor of a chemical sanitizing agent, suggesting an attempt by management to combat the leakage of sewage or industrial runoff.

As Mara was performing her check of the electronics on the door into the suspect quarters, Luke saw two beings—a Gamorrean and a human—leaving other sets of quarters. Both were clad in blue jumpsuits emblazoned with the Zorp House apartment tower logo; they barely glanced at the Jedi before heading off toward the turbolifts.

"Looks as though this floor is mostly quarters for building workers," Luke said.

Mara nodded. "Mostly or entirely. Which makes me wonder how Lumiya got a place here. Did she forge an ID and records, which is certainly within her capabilities, or did she bribe the building manager and it's just a little detail he's conveniently forgotten? Oh, here we go, stand back." She stepped away from the doorway, and though he felt no presence of danger, Luke did likewise.

The door slid aside with a scraping noise suggesting that it needed to be realigned on its rails. The Jedi waited a moment for traps to spring, then cautiously entered.

This set of quarters wasn't a hovel, but it was primitive. The main room, four meters by five, opened via a curtained doorway into a short hall; doors there accessed two bedrooms, a kitchen with minimal facilities, and a refresher. The walls and ceiling were the same blue as the halls outside, and the floor was covered by a thin, springy, off-white pad, scuffed here and there but clean. There was no furniture other than a sleep-mat in one bedroom and a chair in the main room.

Luke and Mara moved cautiously from room to room, inspecting every closet and cabinet, turning the chair over, unscrewing panels from walls to see if anything was hidden.

In one bedroom closet were two Zorp House apartment tower jumpsuits in Lumiya's size. Mara paused while looking through them. Luke saw her nostrils flare, and then she pulled the garments from the closet, tossed them to the floor, and leaned in to study the back of the closet.

"Something?" Luke asked.

"A hidden panel concealing a locking mechanism. I think the whole back of the closet is a doorway. You?"

"The alert diode on the package delivery slot was disabled. Something was delivered since the last time she was here—a datacard."

"Go ahead and run it. I'm going to be a minute or two here."

Luke slid the unlabeled card into his datapad and watched a password prompt and a couple of lines of analysis text pop up on his screen. "Encrypted," he said. "We'll need to run it on a computer with some decryption muscle."

Mara's reply sounded like muttered swearing in Huttese.

Luke didn't know whether she was reacting to his statement or to the persistent unwillingness of the lock she was working on to be opened.

"And speaking of encryption," he continued, "while I was getting at the datacard, I was forwarded a message by the Temple comm system. An encrypted recording from Leia."

Mara glanced back at him, her brows up. "How is she?"

"So-so, I think. She didn't mention Jacen shooting from the *Anakin Solo* and killing her bodyguards. She did mention that Han was getting back to normal from the blaster shot he sustained."

"Good."

"And she asked me to do something." In a few words, he outlined Leia's request about putting a word in Jacen's ear regarding the *Errant Venture.*

Mara turned her attention to the locking mechanism as she considered. "Sounds like a good tactic. But if you do it, you'll be conspiring with an enemy of the GA. I know how you like to keep your nose clean."

Luke offered her a dismissive little sniff. "Han and Leia aren't enemies of the GA—they're suspects in an investigation. If they're ever captured and charged, they'll be cleared."

"That's true. Our justice system is particularly fair and rational these days."

"Also, getting to the truth is always a good idea . . . no matter how it hurts. Besides, if you're ever strapped for credits, you can always turn me in for the reward."

Mara turned again to smile at him. "Luke, you always know the right thing to say."

"I do."

She turned back and made one final adjustment to the locking mechanism. "Ah, here we go." There was a faint rumble from the closet and Mara abruptly bent over backward, flexible as a gymnast, catching her fall with one palm on the floor.

A dart—if a meter-long shaft of polished durasteel could be termed a dart—flew from the closet, passing over her at waist level and burying itself in the wall opposite.

Luke's tone was exactly what he'd use to order a meal he wasn't interested in eating. "Look out, a trap."

"Thank you." Mara rose.

The doorway in the back of the closet opened onto blackness and admitted warm air, pungent with the smells of Coruscant's undercity: native and Yuuzhan Vong plant life, standing water, plascrete so old that it was going to powder in places, distant sewage.

Luke and Mara lit glowrods and entered. The access led to a utilities and repair tunnel; the Jedi explored it for thirty meters in one direction, twenty in the other, just far enough to confirm that its connections to bigger, more traveled tunnels were blocked by new plascrete plugs that looked solid but featured hatches cunningly textured to look like surrounding materials.

"Her own private means into and out of the building," Luke said. "Chiefly as escape route, probably, since we know she didn't use it when she returned here after killing Master Lobi."

"But knowing that doesn't offer us anything." Mara sounded annoyed. "The datacard had better give us something. Or we visit the Neimoidian and get our money back."

CORUSCANT
JEDI TEMPLE, OFFICE OF THE
ALEMA RAR TASK FORCE

Curiously, considering the rigid militarism of his background, Jag Fel ran his task force very informally, and there were times when Jaina was quite pleased with the fact.

Such as now. The office Luke had assigned them was large enough for several desks, floor-to-ceiling displays, and other gear. There was even room for a speeder berth, had the office been equipped with a hatch to the outside, and Jag had filled it with exercise equipment. Today both he and Zekk were shirtless, doing chin-ups, while Jaina sat at a terminal and watched them surreptitiously.

The competition—and it *was* a competition, though neither man would ever have admitted it—was surprisingly even.

Zekk could draw on the Force to boost his reserves of vitality, but he was taller and, though lean, heavier than Jag—it took him a trifle more effort to perform each chin-up. And he was still recovering from his wounds. Surgery, bacta, Jedi healing techniques, and simple rest had worked wonders, leaving a broad, facing scar on his torso the only visible evidence of his injury, but the damage was not entirely healed.

Jag, shorter and more compact, was in better shape, his muscles more clearly defined, and though he could not call upon the Force, he could call upon the stubbornness for which his ancestors, the Fel and Antilles clans, were both known.

Jag paused at the top of a chin-up. "So. Time has gone by and we've seen no sign of Alema. We've added our monitoring program to the security systems of the Temple, the portions of the Senate Building that would permit it, the building where the Skywalkers keep their civilian quarters, and other places where they are occasionally seen, and we haven't seen a single flag drop. Zekk, we're doing this all wrong."

"We should be doing sit-ups instead?"

Jag scowled, then lowered himself and began another ten repetitions. "Jedi humor. No, that's not what I mean."

"He means," Jaina said, "that Uncle Luke isn't Alema's

current target; otherwise she'd have been detected. Meaning that Mom's the target."

"Ah." Zekk finished his set, then dropped to the floor and reached for a towel. "So we track your mother down."

Jaina shook her head. "If it were that easy, Alema would have done it already."

Jag, grunting his way through one more group of ten—which would put him, Jaina noted, exactly and deliberately ten ahead of Zekk—nodded, finished his set, and dropped to the floor. "We need to get the monitoring software installed in places where your parents might show up. Smugglers' havens, casinos, and trouble spots—here, around the galaxy, even on Corellia." He paused to consider that last possibility. "I wonder if Galactic Alliance Intelligence could swing that."

A current from the vent on the far wall carried air to Jaina, and she wrinkled her nose. "It won't take Intelligence to figure out where that smell comes from. You both need to head to the refresher for a sanisteam. Not to put it too delicately, you stink."

Jag looked at Zekk and gestured toward the door. "After you."

"No, after you."

"I'm smaller, so I stink less. A logical calculation. After you."

Zekk frowned but—obviously seeing no way to slide past Jag's stubbornness or superior rank—wrapped the towel around his neck and left.

Jaina sighed to herself. Zekk had declared that he was over her, but as he'd recovered, he had grown increasingly reluctant to leave her alone in Jag's company. He didn't need to bother. Jag clearly tolerated her only because it was his job; he had as much told her so the day Luke had assigned her to him.

And yet, since the discomfort of their first couple of meetings, he had grown less icy, his words less punitive.

She wondered if he had begun to forgive her for her role in costing him—well, everything. About the only things he still possessed were his body and his skills—

—not that she hadn't always admired both—

She stomped on that intrusive thought as though it were a bug in the kitchen. Things were finished with Zekk except for friendship, partnership. Things were finished with Jag except for professional cooperation—and, she hoped, a respect that would someday overcome the resentment he felt.

She was done with men. She was lucky in war, unlucky in love. And she was the Sword of the Jedi. It might take her a lifetime to learn what that meant, what her destiny was, and she couldn't afford to lose her focus just because she was tempted to jump into another doomed love affair.

She became aware that Jag was still standing, waiting. "Was there something else, Colonel?" Inwardly, she winced. Even to her own ears her tone sounded dismissive—and she'd addressed him by the military rank that had been stripped from him, as if it had been her intent to rub salt into an injury.

Jag flipped his towel across his neck, his action mimicking Zekk's, and showed her a forced smile. "*Colonel.* I suppose not, Jedi Solo." He turned and strode from the room.

She rose to follow, then stopped herself. She hadn't meant to sting him–she had inherited her mother's sharp tongue but lacked the diplomatic skills that Leia used to keep it in check when appropriate. But perhaps it was better this way.

She needed to keep him at bay. But she didn't want to hurt him. She didn't know how to achieve both goals.

She didn't even know whether she *wanted* to achieve both goals, or either. Sometimes she wanted to hurt him. Sometimes she didn't want to keep him at bay.

Blast him for getting past her armor.

COMMENOR PRESIDENT'S RESIDENCE

The holotransmission was in the image of a woman—a beautiful woman, her features aristocratic and refined in the inbred Hapan fashion, almost to the point of anonymity. *She's a generic Hapan,* Fyor Rodan told himself, and the startling thought made him more suspicious of her.

"Your War and Intelligence Ministers argue and delay," the woman was saying. She shook her head in sad sympathy, sending her golden curls swaying. "Knowing that your fleet will be wiped out by the Galactic Alliance forces if they make a misstep. And that would be catastrophic. But delaying will also be disastrous. Corellia will fall soon, and then attacking would be suicide. Soon the GA will turn its attention to Commenor, to what it perceives as Corellia's treason, and you will fall, too."

Rodan snorted. "You're clearly proficient at cutting through the layers of disinformation we surround ourselves with to keep people like you from taking up too much of our time, but that doesn't make you correct in your assumptions. Yes, the government of Commenor has spoken out against Alliance aggression and for Corellian independence. That's not an act of war—as readying a fleet would be."

The unnamed woman gave him a slightly superior smile. "For a man, you've done a superb job of instituting on Commenor the kind of government you advocated for the New Republic. There are no loose turbocannons like the Jedi order rolling around on your decks. But the same caution that convinced you to keep the Jedi at bay could doom you now. Though I don't think it will. You're clever."

"For a man," he added, mockingly.

"For a man." Her reply was straight-faced. "I'm going to do you two favors. I'm now transmitting a package of data I have obtained from my sources within the Galactic Alliance Guard. Favvio?"

The next voice belonged to someone not in the holocam view: "Transmitting, Mistress."

Rodan forced himself not to grimace. He imagined the speaker as a Hapan drone male, his body perfectly maintained through exercise regimens for the pleasure of the woman he called Mistress, his mind stunted by the pampered life he led.

The woman continued, "These are the plans by which the GA will conquer Commenor, exactly one month after the fall of Corellia."

"I see," Rodan said, keeping his voice neutral.

"Your people will analyze them and confirm their authenticity," she continued. "Establishing *my* authenticity. Then, in a few days, I will transmit you the time and movements of other fleets that will be moving on Corellia. Fleets that, by themselves, perhaps cannot prevail. Fleets that, with the aid of Commenor, *must* prevail."

"Thank you for your transmission, my lady," Rodan said.

She smiled. Her image winked out.

Rodan checked his comm display to make sure that the transmission had been cut, and that the data package was intact and in his computer. Then he sat for long moments, still on the outside, vibrating on the inside.

Much of what the woman had said was true, especially the part about his ministers' dithering. If the woman also spoke truly about the conquest plans, Rodan *had* to act, his ministers *had* to act.

"Vee Ell Eight," he said.

Instantly his secretary droid was beside him. "Yes, sir."

"Transmit that datafile to the Ministers of War and Intelligence, plus to everyone on our top military analysis list. Encrypt it to top levels and attach a note saying that it must be evaluated. Then set up a meeting for me and all those parties for midday tomorrow."

"Yes, sir."

STAR SYSTEM MZX32905, NEAR BIMMIEL

Lumiya waited until her medical droid was set up beside her reclining chair. She was healing well—she should be fit to return to physical activities within a few days. She was still weak, though, and wanted care to be instantly available if this task caused her to collapse.

She closed her eyes and let the dark side power that suffused the asteroid roll over her, through her.

Then she began looking, through the Force, for a distant target—a mind she had touched many times and reshaped during those contacts, a mind she had made so familiar and distinct she could find it even halfway across the galaxy.

It helped that she knew on what world the mind was to be found, but even so it was long, wearying minutes before she found it—to her inner eye it was a distinctive yellow glow, surrounded by tiny gleaming sparks of red. Fewer sparks than before; the efforts of the enemy to diminish her influence had apparently been successful in part.

But only in part. Lumiya smiled. The enemy's techniques were nowhere near as effective as hers.

She approached the mind until it filled her vision, and she planted herself there, making its location an anchor point for her consciousness.

Now for the second phase of this elaborate Sith technique. She drew back from her target mind, seeking other mentalities in the area. And there they were, glows of various hues, none of them, sadly, decorated with the red sparks of her influence.

She sampled each in turn. Most were awake—firm, more resolute than she could affect at this distance. Others were too fragmented; when she touched them they tended to drift apart into smaller, incoherent glows, and she knew that these were the minds of the inmates . . . the patients.

Then she found one that was firm, grounded, but not so resistant to her touch. Its owner was asleep. Lumiya sampled it further, found it to be the mind of a Quarren female.

Like a spectral parasite, she affixed herself to that mind, forging a connection, drawing energy out of it and the body that sustained it. She could not draw that energy into herself, though she badly needed sustenance now; she could feel her own body begin to shake from the strain. But she could, and would, put the energy to use.

Finally she flowed into the distant Quarren's mind, flowed out through its memory of its surroundings . . . and she could see.

She hovered above the Quarren. The amphibious female was dressed in medical scrubs and leaned across a desk, sleeping there. This was a small office packed with, and lit solely by, computer displays. A window looked out over a facing wall of building fronts, and there were, for once, no traffic streams to be seen. A door, ajar, led into a brightly lit corridor.

Lumiya got to work. Into the woman's sleeping mind, she whispered, "Open your eyes. Stand up. We have work to do. Records to read. Instructions to issue."

And the Quarren rose, her eyes glazed, her face-tentacles twitching.

Minutes later Lumiya restored the Quarren to her desk and true sleep, then drifted from the chamber to find someone. A very useful someone.

GALACTIC CITY, CORUSCANT, VETERANS' MENTAL CARE HOSPITAL

Matric Klauskin, former commander of the Second Fleet's Corellian task force but for the last several weeks a patient in this too-sympathetic prison, awoke. The small room he'd been given was, as always, dark and quiet, its few items of furniture reflecting white gleams from the city lights filtering in through the transparisteel viewport. Everything was as it should be.

Or perhaps not. The door was open.

He frowned. The door opened only when the doctors or nurses came for him, or when his caseworker from the Alliance's naval administration visited to reassure him that all was well; they hadn't forgotten him.

But now the door was open and no one was entering.

He sat up, his sheet falling from his chest, and realized that someone was standing beside his bed. He looked up.

It was Edela. Of *course* it was Edela. His treatment here was all about his wife. Now she smiled down at him, patient and loving as always. Tonight she wore a shimmering synthsilk gown of burgundy.

She had lost weight, diminishing from the pretty but distinctly overweight woman she had been the last time he'd seen her to a figure he could describe as "pleasingly plump." The gray was gone from her hair, too, and he realized belatedly that she wasn't just slimmer, she was *younger*—she looked as she had a mere five or ten years into their marriage.

"Hello, dear," he said. "You realize you're dead."

Her smile broadened. "Of course I'm dead. I've been dead for years. But it doesn't mean I don't *exist.*"

"Well, that's the point, isn't it? The doctors all say that you don't, that your very existence rests only in my mind. But they say I'm getting better."

"I don't exist just in your mind. I exist in fact. Phantoms of the mind can't open a door and free you, can they?"

Klauskin looked again at the door. It remained resolutely open. "That just means I'm dreaming again. It's really not open."

"It is, as you'll find out in a moment." Her voice became urgent. "Darling, you've been lied to, we've all been lied to.

The Corellians have been in the right all along, and we've betrayed our own people by opposing them."

Klauskin frowned. He knew his thinking was muddled, but he couldn't see how he was harming his homeworld of Commenor by opposing Corellia. True, Commenor's government had offered words of encouragement to Corellia, but that was just politics at work.

Edela continued, "Commenor and Bothawui are coming into the war on Corellia's side. And you, darling, have been imprisoned here and convinced that you're ill . . . just so the Alliance can keep you from helping our world."

Klauskin sighed. Truth was such a slippery concept these days that he found it hard to trust—even his dead wife. "You're either here or not."

There was a little curiosity in Edela's voice. "True."

"And I'm either a prisoner or a patient."

"True."

"And Commenor and Bothawui are either in the war or not."

"True."

"I have to know the truth, and the truth is in what can be verified. I'm sorry, darling. I'm going to go through that open door and then wake myself up. If I *don't* wake up, then what you say is true."

"Don't apologize, Matric. I know these are difficult times for you."

Klauskin rose. His bare feet were cold on the tile floor. He walked out through the door, looking up and down the corridor at the other doorways; they were all closed. Edela followed and joined him.

Klauskin raised his hand to his lips and bit the webbing between his thumb and forefinger. It hurt. He kept the pressure on, biting deeper, and tasted blood. He held the bite until he couldn't stand the pain anymore, and finally he let his arm swing to his side again.

Weary, he said, "I'm convinced."

"Good. Because you have a lot to do. I'm going to lead you out of this prison. Outside, a friend will give you clothes, transportation, and documents." Her expression turned to one of sympathy. "You've been a hero of the Alliance for so long. But they turned against you, and it's time to be a hero of Commenor again."

STAR SYSTEM MZX32905, NEAR BIMMIEL

Lumiya gave Klauskin one last, sweet kiss as he stood on the walkway outside the mental hospital. The shaking her real body was experiencing almost reflected itself in trembling in Edela's arms, but she maintained ruthless control.

Then she let Edela fade away to nothingness. Her consciousness roared back into her own body.

That's when the pain and weakness hit hard. She spasmed, sitting upright, and nearly rolled out of her reclining chair. She forced herself to lie down again. She lay there, her limbs twitching—even the artificial ones.

"My lady?" the medical droid asked. "Can you hear me?"

"Yessss." Feebly, she waved fingers at him, trying to dissuade him from unnecessary conversation.

This session had gone longer than most, and had been worse than most. It would take her longer to recover. She wondered what would have happened if she had continued it to the point of her own collapse. Would she have died? Or would she be trapped on Coruscant, in the phantasmal body of a long-dead military wife, forever hovering around a man she had deliberately driven crazy?

She didn't know the answer, and it didn't matter. She had succeeded, and Klauskin would now dutifully go about accomplishing her plans.

The Galactic Alliance had been so circumspect about covering up the details of Klauskin's mental breakdown. They thought they were being merciful; that if Klauskin was able to effect a recovery he could someday resume command, even if a lesser one. His official record said only that he was on administrative leave, which could result from a physical injury or an urgent family problem. He still held his admiral's rank and command rating.

And in not informing the fleet that Klauskin was dangerously delusional, they had doomed—

—had doomed—

On that thought she fell asleep.

DREWWA, MOON OF ALMANIA
DREWWA SPACEPORT

Customs inspections, Ben decided, *are very inconvenient.*

The transport ride to the Outer Rim system of Almania had been long and dull. Ben spent most of it reading Jedi texts on his datapad—texts about his grandfather, Anakin Skywalker, he'd been given as preparation for the document he was supposed to write—or sleeping. He interacted very little with his fellow passengers, preferring not to become memorable to them.

Finally the transport had landed on the heavily industrialized moon of Drewwa, with its high-security spaceport and its carefully regimented customs facility. Ben stood in the inspection line, his small pack and his belt pouch in hand, and prepared to enter the twenty-meter-long sensor tube. There he would be scanned a dozen different ways, and at the end his belongings would be laid out on a table and hand-inspected, with anything the sensors had flagged receiving special attention.

There was no way his lightsaber would remain undetected if he carried it through the tube.

The tube allowed access through a security wall that was seven or eight meters tall, and there was a three-meter gap between the top of the wall and the drafty-looking shell of the ceiling. There were lots of glow rod pods up there on either side of the wall.

Ben could bound to the top of the metal awning above the tube entrance and might be able, with a prodigious leap, to make the top of the wall. He could then run along the top of the tube, clear the wall on the far side, and run out into the nonsecure portion of the customs building to vanish into the night.

Assuming it was night out there. And the holocams all over the facility would record his face, and his image would be on every guard's datapad in an hour. That would be inconvenient.

Then he thought about the Jedi Temple practice droid and its foamsteel balls, and he knew what to do.

He looked up and found a glow rod pod well behind him. He reached out through the Force to grab it, yank it . . .

It rocked a bit.

Ben frowned. It was firmly rooted. He focused harder, putting all his intensity into his concentration.

The pod snapped free of its mooring and crashed to the permacrete floor, its cluster of dozens of glow rods shattering and sending glass pieces skidding along the floor in every direction.

As everyone looked, and one armed guard trotted over to see what had happened, Ben used the Force to send his lightsaber up to the ceiling. There, above the glow rods, it was barely visible. He caused it to slide across the ceiling until it came to rest above a pod on the far side of the wall . . . and then, with meticulous care, he lowered it until it nestled into the cluster of rods.

"You're holding up the line, stupid." The speaker was an elderly woman, as lean as though she were made up just of bone and rawhide, a disapproving look on her face.

"Sorry," Ben said. He trotted forward into the tube.

"Sorry doesn't mean anything. If you were sorry, you wouldn't have done it in the first place."

"Sorry."

"Now you're being insolent."

"Sorry." Ben thought about using his powers to cause her to trip. A face full of permacrete might scrub the disapproval off her face.

No, she was old, and she might really be hurt.

On the other hand, it would teach her a lesson, and she could stand to be taught a lesson.

At the far end of the tube, he handed over his bag and pouch to the gray-uniformed inspection officer and waited, frowning over the question of the old woman. What would Jacen do in this situation? Ben shook his head. The question didn't apply. No one would have spoken to Colonel Jacen Solo that way, even before he was famous.

Why not? Because he was tall and handsome? No, *Luke* wasn't tall and was only as handsome as his scarred face let him be, and yet everyone treated *him* with respect.

Luke and Jacen commanded respect because everyone knew it was a bad idea to mess with them, from either their appearance or their history. Which meant that Ben was out of luck, because he had neither fame nor formidable looks.

The old woman fussed her way up behind Ben. "You're a very nasty little boy," she said.

Ben glared up at her. "I take it back."

"You take what back?"

"My apology. I apologized, but you didn't accept it. You just used it as an excuse to keep being rude. You have the manners of a bantha with digestion problems. If you had children, I hope they were raised by piranha-beetles so they'd be nicer than you."

The woman loomed up over him, her face distorting with anger, and Ben saw in her mind her intent to slap some of what she considered courtesy into him.

But he intensified his glare, and added to it a little push with the Force. *Try it,* he all but said. *See what I become.*

A bit of grayness crept into her complexion, and she

took an involuntary step back. She turned stiffly away from Ben, handing her bag to her inspections officer, and looked at everything but Ben, muttering to herself.

Ben's inspections officer handed his bag back to him. He also offered a silent smile and a thumbs-up.

Surprised, Ben offered a shy smile in return. He turned and trotted toward the door out of the customs facility.

There, he told himself. *That's how Jacen would have done it if he were my age.*

As he reached the door, he let his lightsaber drop into his hands, then moved out into the night air.

chapter eleven

DREWWA, MOON OF ALMANIA

In the silvery light of dawn, Ben stood under a sidewalk café awning beside a nearly deserted city street and stared up at the soaring Crossroutes Business Habitat. It was unlovely in the extreme, a greenish column extending eight hundred meters up into the sky, with decorative yellow-white structures like planetary rings situated every five floors. At least Ben hoped they were decorative—what their function might be otherwise was beyond him. Could they slide up and down the building exterior like massive open-air turbolifts?

The data card Seha had given him included a datafile on Drewwa, including a mention that the Crossroutes building was one of the system's few acknowledgments that there was life outside Almania. Trang Robotics, one of the system's largest industries, traded a tremendous number of computer systems and droids to the Alliance, the Chiss, and other large collectives of planets and cultures, but the locals by and large ignored the fact that anything existed beyond their star system.

The occasional firm like Crossroutes seemed to exist principally to rub such unwelcome news into the faces of the Almanians. The building housed the local offices of hundreds of offworld firms as they tried, usually successfully, to arrange for advantageous purchase deals from local technological firms or attempted, usually unsuccessfully, to market their own goods in this system.

At this early hour there was already a stream of workers entering the ground-level doors of the Crossroutes building. Most looked to Ben as though they were offworlders like himself. At some point he would have to join them, go up to the 215th floor, find and break into the display case, replace the real Amulet there with the fake he carried in his pocket, and get out undetected.

No, that was too much, he decided. For once, it was his mother's voice and not Jacen's that whispered in his ear. "The first step in any intelligence operation," she had told him more than once, "is gathering information. You gather enough information to make your plan. If you're planning without information, you're planning for failure."

"But that's not how the Jedi do things," Ben had protested. "They just go there and solve the problem."

She'd given him a crafty smile. "Which is why they're famous, right?"

"Right!"

"Well, when intelligence operatives do their jobs correctly, they never become famous. Because no one ever learns they've been there. And sometimes that's what *solving the problem* means."

Ben hadn't liked the answer then, because it seemed to preclude igniting lightsabers, bouncing off walls, and stuffing the smiles of bad people straight down their mouths. But now he could see that the intelligence way had merit from time to time. Jacen did things that couldn't always appear on news holocasts; Jacen's duties seemed to be about half intelligence these days. Suddenly, in Ben's estimation, Mara got a lot smarter.

So he'd do an information-gathering run and then decide, when he knew more, whether to continue straight into the actual mission or back off and return at a later time.

The wall behind him slid up, revealing the café's interior. Warm air smelling of fresh-baked goods rolled across Ben, and he abruptly realized that he was hungry.

The proprietor, a tall man with the build and gut of a Gamorrean, stepped out among his tables, looked up and down at the sidewalk foot traffic, and glanced at Ben. "Here to eat, son?" To Ben's ears, his quaint accent made it sound like, *Hierr to eat, sann?*

Ben nodded.

The man tapped a tabletop, motioning for Ben to sit there. The tabletop lit up, four points on it revealing themselves to be displays showing the establishment's morning menu. Ben sat and looked it over, while also watching the front of his target building, noticing the way many people heading toward the building instead veered toward the café.

"Caf, please," Ben said. "And kruffy pot pie."

"Tap it out, son. And put in your credcard. No mistakes that way." The proprietor tapped his ear as if suggesting he were hard of hearing. "You sound Coruscanti."

Ben entered his order and slid his credcard into the slot at the table's center. "I am. Mostly."

"Two kinds of Coruscanti there are. Those that are happy for big open spaces, and those who can't stand not being surrounded by close walls and tight streets."

"I suppose so." The table surface went *ding* and the word DECLINED, in red, was superimposed over the menu. Below it, more text read, ACCOUNT NOT FOUND. PLEASE INSERT ANOTHER CREDCARD.

"Hey," Ben said. "Your table is broken."

The proprietor moved over to look. He pointed at a symbol at the menu's lower left corner, an animation of tiny blaster bolts crisscrossing, right to left and left to right.

"No. Holocomm data link's live. That means it's checking all the way back to wherever your account's supposed to be. And there's no account to find. Got another credcard? Or coin?"

Ben felt in his pocket. There was one credcoin there, his last. He'd planned to get local coins through his credcard. He shook his head.

The proprietor gave him a sympathetic look. "Well, go ask your mother or father for more."

The hunger Ben was feeling was graduating from mild to sharp and painful. "Maybe," he said, "you could let me have my breakfast, and I'd get Dad to pay you back later today." To his suggestion he added a sizable push through the Force.

The proprietor laughed. "I could. But after a year of doing that, I'd be out of business. Off with you, son."

Ben sighed and left the table. He really was hungry now, and perhaps, he reflected, the hunger had kept him from concentrating and being able to affect the man. Or maybe Ben was just too weak because, like his father said, he hadn't had sufficient Jedi training. Or maybe the proprietor was too strong-willed.

It didn't matter. Ben resisted the urge to stomp his frustrations away as he left the café.

And now his plans needed further revision. Before reconnaissance, he needed *food*. And he needed to find out what had become of the special account that was supposed to be available to him for this mission.

Banking kiosks turned out to be no help. Twice he inserted his credcard in their slots and tried to access his account, but all he received was a cryptic ACCOUNT NOT FOUND screen. He tried to send a message to the establishment, but even a tiny data query would cost money if sent over a holocomm connection, and he had no money to draw on.

Well, that had to change. He had to, as his mother had

put it so many times, *acquire resources.* And in this situation, that meant . . . stealing.

He hesitated over that. Stealing was wrong. Sure, everybody in his family had hijacked ships at one time or another, but those were always emergencies. Nobody stole for breakfast credits.

But this wasn't just breakfast credits. He was on a mission, one he was proud to have been assigned, one that was important and might save the lives of Jedi and Guards . . . didn't that make it an emergency?

He decided it did.

He drifted across the street to stand near the doors into the Crossroutes building. Perhaps someone would flash a credcard, Ben would see where he pocketed it, and he could follow the owner—

And what? He didn't have his mother's skills. He couldn't pick someone's pocket clean without that person feeling it. He could follow his target into a lonely corridor or alley, hit him over the head . . . but Ben's already upset stomach rebelled at that notion. Suddenly he was a mugger, injuring or possibly killing someone in an effort to obtain pocket credits.

He shook his head. Hitting someone over the head for breakfast credits would be a mistake, and he couldn't afford to make a mistake right now.

The answer came to him a moment later. A public conveyance airspeeder, striped red and yellow to make it even more conspicuous than the glowdot marquee reading FOR HIRE on the hood, pulled to a landing in front of the building, and its driver hopped out to open a front-end cargo compartment and off-load luggage. The passenger exited and waited on the walkway, a small portfolio of black simulated nerf leather open in his hand. And tucked into many of the numerous little pockets of that portfolio, Ben saw, were credcards. Some were banking institution credcards, the sort that required validation from the institution to access funds, but others were stamped to indicate that they carried their own value in their memory.

Ben knew what he could do. He drifted closer.

When the driver was finished and three pieces of luggage rested on the walkway, the passenger handed him one of the institutional cards. At that moment, Ben flicked a finger and exerted himself through the Force. One of the other cards, the lesser ones, leapt free of the portfolio and fluttered to the street.

Ben edged closer and pinned the card to the ground with his mental exertion. A moment later, the driver handed the other card back to the passenger, entered the driver's compartment, and accelerated away. The passenger pocketed his portfolio, clumsily picked up the luggage, and moved on into the Crossroutes building.

Ben moved over beside the street, knelt as if to fiddle with his boot, and picked up the card.

And that was it. He was a thief, but he'd only taken a little bit of what the man possessed and had hurt no one. He'd made the wrong as small as he possibly could.

Half an hour later, well fed on caf and kruffy potpie, which turned out to be savory fowl meat, vegetables, and gravy in a thick pastry shell, he felt ready to put his troubles behind him and get the mission under way.

A few minutes with his datapad communicating with a public data terminal gave him some of the information he needed.

Tendrando Arms leased the 212th through 215th floors. That suggested to Ben that the floor he wanted, 215, was where the most important employees had their offices. His mother had told him on numerous occasions that one way people liked to feel important was by sitting on top of their subordinates, and the practical way to do this was to have their offices on upper floors.

Since the building had its decorative planetary rings

every five stories, starting with the sixth story, then 215 had to be just beneath one of those rings. Ben searched the building directory and found that Lyster Innovations leased the next three floors, 216 through 218. Lyster Innovations' public records indicated that the firm employed quality specialists and "idea generators" who would visit other companies and tell them how to do their jobs better. Ben frowned over that, dubious, but decided that descending from 216 might be the easiest way to get onto 215 unobserved.

He occupied himself for another hour researching Tendrando Arms' local office and Lyster Innovations, then spent the rest of the morning and some of the afternoon buying things: food and bottled liquids that would not rapidly deteriorate, twenty meters of thin, pliant, strong cable, basic mechanical tools, a box of sweets, a length of red ribbon, and a large backpack. The last of the credits on the card he'd stolen went to buying himself a hot midday meal.

As the workday grew late and workers began streaming out of the Crossroutes building in anticipation of shift change, Ben entered the building, backpack on his shoulders and ribbon-wrapped box of sweets in his hands, and took the turbolift up to 216.

The doors opened into a jungle. Ben stared at healthy trees growing up out of dark, moist-looking soil, smelled the warm, heavy air of a tropical rain forest, saw a distant solar light through the trees that was a whiter hue than Almania's sun. Somewhere in the distance, water splashed. There was no sound of industry, of harassed workers, of overtaxed terminals.

He stepped out onto the jungle floor, and the turbolift doors closed behind him. He turned to look at them and saw only a sheer rock face. It was a perfect illusion.

When he tried to examine it through the Force, he could sense very little. The trees did not resonate with life. He could detect no movement of insects through the air or underneath the soil.

He grinned toward the trees. "It's all mechanical," he told himself.

"So it is." The voice, male, came from only a few meters ahead. "Follow the path, please."

The path, the ground and leaves underfoot convincingly soft and resilient, led forward, then curved right, revealing a clearing that should have been visible from the turbolift but was not. The right half of the clearing was dominated by a stone-lined pool, seemingly natural, into which water from an adjacent waterfall splashed. Next to it was a desk apparently made of black stone. As it came into view, the man who sat behind it, young and pale-skinned, lowered his lizard-skin boots from the desktop and sat forward in a more normal pose. His jumpsuit, though apparently cloth, had the same color and texture as his boots. "Welcome to Lyster Innovations," he said. "Can I help you?"

"What is all this?" Ben asked, gesturing around.

"Corporate culture." The man offered Ben a big, practiced smile to go with his big, practiced words. "One of the things we do is show companies how to establish and maintain their own cultural identities through environmental design. Here in our receiving area, the floor, walls, and decorative pillars are made of or coated with our patented chameleon cover material, which allows the ultimate in decorative versatility. With just a few words, I can establish a new tone, a new work environment. For instance—Décor, Purity."

He'd hardly finished the second word when a change rippled through the chamber. Trees straightened, becoming vertical, absolutely symmetrical, their branches folding up into their sides. The floor flattened into a perfect plane and Ben, balancing, could feel it harden under his feet.

Most objects faded to white smoothness, the trees becoming featureless and gleaming. Even the man's clothes transformed from their green scale texture to pure white. His desk became silver, and the rim of stones around the pool became a silvery seating bench.

Now Ben could see the true dimensions of the room—for a reception area, it was large, about twenty meters by twenty, but it no longer seemed to stretch forever in every direction. Silvery panels on the walls—doors, he supposed—showed him where the boundaries were.

The man was watching him closely, and Ben did not need to tap into the Force to feel that he wanted Ben to be impressed. *He lives for praise,* Ben thought. *And Jacen says that when you give people what they want, they can be more cooperative.*

"Wow," Ben said. "I mean, wow."

"Wow indeed." The man smiled, apparently satisfied. "So, are you looking for someone in particular?"

"Oh, yeah." Ben pretended to consult his datapad. "I have something for, um, Gilthor Breen."

"I'm Gilthor Breen."

I know that, Ben thought. *Your face and your name are on the company's public page. And a whole long list of your likes and dislikes.* "Then this is for you." He put the beribboned box on the desk top.

Gilthor looked closely at Ben, then subjected the box to the same scrutiny. He pulled the ribbon end to untie the bow, then opened the box and gave a brief, uncertain smile when he saw the variety of sweets within. "Uh, is there a note?"

Ben checked his datapad again. "No note. She just left a short message. 'Two days.' "

" 'Two days.' She. Who's she? What's her name?"

Ben shrugged. "She didn't leave one. But she was very short, with long black hair and black eyes. And cute, really cute." This was a description of Aliniaca Verr, a young holodrama actress currently in vogue. She was from the world of Balmorra, like Gilthor himself, and she was his favorite actress, three facts that Ben had found on Gilthor's personal page. Ben wasn't going to try to persuade Gilthor that his admirer was Verr herself; it just seemed reasonable that if Gilthor admired Verr, he'd also be interested in a woman who looked like her.

Apparently he'd guessed correctly. Gilthor practically began to vibrate in his chair. "Two days," he said. "Until what? Maybe she'll be in touch again. That's it." Abruptly realizing that Ben was still present, he dug into a pocket and drew out a credcoin. "Thanks."

"You're welcome. Um, can I use your refresher?"

"Of course, of course. Décor, refresher."

A melodious droid voice to Ben's left said, "Here I am," and when Ben glanced toward it, he saw that one of the silver panels was now cycling between silver and black. Ben smiled and trotted that way.

He spent little time in the refresher, just long enough to determine that its jet-black tiled floor and blue tiled walls seemed content to stay in their respective colors, and that there were exterior windows on one wall. That's what he needed to know.

Moments later he trotted out to the silvery turbolift access and waved good-bye to Gilthor. The man gave him a distracted nod and spoke a couple of words Ben couldn't hear. The lift doors opened.

Now was the moment of truth. Ben took half a step forward but did not quite enter the turbolift. He concentrated on Gilthor and imagined, in some detail and with great conviction, himself getting aboard. As the doors closed, he tried to project the image of the doors closing with him on the other side. *I got on the turbolift,* he thought. *Think about the girl.*

Gilthor leaned back in his chair and put his feet up again. He seemed to be whistling.

Slowly, quietly, Ben moved at a crouch back toward the refresher. *I got on. I went away. I'm gone.*

By the time he reached the refresher door again, he was sweating through his garments, but Gilthor never looked his way.

Ben set himself up in one of the stalls, hand-lettering a sign that read IN NEED OF REPAIR. MAINTENANCE HAS BEEN SUMMONED. REPAIRS SCHEDULED FOR TOMORROW. This he placed on the front of the stall, and he kept his Force-senses and more ordinary senses sharp, straining to hear or feel anyone who might approach this refresher chamber. But no one did, and he could feel Gilthor outside, seated at his desk. He could also feel a steady stream of life moving up and down the turbolift, mostly down as the offices were depopulated by the late hour. But no one came to this refresher before Ben was done.

With his tools, Ben unscrewed one viewport panel from the wall and carried all his equipment through it to rest on the planetary ring structure beyond. Twilight was gathering outside, and from here Ben could see all the lights of the city, the majority of them pale blue, pale green, or white, a striking difference from the nighttime skies of Coruscant in all their spectral beauty.

The decorative ring turned out to be made of plasteel, mounted sturdily to the building exterior. It shifted not at all under the occasional breeze. A gap of about ten centimeters separated it from the building edge, and through the gap Ben could see the regularly spaced mounting struts that held the ring to the building exterior.

Though in the growing darkness Ben didn't think he could be seen, he kept his movements to a minimum as he repositioned the transparisteel panel he'd removed and carefully dogged it back into place.

Then he knotted the cable he'd brought at one-meter intervals. He tied it at about the middle around one of the support struts visible through the gap. He threaded one half down through the gap, tossing the other over the edge.

Carefully he lowered himself over the edge and climbed down the cable.

This put him directly opposite one of the viewports of the Tendrando Arms offices. It was only dimly lit, and hanging there Ben could see it was furnished mostly with sturdy-looking stand-up lockers as tall as a human man. Weapons lockers, he guessed, given that Tendrando was an arms manufacturing firm, and wondered if he should help himself to a weapon or two. But he shook his head. Jedi weren't supposed to need anything but their lightsabers—except when they piloted warcraft, of course.

He descended a few more meters on his cable, bringing him down opposite the 214th floor, and began shifting his weight, causing him to swing toward the building wall and the other half of the cable dangling there. After a few moments, his swings brought him close enough to that cable to grab it. He let go of the first one, leaving him dangling next to the building wall, and climbed back up to 215.

Leaning in close to the viewport, he could see the mechanical control that opened the viewport from within. It seemed, from this angle, to be a simple hand crank, but its handle was now folded against its shaft, and the control itself was snugly fitted within a small transparisteel cylinder with a mechanical lock holding the cylinder to the apparatus.

Ben studied it for a few moments and decided he understood its workings. With the handle up against the shaft and the smooth transparisteel cylinder in the way, an ordinary person's grip strength could probably not develop the torque necessary to open the window.

He half closed his eyes and concentrated on the apparatus. He reached out to it through the Force, gripping it as he'd grip his lightsaber hilt to yank it to him, and twisted.

It didn't budge.

He tried the other direction. Now it did move, a few degrees of arc. He frowned, concentrating harder, and the crank began to rotate, very slowly. It was hard work.

As it moved, a tiny gap appeared at the top of the viewport, and it widened—one centimeter, two—

Ben's grip slipped and he fell.

Ben grabbed frantically, wrapped one arm around the cable, felt its knots bumping their way past his elbow hard enough to leave bruises. He tightened his grip, grabbed with his free hand and the Force, and arrested his fall, the impact of his stop yanking both arms to full, painful extension.

He gulped for a few moments, then looked down.

He'd fallen only two stories. There was still more cable beneath him—he hadn't grabbed the very end. And two stories down was the next decorative ring. Had he missed the cable altogether, he would have hit that—possibly not even with enough force and noise to alert every security officer within a kilometer. Possibly.

Half dreading what he might see, he looked into the viewport where he now found himself, expecting to peer into the alarmed faces of office workers, but instead he saw an unoccupied chamber, a combination lounge and kitchen.

He gulped in a few breaths, then climbed back up, furious at himself. His concentration on the Force had been so great that he'd lost focus on his hands. He couldn't afford to do that. He'd get himself killed.

When he reached the viewport again, he spent a few moments tying the cable around his waist, with a knot he could undo with just a pull, then got back to work.

In a couple of minutes, the viewport was open enough to admit him. He scrambled through, pulled the release length of cable, and dropped to the floor.

He was happy. He could relax for a moment, and all he had to do at this point was make a covert search of the offices, find the display case, swap the amulet, and make his way to the ground again. Easy.

Ben looked at the display case and his heart sank.

It hadn't taken long to find. The Tendrando offices all seemed to have been emptied by the hour, so there were no people to dodge. The display case was not in any of the individual executives' offices, but in the central chamber, dominated by a big desk and a receptionist/protocol droid whose optics were unlit, indicating that it was in sleep mode.

The chamber itself contained a dozen or so displays, chiefly statuettes and plaques commemorating unusually advantageous business deals made on Drewwa. Some of the items were unusual presents given to the local office, such as a set of tiny acrobat droids, each no taller than Ben's hand was wide, even now doing tumbling routines on their shelf of the display case.

But the transparisteel top had been carefully removed from the display case and the Amulet of Kalara was gone.

The red velvet pillow it had rested on was still there, as was the silver-on-black sign next to it: AMULET OF KALARA. PRESENTED TO STONIAS LEEM BY THE GRATEFUL VICTORS OF THE INSURRECTION OF ILIABATH.

But there was no amulet on the pillow itself. Instead there was a hand-lettered piece of flimsi. It read, *I will return the Amulet to where it belongs. Be grateful that I spared your lives.* It was signed, *Faskus of Ziost.*

There was something else in the case, too. It was a trace of emotion Ben could detect through the Force, a sensation of happiness, glee. The gloating of a Sith lifetime had to have infused the amulet, and a little of that emotion had been left behind in the case.

Ben sat on the carpet and tried to sort out what it all meant.

Someone *else* had stolen the amulet he meant to steal. That wasn't fair.

And it had to have been done recently, within the last couple of hours. If it had been done yesterday or earlier, the local authorities would have been here to investigate already, and the case wouldn't have looked like this. It would be closed up, the piece of flimsi removed.

Ben closed his eyes and tried to feel something, anything about the theft. But he couldn't. There was no tragedy here to detect, no vast outpouring of emotion concerning the amulet. He could not see the perpetrator's face or get a sense of his spirit. And he could detect no one in these offices, meaning that the thief had already made good his escape. With only a few minutes' head start, he could be anywhere in the city, and he could have had much more than a few minutes.

Ben opened his eyes and sighed. He'd failed. He'd failed Jacen, and now all the Jedi were at risk.

No, wait a minute—maybe he hadn't, not yet. Perhaps, instead of slinking home and admitting to failure, he could continue the mission, improvising. He might be able to follow this Faskus and take the amulet back from him.

But where would Faskus take it? Ben took out his datapad and accessed files that he hadn't read before, those pertaining to the amulet's origin and history.

The main file on the subject said that it had been fabricated on Ziost some two thousand standard years ago, and that the dark side energies invested in it kept it from corroding or showing wear. Ben frowned. Jacen didn't believe in dark side energies, or the dark side of the Force per se, and so Ben didn't, either . . . but so many of the Jedi they dealt with were so old-fashioned on that point that Jacen did grudgingly employ terms like *light side* and *dark side* to communicate with them effectively.

Stolen by a man from Ziost, crafted on Ziost—Faskus was obviously going to take the amulet back to Ziost.

Ben recognized the name of that planet, and it gave him a little shiver. Ziost was the homeworld of the Sith—the species that had given their name to the later order. In subsequent centuries *Sith* referred to Force-users of any species who followed the order's traditions.

His datapad yielded a little information on Ziost, and Ben was surprised to discover that, as galactic distances went, Ziost was not far from Almania—a few hours' ride away by shuttle. But no shuttles would be going there; worlds noted for their inhospitable weather and ancient horrors just were not common tourist destinations. He'd have to acquire transport some other way.

But what to do now? Leave the display case as he'd found it?

Jacen had said that his core mission was to put the amulet in his, Jacen's, hands. If it were reported stolen, it might be harder to acquire. If the authorities picked up this Faskus of Ziost, it might be very hard indeed.

Ben pulled his copy of the amulet from an inner pocket and laid it on the velvet pillow. He took several looks at the holo of the real amulet on his datapad and was careful to arrange the fake and its chain on the pillow just as they appeared on the image. Then he took Faskus's note and remounted the display case top.

There. Now no one would know that the real amulet had been stolen, unless they took out the fake and studied it. Maybe not even then; it was clear the local Tendrando office had no idea what they'd had, and perhaps they'd never recorded enough information about it to tell the real one from a fake.

Ben spent extra minutes covering his tracks. At the viewport by which he'd entered the offices, he used the Force to untie the cable and drag it in to him, then closed the viewport again.

Now there would be no sign that any unauthorized person had been here.

He left the offices by the front way, summoned the turbolift, and descended to street level.

Two minutes after Ben's departure, the protocol droid in the reception area came alive. Its optics lit up, and its head swiveled to look at the display case. The image its visual sensors picked up was compressed and transmitted over a specific comm frequency.

Kilometers away, at the Drewwa Spaceport, a hundred-meter-long bulk freighter rested in one of the outlying hangars. In the days it had been in port, the inoffensive-looking vessel had attracted little attention, her minimal crew carrying on a small-scale disinterested trade in droids from discontinued lines.

But the squat, inelegant vessel would have attracted more interest had anyone gone aboard to examine her. Inspectors would have found that half the cargo bays had been converted to starfighter bays, and that the black-and-bronze starfighters were well known on the space lanes as pirate vehicles.

The freighter's name of record was false. Her transponder indicated that she was the *High Tide,* while her crew, and victims, knew her as the *Boneyard Rendezvous.*

The comm board's computer received the distant droid's message, interpreted it, and popped a text message onto the display of its captain, whose name was Byalfin Dyur. Dyur, an underfed-looking Bothan with lovely bronze-colored fur, looked away from his holodrama and read aloud to the other crew members on the bridge: "Red Braid in motion. Tracker activated. Confirm handoff." He sat back and sighed, glad that the stopover on this overly law-abiding moon would not be protracted.

Hirrtu, his comm officer, tail gunner, and cook—a Rodian who spent every spare credit having every fifth scale on his body dyed from a light green to a dark blue, giving him a curiously dotted appearance—jabbered a question.

"Yes, answer," Dyur said. " 'The captain and crew of the *Boneyard Rendezvous* acknowledge that your safe, undemanding part in this escapade is at an end, and accept handover of responsibility. Sleep untroubled, and know that parties far more interesting than you shall carry this torch evermore.' Got it?"

Hirrtu stared at him for a few moments. Then he typed HANDOVER ACKNOWLEDGED on his comm board and sent the message.

Dyur sighed and returned his attention to the holodrama. "There is no immortal spark within you."

Hirrtu nodded, admission that the captain was correct.

"Track the boy. I want to know where he is every minute of the day."

chapter twelve

BOTHAWUI SYSTEM
GALACTIC ALLIANCE FRIGATE SHAMUNAAR

The door into the command center slid open and the admiral, a paunchy, middle-aged man who nonetheless looked commanding in his white uniform, entered, flanked by two junior-officer escorts. One of them called out, "Admiral on the bridge!"

Shamunaar's commander, a stocky Devaronian, leapt up from his chair and saluted. "Admiral Klauskin. Happy to have you aboard."

Klauskin returned the salute, his gesture as crisp as his uniform. "Captain Biurk. Good to meet you." He shook the captain's hand and glanced around the bridge. "We need to speak in private."

"At once."

Biurk led the admiral through another door into his private office, which was decorated in shades of deep brown and tan. Rather than take his customary chair behind the desk, he stood by one of the two chairs in front of it and gestured for the admiral to take the other.

Klauskin sat and, as Biurk seated himself, handed the captain a data card. "These aren't exactly orders," he said, "but authorization for you to take my verbal orders. *Shamunaar* has been detached from ordinary fleet activities and assigned to the Galactic Alliance Guard on a special assignment."

"Sir, I don't understand. *Shamunaar*'s current assignment is anything but ordinary. We're coordinating all the Alliance's reconnaissance and fighting forces in the Bothawui system, and we're charged with preventing the Bothan fleets from secretly leaving the system. Our assignment is strategic . . . and important."

"It would have been, if you hadn't been betrayed."

That caused Biurk's spine to stiffen. "Betrayed how?"

"The GAG has been assigned this mission because certain portions of the military have been compromised," Klauskin said. "Not too surprising in a time of war, of course. I've spent the last several weeks on special assignment, ferreting out traitors and planning a response."

Biurk had heard that Klauskin had been hastily removed from his command of the task force at Corellia awhile back. There had been rumors that he had experienced some sort of breakdown . . . but any sudden reassignment of a commander was likely to spawn such rumors.

"Here's the situation," Klauskin continued. "Several of the officers under your command are actually in Bothan employ. On the day the Bothans decide to send their fleet into action, they're going to do whatever it takes to keep Alliance forces from discovering that fact . . . until too late.

"But we're not going to let that happen. You'll supply me with a list of all officers under your command, and I'll indicate which ones are the traitors. We'll reorganize their duty shifts to leave each of them unobserved and unprotected at specific times, at which point we'll capture or eliminate them. Then we, by which I mean *Shamunaar*, will take the observation zone they would have been covering—we'll plug the hole their absence leaves."

"Understood. But, sir, I know many of these officers very well. They're not traitors."

"I'm sure the ones you personally vouch for are completely loyal. When you give me the list of officers, be sure to indicate which ones you're certain of." Klauskin leaned forward to give Biurk a sympathetic clap on the shoulder. "I know this comes as a shock, son. But we'll get it straightened out, very quietly, and it won't reflect on your service record."

"Thank you, sir."

DREWWA, MOON OF ALMANIA

Ben spent the better part of two days planning his trip to Ziost. In that time, he performed his credcard-stealing technique twice more, and was pleased to discover that it became easier, smoother, and less detectable each time.

He did do some planetary database research to find out whether any shuttle carrier or excursion service made trips to Ziost. The answer was a definite, unequivocal no—since Ziost did not appear in any public database. Still, its coordinates were in the files Jacen had given him.

Nor was there, as far as he could determine, much smuggling activity here—there was nothing to suggest that desperate shipowners, as his uncle Han had been so many years ago, lurked in every tavern, willing to take aspiring young Jedi wherever they needed to go.

Well, then, he'd just have to steal a vehicle.

He knew that wouldn't be as simple as sneaking onto some flight line, jumping into a B-wing, and taking off. Vehicles had security codes that made stealing them difficult.

Security around the spaceport was not exactly lax, but neither was it set up to deter a Jedi. The chief danger of detection he faced lay with the small security droids used all across the base—half the height of a human, spindly, with conical head/sensor packages atop a humanoid arms-and-legs arrangement. Scores of these droids wandered individually across the spaceport environs, sometimes hiding in the thrusters of hangared vehicles, sometimes riding on the backs of luggage-delivery vehicles. Ben watched them for an hour or so through the viewport in the waiting lounge outside the secure areas and noticed that they did not react to people wearing the bright yellow jumpsuits of spaceport personnel.

That knowledge made it easier. A touch of Jedi telekinesis kept doors from closing and latching firmly behind port personnel entering secure areas. Ben wandered through, eventually finding a locker room and helping himself to a jumpsuit and the corresponding transponder that kept security droids from paying attention to its wearer.

That gave him the freedom to walk around the port for a day. He still kept well away from most human personnel; they might ask questions about an obviously offworld teenage boy doing what looked like a thorough inventory of all craft on the base. But droids were no longer an issue.

It didn't take him too long to find the craft he thought best suited to carry him to Ziost. It was an old Y-wing starfighter, carefully maintained, its hull paint unscarred. It rested beneath an environment blanket covered by a thick layer of dust.

The hangar's door computer listed the owner as Hemalian Barkid of Drewwa and indicated that his last flight with the Y-wing had been half a standard year earlier. A little time on the planetary net tracked down personal data for Hemalian Barkid. He was an employee of Trang Robotics, and messages to him were now being forwarded to Kuat. Clearly he had been assigned offworld and left his personal vehicle behind.

The Y-wing's astromech was nowhere to be seen, and its weapons systems were dismantled and missing, probably due to local ordinances about private citizens having lasers, ion cannons, and proton torpedoes. But its hyperdrive was intact, and the little glow on the control board Ben could ee through the cockpit canopy made it clear that the computers were charged—probably diagnostics running on a battery.

And this, at last, told Ben what he needed to do to get the Y-wing operational. "In the field, when you can't do something yourself," his mother had told him once, "your obvious solution is to find someone who can do it for you."

He downloaded contact information for Hemalian Barkid into his datapad, then spent several more hours searching on the planetary database for more information he needed and letters like the one he had to write. Carefully, doggedly, he extracted a fact here, a sentence there, and ended up with something that, to his eye, seemed authentic.

From: Hemalian Barkid
Account 7543 BH (Hangar 113)
To: Hangar Manager, Drewwa Spaceport

I will be returning home tomorrow. I'd really like my Y-wing to be ready when I get there. Please do a power-up, standard maintenance check, and astromech analysis of the computer, particularly the nav computer, and bill at your standard rate to my account.

It was that last part that Ben thought would sell the spaceport managers on this task. Everyone said that people loved doing last-minute tasks at their standard rates, because last-minute standard rates were always three or four times what standard rates would be if arranged in plenty of time.

Ben sent the message from the hangar door computer, which could plausibly have received and relayed the message from the real Barkid. He took his pocket holocam, the one he'd been carrying ever since his mission with Jacen to Adumar, and affixed it to the rafters, pointed down at the

Y-wing's security access panel, then made sure it would accept commands transmitted from his datapad. Finally he restored the environment blanket to the top of the Y-wing, smoothed out the dust as much as he could, and made himself a hiding hole behind some discarded plasteel crates to wait.

It didn't take too long. Three hours later, the hangar door rolled open and two shapes entered—a female human mechanic in the standard yellow jumpsuit and an R2 astromech.

Ben's heart sank. He'd assumed, based on how automated things were around here, that an operation as simple as a routine vehicle check would be handled by a mechanic droid. He'd planned to wait until the droid was finished with its task and then cut its head off, preventing it from leaving with the R2.

But he couldn't cut the woman's head off.

Well, technically he could. He just shouldn't. Though if it came down to a question of doing that or failing in this mission—an important mission—what would he do? He frowned, struggling with the answer.

The woman—thirtyish, muscular, dark hair up under a yellow cap—swept the environment blanket off the Y-wing, sending a tremendous amount of dust into the air. She immediately began sneezing. Her R2 unit tweetled at her.

As the airborne dust reached Ben, he felt like sneezing, too. He held a finger under his nose and scowled at the woman.

As the woman moved up to the cockpit, Ben activated the holocam. The R2 unit tweetled again, spinning the dome-like top portion of its body around, its sensors obviously searching for something. Ben crouched further, as if it would make him even more invisible.

"Don't be silly, Shaker," the woman said. "What do you bet the owner has anti-theft sensors set up? We probably set one off."

Mollified, the R2 unit tweetled again and returned its attention to its companion.

In a matter of a few minutes the woman punched her security code into the cockpit side panel, raising the canopy, and then used the hangar's magnetic winch to lift up the astromech and lower it into its berth behind the cockpit. Ben watched as she undogged side panels along the Y-wing's fuselage and plugged her own oversized datapad into them, one by one, checking readings as she went. As the R2 went through its own series of checks and analyses, the woman left the hangar for a few minutes; she returned behind the controls of a small fuel tanker and proceeded to refuel the starfighter.

Anxiety began to grow within Ben. The woman and the astromech had to be reaching the end of their duty. Soon she would be removing the R2 from its housing behind the cockpit. Ben needed to decide right away what he was going to do about the woman.

Well, he certainly wouldn't cut off her head. But he would have to incapacitate her. When both she and the R2 unit were looking away, Ben leapt up into the rafters, made his way to where his holocam was strapped and retrieved it, then worked his way over to a spot directly above the hangar door and waited. When it seemed that both woman and droid had their attention fixed elsewhere, he dropped silently to the permacrete and used that momentum to roll outside the hangar.

Then he walked right back in again, datapad in hand. The astromech was still behind the cockpit; the woman was now readying the refueling vehicle to be driven away.

"Hello," Ben said.

The woman looked him over. "Hello. Aren't you a little young for a port worker?"

"Trainee." Ben made his voice sound sullen. "All I'm good for is delivering messages, I guess. And I have one for you."

"Go ahead."

"The owner of the Y-wing says his astromech went through a messy programming breakdown and is having its memory wiped. So he needs another one temporarily. He'd like to rent whichever one was used for the vehicle's computer calibration."

She wiped her hands on a rag and shrugged. "So why are you telling me?"

"So you can leave the droid here."

"Oh, he's getting here *that soon.*"

Ben nodded.

She looked back over her shoulder at the droid. "Looks like you get to go tootling around the solar system for the rest of the day, Shaker. Lucky rodder." She tossed the rag aside and returned her attention to Ben. "Got the authorization code for that?" She retrieved her datapad from the refueling tanker's front seat and held it toward him.

"Right here. Prepare to receive." Then Ben scowled at his datapad. "Stang. My screen light's gone out. We have to do it in the sunlight."

With a sigh—whether for the reliance of others on inferior devices or for the inconvenience of having to walk ten paces, Ben didn't know—the woman headed toward Ben and the door out.

He led the way and turned left past the door, stopping when they were just out of sight of the R2 unit. In the second he had available before the woman reached him, he took a look around. The closest person he could see, a jumpsuited worker, was at another hangar more than fifty meters away. That was good.

"All right," the woman said. "Transmit."

Ben pressed a button on his datapad, though he'd switched the device off. "Transmitted. Anything I need to do to prep the droid?"

"Just take the restraining bolt off. And I'll do that. Hey, I didn't get the code."

Scowling with pretended annoyance, Ben pressed the button again. "How about now?"

"No."

He stepped closer and was now within arm's reach of her. "One more time," he said, and drove his fist into her solar plexus.

Her eyes got big, all the air went out of her in a painful-sounding "Oooosh," and she involuntarily bent forward.

This time he struck upward, an open-palm blow that caught her on the chin. He felt her jaw break under the impact. She went down as limp as a cloth bag full of bantha fodder, her datapad clattering against the duracrete beside her.

He felt bad, even nauseated, for a brief moment, then elation replaced that feeling. *There,* he told himself. *Not too much damage. Jacen would have forgiven me if I'd killed you, and I didn't even do that.* Moving quickly, he hoisted her up to a sitting position, then drew her up and onto his shoulders, a basic rescuer's carry that all Jedi apprentices were taught.

He carried her around to the side of the building, into the narrow alley between two hangars, and laid her down there. Then he went back to the front of the hangar, retrieved the woman's datapad, and got behind the controls of the refueling tanker.

In the few moments it took him to familiarize himself with the controls, the droid tweetled at him.

"Everything's set up," Ben assured the R2 unit. "She's doing the last details and asked me to move this." He powered up the vehicle, then carefully backed out of the hangar and immediately parked the tanker where it would block any line of sight on the unconscious woman.

He had a stroke of luck then. The woman had apparently opened her datapad to the job file for the task of maintaining the Y-wing. All the data he needed, including full maintenance specifications for the Y-wing and data on the R2 unit, was there.

So he was whistling when he returned to the hangar. He used the woman's own tools to remove the restraining bolt from the droid. "I'm supposed to take the Y-wing out on a test flight," he told the R2. "That way, if it blows up, the owner isn't inconvenienced."

The droid whistled and chirped at him, its musical tones suggesting that it was indifferent to the change in plans but more than happy to go.

"Good. Let me get my backpack and we can start the preflight checklist."

CORELLIAN SYSTEM EXCLUSION ZONE
ERRANT VENTURE

In the first few days after *Errant Venture* was authorized to ply its trade for Alliance military personnel in the Corellian system, its casinos and other entertainments did great business. Booster Terrik, the Grand Old Man of the operation, though he was theoretically retired from day-to-day duties, was often seen in the casinos, flitting around in his hoverchair, greeting patrons and encouraging workers, his eyes alight in the way that only commerce could make them.

His new, unpaid workers didn't hurt things, either.

Iella and Myri worked as dealers. Iella wore enough makeup to disguise her true identity; Myri did not need that precaution, but did change her hair color with spray-on hues and combinations each day, just because it was her custom. Two attractive women a generation apart, skillful conversationalists and card handlers, they drew good-sized crowds at their tables each day, and their tips were grand enough to make Myri wonder whether intelligence was the career she wanted for herself after all.

Lando and Han worked the casinos, too, but not as dealers. Each day they set up, in different casinos, at sabacc tables. Lando maintained his Bescat Offdurmin identity, and Han continued to put on his yellow-skinned, thin-mustache makeup each morning. At the end of each day they compared their winnings; after the first week Lando was slightly ahead.

Mirax spent most of her time with her father. During

years of retirement on Corellia, she had cheerfully ignored her father's efforts to bring her to the *Errant Venture* to learn and perhaps take over its operations. Now her homeworld was for the time hostile to her and she had nothing to do more suited to her talents, so she threw herself into these new studies with typical Mirax obsessiveness, delighting her father.

Leia, Wedge, and Corran concentrated on the data interpretation side of things. Seldom venturing into the ship's public areas—each such trip, however short, would cause them to have to don disguises—they confined themselves to an auxiliary computer cabin provided by Booster and began meticulously assembling and analyzing the data the others provided them.

Data came from the drunk patrons and the sober ones, from the happy ones and bitter ones, from the officers with marital problems and straying eyes, from the personnel with accumulated resentments and inadequate filters between their brains and their mouths.

The most valuable data often came from patrons who, at the end of their rest-and-recreation leaves, were dead broke and too drunk to stand. The special circle of *Errant Venture* employees took care of them, letting them sober up in quiet little lounges, giving them enough credits for a return shuttle flight to their military units—assuming they hadn't bought round-trip fare in the first place, which often they hadn't—and even half carrying them to the shuttle docks for their outbound flights. Han, Lando, and the other data gatherers became new best friends to an immense number of young soldiers, pilots, and technical personnel.

But the information they farmed was frustratingly tenuous. One week into their operation, the data gatherers assembled to see if there were any informational gemstones to be found.

"I say we start with you," Lando said, pointing to Wedge. "You look unhappiest. And that means results."

Wedge did look surly, and the look he shot at Lando did nothing to diminish that impression. "Unhappy, yes," he said. "Results, not really. Syal is here today, gambling in the Maw Casino." Syal, Wedge's eldest daughter, was a pilot with the Alliance forces, and Lando felt a rush of sympathy for Wedge—to be so close to her, yet unable to approach her, all for the silly little reason that he was technically regarded as enemy personnel.

Then Wedge added, "With a boy."

Lando snorted. "A boy? What, twelve, thirteen years old?"

Wedge's glare did not waver. "About her age. And a pilot. There are two types of male pilots. Good men, such as the ones I never tried to break or run out of my squadrons, whom I would shoot before I ever trusted them with my daughter. And worse men, whom I would shoot if I caught them *looking* at my daughter."

"Thirty seconds in," Corran said, "and we've already strayed from our topic. War, right? People are still interested in war and puppet masters?"

Wedge sighed and turned his glare onto the tabletop.

"I know this is going to sound strange," Leia said, "but I haven't found any indication that this war was precipitated by outside forces. I've been reviewing news reports, historical analysis, all the data we have on hand, and it looks like the central conflict between Corellia and the GA was the inevitable conclusion of their respective political directions."

"Fewer syllables, please," Lando said. "Remember, your husband is at the table."

Han gave him a faintly amused *you're-next* look, then turned his attention back to his wife. "So that means no puppet master?"

She shook her head. "It means that war itself is not the puppet master's original plan, or at least not his fault. But the manipulations we think we've detected do add up to *something.* We can see a cause-and-effect relationship . . . we just have to figure out the *motive.*"

Iella opened her datapad. "Events like the Corellian ambush of the GA Fleet that came in to intimidate it. The outcome? Corellia remained independent awhile longer. If it hadn't, another world would probably have become the focal point of the independence movement. Bothawui or Commenor would be likely candidates, but Corellia had something they didn't."

Wedge nodded. "Centerpoint Station and a secret assault fleet."

"Correct," Iella said. "Then we have Admiral Klauskin, who pretty clearly was meddled with, if we're right that these Force ghost manifestations are evidence of our puppet master. The result of that interference? The situation here was worsened, the Alliance was cast in a bad light, Corellia received a lot of sympathy."

"Speeding up the process by which other worlds considered coming in on Corellia's side," Leia said. "Then the whole thing at Toryaz Station, the death of Prime Minister Saxan. It caused a change in Corellian leadership, permitting Thrackan Sal-Solo to boost himself from Minister of War to President. And with war preparations accelerating, he had to put his secret fleet on the resources list."

Her voice quiet, as though she was hesitant to speak up in this exalted company, Myri said, "It also scattered the Jedi."

Leia frowned. "What?"

Myri looked uncomfortable. "Well, it didn't scatter the *Jedi,* really. I mean, the Jedi Council on Coruscant wasn't affected. But if you look at family ties, which have made so much of a difference over the years with the Solo-Skywalker extended family, one minute you were all together, and then, boom, you were scattered across the galaxy. Some of you at odds. It was like a secret grenade."

Leia and Han exchanged a suspicious look, and Iella regarded her daughter with interest.

"That's an interesting interpretation," Leia said. Her tone suggested caution, reserve. "I hadn't considered that as a factor."

Myri, her idea not having been shot down by the accumulated aces, began to look more comfortable. "At school, we were taught the *follow the* principle. Follow the money. Follow the lover. Follow the resources. The trick is sometimes in identifying the resources."

Corran had been nodding ever since the first *follow the* left Myri's lips. "You're saying the Solo-Skywalker clan is a significant resource, and that it has been eliminated."

"Yes."

Leia wasn't able to keep a little anger out of her voice. "We have *not* been eliminated."

"Not as individuals, no." Corran gave her a sympathetic look but didn't yield. "But as a family—tell me that you can send out a call, as you could have done six months ago, and focus the attention and skills of your entire family on a single problem or enemy. Tell me that."

Leia thought about it, then seemed to wilt just a little. "I can't."

"You've been taken out of the picture. As a united force." Corran gave Myri a little nod of respect. "Good work, girl."

"Thanks." Myri seemed both pleased and uncomfortable with the praise. "So maybe we assume that breaking your family into pieces that don't fit together anymore was one of the puppet master's major goals. Because in the long run, if recent galactic history is any evidence, that will make a big, big difference."

"And you've got to put that clan back together again," Lando said.

Han couldn't keep the pain from his face or his voice when he said, "I'm not sure it's possible. I'm not sure some of the pieces will ever fit together again."

"Lando's right, though." Leia's expression became set,

determined. "Han, we've been concentrating on the wrong things. Proving our innocence, figuring out which of Dur Gejjen's cronies need to go down when he does . . . none of that is really important, not compared with fixing things. I think we need to give up on the Corellian conspirators—"

"At least," Wedge interrupted, "until the war trials."

"Right. Give up on the conspirators, relegate the puppet master to secondary importance, and concentrate on solving the real problems. Putting the Skywalkers and Solos back into play as a united front."

"Sure, why not?" Han offered a crooked smile. "All Luke and Mara have to do is get themselves exiled, too. And then we can cruise the spaceways as one big, happy family."

But something in his eyes suggested he had left something unsaid, and Lando was pretty sure he knew what it was: *Except for Jacen.*

Dozens of decks below, a small cargo craft rose into the main hangar bay of the *Errant Venture.*

It wasn't a pretty vehicle. About forty meters in length from bow to stern, it had a front end—its main cargo hull—that was as elegant and aerodynamic as a thick nerf steak cut into a rectangle and stood up on its edge. Behind that, constituting about a third of the length of the craft, was the maneuvering shaft, a low cylinder housing the main thrusters and the servos that positioned the maneuvering fins, long wing-like surfaces that stretched laterally from the shaft.

In short, it looked like the mutant offspring of a bird and a brick, reengineered by Verpines to fly backward.

This example of the YV-666 line had dents, blast scars, and rust patches all over its hull, making it especially unlovely.

At the forward portion of the top deck, Captain Uran Lavint carefully maneuvered the awkward craft up into the hangar, then followed the glowing spherical droid above a trail of blinking lights on the hangar floor to her assigned berth. "Soon as we land," she said, "you'll want to get into the smuggling compartment. They'll do a basic scan from outside."

"We understand." Alema's voice came from a patch of shadow, impenetrable by ordinary sight, at the back of the bridge. "Why do they care if there are undeclared passengers?"

"It's all money." Lavint set the craft down with only the faintest of thumps, though that noise was joined by the squeal and creak of durasteel components settling. She grimaced at the noise. "If they don't know about you, they can't charge you for, well, anything. Soon as I get my cabin assignment, I'll comm you where it is."

"Good. Why this ship, Captain? What is so special about a gigantic casino and shopping complex?"

"It'll take too long to explain now. But remind me sometime to give you my speech about Corellian smugglers."

"We will."

Lavint didn't see the shadow fade, but the bridge seemed to brighten, and she knew Alema was gone.

Three stories below, hangar workers came forward. In a moment they'd be plugging into an exterior hull comm port and asking which of their many overpriced services she wished to avail herself of—refueling, de-rusting, painting, transmission of the latest holodramas . . . She waved and smiled down at them as if she didn't mind their presence.

And she wished that the *Errant Venture* would be where they found the Solos, so she could leave Alema Rar and her craziness behind forever.

chapter thirteen

CORUSCANT
JEDI TEMPLE

Mara leaned forward, elbows on the table on either side of the datapad retrieved from Lumiya's quarters, and rested her chin in her hands.

From the other side of the table, Luke looked at her. "You cracked the encryption on the data card?"

"Finally."

"But you don't look happy."

"You don't need a Force-bond to tell that, farmboy."

"Tell me."

"Some of it's an invoice. The sender seems to have been a bounty hunter working for Lumiya, and the invoice is an itemized list of expenses: hours worked, fuel expended, blaster shots taken. The main part, though, is a mission status and event report. Even decrypted, it's hard to puzzle out—everything is referred to by code words. But assuming I'm putting the right names to some of these code words, the information is . . . interesting."

"Such as?"

" 'Confirmed that the Lady's daughter succumbed to injuries inflicted by Grandson Three-two-seven-oh-seven,' " Mara recited. " 'Please inform if Lady's mission changed from insertion/observation to revenge.' "

Luke frowned over that one. "*Lady* has to be Lumiya. She used to style herself the Dark Lady of the Sith . . . after Emperor Palpatine and my father were no longer around to slap her down for presumption."

"I agree. And if that same-time context is the basis for more than one of these code names, *Grandson* would therefore have to be one of Darth Vader's grandsons, right? Jacen or Ben."

"Three-two-seven-oh-seven," Luke said. "Just a second." He pulled out his datapad, connected it remotely to the Temple's computer, and went searching for a report Ben had filed weeks earlier. "Here it is. Bee-em-ex-three-two-seven-oh-seven. An uninhabited star system near Bimmiel. That's where the woman Syo led Jacen and Ben, where Jacen defeated some sort of dark side Force-user within the asteroid under her habitat."

"Where Nelani Dinn died." Mara looked confused. "Nelani was Lumiya's daughter?"

"No. Nelani's parents have files in the order database, and Nelani looks—looked—a lot like her mother. Besides, Nelani died the same day Jacen and Ben arrived at the habitat. Your file there suggests that 'the Lady's daughter' lingered for a while." Luke frowned. "The other woman who was there, Brisha Syo. Brisha could be an anagram for Shira B—Shira Brie."

"Lumiya's real name."

Luke nodded. "I didn't make the connection at the time, because then it had been years since we'd heard anything about Lumiya." A thought was growing within him, and alongside it a worry, a big one. "Let's say Lumiya has a daughter. She names her Brisha, a self-tribute, and Brisha works with her. Brisha lures Jacen and Ben to an ambush.

She and the mysterious Sith she claims is living in her basement—maybe he's just a Dark Jedi she's hired, maybe he's Lumiya's Sith apprentice—are going to kill Ben, an act of revenge for everything I've done to Lumiya. Or maybe to capture him, train him to be a Sith. Which is just as much revenge, and twice the evil."

"I did a thing or two to her, as well."

"Right. Revenge against both of us. But Nelani is there, too, and throws the odds off. The dark sider and Nelani are killed, Brisha is badly wounded, Ben gets a knock in the head and forgets what happened, and Jacen presumably never figures out that Brisha was one of the bad guys. Jacen and Ben leave . . . and weeks later, Brisha 'succumbs to injuries.' "

"And her mother . . ." Mara winced. "Her mother would want revenge. Against Jacen. He's racking up quite a body count against daughters of dangerous opponents of ours."

Luke shook his head. "We don't know that Jacen wounded Brisha. How could he have done so and then left the habitat without thinking of her as an enemy? Ben must have done it, during one of the periods of time his memory doesn't cover. Which would make Ben the target." His stomach began doing flip-flops. In addition to being a cocky teenager alone in a galaxy at war, Ben might now be the target of one of the galaxy's deadliest killers—a woman who had fought Luke to a standstill mere weeks before.

"Your theory spooks me, farmboy. Because it answers a *lot* of the questions we've been asking. Why Lumiya would have infiltrated the Galactic Alliance Guard—to gather information about Jacen or Ben and prepare for revenge if she needed to take it. Why she would have been around for as long as we've known she has been but didn't attack you until a few weeks ago—because that's when she received the word about her daughter dying." Her frown deepened.

"And what if this is the reason for all Jacen's bad decisions? What if Brisha or the Sith apprentice on that planetoid got to him, affected him—*infected* him in some way?"

"Then whatever's afflicting him might be easily curable."

Mara slammed her fists down on the tabletop and turned away from Luke. Far from being pleased by that possibility, she'd been angered by it, and even without the benefit of their Force-bond, Luke thought he knew why.

Because if Jacen were the victim of some Sith brainwashing technique, he wasn't responsible for his recent actions. In which case Mara couldn't forge and sharpen her emotions, her dedication, to oppose and eliminate him as a former Emperor's Hand should be able to.

"We have to find out what happened on that asteroid," Luke said. "And we have to confront Jacen face-to-face to do that. We can't be in a position where all he has to do is press an OFF switch to shut us out."

"I agree." Mara's voice was strained.

"I'll make the arrangements."

"Before you go . . ." A little pain crept into Mara's voice. "Luke, who was Brisha's father?"

Luke shrugged as he rose. "How would I know?" Then he caught the look on her face, a combination of suspicion and an eagerness to let any answer wipe that suspicion away, and he said, "No."

"You're sure."

He offered her a reassuring grin. "Mara, we were involved emotionally, but not physically."

"All right." The suspicion eased from her expression, but through their Force-bond Luke could still feel a touch of disquiet from her.

As Luke hurried off to make flight arrangements to Corellia, he cursed Lumiya—for managing to introduce strife, however fleeting, into his life, this time without even trying.

CORELLIAN EXCLUSION ZONE
ERRANT VENTURE

The universe was not cooperating, and Alema Rar was becoming impatient with it.

There was a Jedi—other than herself—aboard *Errant Venture*. She was sure of it. As she stalked the darkened passageways and shadow-filled casinos, as she wandered, wrapped in robes that concealed her disfigurement enough to allow her to mingle with drunken gamblers and revelers, she would occasionally feel little pulses and eddies in the Force that were characteristic of Jedi presence.

But she never spotted the Jedi. To the logic she employed in her calculations, that meant one thing: the Jedi was hiding—hiding from *her*—and therefore it was Leia.

That evening, in the cabin she surreptitiously shared with Captain Lavint, she spoke of these matters. "You are almost free of your debt to us," she said. "You have brought us to where the Solos, at least Leia, conceal themselves. But we cannot find her. Them. When we *see* them, then you are free."

"I'm in no hurry," Lavint said. She sat cross-legged on the bed, a small bottle of expensive prewar Corellian whiskey trapped between her ankles. "We—you and I, that is, not just me—are making a killing at the gambling tables. Did you ever think about giving up your quest, whatever it is, and turning pro?"

"No."

"All right. Here's a hint, then. You're using only your Jedi magic and your royal *we* instead of your brain."

Ordinarily Alema would have been offended by such a declaration. She would not necessarily have demonstrated it, except to exact a little revenge. But Lavint was not trying to insult. She simply had no filter between her brain and her mouth. Whatever she thought came tumbling out, particularly when she had some alcohol in her.

"Tell us, then, what we are doing wrong. What we are not thinking."

Lavint raised a forefinger. "One. What is Han Solo?"

"Adventurer, friend to Jedi, husband, father, smuggler, general, ship captain —"

"Those are all the branches. Except smuggler. That's the trunk. *Corellian* smuggler." She raised two more fingers. "Two. Wedge Antilles, who just vanished from Corellia. What's he?"

"That's three."

"Eh?"

"That's three fingers, not two."

Lavint glared down at her hand and folded one of her fingers down. "Antilles."

"General, admiral, pilot, husband, father, friend to Jedi—"

"And when he was just starting, a Corellian smuggler."

Alema looked at her suspiciously. "Is this the speech about Corellian smugglers?"

"Yes." Lavint raised the third finger into place again. "Three. What's Booster Terrik?"

"Businessman, shipowner . . . and, we must guess, Corellian smuggler?"

"Retired." Lavint smiled. "You're catching on. Also father of a daughter named Mirax Terrik. What's she?"

"Corellian smuggler."

"Good. We've got the trunks all laid out. They grow from the same ground. Corellian-smuggler-hood. Now, where do the branches come together? Han Solo is married to Leia Organa, so there's a Jedi connection—and not just any Jedi connection, because Leia's the sister of the Grand Master. Antilles is married to an ex–New Republic Intelligence agent, so he's got branches into Galactic Alliance Intelligence. Booster's daughter is married to Corran Horn, another Jedi, with branches into CorSec. Horn and Antilles flew together. I've been doing more research on them. Antilles has a daughter named for Terrik's daughter. You see how tight the branches are?"

Alema added it up. "So the Solos are here because of all their friends, the security they represent—"

"And money, and resources, and you're not going to find them in the Deepcore Lounge because they don't have to mingle, they're all in it together with the owner of the entire establishment. You've been wandering the public areas while they're probably all on the bridge, drinking and laughing together."

Alema felt a sudden flush of gratitude that she had not killed this woman. It was a rare emotion for her. "We must begin to search other places."

"Yes, and right away, so I can get some sleep."

BOTHAWUI SYSTEM
SHAMUNAAR

On the records and assignment sheets, a thin screen of starfighters and armored shuttles equipped with long-range sensors guarded the Rimward edge of the star system. If the fleets that were assembling, performing maneuvers and war games, and otherwise rattling their lasers deep within the system were to head out in the direction of the Outer Rim—toward, say, Kamino, directly opposite the direction a fleet would most logically take if headed toward Corellia—this screen would detect it and transmit that information to *Shamunaar* for retransmission to the Second Fleet. The Bothans would not be able to take the task force at Corellia by surprise.

In theory.

In fact, Admiral Klauskin had identified a number of this task force's pilots and officers as traitors. He'd been very careful to flag the ones whom Captain Biurk had already written up for various disciplinary reasons, and to avoid those Biurk indicated he trusted implicitly. Then Klauskin had assigned each of them to the Outer Rim screen. He and Biurk had positioned *Shamunaar* at the heart of that coverage area, and had called in each of those on-duty pilots in turn, arresting them and seizing their vehicles.

Now, though they were still officially onstation, each of the alleged traitors was in the brig, and *Shamunaar* floated alone, doing the work of the entire screen by herself.

She was more than fit for the job, of course. She had been fitted with the best long-range sensor suites a frigate could boast. It was unfortunate that she couldn't remain at her usual station, well outside the Bothawui system on the Bothawui–Corellia approach corridor, but there she was merely redundant. Here she was doing critical work.

"Don't worry," Klauskin told Biruk. "I've transmitted news of our success to Admiral Niathal. She'll be sending replacement vehicles immediately."

"Good to know." Biurk stood in the middle of the bridge and turned to look at each officer's display in turn. He was restless, and would continue to be until all those replacement forces were in place.

"Your officers look bored."

Biurk gave the admiral a surprised look. "I don't think so, sir."

"Still . . . let's shake them up a bit. I spent part of yesterday putting together a simulation. In the sim, the three Bothan fleets stage a simultaneous breakout, and one heads straight for *Shamunaar.* There's opportunity for a stand-up fight, or for picking off their weaker units."

Biurk smiled at the admiral's mistake. "Just telling me that affects my tactics, Admiral."

"So it does. Well, put your second in command in charge. You and I will run things from the auxiliary bridge."

"Right." Biurk turned toward his second, a tall Gotal. "Lieutenant Siro! You have the bridge for a sim. The admiral and I will be running it from the auxiliary bridge."

Moments later Klauskin and Biurk walked into the auxiliary bridge, a small, seldom-used chamber, its walls more thickly lined with displays than any other compartment on the frigate. These displays were just now flickering into life, as were the overhead lights. The bridge doors slid shut behind the two men.

"All overrides default here, correct?" Klauskin asked.

"It wouldn't be much use as an emergency bridge if they didn't," Biurk said. "Oh, sorry, Admiral. I didn't mean to sound sarcastic."

"You really ought to watch your mouth, son," Klauskin said. From his pocket, he pulled a hold-out blaster.

Biurk's eyes widened as if he thought the admiral's gesture were a not-too-funny joke about disciplinary measures.

Klauskin shot him in the chest.

Biurk went down on his back, the impact making the floor panels ring. Smoke curled up from the scorched patch over his breastbone, and a little blood oozed from the burned flesh.

He tried to speak, to reach for his comlink, but Klauskin sadly shook his head and fired two more times.

There. One grim task out of the way.

Using the codes he'd just heard Biurk use to open and activate the auxiliary bridge, Klauskin ensured that the doors could not be opened again.

Then he moved to the communications board. He activated a line to the main bridge and said, "Lieutenant Siro. I'm cutting all external communications. From this point on, any communications you make will actually be going to the sim program. If you get an override message from the fleet, it will be accompanied by a red blink that indicates *I'm the real thing*. Understood?"

"Yes, sir."

Klauskin punched in controls that would disable all communications antennas aboard the frigate—all but one, which he reserved for use of his own comm board.

He moved to the main computer and inserted a data card into its slot. The computer accepted the program and activated it.

All over the ship, every internal door or hatch controlled by a servo slid and locked open. Klauskin imagined the officers on the bridge staring in puzzlement at the doors as intership communications began buzzing with questions.

The door into this bridge remained resolutely shut, of course. It wouldn't do for Klauskin to die with the others, though even if he did, his primary mission would still be successful.

The main computer display came up with a text message indicating that all safety protocols concerning exterior hatches had been overridden. Klauskin nodded. All he had to do now was stand by, though he did have ten seconds in which he could abort this sequence—

He didn't. And when the tenth second counted down, warning lights and chime alarms began to fill the air.

Klauskin switched the main display from view to view. First was the interior of the frigate's small starfighter bay, where the force field holding the atmosphere had just dissipated. Atmosphere rushed out through the great gaping hole through which starfighters normally launched or landed, and some of the starfighters in the bay rocked slightly. A lone mechanic standing too close to the main opening stumbled, forced along by the air currents fleeing into space, and was swept into the void. Her arms flailed as she drifted out toward explosive decompression and death.

The next view showed personnel in the ship's mess. They stood, looking around, their eyes wild, as they began gulping for air. Some began running for emergency control panels and wall comm boards. Others turned around and around, looking for the source of their trouble.

All over the frigate, it was the same. Every exterior hatch or portal was open and was pouring precious atmosphere into a vacuum that would drink until it was all gone. Only the auxiliary bridge was safe, and Klauskin could feel cool air blowing onto his neck from an overhead vent.

He switched the display to look at the bridge. The holocam view from the bridge was dominated by the face of the human communications officer. He was so close to the holocam that his features were distorted. To either side of him, other bridge officers stood, shouting, clutching their throats.

This wouldn't take long. And when it was done, he would be a hero of Commenor. Somehow the thought, so reassuring across the last several days, failed to lighten the heaviness he felt in his chest.

He returned to the comm board and punched in a frequency, then activated it. "Klauskin to K'roylan, please respond."

A moment later the face of a black-and-tan Bothan appeared on the display. "K'roylan here."

"The eye is closed, and *Shamunaar* is ready for a prize crew. She'll be repressurized by the time you get here."

K'roylan smiled. "And exactly on time, Admiral. I admire your punctuality." Then his expression became one of concern. "Are you all right?"

"Yes, of course. Why?"

"You seem to be . . . crying."

Klauskin reached up. His fingers found tears on his cheeks. That startled him, but it would not do for this Bothan to see him discomfited. "Ah, yes. A result of the atmospheric pressure changes aboard."

"Of course." The smile returned. "My crew will be there soon. K'roylan out."

CORELLIAN EXCLUSION ZONE
ERRANT VENTURE

Leia and Luke embraced for a long moment, uncaring that they were surrounded by observers—those observers were family and friends. And though the private conference room Booster had set aside for his secret guests wasn't exactly as cozy as the vessel's more sumptuous suites, its shortcomings of comfort did not matter.

Luke drew away from his sister and followed Mara's lead in shaking hands or offering embraces all around: Han, Lando, Wedge, Corran, Mirax. "It's good to see you," he said. The words were simple, but they came from his heart. It startled him to feel this level of relief at seeing people in person when he already knew they were alive and well—but, he supposed, the heart did not always believe what the mind knew to be true.

"Us, too," Han said, and it was apparent that the distance that had developed between the two men, back when it became clear that Han supported Corellian independence while Luke remained loyal to the Alliance, had finally closed. "Though we're kind of surprised to see you here."

"We were in the neighborhood," Mara said. "Not a joke. We're in the Corellian system to see if we can pin Jacen down, get a few answers from him. Ben is missing." Leia did not miss the little flash of pain visible in Mara's face, detectable through the Force. "We don't think Jacen knows where he is, but he has some information that might lead us to Ben."

"You've chosen a good time to visit, then," Wedge said. "Jacen is here. Aboard *Errant Venture.*"

Luke gave him a dubious look. "Jacen, gambling?"

"No." Corran shook his head, clearly annoyed. "He's wandering around, looking things over. Maybe he's come to the same conclusion we did—that *Errant Venture* is a very useful tool for gathering data. Seems a very GAG thing for him to think of. Or maybe he wants to make sure that the ship doesn't constitute a security leak that would help the Corellians. Either way, he's here, so those of us he knows are having to keep even more out of sight."

"No more gambling, even in disguise, until he goes away," Han added.

"There's something else," Leia said. "Something I've been sensing through the Force for the last few days. There's a presence aboard ship, someone or something I can't identify . . . but it's here. Watchful."

"I'll keep that in mind," Luke said. "You won't be offended if Mara and I go to pin Jacen with some questions in a few minutes."

Leia shook her head. "Just be careful."

"Count on it." Luke seemed to hesitate before continuing. "In the meantime there are some things we need to bring you up to date on."

"Such as Alema Rar and Lumiya, Dark Lady of the Sith," Mara said. "And we now have a little Force technique, developed by Master Cilghal, that will help us counter the way Alema meddles with memory. We'll teach you."

Jacen stopped a few meters from one of the tables in the Maw Casino. Like so many of the individual dens on this ship, this one was named for a particular planet or region of space and decorated accordingly. As the Maw was an area where clustered black holes surrounded a hidden region, swallowing all light, the Maw Casino was dark, its walls black. Its silvery tables were edged with dim glow rods, and there was no overhead lighting; the servers and other casino personnel wore piping, jewelry, and accoutrements that glowed. The décor made the casino an intimate one, a place where conversations could be nearly private, where trysts could be arranged or conducted with little fear of discovery.

The table Jacen stopped to watch was a microdroid-wrestling betting table. Inset into the glowing tabletop were numerous displays. Several showed combat taking place in another chamber aboard ship—combat between droids no longer than ten centimeters, droids designed and programmed by hobbyists whose chief occupation was pitting their designs against one another. Other displays showed the odds of bets being laid on the combatants. In the duel currently taking place, a droid shaped like a piranha-beetle on treads exchanged fire with one shaped like a Tatooine sandcrawler; they were separated by a few meters of artificial terrain resembling the towering forests of Kashyyyk.

But it wasn't the droid fight that drew Jacen's attention. It was the woman facing him from the center of the long edge of the table. He knew her face, and he'd never expected to see it again.

He circled the table so that it would not be between them and stepped up next to her.

Captain Uran Lavint looked up from her betting and her drink to nod at him. "Colonel Solo."

"Captain Lavint. How did you get here?"

"That's a silly question, isn't it? I got here on the cargo vehicle you gave me." She lifted her drink, tilted the container toward him in salute, and took a sip. "Please forgive me for not thanking you before now. The *Duracrud* has become a good-luck charm for me. My fortunes have been improving ever since I took command of her. I've run three cargo routes, all at a tremendous profit."

"You haven't had any difficulty with her?"

"Well, she's old. I spent part of your payment to me giving her an overhaul. But nothing catastrophic."

Jacen stared down at her, baffled. Jedi could often tell when someone was lying, and Lavint was clearly withholding information, but she didn't manifest any of the emotion that should accompany the lies he expected. If her hyperdrive had failed, she should be angry with him. She was not. If she were covering up the fact that he had ruined her financial fortunes with his actions, she should radiate resentment. She did not. Something had gone wrong with his final instructions concerning her. But he'd sort that out with his next few questions.

Then he felt a slight flicker within the Force. He looked up to see Luke and Mara standing just inside the casino entrance, staring at him.

He gave the captain a purely artificial smile. "We'll get caught up later."

"Looking forward to it. You can buy me a drink."

Pushing Lavint from his mind, he approached Luke and Mara, offering each a civil handshake. "Masters Skywalker. You should have told me you were coming to Corellia."

"Where would you have been if we had?" Mara asked.

Jacen blinked at the question. "Aboard the *Anakin Solo,* probably." He did not add, *And able to limit the time I would have to spend with you.*

Luke gave him a cheerful smile. "Well, it's nice that we could find you when you have more time for socializing. Let's get a table, order drinks." Not waiting for a reply, he turned and led the way into the ranks of small tables closer to the bar. He chose an empty one that appeared to have been recently cleaned—its glowing, glossy surface was still damp—and sat.

Mara and Jacen joined him. Jacen had to struggle just a bit to keep annoyance from his face. This encounter was inconvenient. The server, a Bothan female with silver-gray fur, not much of it covered by her abbreviated black dress, materialized to take their drinks.

Once she was gone, Luke leaned in close. "Jacen, this is important. We need to know exactly what happened on the asteroid near Bimmiel."

Jacen kept his emotions under tight control and attempted to project nothing more than additional annoyance. But inwardly he felt relief, a return of confidence. Luka and Mara had obviously already found the leads Lumiya's people had planted. All he had to do was keep straight the details she had sent him. "It's true I haven't had time to write a report. My Guard commission came in too soon after our return to Coruscant. Was there something wrong with Ben's report?"

"Well, it's incomplete," Mara said. "It doesn't cover what happened while he was unconscious, or what happened to you while you were separated from him."

"Oh. Of course." Jacen frowned as if trying to dig up memories buried beneath tons of more recent events. "Well, let's just concentrate on those two periods, then. Brisha Syo, Nelani, Ben, and I boarded a sort of railcar that took us into the asteroid's interior. A pulse of Force energy yanked Ben and Nelani out of the car. After a moment Brisha was yanked free. The car stopped in a deep cavern, and there I was attacked by a Force-user who radiated dark side orientation and wore your face, Luke."

Luke nodded. "At the same time, I was fighting a Force projection with your appearance. An altered appearance. And Mara and Ben were fighting distorted versions of each other."

"That's right." Jacen's mind clicked its way through the details Lumiya had so recently provided as he tried to figure out the best order in which to present the information. "My duel ended when the false Luke hurled some boulders at me and I inverted into a spin with my lightsaber. We both connected. I took a rock to the head and was out for a while. But when I woke up, my opponent was in two pieces, and once I found his head, several meters away, I could see his true features. A Devaronian. He had no identicard on him. His lightsaber was gone."

"Gone?" Mara frowned. "So someone came while you were unconscious and took it."

Jacen shrugged as if the detail was of no importance. "Probably it just went flying into a cranny somewhere and I couldn't find it. It was a very low-gravity environment. You could throw a lightsaber hilt a kilometer if you tried."

"And Ben?" Luke asked.

"I found him in an upper cavern," Jacen said. "Unconscious. Brisha Syo was nearby. She'd lost an arm and had sustained a head injury and sucking chest wound, all of them lightsaber-inflicted. I stabilized her. She seemed pretty sure her habitat's medical droids would be able to fix her up. She said she found a wicked-looking redhead—her description matched Ben's 'evil Mara'—preparing to behead Ben, and that she interfered. She was badly wounded but drove the false Mara into retreat."

Luke and Mara exchanged a glance. "So," Luke said, "if she was telling the truth, the timing can only work out one way. The Dark Jedi, or whatever he was, impersonated Mara and attacked Ben. He won that fight, Brisha stopped him from killing Ben, and he ran off. Then he took my face and attacked Jacen, and Jacen killed him."

Mara shook her head. "That doesn't work, though, if we assume there was some link between the two Jacen–Luke fights and the two Ben–Mara fights. Because my fight with the false Ben and your fight with the false Jacen were simultaneous."

"Suggesting that my fight with the false Luke and Ben's with the false Mara were, too." Jacen pretended to puzzle that one over. "The only logical conclusion is that there were two enemies in those caverns, not just one."

"That's right." Luke returned his attention to Jacen. He hesitated a moment before continuing. "Jacen, we have evidence that Brisha Syo was Lumiya's daughter."

Jacen sat back and allowed a look of startlement to cross his features. "I don't believe it. I'm not that easy to deceive."

"She'd be very good at deception," Mara said. "If she were trained by her mother."

"So . . ." Jacen pretended to think it through. "So Brisha probably killed Nelani. And Brisha dueled Ben."

"And Ben cut her to ribbons." A little pride crept into

Mara's voice with that remark. "But she defeated him with some ploy. And she probably did something to him, altering his memories, maybe making him vulnerable to other techniques, just before you came across them."

And now, Jacen told himself, *the test of courage. Do you propose to me that my memories were meddled with, too? That my thinking has been altered?*

Luke did seem to be on the verge of saying something else when he looked up and around. A moment later Jacen and Mara felt it, too—a massive surge of surprise, consternation. Other emotions, from another direction, joined the mix: fear, exultation, anger.

Those emotions had to be projected by hundreds, even thousands of people simultaneously to manifest like this through the Force.

Jacen grabbed his comlink and spoke into it. "Colonel Solo to the *Anakin Solo*. Status check."

"Sir." Jacen recognized the voice; it belonged to one of the *Anakin Solo*'s communications officers. "It's, ah . . ." There was silence for a few moments. "Fleet action, sir. There's a fleet, incoming, they're everywhere, they're already hitting the task force around Corellia proper—"

Jacen stood and ran toward the door leading from the Maw Casino. He grazed the returning Bothan server, spinning her, sending three full drinks to the carpet.

chapter fourteen

Across the darkened casino chamber, in a shadow caused by the room arrangement but deepened by her own abilities, Alema Rar hesitated as Jacen Solo bolted for the exit.

She had noticed Jacen enter and had followed his movements with mild disinterest. After hours of prowling secure hangar bays with no sign of the *Millennium Falcon* to show for it, she had sought out Captain Lavint in order to help the woman's gambling success. She had seen Jacen talk to Lavint, then move toward the door to approach two people silhouetted there.

A minute later a little twitch in the Force convinced her to move closer and get a good look at Jacen's conversation partners—which was when she had recognized Luke and Mara.

That recognition sent such a jolt of adrenaline through her that she had to spend several moments calming herself. She brought out her blowgun as she savored the opportunity fate had presented her.

Luke Skywalker was here. And if he was here, the odds improved that Han and Leia Solo were here, too, or would be soon. It was possible that Alema could finish her mission—could strike down Han and Mara before the disbelieving eyes of their loved ones, causing Luke and Leia the anguish that would return Balance to the universe, to her soul.

She tucked her blowgun under her bad arm and fumbled for her darts. Just a few more seconds and she would spit poison toward Mara.

But the disturbance she'd sensed had obviously upset Jacen, and it had to have made Luke and Mara alert; Mara was pulling out a comlink, but Luke was vigilant, looking after Jacen and then around the casino. An assassination attempt now was likely to be detected. But when would she have a better chance?

She got her dart in hand, placed it into the mouthpiece of her blowgun, and was just raising the weapon to her lips when Luke stood and looked straight at her.

She froze. He couldn't possibly see her, not in these conditions. But if she attacked now, when his senses were obviously at their keenest, he couldn't possibly fail to detect the attack.

Comlinks all over the casino began to beep and chime. Military personnel stood up from their tables, from their drinks, many of them now in the direct line of fire between Alema and Mara. She hissed, vexed.

She needed to be closer. She moved forward, still cloaked by the chamber's natural shadows.

Then Mara rose, saying something, and she and Luke ran toward the exit. Uniformed personnel also began crowding that way, most of them listening to or speaking into their comlinks.

Alema picked up the pace, but she was slowed by the crowd, by the fact that one of her feet, little more than a stump, caused her to limp. She shoved gamblers out of her way, using the Force to add a little strength to her efforts.

But still, it was long, frustrating seconds before she got through the exit, in the middle of a pack of military men and women. Not a tall person, she hopped up and down, looking along the access corridor in both directions for her target.

There she was, Luke beside her, at a full run in the direction of the bow, almost at the limits of the blowgun's range. Alema put the weapon to her lips, paused half a second to calm herself, elevated the weapon's tip to give her dart a trajectory that would carry it near the corridor ceiling, and blew.

The dart was lost to her sight the moment it left the blowgun. She hopped up twice more to maintain a line of sight on Mara's retreating back. *The dart should hit just about—*

Luke and Mara passed the entrance to a cross-corridor and turned left into it. An Ortolan—blue-furred, big-boned, and squat, with drooping oversized ears and a nasal trunk that reached to midchest—came trotting out of that corridor, turning toward the Maw Casino. Then the Ortolan stumbled and fell face-first onto the corridor floor.

Alema snarled. Her dart had found the wrong target.

The moving crowd had grown so thick that without exerting herself fully, and very obviously, through the Force, she could make little headway through the mass of military personnel heading toward the *Errant Venture*'s vehicle bays. By the time she got to the cross-corridor, there was no sign of the Jedi.

A human male emerging from the side corridor bumped into her. He was dark-skinned, good-looking, with thick white hair and a trim white beard and mustache; he carried a silver-tipped cane, and his flaring silken cloak slid across the bodies of everyone he passed, Alema included.

Alema was twenty meters down the side corridor before she realized who he was.

Lando Calrissian.

She all but screamed where she stood. If Lando was here, there could be no question about Han and Leia. She turned back and forth, trying to decide whether to follow Lando or the Skywalkers, and finally turned back to pursue Lando.

BRIDGE OF THE DODONNA

"Recall all scouts," shouted Admiral Tarla Limpan. The gray-green skin and red eyes of her Duros ancestry made her a striking figure on the Star Destroyer's bridge—a benefit to her now, in the thick of battle. "Launch squadrons as they come ready. Threat assessment! What are we looking at?"

Finally, a hologrammic schematic of space directly around the planet Corellia sprang into existence above the bridge walkway. Admiral Limpan was actually within the hologram; she took two steps backward to be clear of it. On the schematic, the sphere of Corellia was a blue wire grid; Alliance ships were small green symbols, Corellian craft on the planet's surface or within her atmosphere were yellow, and unknowns were red. There were lots of unknowns, some of them already streaking down into the atmosphere on the far side of the planet from the *Dodonna.* Far too many were approaching *Dodonna* along orbital vectors.

Though Colonel Moyan, her starfighter coordinator, was not on the bridge—he remained in the starfighter control salon, a nearby compartment—his growling voice echoed over the bridge's speaker system: "We have two cruisers, a frigate, and a minimum of twelve starfighter squadrons headed our way. That's only the newcomers. There are at least as many starfighter units rising up from Corellia's surface. This is an all-out push. Our deployments around Centerpoint Station and the other four worlds are reporting similar mismatches."

Limpan looked up, toward the high speakers, as though Moyan were up there. "Who are they?"

"They're Bothan Assault Cruisers, Admiral."

No expression crossed her face, but Limpan felt a twinge of sympathy for Moyan. He was Bothan.

"All right," she called. "Navigation, plot a course for Centerpoint Station. Order our forces already there to hit the station as hard as they can. Denying it to the Corellians is our top priority. *Dodonna* will join in that action." *If we're still functional when we get there,* she added silently. *And assuming we are, we can get a sense of whether we need to stay there and keep pounding, or run with our tails between our legs.* "Where's the *Anakin Solo*?" That Star Destroyer, assigned to Jacen Solo and the Galactic Alliance Guard, didn't answer to her, and she didn't always know its location or current task.

Her sensor operator called out, "It *was* at its usual station, just outside the Soronia orbit, on the direct approach from Coruscant. Now its coming in."

"Ask it to join us at Centerpoint." Limpan could feel the subtle changes in the ship's artificial gravity, and see through the viewports at the bow, as *Dodonna* slowly wheeled away from her orbit and oriented herself away from the planet's surface. "How many starfighter squadrons do we have on-station?"

"Three, Admiral."

Limpan shook her head, rueful. They were going to take a pounding. In fact, a mere pounding was the best they could hope for.

As if reading her thoughts, one of the junior officers said, her tone just loud enough to reach Limpan's ears, "We're borked."

"Enemy starfighters now reaching our maximum firing range," Moyan said.

"Open fire," Limpan said. "The order is fire at will."

ERRANT VENTURE

Wedge and Corran angled into the Flag Hangar, each skidding as he made the hard turn from the corridor. Their astromechs had done a preliminary power-up, and the canopies of both snubfighters were already open. Wedge was first to his vehicle, but Corran, rather than climbing the ladder hanging from his cockpit, leapt lightly into his pilot's couch. Wedge swore at the Jedi under his breath and climbed his ladder. "What've we got, sweetie?"

Iella's voice crackled back across his comlink. "Unknown forces hitting every major position held by the Second Fleet in the system. Wait, not unknown. The Centerpoint Station task force is reporting Commenorian markings on the assault forces. The Tralus and Corellian blockade forces are reporting Bothan markings. *We* have a small force, one frigate and one squadron of starfighters, headed our way. And the *Dodonna* has ordered *Errant Venture* not to enter hyperspace until every spaceworthy fighting vehicle aboard has launched."

Wedge swung nimbly into his cockpit. *Dodonna*'s order meant Booster would have to play a game of careful calculations. If he did jump before the military personnel aboard had all launched, he risked certain punishment from the Galactic Alliance—crushing financial penalties that could bankrupt him. If he didn't, and the forces headed this way were too strong, he risked losing the *Venture*—and his own life, and the lives of thousands of employees and guests—as the underarmed Star Destroyer was vaped.

Wedge yanked the ladder free of his fuselage and dropped it to the hangar floor. He slid down into the couch, clamped his helmet on, closed the canopy.

Corran's voice came across his helmet speakers. "Silly operational question. What's our squadron designation?"

Wedge snorted. They ought to have one for purposes of coordination and efficiency, but the question seemed just slightly ridiculous under the circumstances. "Ganner. I'm Ganner One, you're Ganner Two." He checked his status display. "Four lit, four green. Open hangar doors."

"Say *please,*" Iella said. "Just kidding."

The Flag Hangar's lights dimmed, and the outer doors

slid aside. Wedge activated his repulsors, sending his X-wing into a wobbly two-meter climb, then hit his thrusters and punched out through the opening before the doors were completely withdrawn.

It was an awkward launch, and thrust wash would have scorched the hangar bulkhead behind the X-wing. Such a launch would have earned him a reprimand back when he was still flying for the Rebel Alliance or the New Republic. Here he didn't care—he needed to be outside, where the action was.

He and Corran circled to run the length of *Errant Venture,* heading toward the stern. They could see starfighters and other vehicles dropping out of the ship's belly bays like explosives dropping from a bomber. The starfighters ignited thrusters, turned toward the world of Corellia, and blasted in that direction. The more distant ones were already leaping forward and vanishing, the visual effect to outsiders of their entering hyperspace.

Two X-wings from the main hangars came alongside, matching speed and vector. Wedge was startled—they hadn't appeared on his sensor screen until they were a few hundred meters away, but as they drifted into visual range, he saw why. They were StealthX craft, their surfaces looking dark and oddly mottled because of the sensor-defeating coatings they wore.

Wedge changed his comm frequency to a general military hailing range. He thought he knew the answer, but asked anyway: "Who've we got there?"

"Hello, Wedge."

"Luke. I take it your talk with the colonel was cut short. Mara's your wing, correct?"

"Yes. Going to deal with *Errant Venture*'s pursuit?"

"Just until the *Venture* can jump to a safe zone."

"Makes sense. You do realize that you're attacking your own allies, don't you?"

"No one trying to blow up the old man who became my

benefactor when I was orphaned is my ally, Luke. By the way, you're now Ganner Three, and Mara's Ganner Four."

There was a short pause. "For Ganner Rhysode?" Luke asked. Rhysode, a Jedi Knight, had died on Coruscant during the Yuuzhan Vong war, fighting—and killing—more enemy warriors in personal combat than perhaps any other combatant in the war.

"Can you think of a better name for someone fighting a delaying action?"

"No. Who's Ganner Two? Corran?"

Corran's voice was crisp across the comm channel. "Hello, boss."

CORELLIAN SPACE

Jacen's shuttle was on the verge of entering hyperspace and jumping toward the *Anakin Solo*'s position, just outside the star system on the most direct trajectory toward Coruscant, when he received a new message from the Star Destroyer, relaying Admiral Limpan's request for assistance at Centerpoint Station. Jacen authorized the change in plans, quickly plotted a new jump for Centerpoint, and launched into hyperspace shortly afterward.

When he dropped from hyperspace, the Centerpoint engagement was spread out before him. In the background was the station itself, the ugly, cylindrical, kilometers-long mass of it. Nearer were the Galactic Alliance Mon Calamari heavy carrier *Blue Diver* and two sturdy-looking *Carrack*-class gunships. Compared with the curved, organic-looking Mon Cal vessel, the Carracks looked antiquated and impossibly primitive, like thick guard batons slightly larger at either end than in the middle. *Blue Diver* was exchanging turbolaser and ion cannon fire with the newcomers, and, curiously, it looked as though any of its turbolasers that could not be brought to bear on the gunships were being used to strafe Centerpoint. Surrounding the three capital ships were tiny glimmers and streaks of light, evidence of starfighter action taking place all around them.

Jacen stayed well back—the light laser cannon on his shuttle would not add much firepower to the Alliance forces, and he might not be able to detach himself from a skirmish when he needed to.

His sensor screen blipped with the arrival of a new force and showed him the blue triangle of the *Anakin Solo,* just arrived from hyperspace, racing toward the engagement. He heeled over, taking an intercept course that should bring him alongside the *Anakin* before it reached the engagement and allow him to get aboard before the *Anakin* had to open up with its weapons batteries—assuming that enemy starfighters didn't rush to engage.

He was in luck, though. None of the enemy forces at the station disengaged to meet the *Anakin,* and Jacen reached the Command Salon within minutes.

There Commander Twizzl, commanding officer of the *Anakin Solo,* greeted him with a simple nod. A big silver-haired man who looked as though he should be appearing on holocasts advertising exercise equipment and protein-boosted foods, he spoke with a Coruscanti accent that had been diminished by decades of service spent among many species and social classes. "We're preparing to bring the long-range lasers to bear against the gunships."

"Belay that," Jacen said. "Use them to reinforce *Blue Diver*'s fire against the station."

Twizzl scowled. "Kill more enemy troops rather than preserve the lives of our own? Colonel, that's a bad choice under these circumstances."

"It's our only choice. Can't you see what's going on? Admiral Limpan wouldn't have ordered the attack on the station if she weren't sure that the enemy forces could drive us out of the system. And if we are driven out, and leave an intact Centerpoint Station behind—"

"Yes, Colonel." Twizzl didn't sound convinced, but

turned to the weapons officer. "Take a new target: Centerpoint Station. Continuous fire. Inflict as much damage as possible." His voice was grudging.

ERRANT VENTURE

Well away from the public areas frequented by *Errant Venture*'s clientele and guests, Lando stepped from a shadowy passageway into a small turbolift. Its doors closed behind him and its service program spoke: "Deck, please."

"Subcommand Three."

"Please press a fingerprint, eyeball, or other individual identifier to the sensor."

Lando raised his hand to do so, but the doors hissed open again and a woman in a dark hooded cloak limped in to stand on the far side of the lift.

Lando gave her a polite nod. It would be both suspicious and rude to order her out of the turbolift, so he'd let the lift take her to her destination, then lock it down against further entry and get back to his group's operations center at the conference room.

"Deck, please."

The newcomer ignored the service program. She pulled the hood from her face, revealing the features and lekku, one of them a stump, of Alema Rar. "Hello, Lando."

Lando rocked back against the turbolift wall and drew his hold-out blaster, but before he had even cleared it from its hidden pocket she reached for it. The weapon flew from his hand into hers.

Alema looked at the blaster before dropping it to the floor behind her. "We are disappointed. This is not an appropriate greeting for an old friend."

Lando cleared his throat. "You're right, of course. Sorry. A bad reflex." Looking at her now, he had to force himself not to wince. He'd met her for the first time years ago, at the height of the Yuuzhan Vong war, when she was still a teenager, still mourning the death of her sister Numa, still physically perfect.

Still sane.

Now she stood before him, a weird gleam in her eyes, her shoulders at different angles. He'd heard the list of mutilations she had sustained and knew them to be matched by the savage injuries her mind had endured.

Her tone remained curiously friendly, nonthreatening. "Where are the Solos?"

"Oh. Um . . . Corellia?"

"No. Here. Aboard. Where?"

"If I tell you, you won't kill me?"

"We would never kill you. We have always admired you." There was almost a purr to her voice.

"That's comforting." He pointed his cane at her.

It, too, was yanked from his grip by invisible forces and flew into her hand.

Now Alema really did look hurt. "You were going to shoot us with a concealed blaster?"

"Not exactly. Zap-zap."

At Lando's command word, electrical arcs, tiny and blue, curled from the ends of the cane and flowed across Alema's skin. Her eyes widening, she convulsed, her muscles locking in a tetany caused by the charge flowing through her.

But she didn't fall unconscious. Lando cursed under his breath. The weapon maker who'd built the cane to Lando's specifications had assured him that the charge would take down a good-sized Wookiee.

But the weapon maker had never dealt with Jedi.

Alema fell, landing atop Lando's blaster, but clearly was still struggling against the shocks paralyzing her even as wisps of smoke began to rise from her body. And the electrical arcs seemed to be getting weaker . . .

The turbolift doors *whooshed* open and Lando ran back down the passageway, toward cross-corridors filled with people, filled with light.

He wouldn't waste breath on a comlink call until he was surrounded by people. He put every effort toward running.

Something seemed to move within his head, as though there were a greased worm writhing in his brain matter, heading toward the exit of one of his ears. He ignored the sensation. He ran.

The first cross-corridor was ahead, lightly trafficked. He turned rightward into it, toward heavier concentrations of people. His rapid movement didn't attract much attention; a lot of people were running. A few moments later he was in the midst of a thick crowd of *Errant Venture* personnel streaming out of a casino now being evacuated.

He pulled out his comlink. *Now* he could . . .

He could what?

Call someone, he supposed. But who? And why did he need to call anyone? What had he been running from?

And where had he lost his blasted cane?

Shaking his head, and wondering whether age really was beginning to affect his faculties, he put his comlink away and looked around for the nearest turbolift.

CORELLIAN SPACE

Luke had to agree that Wedge's improvised plan was a good one—or would be, if it worked. But then, he decided, that was true of all plans: in retrospect, they were only as good as they were successful, regardless of how brilliant they might have appeared before execution.

He and Mara were many kilometers out ahead of Wedge and Corran and a few kilometers to one side of the straight-line approach the enemy force was taking. As soon as their sensors detected the incoming frigate, he and Mara shut down all active systems and went dead in space, merely drifting. From this point until they rejoined Wedge and Corran, they would not use their comm systems; their

Force-bond, undetectable by sensors, would be their only means of communication.

Passive sensors showed Wedge and Corran approaching the enemy force, showed the enemy's starfighters arraying themselves out in front of the frigate as a defensive screen. Luke nodded. These were wise, basic tactics. The frigate and starfighter screen passed Luke's and Mara's position, and Luke's sensors showed the frigate to be an ax-shaped Nebulon-B.

The Jedi waited there and watched the battle begin. Wedge and Corran, staying so close to each other that they were sometimes one blip on the sensors, darted to one edge of the starfighter screen. There was a swirl of activity there, and suddenly Wedge and Corran were in retreat. Eleven enemy starfighters remained, and one was dead in space, its pilot requesting shuttle pickup over open comm frequencies.

Luke gave Mara a simple prod through the Force, then lit his thrusters and began to maneuver in behind the frigate. She tucked in beside him, and he could feel a cool readiness flow from her—a dispassionate willingness to inflict damage, kill, even die as necessary.

Their approach was smooth and slow, designed to benefit from these X-wings' comparative invisibility to sensors. They needed to come as close as possible and launch their proton torpedoes before the frigate's crew realized they were there. At the moment, the frigate was running with its shields more powerful at the bow, weaker at the stern—a sensible measure, as Wedge and Corran were keeping the starfighter skirmish out ahead of the frigate.

Closer they came—now one hundred kilometers behind the frigate, now ninety . . .

When they were so close that their attacks would take less than a second to reach the frigate, but not so close that retaliatory laserfire would be at point-blank range, Luke fired a torpedo. A split second later Mara fired hers. Luke activated his X-wing's shields and, through their Force-bond, felt Mara do the same.

The torpedo thrusters drew a near-instantaneous straight line to the frigate's stern. Luke's torpedo detonated against its rear shields. Then Mara's disappeared into the blast zone and detonated, as well.

It took a few moments for the superheated gases of the explosions to dissipate. As they cleared, they revealed a frigate stern that was badly damaged, deeply cratered. Luke couldn't see a single functioning thruster. He gave a little whoop. One enemy was out of commission, and the loss of life had to have been low—if luck was with the frigate, it might have lost no personnel at all.

Luke and Mara accelerated in an arc toward the star-fighter engagement. Sensors now showed eight actives in the engagement zone—Wedge, Corran, and six hostiles. On Luke's sensor screen, the computer finally identified the hostiles—I-7 Howlrunners. Luke was familiar with the star-fighters: sleek rectangular hulls with stubby maneuvering wings at one end and two forward-projecting laser cannons at the other. Luke knew them to be shielded and tough, but they also lacked much firepower. Still, the original escort of twelve starfighters would ordinarily have been more than sufficient to destroy two X-wings . . . just not X-wings flown by pilots of the caliber of Wedge and Corran.

And now they were to be joined by pilots of the caliber of Luke and Mara.

The StealthX fighters were only a few kilometers from the engagement zone when the five still-functional Howl-runners broke away, roaring back toward the frigate. Luke and Mara let them go. The Howlrunners took up position circling the crippled frigate, a far more pathetic defensive screen than they had been mere minutes before.

Luke reactivated his comm transmitter. "What now?"

"Back to the *Errant Venture* for me," Wedge said. "To

give protection until it makes the jump into hyperspace. I'm not going to get involved in the main battle. Honestly, I wouldn't know whose side to be on."

Mara asked, "How about you, Corran?"

Corran sounded just a little uncertain. "It's kind of up to you, Luke. I've tended to all my personal business on Corellia, I don't need to go back . . . where do you need me?"

"Coruscant," Luke answered instantly. "We need all the good sense and sharp thinking we can get at the Temple. But for now, Mara and I will be heading to the main engagement to see what good we can do for the Alliance forces. You want to come along or head back to the Temple?"

"I'll fight."

Wedge said, "Luke, you're Ganner One now. Best of luck."

"Likewise."

As Wedge peeled off from their formation and set a course for the *Errant Venture,* Luke opened his comm board to listen across military frequencies to find out what was happening and where.

DODONNA

Admiral Limpan retreated to the command salon, which was smaller, quieter, and less frantic than the bridge. Now she could hear herself think again—and could more easily track the battle's progress.

And *Dodonna*'s probable death. The *Galactic*-class battle carrier, commissioned less than a year before, was being chewed to pieces by the Bothan forces pursuing her; she might not last long enough to flee the solar system. The constant pounding by the laser batteries of enemy cruisers—and just as damaging, the missiles and torpedoes of enemy starfighters—was taking a terrible toll on Limpan's flagship.

"Ready to enter hyperspace, Admiral," her navigator announced.

"Launch," she said.

The exterior view, brought in by the salon's displays, showed the stars twist, become streaks of light—and then instantly revert to stars again, because this hyperspace jump was very short, not even leaving the system.

Centerpoint Station and the furious fight being waged around it appeared on the main display.

"Navigation," Limpan said, "plot a course to send us on an approach close to the station—at optimal range for our batteries. We'll make one pass and pour as much damage as we can into her. Then we're outbound. Our next jump will take us to—Fenn, what's the designation for the muster point you used for your initial assault on the system?"

Colonel Fiav Fenn, a female Sullustan, turned from her station computer. "Point Bleak," she said. Fenn had been the aide to Limpan's predecessor, Admiral Klauskin; Limpan had her own aide, but had transferred Fenn to starfighter coordination duty and was pleased with her work in that role.

"Once we're past Centerpoint"—*if we survive,* Limpan thought—"our next jump will take us to Point Bleak. Communicate with all other Alliance forces, tell them to break off the engagement and join us there. Tell *Errant Venture* they have the option of joining us there."

"Recommend against that course of action, Admiral," Fenn said.

Limpan fixed her with a harsh look. "Explain that, Colonel."

"If every Alliance force at the Centerpoint engagement zone jumps to the same spot in space, fine—the enemy can plot our direction but not the distance of our jump, so following us would be pointless. But if Alliance ships from six different engagement zones jump to the same location, all the enemy needs to do is triangulate, and they can find us within minutes."

Limpan seethed quietly for a moment. She'd been promoted to admiral from captain during the peacetime after the Yuuzhan Vong war. During that war, she'd had to lead New Republic forces in retreat on more than one occasion, but she'd only commanded one ship at a time then. She knew the tactics of a full task force retreat in theory, intellectually, but they weren't second nature to her.

Into the silence that had fallen in the command salon, Limpan said, "You're right, Fenn. Good call. Navigation, relay the Point Bleak order to all our forces in this engagement zone. Communications, tell the coordinator of each separate engagement zone to find its own arrival spot just outside the system and communicate with us from there. Tell the same thing to the blasted gambling ship."

"Yes, ma'am."

Limpan settled into her command chair and scowled at the main display, scowled at Fenn's back. The chair vibrated beneath her as *Dodonna* sustained another torpedo hit. More red lights flashed on the diagnostic displays.

Whole banks of turbolasers were failing. Shields were down to 68 percent efficiency and weakening. Life support was out on a dozen decks, the personnel there scrambling to get to safer areas. Several thruster banks had been destroyed, and more were being stressed past their operational limits. Persistent vibrations shook the *Dodonna*, a sign that accumulated damage was twisting her very framework.

Dodonna might survive this engagement, but she would do so in such bad shape that she would have to return to the shipyards immediately for repairs. She would be out of commission for months.

More quietly, Limpan added, "Communications, let *Blue*

Diver know that as soon as we reach Point Bleak, she's to come alongside. I'll be transferring the flag to *Blue Diver.*"

"Yes, ma'am."

Limpan saw several spines stiffen at the announcement. *Good,* she thought, *they still have their pride.* It was one thing they hadn't completely lost.

Dodonna poured damage down onto Centerpoint Station, digging a latitudinal trench of melted metal and scoring to match the longitudinal one *Blue Diver* had gouged. But the pursuing Bothan and Corellian starfighters, unchecked by a sufficient starfighter screen, continued to hammer away at the battle carrier. *Blue Diver* broke away from the station to follow the flagship, using her batteries to eliminate as much of the starfighter pursuit as she could, but it was like a novice Jedi trying to protect a haunch of blood-warm meat from a swarm of piranha-beetles.

Finally *Dodonna* jumped, joined shortly thereafter by *Blue Diver* and the hyperdrive-equipped starfighters supporting them. *Anakin Solo* was the last to enter hyperspace.

Arriving at Point Bleak, the three capital ships maneuvered close to one another, the better to exchange aid and support with overlapping fields of heavy-weapons fire.

But no enemy vessels followed them out of hyperspace. They had time to assess damage, to communicate with Coruscant, to gather data.

It wasn't long before the HoloNet churned with news reports from Corellia. Prime Minister Dur Gejjen almost glowed with the victory of "casting free the yoke of Galactic Alliance oppression," and offered praise to the forces of Bothawui and Commenor, and to his own battle coordinator, Admiral Delpin, who was conspicuously commended for doing "what Admiral Antilles could not"—as if she'd had any role in bringing the Bothans and Commenorians to the table.

Admiral Niathal ordered *Dodonna* back to Coruscant.

She ordered Limpan's task force to effect repairs, stand by, and use its resources to monitor activity within the Corellian system. She also warned Limpan of possible treachery or sabotage—it was clear that the Bothan fleet's departure from the Bothawui system had been kept secret owing to some catastrophic failure of the Alliance forces monitoring that system.

Within a day the Galactic Alliance declared that the state of war previously enacted against Corellia now extended to Bothawui and Commenor as well. Holonews political analysts, sober or gleeful depending on the political and exploitative leanings of their own news services, speculated on which systems would be next to join what they now referred to as the Corellian Confederation.

Commendations were offered on both sides. Memorial services for the dead took place.

And with the political climate changed—with a negotiated peace between an isolated Corellia and the Alliance no longer possible—Jacen Solo and the *Anakin Solo* were ordered back to Coruscant.

chapter fifteen

ZIOST

From high orbit, the world of Ziost didn't look like a place of evil.

It was a typical blue-green world, a good mix of landmass and open water, ice at the poles, white cloud formations everywhere, including the characteristic spiral of a hurricane over one of the oceans. The landmasses at the equator seemed to be almost entirely green, graduating to green-white up through the temperate zones and turning to pure white soon after, giving the world large polar ice caps. There was no hint of desert or any terrain other than forest and tundra.

It was, in fact, a beautiful place, if one looked only with one's eyes.

But Ben had other senses, and through the Force he could feel something else, something malevolent about the planet. It seemed to be staring at him, as if it were a mottled eye belonging to a hideous, hate-filled face he couldn't quite make out.

Ben stared at Ziost, and Ziost stared at Ben. Ben gulped.

"Shaker, do you pick up any thruster trails?" Ben asked. He didn't really expect much help there. Thruster emission trails dissipated rapidly, and since a planet's vehicle and vessel traffic was heavy, all the trails tended to blur into one another.

The astromech tweetled an affirmative noise, and lines of text popped up on one of the Y-wing's cockpit displays:

> HEAVY ORBITAL TRAIL INDICATES ONE OR MORE VEHICLES IN SPECIFIC ORBIT FOR CONSIDERABLE TIME.
>
> VEHICLE(S) LEFT ORBIT APPROXIMATELY EIGHT STANDARD HOURS AGO AND MADE PLANETARY DESCENT.

The cockpit sensor display switched from a live sensor feed to a diagram of the planet's surface, with dotted lines showing the abandoned orbit and the descent path.

Ben felt a wash of relief. Of course, Ziost was a dead world, in terms of planetary civilization. Few vehicles ever arrived here, and thruster trails would be distinct for a longer time. That changed the prospect of finding a single vehicle in an area the size of a planetary surface from "crazy" to "possible."

He switched the R2 unit's data over to his navigation computer and plotted his own descent.

From an altitude of a few kilometers, traveling slowly enough that the Y-wing would neither cause sonic booms nor pull contrails visible from the ground, Ben studied the vehicle that must have brought Faskus back to Ziost.

It was a Corellian YT-2400 light transport—disk-shaped, like Uncle Han's venerable *Millennium Falcon,* but with its cockpit at the end of a starboard-side outrigger-style projection.

At least it had once been a YT-2400. Now it was a scorched heap of buckled durasteel, blackened in numerous places by fire; smoke still curled up into the sky from spots where the hull had ruptured. The cockpit and its access tube had separated from the transport's main body and had rolled, or been hurled, down a gentle incline, putting them twenty meters from the main hull. A light snowfall drifted down across the two main portions of the destroyed craft.

Had it crash-landed? Ben increased the magnification on his visual display and shook his head. No, the scorch patterns on portions of the hull showed clear sign of turbolaser strafing. The transport had been fired upon multiple times, and then had burned.

Ben quickly switched back to primary sensors, but there was no sign of other air traffic in this area. The attacker was long gone.

Ben spiraled down to a landing in the same clearing Faskus had chosen. He set the Y-wing down well clear of the burned wreckage, then investigated on foot.

Portions of the transport were cool enough to approach, and he was even able to enter one or two places where hatches had been blown off or the hull had gapped open wide enough to admit him. There was nothing within but lingering smoke and the smell of burned plastics and pseudoleathers.

Seeking more clues, he opened himself up to the Force . . . and shivered. The sensation of being stared at was stronger here than it had been in orbit. He tried to set that sensation aside, to feel around and beyond it, and he could detect no hint of death. He didn't think the pilot had died in the transport.

Where was he then? Ben wasn't an accomplished tracker. He didn't think he could follow a target—particularly one who had recently been fired upon, and was probably cautious and deceptive—through heavy forest.

And then he felt it, just at the periphery of his Forcesenses, a little hint of wicked glee, just as he'd felt it at the display case on Drewwa.

That glee remained steady, if distant, as he returned to

his Y-wing. "Shaker, I'm going extravehicular for a while. Maybe days," he told the astromech.

Shaker offered him a musical interrogative. Ben didn't need to pull out his datapad and read the transmitted text to understand. *What do you want me to do?*

He thought about it. On this hostile world, an R2 unit's sensors, tools, and other capabilities could be very useful, assuming the little droid didn't become stuck in a bog or something. But Ben didn't have the winch needed to remove Shaker from his housing on the Y-wing. Some astromechs had modifications that would let them climb free and make a safe descent, but Shaker seemed to be a stock model, with no mods of any consequence.

Still, Ben did have the Force available to him. He just wasn't sure he could manage a precise feat of telekinesis with something as heavy as an R2 unit.

"Hold on a moment, little guy." Ben closed his eyes and concentrated.

Through the Force, he could feel the looming mass of the Y-wing, even trace its contours. And there was Shaker, too, but he couldn't separate the droid in his mind from the starfighter. He didn't want to pick up the whole starfighter, didn't even want to try.

Then Shaker made a noise of curiosity, and suddenly the droid was distinct from the starfighter, its own lines clearly defined. Ben grinned and focused on the astromech.

He gently pulled upward, as if trying to extract a plug from an engine. The plug proved to be stubborn, so he pulled harder.

Shaker's sudden squawk of alarm almost broke Ben's concentration, but he frowned and kept at it, and could sense the astromech rising into the air and floating free of the Y-wing. Ben gestured laterally, and Shaker drifted to one side.

Carefully, Ben brought the droid down to the ground

and opened his eyes. Swaying a little, tired from his effort, he said, "I guess you're coming with me."

The droid chirped, its tones suggesting relief.

Heading westward, the direction in which Ben felt the distant glee, they plunged into the forest of Ziost.

It was a cold day. Though Ben had felt comfortable out in the clearing, in the cloud-muted sunlight, here the forest canopy cut off most of the sunlight, and Ben felt a chill. The massive, dark, twisting tree trunks, looking like pain-racked bodies flash-frozen and preserved in their agonies, added to his unease. He pulled his Jedi cloak from his backpack and donned it, grateful for both its warmth and the symbolic protection it offered.

There were no trails through this forest, just dense undergrowth. Shaker's limitations in the environment—the droid could move briskly on its wheels on flat, hard surfaces, but had to waddle slowly on legs on uneven terrain—kept their progress slow. But in the first hour of travel, Ben did not feel the glee he was pursuing become more distant. If anything, he and Shaker seemed to be closing, very slowly, on his quarry.

Then he heard sounds from the direction they'd come. The sounds were far away, muffled by distance and the oppressive forest, but Ben thought he recognized the scream of ion engines, the *thoom* of laserfire.

Shaker began tweetling a complicated message. With a sinking feeling, Ben pulled out his datapad and opened it. A series of diagnostic reports scrolled by on the screen too fast to read, but then the message scrolled to a stop.

The last line read:

Y-WING DIAGNOSTIC SUMMARY: ASSESSED DAMAGE PRECLUDES FUNCTIONING. COMMUNICATIONS ENDED. PROBABILITY 84% THAT Y-WING HAS BEEN TOTALLY DESTROYED.

Ben sank down to sit on the powdery snow cover on the forest floor. Faskus's enemies had come back and destroyed his transportation, the only way he knew to get back offworld.

The files he had suggested that no one was sure of any sentient beings still left on Ziost. There might not be anyone to help him get offworld, ever . . . and no one who cared about him knew he was here.

He was going to die alone on Ziost.

He forced himself to stiffen up. Whether he died or not, he had a mission to finish. And once it was done, he had a second mission, a personal one.

To punish the people who had tried to exile him on this lonely world.

CORUSCANT
JEDI TEMPLE, COUNCIL CHAMBER

They met in their circle of chairs—elegant stone seats, far short of thrones in lavishness, and not comfortable enough to encourage meetings that lasted for hours. The others—Mara, Corran, Kyle Katarn, Cilghal, Kyp Durron—waited for Luke to sit, a tradition they'd informally adopted and which he wished, just a bit, that they'd abandon.

When all were seated, Luke said, "Cilghal, I'd appreciate it if you'd take the role of taras-chi for this gathering."

The Mon Cal Jedi Master blinked at him. Her protruding eyes made the action more impressive than it would be from a human. "I'm sorry, Grand Master. Take the role of what?"

Kyp made a tiny noise. It could have been a noncommittal grunt. Luke glanced over to see that Kyp's face was locked up with the effort not to laugh. Luke continued, "Taras-chi. A tradition we haven't observed recently. You find a challenge for any idea or proposition you think isn't being adequately tested."

"Ah," Cilghal said. "Yes, of course."

Kyp twitched just once, a final suppression of laughter, and then relaxed.

"We have several items to consider," Luke said. "In no particular order . . . Though we have no restrictions on how many Jedi Masters there should be, the war has clearly taken up additional time from each Master, and the worsening of the war will probably take still more. This means the teaching will suffer. I propose, then, that we consider whether any senior Jedi Knights are suitable for advancement. We don't need to debate candidates today, but you should all prepare lists of those you think are suitable." Most of the Masters present nodded, all but Cilghal, who considered the question, her bulbous eyes elevated to different levels, but offered no objection.

"Second," Luke continued, "as many of you know, Ben is missing. He may have run away to reach Jacen. He may have left on some personal mission to prove himself. He may . . ." It took him a moment to force the words out. "He may have been taken. Evidence Mara and I have uncovered suggests that he may have injured a woman who later died from her injuries . . . and that the woman's mother was Lumiya."

That drew some murmurs from Kyle, Corran, and Kyp. Cilghal was quick to ask, "Was this reason for Lumiya's attack on Master Lobi?"

Luke nodded. "Presumably. Lobi was shadowing Ben. If Lumiya did something related to Ben—spoke with him, planted a tracer on him, and so forth—she would want to eliminate witnesses."

"So," Cilghal said, "this isn't just a case of two Masters demonstrating excessive attachment to an apprentice. The situation could result in the deaths of more Jedi."

Well done, Luke thought. *Already a salvo launched at an accurately identified problem.* "Correct."

"But I must ask," she continued, "whether you and the

other Master Skywalker are dispassionate enough about Ben to make good decisions on this issue."

Mara leaned forward as if to offer an angry reply. Luke glanced at her and, through their Force-bond, reached out with a touch of caution. Mara retained her pose but did not speak.

Luke answered, "I think so. In any case, Mara and I have very little to go on in terms of Ben's disappearance. As of this morning, I have been unable to find Ben in the Force. Which could mean that he has learned to conceal himself; that he's in a place, like Dagobah, where the Force characteristics of his surroundings mask his presence; or . . ." He didn't finish that painful thought. "But to be sure, I call upon the Masters to speak up if ever you think we're behaving inappropriately. I'll be the first to admit that we need to rely on your more objective judgment on this matter."

"And other matters of attachment, if I may," Cilghal continued. "Master Horn, the issues with your family are resolved?"

Corran nodded. "All Jedi except those helping the Alliance armed forces in intelligence gathering are off Corellia, as is my wife. Though she may divorce me, since I left without kissing her good-bye."

Cilghal did not offer the statement that had predicated her questions. *Jedi should abandon attachment.* It had been a basic tenet of Jedi philosophy in the Old Republic era and earlier times. Luke had, as an experiment across the years, relaxed it, describing to his students its role in Jedi history but not insisting that it be observed by the modern Jedi generations. Having himself chosen a life with a wife and child, he could hardly rule that out for others, and these days many were formally married and often raised their own children, with varying degrees of proper Jedi detachment. He had to admit that in such cases—even in his own—true detachment could at times be nearly impossible.

Cilghal was unlikely to offer that criticism, because she had never indicated that she believed in the absolute merit of the old tradition. But she was obviously taking her role as taras-chi very seriously.

"Also on my agenda," Luke said, "an update on Leia. You've all been patient and forward looking in allowing her to remain with Han. And I continue to think this serves both the interests of the Jedi order and the Galactic Alliance in allowing us to keep an eye on other perspectives, and on facts not otherwise available to us. Mara and I did see her during our visit to Corellian space. I wanted to put forth the idea that we continue to do so, and offer her no censure for apparently being opposed to Alliance goals . . . even when the Alliance continues to insist on punitive measures."

This time it was Kyle Katarn who brought up the likelihood of argument. Lightly bearded, a few years older than Luke, he actually looked a touch younger because he had not picked up as impressive a collection of facial scars. "You're certain that your attachment to your sister doesn't influence the way you're handling the issue?"

Luke nodded. "Unlike the situation with my son, I'm at ease with this issue, comfortable with all my decisions."

"The Galactic Alliance has valid points on this matter," Katarn said. "Not necessarily a durasteel-clad case, but valid points. They're not asking us to bring her to justice in chains. But if the Jedi order supports the Alliance, and a Jedi Knight is actively supporting the enemy, their contention is that the Jedi Knight in question should be expelled from the order."

"Maybe we should," Mara said. "Once a fair trial has proven that she has aided the enemy. It hasn't been proven yet. Her presence with Han at several events has been noted, yes. But not even Tenel Ka, the intended victim of their alleged assassination attempt, believes them to be guilty of it."

"And," Kyp added, "there's the question of whether they can get a fair trial in the current environment."

Katarn waved their comments away. "Considering it dispassionately," he said, "what would it change if Leia Solo were expelled from the order? She'd continue to stay with Han, continue to provide you with crucial information—she wouldn't stop being your sister, after all—and we could readmit her once the trial ruled for her innocence."

"Thereby making the Alliance government happy," Luke said. "But would it be *right,* Master Katarn? Expelling her for taking the initiative and investigating things she sees that no one else does? Which one of us hasn't done that?" No one raised a hand, and he continued, "Are you really advocating that, or are you assuming Cilghal's role as honored debate opponent for a moment?"

Katarn smiled, flashing white teeth. "Does it matter? The proposal has merit, or lacks merit, on its own, regardless of whether I believe in it."

"He's right," Cilghal said. "We need to analyze the proposal on its own merit, and the Grand Master's response to it likewise."

"Well, here's my response," Luke said. "If we strip Leia of her Jedi Knighthood because of allegations, and in so doing prevent the Alliance from visiting penalties on us, penalties that could reduce our effectiveness, then we'd be doing a small wrong to prevent a potential larger wrong. But it's not the mission of the Jedi order to do evil. Our job is to identify things that are wrong and get in their way. Even when it costs us our resources, or happiness, and our lives. That's what I propose we do here."

Katarn nodded as if pleased with the answer. He turned to Corran. "Master Horn, I notice you haven't been saying much."

Corran had been sitting with his brow furrowed for

most of the discussion. Now he nodded. "I was under the impression that the taras-chi was some sort of bug on Kessel. Booster said they tasted like muck dripping from a badly maintained engine."

Mara gave Corran a scowl that all but said *Not now, you idiot.*

Kyp lowered his face into his palm. "Talk about straying from the topic," he said.

Corran relaxed, his expression becoming more neutral. "All right. Back on topic. We've all been talking about dispassionate analysis in this argument. Now, I approve of dispassionate analysis. That's how criminals get caught and convicted. But we're also Jedi, and encouraged to trust our feelings. I just spent several days in Leia's company, and, friend or not, I came away convinced that she *wasn't* supporting Corellia, any more than she's supporting the Alliance. She wants to find out the truth. The truth behind the war, the truth behind her son's questionable decisions—which *also* reflect badly on the order, despite the fact they're government-approved, I might add. She's trying to identify the wrong and to maneuver herself in front of it. I don't think that we should discourage her from that, even by a reprimand some of us consider irrelevant. I think we should trust our feelings."

They were all silent for a moment, and Luke wanted to cheer.

Finally Katarn said, "I'm probably the Master present who has the fewest connections of family or long-term friendship with Leia Solo, and I formally recommend that we take no action against her for the time being."

The others agreed.

"That's my agenda," Luke said. "Anyone else?"

"I have something," Cilghal said. "The war, limited as it has been so far, has increased the rate of Jedi injury . . . and, sadly, death. We have had no trouble dealing with the increase with our available resources. But now the war is spreading . . ."

ZIOST

Ben spent a cold night.

In the first part of the night, he found a low hollow spot where the wind couldn't reach him. He rolled up tight in his Jedi robe and fell almost instantly asleep.

Then, two hours later, he woke up, so cold that it was his own body shaking that had jarred him from sleep. He was also blind, or so he thought, unable to see Shaker less than a meter away; but when his cold-stiffened hand was able to extract a glow rod from his pocket and ignite it, he realized that he was surrounded by fog.

Together he and Shaker clambered their way out of the hollow, and he found that the temperature rose by several degrees as they ascended the slope.

Toward the top, he used his lightsaber to cut dead branches from some of the trees. With them and leaves he built a fire, igniting it with his lightsaber. After a few minutes of warming himself, he made a sort of nest out of snow and more leaves. Only then did he allow himself to fall asleep again.

The cold awoke him several times during the night—and once distant screams, like a primate being tortured, jarred him from his rest. Each time he was able to doze off again, though it was to formless dreams in which dark shapes crawled close to his sleeping body and whispered into his ear in a language he did not know.

By morning he was slightly more rested, but he would have traded a month's service to a Hutt refresher-cleaning firm in exchange for a tent and a portable heater.

Once the sun was up high enough to provide some sparse heat to his surroundings, he and Shaker set out again. He could still feel the distant glee.

At midmorning he ran out of the food he had bought himself on Drewwa.

"I don't suppose you have anything stored in an inner compartment?" he asked Shaker.

The droid responded with a low, negative trill.

"Know anything about hunting?"

Shaker gave him the same answer.

"I mean, I'm not asking you to *hunt,* I was just wondering if you had any texts on hunting, something I could read. To learn how."

Shaker's answer this time was a more excited series of beeps, but the R2 unit lurched forward, waddling faster. They were now at the edge of a large, snow-filled clearing, and Shaker moved into that open space.

Following, Ben saw the reason for the astromech's agitation. In the distance, beyond the next verge of trees, a plume of smoke rose into the sky. Someone had built a fire—and that beacon was in exactly the same direction as the sense of glee Ben sought.

An hour later, they were at the edge of another clearing, looking at a camp. There was a tent, improvised from several bright red emergency blankets and yellow cord. There was a fire, as paltry as Ben's own from the previous night. There was an enormous backpack, rigged from an oversized carry-sack, a few durasteel spars doubtless salvaged from the downed YT-2400, and more yellow cord.

And there was a man.

Leaving Shaker behind, Ben crept forward, keeping low behind snow mounds. When he was close enough to get a good look at the man, he felt a sense of disappointment.

Faskus of Ziost didn't look much like a protector of Sith artifacts. He was a pale-skinned human with a chin that was just two steps short of being adequate and a thick, curling black mustache that only emphasized his chin's inadequacy. He wore gray garments that were the height of anonymity. He moved slowly, adding branches to his fire, and talked to himself, words that Ben could not hear.

And the first time he turned in Ben's direction—to add another handful of sticks to the fire—Ben could see that he wore the Amulet of Kalara on its chain around his neck.

Ben froze. If Faskus knew he was here, the man could vanish from his perceptions, could track him down and kill him with little effort. Ben had to obtain the amulet without alerting Faskus.

And that meant waiting for an opportunity . . .

No. Ben was hungry now and would only get hungrier. And colder, exercise being counterproductive when an agent was trying to remain undetected. If he waited, he would either become so weak and stiff that he could not complete his mission, or he would freeze to death.

So the situation meant that he would have to attack—and attack soon.

And attack without mercy. Anyone who could steal the amulet and wield its power had to be formidable.

When Faskus turned his back again, still mumbling to himself, Ben crept closer. A depression in the terrain allowed him to approach within ten meters of the tent. He could hear some of Faskus's words: " . . . worry at all . . . got to be shelter . . . not bad as it looks . . ."

Ben rose up to peek over the edge of the depression. Faskus had his back to him again.

Ben sprang forward, shoving himself through the Force, giving his leap extra distance, extra altitude. In the middle of his arc, he brought up his lightsaber. As he began his descent, he ignited it.

The sound alerted Faskus, who began to turn.

And in the final quarter second before impact, Ben saw, beyond Faskus, sitting on blankets at the front of the tent, staring up at him with wondering eyes, a little girl.

He was going to cut off the man's head in front of this little girl.

Ben landed foot-first, kicking Faskus back across the girl. Landing astride the man, he heard Faskus's grunt of pain, heard the girl's muffled shriek. Ben's lightsaber cut into the tent's top blanket, setting the edges afire. He shut the weapon off.

Then he got his free hand on the amulet and yanked. The chain didn't give way, and neither did Faskus's neck. Ben swore and yanked up, drawing the chain free of its wearer. Only then did he retreat, scrambling backward from the tent mouth, and dropped the amulet into his pouch.

The little girl squeezed herself out from beneath Faskus's legs and looked around wild-eyed. She had dark hair cut short and blue eyes; she might have been six standard years old, and she wore a garment that was a child's copy of an orange X-wing jumpsuit. When she caught sight of Ben, she shrieked again. She reached down and her hand came up with a few twigs and leaves, which she hurled at Ben. One stick flew as far as his foot; the rest of the debris fell well short.

"Shut up," Ben said.

The girl hurled herself on Faskus. "Daddy, wake up. Daddy . . ."

"Daddy?" Ben rose and moved forward again.

The girl turned and grabbed more debris from the tent interior to hurl at Ben. This time it was a duralumin cooking pan. He batted it to one side, not breaking stride, and entered the tent. "Stop that."

"Don't hurt Daddy." She grabbed for something else—a blaster. Ben, suddenly alarmed again, tugged at it through the Force and it flew to its hand.

It was light, too light. He looked it over. It was a child's toy, a miniature copy of the classic DL-44 blaster pistol, like the one his uncle Han usually carried. Ben tossed it out through the opening. "Stop throwing things. I mean it."

The girl froze, her hand up with a fork in it.

Keeping an eye on her when he could, Ben looked at

Faskus. The man was unconscious—odd, since Ben didn't think he'd hit him that hard. But that would help. Ben returned his lightsaber to his belt, then patted Faskus down.

The blaster in Faskus's belt holster was real. So were the smaller ones in his boot and in the small holster under his right sleeve. So was the vibroblade in the sheath in his left sleeve. Ben appropriated all the weapons, then looked around.

There was a coil of yellow cord in one corner of the tent. Ben snatched it up. Then he rolled Faskus over, discovering, and appropriating, another blaster in a holster at the base of his spine, and got to work tying his hands.

The fork hit him in the cheek, stuck for a moment, then fell free. "You're hurting him!"

Ben rubbed his cheek. His fingers came away with a smear of blood on them. "No, I'm not. I'm just tying him up."

"He's already hurt, you're making it *worse.*"

Ben finished with Faskus's hands and got to work on the man's feet. "Where?"

"His stomach."

Ben rolled Faskus over again and pulled up the man's gray tunic.

He whistled. An improvised bandage—thick layers of shirt cloth held on by bindings made from torn cloth strips—covered the lower left portion of Faskus's stomach. It was soaked with blood.

Carefully, Ben untied the strips and lifted the bandage free. A look at the blood-washed skin beneath showed him that Faskus had suffered a penetrating wound at least seven centimeters long. More blood welled from it as the bandage came away. Faskus groaned but did not wake up.

Ben replaced and retied the cloth. He'd received training in first aid from both his Jedi teachers and the Guard, but more than first aid was called for here.

He put his hands on Faskus's chest and brow and sought

what knowledge and feelings he could through the Force. He didn't know much about Force healing, but Master Cilghal and his father had taught him a few things, bare necessities.

Faskus was not strong in the Force, not strongly *here*. He was like a flickering candle compared with his daughter. There was turbulence from the wound. As Ben peered deeper, he sensed blood flowing where it should not. He sensed life ebbing.

He didn't know much about stomach wounds. Other Jedi had told him they sometimes didn't bleed much, but that they usually hurt a lot.

Faskus should be dead now, and it was clear that only willpower and a desire to protect his daughter were keeping him alive. And even they wouldn't be enough for long. Ben hesitated, wondering how to tell the girl. "What's your name?" he asked.

"Kiara. Are you going to make him better?"

"I can't."

Faskus's eyes opened. They were glassy. He tried to roll to one side and failed. His vision cleared a bit, and he looked at Ben. "Who are you?" he asked.

"Ben Skywalker. Galactic Alliance Guard."

"Any relation to Luke Skywalker?"

"I'm his son."

"Good." Faskus lay back and closed his eyes for a moment. Ben thought the man might die then and there, but this was only a gesture of relief, and Faskus opened his eyes to look at his daughter. "Guardsman Skywalker will take care of you from now on."

"No, Daddy." Kiara hurled herself onto her father's chest. "He hurt you."

"He just knocked me down. I was already hurt. The starfighter hurt me."

Uncomfortable with the exchange, with what was coming, Ben interrupted. "Why did you steal the Amulet of Kalara?"

Faskus looked at him, confused. "I didn't."

"Yes, you did. From an office building on Drewwa."

"Drewwa is where they gave it to me, yes. That's where I live and work."

"I thought you were from Ziost."

Faskus shook his head, not an energetic move. "I'm from Almania. I'm a courier."

"Who gave the amulet to you?"

"A Bothan. Named Dyur. He told me to bring it here. To land at specific coordinates and carry the amulet to a nearby cave. To come alone." He laughed, one short bark that ended in a gasp of pain. "I'm sorry, Kiara. I wish I had. I'm so sorry."

"And you were strafed?" Ben asked.

Faskus nodded. "I was partway to the cave when I heard the engine roar. I ran back to the *Blacktooth*. They were firing on it, a TIE fighter. Kiara was still inside. I had to reach her . . ."

Ben didn't need to ask anything more. The rest of the story was clear to him. Faskus has gotten his daughter clear of the transport, but some calamity, an explosion perhaps, had sent a shard of durasteel into his guts.

And killed him. Slowly.

"Please." His voice was weak, wavering. "Untie my hands. So I can hold her."

Ben thought it over, then nodded. Using Faskus's own vibroblade, he cut the bonds on the man's hands.

Then, while Kiara sobbed and Faskus spoke soothingly to her, in ever-quieter tones, Ben began to break down the man's camp and inventory his goods.

And to think.

I have the amulet and it can't be used against me. This stage of his mission was accomplished; Ben could check it off his list. Now he needed to find a way to get offplanet, or at least to send a signal to Jacen.

If Faskus, or whatever his real name might be, didn't steal the amulet, who did? Dyur, whoever he was. And Dyur had framed Faskus by leaving the note behind. But why would Dyur give Faskus the real amulet to bury in a cave? This had to be the real thing; up close, it reeked of dark side energy and the creepy happiness that had allowed Ben to follow it. Something did not add up.

Ben counted six oversized blankets, one of them slightly damaged by his lightsaber; several wooden poles being used as tent poles; four durasteel spikes anchoring the tent to the ground; three blasters and a vibroblade, each one with extra power packs; food rations, possibly as much as a week's worth; a quantity of cord; the backpack; the contents of Faskus's pouch, including a datapad, numerous credcoins, credcards, data cards, and identicards; and the man's clothes, if he wanted them. But he didn't. He carefully broke down the tent, exposing the girl and her father to the first snowfall of the day, and folded all the blankets except the ones constituting the floor, on which Faskus and Kiara still lay. Faskus's eyes were still open, but he no longer spoke, and Ben could not feel him through the Force.

The astromech came waddling down from its position of concealment as Ben began dividing all his new goods between his own pack and the larger backpack Faskus had made. "Good news, Shaker," Ben said. "Several power packs. If you have adapters, we can keep you going for a long time."

But Shaker's response didn't sound happy. The droid kept its optics trained on Kiara and Faskus, trilling a discordant note.

"Yeah," Ben said. "It's sad."

Even sadder was what he'd have to do in a minute. But

his duty was clear. He had to get the amulet to Jacen. And that meant not taking chances with his resources.

He thought about asking Kiara to move so he could claim the final two blankets, but decided that such a request was unnecessary. Four blankets would be enough for just him.

He spent a few minutes using more cord to tie the big backpack to Shaker's dome, and then he began walking.

He didn't hear Shaker following. He turned to see the R2 still in place. Its optic sensor glided back and forth, staring first at him, then at Kiara. "C'mon, Shaker."

The astromech began waddling in his direction. Ben imagined that he could sense reluctance in its pace, but he pushed the thought away. Shaker had never met these people before, and therefore it could not care about them.

"Hey!" Kiara sat up. Snow was accumulating in her hair, and tears were freezing to her cheeks. "You can't go. Daddy said you were going to take care of us."

"I'm sorry," Ben said. "But I didn't say I would."

"You can't leave him! The animals will eat him!"

"I'm sorry."

Turning his back on the girl a second time took an act of will, but recognition of his duty gave him the strength to do it. He began walking again, slowly, and Shaker followed.

The droid trilled, a long and complicated communication. Ben opened his datapad, and it had received Shaker's message:

WHAT IS OUR DESTINATION?

"I had a look at Faskus's datapad." Ben tapped his pouch to reassure himself that the 'pad was still there. "There's information on Ziost that I don't have. Like the coordinates where he was supposed to set down, the cave where he was supposed to leave the amulet—I guess he abandoned that part of the plan after he got hurt—and a lot of locations marked RUINS. I bet that wherever there are ruins, there's stuff to find. Maybe even people. Maybe even the base that TIE fighter is from. We're headed for the nearest ruins site. I bet Faskus was, too."

WHY ARE YOU LEAVING THE GIRL BEHIND?

That caused Ben's stomach to knot up again. "Because if she's with us, we'll go through our resources faster, like our food. And we might not get to where we need to go. Our mission is more important than her life."

IS THE MISSION MORE IMPORTANT THAN YOUR LIFE, TOO?

Ben thought about it for fifty meters of travel. "Yes."

THEN TELL ME YOUR MISSION SO THAT IF YOU FALTER I CAN ABANDON YOU AND COMPLETE IT.

Ben turned and round-kicked the astromech in its dome. Shaker squawked and fell over. But the bindings Ben had used to lash the big backpack in place did not loosen. "Shut up, you, you walking hot plate. If you didn't have a few useful systems to go along with that malfunctioning droid brain of yours, I'd leave you, too."

Shaker didn't offer a response. It didn't try to right itself.

Ben forced himself to calm down. He'd wait until he was sure he didn't need the astromech anymore, then he'd crush it in a vise or throw it out an upper-story viewport.

No, that made no sense. It was valuable property. He could sell it for passage to another planet, if he could find someone willing to take him.

With a sigh, he righted the astromech, then continued walking.

* * *

An hour later, as they crossed a lightly forested ridgeline, Ben's datapad beeped. But Shaker hadn't made any noise indicating he was trying to communicate. Ben stopped and opened his datapad.

Images of his parents swam into focus on its diminutive screen. They were both smiling.

"Ben," Mara said. "In case you hadn't noticed—you're fourteen!"

"Congratulations on another birthday," Luke said. "So whatever torture your teachers, including me, had in store for you today—forget it. Report to me for some birthday credits, and the rest of the day is yours to enjoy."

Their images faded to blackness.

Shaker came up behind Ben and waited with a droid's patience.

Oddly, Ben felt as though there were nothing inside him, as if he had suddenly become a Ben-shaped balloon filled with gas. Gas could not think, and neither could he, for a long moment.

They had to have recorded this shortly before he started this mission.

"Hi, Mom," he said. "Hi, Dad. For my fourteenth birthday, I killed a little girl."

He sat down, his lower back resting against the astromech. He leaned forward, wrapping his arms around his knees.

And he began to cry.

Kiara stabbed at the ground with the knife. It was an eating utensil, not a vibroblade, and when it hit the ground, it made a ringing noise. Sometimes it scraped away a little of the ice-hard soil. Sometimes it didn't. After more than an hour of digging, punctuated by fits of sobbing, she had dug a hole a little larger than her hand.

But she'd keep digging. Her father was dead, and she

had to put him in the ground so the animals wouldn't come and eat him.

Through the snowfall, she could see that there were booted feet in front of her. She looked up into the face of Ben Skywalker. The waddling astromech was entering the clearing from the far edge.

Ben didn't say anything for a few moments. Then he took a look around. "I think," he said, "we need to wrap him in one of the blankets, then pile rocks on top of him. That will keep the animals away."

"They won't eat him?"

"They won't eat him. I'll wrap him up and find the rocks. You put the other blanket around you and go sit with Shaker."

Kiara did as she was told. Her tears didn't stop flowing, but now she knew her father would be safe under the rocks.

chapter sixteen

CORUSCANT

The weeks after the military disaster at Corellia did not argue for a quick resolution to the conflict.

Fondor, a world well known for its orbital shipyards—a world whose economy had been chafing under Galactic Alliance military production restrictions—announced its resignation from the Alliance and signed articles of friendship with Corellia and her allies. It was just one more world, increasing the size of the Confederation—no longer being referred to as the Corellian Confederation, at the indignant insistence of Bothawui and Commenor—from three systems to four. But of those four systems, two, Corellia and Fondor, possessed ship construction yards that were critical to Alliance military development. Fondor's loss lit up the holonews services. Soon after, Bespin, with its crucial production facilities for Tibanna gas, and Adumar, with its munitions industry, also joined the Confederation.

And other worlds were wavering. The worlds of Hutt space made no secret of their preference for the Confederation—or of their willingness to remain staunch, warm friends of the Alliance, so long as they received special trade and aid privileges that would pour wealth into their accounts. Several planets of the Imperial Remnant, long uncomfortable with being part of the Alliance, suggested that they favored the Confederation, but the Moff Council continued to abide by its treaties with the Alliance. Grand Admiral Pellaeon, recently retired and returned to the world of Bastion, participating in the ongoing process of rebuilding and repopulating the Imperial throneworld, spoke openly and often of the Empire's need to remain associated with the Alliance.

During these weeks there were only sporadic clashes between the Alliance and the Confederation. Admiral Limpan's task force at Corellia made frequent raids against the Corellian shipyards, the still-intact Centerpoint Station, and industrial facilities on the other worlds allied with Corellia, though these were largely inconclusive. The Confederation forces in the Bothawui system succeeded, with minimal effort, in driving Alliance observation vehicles into retreat.

Neither side pressed an assault. The Confederation worlds sat back, tightened their defenses, sent diplomats with offers of friendship to scores of systems, and cranked up their ship production to epic levels. The Alliance brought military forces back from distant stations and patrols, gathered information, and enhanced security. Mostly the war was fought in the news feeds, with analysts predicting where the next major action would be fought, who would start it, and how it would end.

Admiral Matric Klauskin, recently vanished from a hospital on Coruscant, turned up on his homeworld of Commenor. His handlers transmitted to Coruscant the resignation of his commission with the Galactic Alliance military. At a dinner on Commenor, he was recognized as a hero of his planet and was ceremoniously retired. He was not observed to speak much during the celebration, and close observers described him as unresponsive and glassy-eyed.

GALACTIC ALLIANCE
MILITARY HEADQUARTERS
SENIOR OFFICERS' BRIEFING ROOM

"The so-called Chasin Document," said General Tycho Celchu, "is authentic." A tall, elegantly handsome man with blond hair frosting to white, he radiated confidence and competence.

Admiral Niathal was not concerned with what the human military analyst radiated. Her eyes vibrated with her agitation. "It can't be, General. We *had* no plans to invade Commenor."

"Yes, we did," Tycho assured her. "Thirty years ago."

That settled Niathal a bit, piquing her curiosity. The statement obviously had the same effect on the other senior officers present; Niathal heard muttering from up and down the long table. "Please continue," she said, cutting off the side conversations.

"Back when the Rebel Alliance was mounting its campaign for the liberation of crucial planetary systems of the Empire," Tycho said, "General Garm Bel Iblis drew up a number of plans for individual systems. The Chasin Document, recently obtained for us by Intelligence, is a revision of Bel Iblis's Operation Blue Plug. Blue Plug was never launched, because Commenor voluntarily ousted its Imperial governor a few months after Coruscant fell to us."

"Were the details of Operation Blue Plug ever made public?" Niathal asked.

Tycho shook his head. "No, they've been classified top secret for decades. Classified, and forgotten, owing to their irrelevance. I wasn't aware of them. But when I began doing my analysis of the Chasin Document, I was struck by how thoroughly it resembled General Bel Iblis's preferred logistical patterns. At first I thought it must have been drawn up by a student of the general's . . . but then it occurred to me that the plan made no provisions for the use of the most modern classes of ships, and that made me suspicious. So I went looking through the records."

"I see. And do we have any indication of how the original plan fell into the hands of someone who might revise it and pass it off to the Commenorians?"

"Yes." A touch of dismay was visible through Tycho's controlled manner. "Our security has been compromised. An analysis of the data banks where that file was stored indicated that the only times it had been accessed in recent years was when automated backup programming refreshed it and compared it with static stored copies. Military programmers could find no other signs of intrusion, so I requested assistance from Intelligence, which revealed the method used—"

Murmurs from other active-duty officers cut him off. Tycho glanced impassively around the table. Niathal knew the general was in disfavor with his colleagues for bringing in an outsider. She, too, regretted that General Celchu had exposed a security flaw to outsiders, but she also applauded the fact that he'd solved the problem. "By *Intelligence* in this case," Niathal said, "you mean your wife."

"Yes." Tycho's wife, Winter, was a longtime operative. She'd been a field agent back when the New Republic had been an ideal rather than a reality. She had helped rear the Alliance's most popular son, Jacen Solo. Solo was one of the officers at the table, and he listened dispassionately, not reacting when Winter was mentioned.

Tycho continued, "Winter discovered that the backup code had been replaced. It was still doing its job, but it was additionally sending those files to an off-site location. Once we knew what to look for, we found similar programs backing up other banks of data. This programming was self-replicating and could have spread itself through our entire military network, but we caught it in time. It had accessed only older files and some ordnance inventories."

"And your actions?"

"We scrubbed the malignant code and turned over pertinent details to Military Intelligence, Galactic Alliance Intelligence, and the Galactic Alliance Guard. We could have used their intrusion for disinformation purposes, but this would have been a massive undertaking—the enemy would presumably have noticed if their code had stopped spreading through our network, so maintaining the secret would have called for building an entire second network, full of a combination of false data and noncritical genuine data, and updating it at the same rate the real network is updated."

Niathal nodded. Such an operation was possible to execute, but it would have been a tremendous drain on resources. "Do we know how our systems were violated?"

"In part," Tycho said. "Verifiable records suggest that the initial code slicing took place during a routine data inquiry using a GAG passcode."

That did get Jacen's attention. "Ridiculous," he said.

Tycho regarded him steadily. "But verifiable."

"No one with access at a high enough level to make significant requests of the military network is a security risk." Jacen kept his voice hard. "In addition to all the security measures we employ, I'm a Jedi. It would be next to impossible for one of my senior officers to deceive me that way."

"*Next* to impossible," Tycho said, "isn't impossible."

"Give me the passcode," Jacen snapped.

Reciting from memory, Tycho said, "Three seven nine aitch oh ell forty-four underscore bee nine two one."

Jacen whipped out his datapad and accessed a file. He scrolled through it for a few moments. Then his expression went from merely angry to angry and confused. "Unassigned," he said. "Toward the bottom of the unassigned list."

"I suggest," Niathal said, "that you run checks on the other unassigned codes to be sure they haven't been used, as well."

Jacen snapped the datapad shut. "I'll do that."

"And report your findings."

"Yes, Admiral." Clearly furious, Jacen turned away and avoided eye contact.

"Is there anything else?" Niathal asked.

"Yes." The speaker was a dark-skinned, dark-haired woman dressed in somber civilian dress rather than in uniform. She was Belindi Kalenda, the Galactic Alliance's director of intelligence since the end of the Yuuzhan Vong war. "I have one item pertaining to the military. Information has reached me suggesting that the Confederation is experiencing growing pains—an increased difficulty, as more planets join, with coordinating their respective military forces."

Niathal cocked her head at the director. "The only surprising part about that is that they haven't selected a Supreme Commander already."

"Not the only surprising part. Admiral, what I'm hearing is that the Bothans have demanded that the Supreme Commander be elected at a face-to-face meeting of representatives from each world in the Confederation."

Tycho whistled, Jacen nodded, and other officers began whispering among themselves. Niathal said, "That sounds very much like the Bothans. Face-to-face, rather than communicating across the HoloNet, they can influence the outcome."

"Even more than that," Kalenda said, "it appears that the Confederation is using this as a recruiting ploy, telling worlds that are still on the fence, 'Join now and you'll have a chance to send delegates to the election meeting; your candidate might be our Supreme Commander.' "

"Interesting." Niathal mulled that over. "How accurate is this information?"

"It's an absolute that the Hutts have received a *Join now* communication referring to the election, and that the Bothans are in a mad scramble to select the candidate agreeable to the greatest number of relevant politicians."

"We have to be there," Jacen said.

Niathal nodded. "Colonel Solo is correct. The delegations will include some of the Confederation's best military leaders and brightest minds. Not to mention politicians who are very knowledgeable about their worlds' plans. If we can eliminate the attendees, we reduce the Confederation's planning abilities by a noticeable degree. If we can *capture* them, we stand to obtain a tremendous amount of critical knowledge. Director Kalenda, please bring a maximum effort to bear on obtaining that information. Don't hesitate to call on us for resources."

"Understood, Admiral."

CORUSCANT
JEDI TEMPLE TRAINING HALL

"I think you're taking the whole 'Sword of the Jedi' thing too seriously," Zekk said.

In response, Jaina darted in, raising her lightsaber in a horizontal hold. She began a high sweeping slash, visualizing her attack as she did so. But hers was a feint, and, contrary to her visualization, she dipped the tip of the blade well beneath Zekk's blocking maneuver and tagged him along his right ribs.

The weapon made a *zap* noise. A practice saber, it gave Zekk an electrical jolt instead of a new burn scar to match the one he'd earned not so long ago.

He stepped back, rubbing where the blade had touched him. "Hey. You cheated."

Jaina nodded. "I relied on the fact that you anticipate me all the time. Because *you* rely too often on anticipating me."

"Maybe so."

"And I'm not taking the Sword of the Jedi designation too seriously. How can I, when I don't even know what it means? Not even Uncle Luke really knows what it means.

He's never been entirely sure why he said it. Maybe it was the Force speaking through him."

Zekk readied his practice saber again. "Maybe it means you're the new Chosen One."

Jaina shuddered, then went on guard again. "I hope not. It took my grandfather decades, multiple amputations, and a lot of tragedy to achieve his destiny." She advanced and threw a probing downward slash that turned into a skittering thrust across the top of Zekk's blocking blade.

But Zekk used his greater reach and height to his advantage, flicking Jaina's point upward, so the thrust ended several centimeters to the right of his face. He tried a lateral sweep, but Jaina stood her ground and brought her blade down, catching Zekk's attack near her hilt.

"Besides," Jaina continued, her conversational tone suggesting that there was not a lightsaber duel in progress, "there's no Emperor for me to hurl down a well."

"There's Lumiya." The voice came from several meters away.

Jaina and Zekk drew away from each other and looked toward the speaker.

Jag Fel sat cross-legged on a practice mat, dressed in his usual black city garb. Jaina realized she hadn't seen or felt him enter.

"I wish he wouldn't spy on us," Zekk said. His voice was a murmur, not loud enough to carry to Jag.

Jaina deactivated her practice saber. The blade, an electrically charged piece of durasteel, did not retract. "What about Lumiya?"

Jag shrugged. "The Chosen One destroyed the leader of the Sith. Lumiya's Sith, correct?"

Zekk deactivated his own blade. "She's what's *left* of the Sith. I doubt that it will take someone who fills a once-in-a-generation prophetic role, if that's what the Sword is, to eliminate her."

"I'll admit I don't have enough knowledge of the Jedi even to speculate in an informed manner—"

"Good for you."

Jag grinned as though Zekk's words were humor rather than insolence. Then he continued. "But I look at it this way. A sword is a weapon. A weapon of the Jedi would be used by the will of, or against the enemy of, the Jedi. The enemy of the Jedi are the Sith and other anti-Jedi, whatever they choose to call themselves. The Sword of the Jedi would therefore be someone who is wielded against the Sith. So is that simple, simplistic, or just wrong?"

"I vote for simplistic." Zekk returned his attention to Jaina. "Another round?"

Jaina shook her head. "I want to hear this. I've never really gotten the perspective of someone outside the order. And Jag always has an interesting perspective."

Zekk sighed, long suffering, and reached out a hand. Jaina passed her practice saber to him. Zekk dutifully headed toward the rack where practice weapons were stored.

Jag offerred Jaina an apologetic look. "I'm not sure I have a perspective other than what I just said. But I can speculate."

"Please." She moved up to sit on the mat in front of him, duplicating his cross-legged posture.

"I'm no more suited to analyze the Force than I am to composing ultrasonic music, since I can't experience either. I just know the little bits I've heard, and that's been added to quite a lot since I've come here. But if the Force was speaking through the Grand Master when he pronounced you the Sword of the Jedi, and if the Sword is anything like the Chosen One, then there's some sort of imbalance that needs to be addressed. And that would seem to point to Lumiya."

Jaina nodded. "Maybe our task force needs to be pursuing her instead of Alema Rar."

"Or in addition to, since the two of them were clearly cooperating against the Skywalkers at Roqoo Depot."

Zekk returned to stand over the two of them. "I don't think the three of us are a match for Lumiya. She fought the Grand Master to a standstill. She's Master level. We're two Jedi Knights and one Force-blind space jockey."

Jaina frowned up at him. "Zekk, that was uncalled for."

"I'm just explaining, correctly and logically, that Fel is not an asset when it comes to matters of the Force."

"Zekk, stop it!"

Implacably, Zekk continued. "And this sort of analysis is something that Fel knows quite a lot about." He turned his attention to Jag. "Didn't you once tell Jaina I wasn't a good enough pilot to join her squadron? Wasn't that cool, level-headed analysis?"

Jaina winced. That event had taken place during the Yuuzhan Vong war, on Borleias. And Jaina had let herself be convinced of Jag's point, even though she'd known better.

Jag's expression did not change, but he took a long time to formulate a reply. "No," he admitted, "that wasn't analysis. That was me being a jealous lover, trying to keep you out of the way."

Zekk looked startled. Obviously, candor was not what he had expected.

Jag gestured up toward Zekk. "And that's something *you* know all about. A lover's jealousy. Otherwise you wouldn't hover like a brooding hawk-bat whenever I walk up to ask Jaina the time."

Jaina felt herself redden. "Jag—"

"You always know the time. You're just making excuses to talk to her."

"Boys, you're making me angry—"

Jag began beeping. Rather, some electronic device on his person did, and the beeps were a complicated swirl of musical tones, like an astromech trying to recite poetry, a more elaborate signal than any of the ones either Jedi had heard from any piece of Jag's equipment.

Looking startled, Jag pulled his datapad from a pocket. "High-priority flash traffic." He opened the device, read a few lines . . . and then began reading aloud. "From the central computer of the *Errant Venture*. 'Jedi Temple holocam recognition and analysis code assigns ninety-four percent probability of match to target Alema Rar for attached sequence.' "

The argument forgotten, Zekk sat beside Jaina. "Put it on the big display."

Zekk oriented the datapad toward the display that dominated the wall opposite the hall's entryway. He pressed a button, and a moment later the screen glowed into life, playing a holocam recording.

It appeared to be from a ceiling-mounted security holocam. It showed a crowd of people, most of them uniformed Alliance military personnel, rushing toward a door. In the midst of them was a well-bundled humanoid female—definitely blue-skinned, possibly Twi'lek, but her face was not large enough on the image for Jaina to recognize.

Then Jag's code went active. A wire-frame representation of a female Twi'lek body was superimposed over the target. As it conformed to her posture, smaller lines stretched from body parts—foot, shoulder, head—and words and percentile numbers flashed by too fast to read. The wire frame adapted itself further, shortening one foot by half its length, causing the left shoulder to droop in a fashion suggesting permanent physiological damage.

That sequence ended and another began. It seemed to follow shortly after the first. The holocam view showed a ship's broad passageway. Uniformed personnel poured into it from a larger chamber; their movement was restricted by their numbers. The blue female was toward the center of the mass of them, jumping up and down. This holocam view zoomed in and held a still frame.

The woman's features were very much like Alema's, the Alema of the Dark Nest.

Jag brought up a third file, but it was not a holocam sequence. It was a log of instances of holocam recording glitches recorded aboard *Errant Venture*—in the areas where the deck plans were not classified, at any rate. The log cited thousands of instances, and a schematic plotted them on those deck plans, showing definite patterns of progression along corridors, through air ducts, through casinos and shopping centers.

Clearly, Alema Rar was on *Errant Venture,* or at least had been when the raw data from this report was compiled, no more than a few days earlier.

And *Errant Venture* was now in the Coruscant system, having been granted the right to ply its trade here after having fled Corellia.

Jag stood so fast he could have been yanked to his feet by invisible springs. "Hunt's on." Expressionless, he ran toward the Training Hall's exit.

CORUSCANT SPACE
ERRANT VENTURE

Walking—half staggering, because the great gambling ship's artificial gravity generators seemed to be phasing on and off, right and left, and had been doing so since she'd downed her sixth whiskey of the evening—Captain Uran Lavint turned a corner into the narrow passageway where her cabin was located.

The thought of returning to her cabin drew a sigh from her. There was an even-odds chance that Alema would be there, skulking, ready to discuss her day's worth of spying failures, ready to offer another set of threats. Upset by the ritual, Lavint would take hours to fall to sleep. Nor could she have any company over while the mangled blue Twi'lek was present.

Still, it was Alema's Jedi powers that gave Lavint the edge at the betting tables. Whenever Alema watched from a shadowy place, and communicated with Lavint with little telekinetic prods, giving Lavint a much-improved sense of how good the other players' hands were, Lavint won big. She won enough to maintain a cabin aboard this pricy flying hotel, enough to buy cargo that would make her next smuggling run a very profitable one, enough to surround herself with the trappings of a life well misspent.

She just wished that Alema weren't one of those trappings.

But now, as she weaved her way to her door, a shadow seemed to flow off the opposite wall of the passageway and stand over her.

Lavint reached for her hold-out blaster and was bringing it in line to fire, or at least threaten, when the stranger snatched it from her hand. He didn't aim it back at her; he just held it, barrel down.

Lavint peered at him, alarmed and suspicious, for the seconds it took to bring his face into focus. Then she recognized him and laughed. "Colonel Solo," she said. "Here to kill me?"

He shook his head and handed her the blaster. "No, I need you."

"Well, I'm not at my best right now, but I'm up for it if you are."

An expression of distaste crossed his face. "Not what I meant."

"I didn't think so. I was just checking." She replaced the blaster in its hideaway holster—on her third try—then drew her datapad from its pocket and used it to open the cabin door. Beyond was a small chamber, minimal furniture, and no Alema, unless she was under the bed or up in the ceiling somewhere.

Lavint led her visitor in and immediately sat on the

chamber's one chair, leaving Jacen to decide whether to take the bed or stand. He elected to stand.

"I have need of your services."

"I don't think so." She started to shake her head but, as the motion caused the cabin to sway violently, thought better of it and stopped. "I distinctly remember you saying, 'I'd never prolong a business relationship with someone who sells the Falleen.' "

"Sells out her fellows," Jacen corrected. He looked annoyed. "Circumstances change."

"And ethics with them. Congratulations! That makes you a smuggler."

He was quiet a moment, as if settling his emotions, then continued. "It's your services as a smuggler I need. Most people connected with the smuggling culture are either staying clear of the war or siding with the Confederation."

"And with good reason. You want to put us out of business."

"No, I want you all to take up a legitimate business. And if *you* help me, I'll help *you* do just that."

"Keep talking."

"There's going to be a gathering of Confederation warships in a few days. From different systems. Their leaders will meet, they'll elect a joint leader, and then they'll launch against a common target. I need to be at the meeting site to find out who's there . . . who's a conspirator."

"Just ambush the fleet and sort them out when they're dead."

He waved her suggestion away. "What will it cost me for you to get me there?"

"I won't do it. You can't be trusted. You sabotage hyperdrives."

A flash of anger crossed his face. "Your hyperdrive *did* fail."

"Of course it did. And I spent several long, long hours thinking I was going to die alone in space. Considering that was on top of having my ship stolen—by *you*—it wasn't a good day. Really it wasn't."

"I ruined two good men because you lied to me the last time we talked."

Lavint shrugged. "They weren't good men. They were saboteurs. Incompetent ones, too, since I eventually fixed the drive they sabotaged. They were scum. Like me, remember? You shouldn't rely on scum, nice boy like you."

Jacen closed his eyes and seemed to be counting. Finally he opened them. "Whatever price we agree to, I'll deliver fully, in advance. To you or your agent of choice. Irretrievably."

"All right." Lavint didn't have to think for long. "I want the *Breathe My Jets* back."

"I can't do that within our time frame. It's been overhauled, recommissioned, put into service as a GA transport. It would take weeks or months to detach it from service, bring it here, and work the ownership records." He thought about it for a moment. "How about a Gallofree Yards medium transport, twelve years old, seized from Corellia, freshly reconditioned and repaired at the Coruscant yards but not yet assigned? I can claim it for GAG and divert it to you. Ownership free and clear."

"I agree. Assuming it's fully fueled, armed, provisioned . . . and not sabotaged."

"Understood. What else?"

"I'm going to need to lay some credits around to buy the information you need. Fifteen, twenty thousand."

"Done."

"And I want you to get a message to your parents for me."

"What?"

"You can do that, can't you?"

"What message?"

"I want them to send me a way, any way, to reach them. At my leisure. Just for one transmission."

"Do you know them?"

"No."

"Then why—"

"None of your business. I'll swear to that. It doesn't involve you; it won't do you any harm." She looked steadily at him.

He considered, then said, "All right. I'll find a way."

She smiled at him. "That's it."

"I expected you to ask for a lot more than that. Because of injured feelings."

"The trick to negotiations," she said, "which you'd know if your father had raised you right, is never to ask for so much that the other party would prefer to kill you than to go through with the deal."

Jacen considered that, looking at her, for a long moment. Then he simply said, "Thank you," and left.

Still smiling, Lavint stretched out on the bed. Now she had to figure out just what she'd accomplished. If Alema were here, then that last bit of negotiation was going to get the Solos killed, and Lavint freed—unless Alema decided to kill her, too, which Lavint fully expected the crazy Twi'lek to do. But if Alema hadn't heard this conversation, those negotiations would probably get Alema killed, which was the outcome Lavint preferred.

"Hey, crazy girl," she said, "are you here?"

There was no answer. Lavint relaxed.

Her eyes closed, and within two minutes she was snoring.

chapter seventeen

ZIOST

Every morning Ben awoke with the memory of the voices in his ears. Some part of his mind tried to listen to them, to puzzle out what they were saying. The rest of him worked harder to avoid comprehending. He knew, deep down, that if he listened long enough to understand, he'd want to do what they told him, and that what they told him would be very, very wrong.

So sleep was not restful for Ben, even on the nights when his fire burned through all the darkness hours and Kiara huddled against him, sad but trusting.

During those nights, he often awoke to a sense of worry or a beep from Shaker to see eyes gleaming from the other side of the fire. Nocturnal predators, Jacen would have called them, and Ben could feel them in the Force. They were big, powerful presences there, suffused with energy . . . and wrongness. He could feel that they were as twisted as the blighted trees of this place.

So far they hadn't attacked, but Ben made sure that Kiara was never more than a step or two from him—except when either of them needed to perform some private business in the trees. Then he made sure Shaker stayed near the girl. The droid's presence seemed not to violate her sense of privacy.

There was another presence, too. The day after Ben found Kiara, at about noon, they had stopped for a quick meal of canned rations. Ben sat, consuming some grease-packed meat product, and eating quickly so that he wouldn't taste the stuff. Wary of the wild beasts he still had not seen, he had his physical and Force-awareness stretched to their limits, and abruptly he was certain that someone was looking at him.

He stood, looking around, and grabbed his lightsaber, but nothing approached. And after a few moments the sensation faded.

The next day, again at planetary noon, it happened once more, this time as they reached the remains of what must have once been a road. Now trees protruded through it, but there were long stretches where it remained flat and level, and Shaker could make much better time. The astromech had just assumed its tripodal wheeled configuration for greater speed when Ben felt the eyes upon him again. Once more, after less than a minute, the sensation faded.

The next day at noon, he was waiting for the sensation, and it did not fail him. In the few seconds he had, he sought the viewer through the Force.

And he was successful. Whoever was staring at him was doing so from straight up. Ben peered up through the canopy of leafless branches. But there was nothing for him to see, just the sun gleaming dimly through a layer of clouds. He said, "Shaker, passive sensors only, look straight up."

The astromech chirped an affirmative.

Again the sensation faded. Ben pulled out his datapad. "Did you see anything?"

I DETECT A FAINT ION TRAIL.

"The ion trail—the kind that a TIE fighter would leave?"

CORRECT.

So the person who had blown up both the YT-2400 and the Y-wing was shadowing them. But why—and, just as importantly, how?

Ben spent part of the afternoon disassembling and checking every piece of equipment he had taken from Faskus's camp, especially the electronics. He found no mystery transmitters in or on them.

There was Faskus's datapad, of course, and it, like Ben's, was a short-range transmitter. To determine whether it was transmitting to their shadow, Ben would have to catch it in the act—its programming could cause it to transmit a single recognition pulse at great intervals, and Ben would have to have Shaker listen on all comm frequencies all the time to detect it.

But instead he could simply remove the battery from the device, restoring it on those occasions he needed to consult its files. That he did. Then, no more informed than before, he led the way onward, through the snow and the twisted trees.

STAR SYSTEM MZX32905, NEAR BIMMIEL

The hologram of the scrawny, bronze-hued Bothan flickered and jittered. Lumiya pretended not to notice. She'd chosen Dyur and crew in part because their ship had a holocomm, but it clearly wasn't a very good one. "Right on time," she said, forcing a note of commendation into her voice. "What do you have to report?"

"Faskus is dead," Dyur said. "The boy and the astromech appear to be heading toward one of the old settlements. And there's a complication."

"Go ahead."

"It looks as though Faskus took his little girl along. She's still alive. The boy has taken her with him."

Lumiya sat back and considered. That was . . . unfortunate.

The orders she had meticulously structured with Jacen didn't specify what Ben should do in such a case. And while rescuing a little girl might initially give him a warm feeling of satisfaction, continuing to protect her had to be a considerable drain on his attention and energies. Taking her along was not survival thinking, not mission-success thinking, not Sith thinking.

And the boy must know it. He was just too much like his father.

And that meant he'd never be good Sith material.

"Kill them," she said.

"Consider it done."

"I'll consider it done when you report that it's done. Anything else?"

"No, my lady."

Lumiya made a subtle gesture with her fingers, which would be beneath the view Dyur had of her, and the hologram disappeared.

She winced just a bit, though her servitor droids would not be able to see it beneath her facial scarf. She'd just ordered the death of Luke Skywalker's son. One more reason for him to kill her if he found out about it.

Ah, well. Perhaps he never would. Even if he did, this was all about Jacen, and now Jacen would not be saddled with an apprentice with a fuzzy, sentimental mind.

ZIOST

The next day, at midmorning, they found the first location marked RUINS on Faskus's map. It was a mass of collapsed stone—dressed stone blocks that had once formed the wall of a small citadel before some tremendous force had pushed them over. Ben found weathering on all exposed surfaces of the stones, but no sign of blaster scoring, melting, or other recognizable indicators of violence.

And he found no way into the mass. Neither his eyes nor his Force-senses suggested a place he might enter to find intact chambers, nor did Shaker's sensors.

"We'll rest and eat here," he said. "Shaker, set up to detect ion trails and communications, please."

The droid acknowledged with a musical chirp. And fewer than ten minutes later, just as Ben was finishing a chilled can of nerf steak stew, Shaker beeped again, a complex series of notes.

Ben pulled out his datapad and read:

YOU JUST SENT A COMM SIGNAL.

Ben scowled. "I did?"

OF LESS THAN ONE HUNDREDTH OF A SECOND'S DURATION.

"Was there a return signal?"

NO.

Ben glanced at the time in the corner of the datapad's screen. There were two listings there, one local and one Coruscant, and the local time was exactly one standard hour short of noon.

Could his own datapad be betraying him? Or some other item of his gear? Quickly he unpacked everything from both backpacks, segregating the items into two stacks—everything he had examined before, and everything he hadn't. He attacked the second pile, minutely scrutinizing each item.

He could probably find out the next day if his datapad were the tracking device. Assuming that the communications were taking place at the same time each day, he'd set his datapad aside just before noon, and he and Shaker would move several meters away. If the datapad sent a signal, Shaker could determine that it was that device and not something else on Ben's person.

He methodically checked all the other items, too, to the point of shaking out his belt pouch over the pile of goods to make sure it was empty.

It wasn't. Nothing more fell out, but the bottom of the pouch sagged oddly in his hand. The pouch seemed to weigh more than it should, if only fractionally.

He turned the pouch inside out and found the tracking device.

It looked like a small steel marble, albeit one with spindly spider legs that were threaded into the cloth of the pouch, holding it securely in place. One leg stretched to a length of six or seven centimeters.

Ben stared at it, perplexed. When had this been planted on him? Or, more to the point—since it looked like a mobile unit—when had it crawled into his pouch? It could have been at any point between the Jedi Temple and his arrival at Faskus's camp. His mother's words about spies accomplishing their tasks without ever being noticed came back to Ben, and he smiled. "Good job, spy," he said.

Then he felt the eyes in the sky again. He checked his datapad. High noon exactly.

Except this time, the sensation of being watched did not fade after a few seconds. It intensified, and Ben could feel something with it, emotions of wicked amusement, a desire to commit mayhem.

He glanced up. There was a tiny dot up in the sky, in the center of the cloud cover blocking the worst of the sun's rays from reaching the ground. "Shaker," he said, "get under cover!"

Kiara, who had been disinterestedly finishing her can of spiceloaf sausages, looked up. She hadn't said much in the last few days and didn't say anything now, but she hopped up as Ben reached her.

That was when the first streaks of laserfire scorched the ground. Green bolts strafed the stand of stones a few meters to Ben's right. Kiara shrilled a scream. Ben caught her up and leapt leftward, toward the near line of trees, sixty or more meters away.

The TIE fighter screamed past and began to loop around for another strafing run. Ben saw it as a blur—it was black, with some details, such as the ribs separating the panels on the solar wing arrays, in gleaming bronze.

He stopped. If he continued toward the trees, he'd be caught out in the open for the next pass. He reversed direction and ran toward the mound of stones; it offered the only protection close enough to reach.

He leapt behind a partially intact stand of rocks and peeked over. The TIE fighter was low, barely fifty meters aboveground, and coming straight at them. Shaker, waddling back toward the flat roadway, was an easy target, but the starfighter pilot ignored the droid.

Ben ducked down again as the TIE fired. The stones immediately to his right rocked and fell backward, landing next to him, propelled by the tremendous energy of the fighter's turbolasers. Black smoke, accompanied by a sharp smell, curled up from the points of impact.

He glanced down at Kiara. She was huddled against the ground—against the stone surface she lay on, rather—and her face was turned upward, her eyes full of fear.

For a moment Ben was somewhere else, in a hundred other places with shivering refugees as squadrons, fleets of TIE fighters roaring past overhead. *So that was the Empire,* he thought distantly. Jacen had shown him that there were some things to admire about the old Empire, including the unwavering fashion with which it had imposed order, but now he could feel what that order was like from the other side.

He shook his head to clear the images away and looked up. He found the TIE fighter coming around for another pass. He reached for Faskus's blaster pistol—

It was still out there on the snow, where he'd dropped it when examining his possessions. He bit off a curse and reached for it. Though he'd never summoned his lightsaber or any other object to himself from that distance, the blaster flew to his hand and he took aim with it.

Then he shook his head. A blaster pistol against an armored starfighter? He had exactly no chance to harm his opponent. He needed bigger weapons—

He needed the Force. He was a Jedi, after all, even if only an apprentice, and the Force was his great weapon, his great armor.

He looked around for a missile, then realized he was surrounded by them. He closed his eyes and concentrated as he had the other day, when freeing Shaker from the Y-wing.

He heard Kiara's gasp as the stone that had just fallen over rose a few centimeters into the air.

The TIE fighter came on. Ben couldn't so much sense it as he could sense the pilot at the heart of its ball-shaped cockpit. He felt the stone, he felt the pilot . . . and he tried to send one to the other.

Sluggishly, the stone rose into the path of the TIE fighter. Ben heard the scream of the lasers firing again and opened his eyes in time to see one green bolt hitting the wall far to his left, the other hitting the floating stone dead center, shattering it into a thousand shards.

The TIE fighter veered but could not get entirely clear of the cloud of debris. Ben heard the high-pitched *klunk*s and *ping*s as the left solar array wing hit the shards.

The TIE fighter suddenly gained a lot of altitude, circled once, and then climbed again until it was out of sight.

Ben looked down at Kiara again. "We're fine for now," he said. "The bad man went away."

She nodded, half believing.

"No, really." He paused, trying to think of what to say to convince her. Then he leaned down and embraced her, felt her shaking. "It's all right. It's all right."

Her reply was muffled: "Will he come back?"

"Yes, he will. But next time I'll be ready for him."

"Why does he want to shoot me?"

"Shoot *you*?" Ben drew back to look at her. "He doesn't want to shoot you. He wants to shoot *me*."

She shook her head, solemn. "No. He shot the *Black tooth* while I was inside. That's how Daddy got hurt. Daddy said they wanted to shoot him, but now they want to shoot me. They want me to be dead."

"No, they don't."

"You wanted it." Her tone wasn't even accusing, just hurt.

"No, I didn't. I just . . ." Ben paused to try to sort his words out. "I'm on an important mission, and I thought that leaving you, even leaving you to die, would make things work out better."

"You changed your mind?"

"I did. I was wrong."

Suddenly Ben felt dizzy. He sat down on the stone beside Kiara.

"What's wrong?" she asked.

He couldn't tell her, though he had a sense of it. He'd done just what Jacen had been doing, deciding that one thing was more important than another, one goal more important than one life, and he'd been too ready to sacrifice one, not willing enough to try to protect both.

He'd been wrong. Perhaps, sometimes, Jacen had been wrong, too.

Ben shook his head. No, Jacen was more than twice Ben's age. He was older, wiser, more powerful. He wouldn't make that kind of mistake, ever.

Unless he was human.

Shaker's trilled query jarred Ben from his thoughts. "We're all right," he called out. "Be with you in a minute."

ZIOST ORBIT
BONEYARD RENDEZVOUS

Dyur looked at the helmeted face in the display and couldn't keep from laughing. "He did what?"

The person he addressed, a man anonymous in the uniform of a TIE fighter pilot—though this uniform was bronze rather than black—sounded abashed. "He threw a rock at me."

"And now you're running back to us."

"It's not like that, Captain. He used Jedi magic to hurl a quarter-ton slab of stone at me. If I hadn't hit the stone with my lasers, he'd have brought me down."

"Ah. Well, that *is* different."

"Orders, sir?"

Dyur's voice turned hard, and like any Bothan who intended to sound angry, his tone became very fearsome indeed. "Keldan, you should have gone back immediately and finished him. Without wavering, without asking. Now you won't get the chance, or the bonus for the kill. Your orders are to report back immediately. Myrat'ur will go down tomorrow at the regular time and finish the job."

The pilot sounded appropriately chastised and resentful. "Yes, sir."

"We don't reward foul-ups here, Keldan. *Boneyard* out."

GYNDINE SYSTEM, TENDRANDO REFUELING AND REPAIR STATION
COCKPIT OF THE MILLENNIUM FALCON

Han finished the preflight checkup.

Lando's repair workers appeared to have done a great

job. All systems checked out as functioning optimally—except, of course, for the occasional fluctuations in the communications among the vehicle's droid brains, which were so idiosyncratic, and which interfaced in what was partly a self-taught, self-programmed fashion, that the efficiency of their intercommunications varied anywhere from eerily high to catastrophically low, like Jedi triplets who could go from an undefeatable battle array to a squabbling trio in seconds.

He flexed his left shoulder experimentally. It felt good. He was healed.

Everything was fixed. But nothing was tested.

He forced a crooked smile for Leia, who was once more in the copilot's seat. "Ready to go, sweetheart?"

She finished strapping in. "Ready."

"Lando?"

From behind him, in the navigator's seat, came Lando's voice: "Oh, I suppose. It just won't be the same, not being able to order you around."

"Leia, remind me to get the navigator's seat rigged with an ejector option."

"You didn't ask *me*." C-3PO's voice sounded just a touch petulant. The protocol droid stood in the entryway to the cockpit.

"That's because I'm looking forward to hitting the thrusters and hearing you roll around for a while." Han brought the *Falcon* up on repulsors and sent her gliding forward to the exit from the repair hangar. "Which is going to happen in about five seconds."

"Oh. Oh, dear. Perhaps I should find a seat."

"Two seconds." They passed through the atmosphere containment field at the end of the hangar and emerged into gleaming starfield. Han heeled over, putting the stars to starboard and the night side of Gyndine to port, and, despite his words, began a slow, smooth acceleration into a sample high orbit.

The engines sounded sweeter than they had in quite a while. He grinned, experimentally increasing the thrust, accelerating the transport faster and sending her up into an ever-higher orbit. "Not bad, Lando."

"One of the virtues of being rich. You can afford to hire the best."

Gyndine's sun came into view, no longer eclipsed by the planet, and the cockpit viewports polarized dramatically, making vision useless. Sensors showed the main cluster of the planet's orbital shipyards—far less numerous than those of Kuat or Corellia, but well respected—at a lower orbit.

They were passing directly above those shipyards when the enemy task force appeared.

The *Falcon*'s threat sensors howled as a tremendous mass appeared directly in her flight path. Han hauled back on the yoke, a hard maneuver that pressed him and his crew deep into their seats, and cringed as he heard something scrape on the *Falcon*'s underside.

"Shields, we grazed her shields," Leia muttered.

Their new course wasn't much better. The *Falcon* flashed through a squadron of starfighters, at right angles to their course, too fast for Han to have anything but a vague impression of them.

"Shields up," Han shouted. "What the *brix* is going on?"

Leia remained cool. "Sensors say it's a Bothan Assault Cruiser and six squadrons of Howlrunners."

And the squadron Han had flown through was turning in the *Falcon*'s wake. The capital ship gunners, doubtless caught unawares by the proximity of the *Falcon* when they arrived, now begin firing turbolaser batteries. Han sent the *Falcon* into a dizzying spiral of evasive maneuvering. "Sweetheart, Lando, I hate to ask—"

Leia unbuckled. "Yes, we'll go shoot down the bad furry people for you." Then she and Lando were gone.

The first shots from the pursuing Howlrunners battered at his rear shields, and Han growled. He'd had a beautifully restored, intact *Millennium Falcon* in his hands for ten minutes before someone was trying to shoot her to pieces again. "Threepio!" he shouted. "Get up here, operate the sensors and comm board."

"Yes, Captain Solo." The protocol droid, rocking wildly back and forth as Han's maneuvers nearly took him from his feet, managed to slide into the seat Leia had vacated. Very prudently he strapped himself in. "If I may ask, sir—"

"Don't." Han rolled ninety degrees to starboard and arced around to a course straight out from the planet. Laserfire from the pursuers bracketed the *Falcon*, missing by meters. But now he could hear the *Falcon*'s own turbolasers firing.

"—what's happening, sir?"

"Bothans have sent a task force to destroy or capture the shipyards here," Han said. "They must have jumped straight at Gyndine and let the planet's gravity well yank them out of hyperspace. That's why they appeared so close."

"Your pursuers are ten in number—no, nine. Someone appears to have scored a hit, and one of them is heading in a different direction."

Distantly, Han could hear Lando's shout of "Nice shooting!" He grinned. That was his lady, always blowing up people who intended to cause him grief.

"And," C-3PO added, "you're getting a message."

"From the Bothan ship. Demanding surrender."

"Well . . . no, actually. It's from a Captain Ural Lavint."

Han grimaced. Jacen had, through circuitous means—via Winter Celchu, via Iella Antilles, all because he no longer had any direct communication access to his parents—recently sent word that this Lavint wanted to get in touch. Han had heard of her, a crusty old smuggler from the Corporate Sector, but had never met her. "Tell her I can't talk now."

"Oh, it's not live. It's recorded. I'm saving it both to the *Falcon*'s computer and to my own memory. I believe in redundancy."

"You don't say." Something belatedly occurred to Han. "Communicate with the personnel on the repair station and tell them to get out, to jump in the closest escape pod and get down to the planet's surface."

"Oh, I already did that, sir. Master Lando communicated those instructions to me through ship's intercom. By the way, you are down to seven pursuers. If I calculate it correctly, that's one damaged, two destroyed."

Han sent the *Falcon* into another series of jinking, juking moves. The hammering his rear shields was taking lessened, but he could see the protocol droid's head whipping back and forth on his metal neck.

"Sir, Master Lando requests a little more stability."

"Does he?"

"Well, that's what I interpret from the rather florid language he's employing. Six pursuers. Two damaged, two destroyed. I—I say! The rest are breaking off!"

Han glanced over at the sensor screen. C-3PO was right: the remaining half squadron of Howlrunners was disengaging, turning back toward the planet. "We're not their mission," he said. "But we ran when they appeared, and like neks, they chased us. Until their commander figured out we were a waste of time." He leveled off. "Leia! Come plot me a course. Let's get out of this system."

Leia's voice was artificially sweet. "Shall I bring you a bottle of ale, too? Maybe your slippers?"

Han grimaced. "Didn't mean it like that."

While they were in hyperspace, Han reviewed the message Lavint had sent him, then he put it on one of the large displays for everyone to see.

It seemed to have been recorded by the cheapest variety

of pocket holocam. The image of the woman's leathery face, when stretched to fill the large display, was heavily pixilated. "Greetings," she said. "I'm sending you this message to do you a big favor and hope you'll do me one in return."

"Smuggler economics," Leia whispered.

"I'm on the *Errant Venture* under my own name. There's someone else here, too. A Twi'lek by the name of Alema Rar."

Han glanced at Leia. Her face set into hard lines.

"I think she has plans for you, and I don't think they're nice ones. So I'm sending you this message. I'm betting that she'll kill me, too, when I'm of no more use to her. So I'm hoping you'll do her first. She says she's a Jedi, otherwise I'd try myself . . . but in my experience, it doesn't pay to try to knock off a Jedi.

"And I have a favor to ask. There are rumors that there's an important meeting planned of Confederation bigwigs. For personal reasons, I really need to get somebody there. I don't know what your affiliations are, and I don't care, but I don't plan to do anything to disrupt the meeting.

"You're one of the best-connected people in the galaxy. If you could let me know the where and when, I'd appreciate it.

"Please erase this message once you've reviewed it. A bunch of people would kill me if they knew I'd sent it."

The message ended, fading to black.

"Huh," Han said. He glanced at Leia. "What do you think?"

"Hard to tell with a low-resolution message," Leia said. "I'd need to speak to her in person to get a real sense of whether she's telling the truth. But her story makes sense. That would explain the presence I felt aboard *Errant Venture*. After our last talk with Luke, I've been wondering if it might have been Alema, or Lumiya."

Han nodded. "Let's go back to the *Errant Venture*."

Lando sounded hurt. "You're not asking *my* opinion?"

Han sighed. "Lando, should we go back to the galaxy's largest mobile gambling and shopping enterprise?"

"What kind of stupid question is that?"

chapter eighteen

ZIOST

Ben dreamed of red eyes springing across the fire he had built, and the dream was so powerful, so immediate, that he woke up out of it in midkick.

His foot connected with something muscular. His blow deflected it in the air, but Ben took enough of the force of the impact that he was rolled backward, away from his blanket.

Shaker was tweetling sounds of alarm. Ben could see the droid's lights, dim glows where the fire was dying—nothing else. There was darkness all around. He grabbed his lightsaber from his belt and activated it, casting a soft blue glow on his surroundings.

Kiara was still wrapped up in her blankets, just now coming awake, her eyes wide. Two meters beyond, between her and the nearest tree, a shape struggled back to its feet and whipped around to face Ben.

It was extremely broad in the chest, with four stubby legs that ended in three-toed feet. Its neck was protected by a bony plate or ridge that circled it like a collar, and its head was dominated by a long jaw filled with triangular, pointed teeth. It looked a lot like holos Ben had seen of neks, but there were no cybernetic enhancements to be seen, and this example was covered in short gray fur.

The fur did not make it look like a plush toy. It crouched and roared at Ben, a roar that echoed from several directions, outside the light cast by the lightsaber.

When it roared, Kiara turned involuntarily to look. The creature glanced over, and, instead of jumping for Ben, lunged at her.

Ben jolted forward, but his reflexes were dulled by sleep and exhaustion. He could not reach her in time.

Shaker's protruding arc-welder arm touched the nek's side. There was a flash of light and the beast howled. It twisted, biting Shaker, taking the droid's extended arm off with a snap of its jaws.

And then Ben reached it. With a hard downward stroke of his lightsaber, he cut through the nek's armor and into its neck. He only sliced halfway through, but that was enough to sever the spine. The beast collapsed, leaving others out there in the dark, close. He could hear them moving, hear their little growls and yips.

They were communicating.

Ben's initial flush of anger began to fade and he started to think.

He reached out through the Force, looking for his enemies. He found them, six in all, circling. He sensed that they were waiting for a moment's inattentiveness on his part, waiting for the lightsaber to go out. They understood that it could only bite them when they were close to him.

He offered them the Jacen Solo *you've-underestimated-me* grin. Left-handed, he drew Faskus's blaster. Aiming through the Force, he fired.

There was a howl of pain out in the darkness, and he could both hear and detect through the Force the wounded nek bounding away.

He chose another target, not bothering even to look in

that direction, and fired a second time. The result was the same: one animal wounded and fleeing.

The rest turned and faded away into the surrounding forest. Comparative silence fell on the camp; the only thing to be heard was the buzz of Ben's lightsaber. Now the cold began to eat into him again, and he shivered.

"Are they gone?" Kiara asked.

Ben holstered the blaster, drew his glow rod from his pouch, and switched it on and the lightsaber off at the same moment. "Yeah. But we're going to spend the rest of the night up in the tree, to be sure." He looked at Shaker. The droid had withdrawn its arm stump and shut the cover plate over it; the rest of the arc-welder arm lay on the snow. "Sorry about that, little guy," Ben said. "You did good."

Shaker gave him a pleased-sounding trill.

Minutes later, once he and Kiara were nestled together up in the tree—high enough, he hoped, that these neks could not reach them—Ben had time to think again.

He wouldn't have been so oblivious to the neks' arrival, but he had been deep in sleep. He was getting more tired every day, and not sleeping as lightly as he used to, as lightly as a Jedi or an Alliance Guard needed to.

And he'd been dreaming.

In the dream, the voices that pressed close all around had finally learned his name. "Ben, Ben, Ben, Ben," they had chanted, and it was so much harder to ignore his own name.

He couldn't, in fact, and once they knew he was listening to them, they learned to say other things. "Protect girl," they whispered. "Protect girl."

That seemed so strange, that in this place famous among the Jedi for evil deeds, the ghostly voices would offer such a positive message. Was it because they cared?

Or because they knew he would listen to a message like that?

On that thought, he fell asleep again, and the voices returned.

"Ben . . . Ben . . ."

CORUSCANT SYSTEM
ERRANT VENTURE

This time there was a kind of electricity to the conversation, as if everyone involved knew they were steps closer to their goal. The interesting thing, Wedge noted, was that there were so many goals, but everyone was making progress.

"So Lando and I have been cashing in old favors," Han was saying. "Sometimes *very* old. And it turns out Captain Lavint is right. There's a major Confederation gathering being put together. And it's not just to elect their warlord. News trickling out of that whole mess suggests they're assembling a fleet at the election spot, and from there the new warlord will lead some sort of fleet action. But no one knows where or against what."

"Shipyards." Wedge and Jag said the word at the same time, and looked at each other.

"Kuat, Coruscant," Wedge began.

"Sluis Van, Thyferra, any number of places. But shipyards," Jag said.

Zekk frowned. "How do you know?"

Wedge had noticed that Zekk frowned just about every time Jag spoke, and Jag frowned just about every time Zekk spoke. "The pattern of the last several days' worth of Confederation attacks and raids," Wedge said. "Mostly against orbital shipbuilding facilities. Their clear strategy is to diminish the Alliance's production and repair of warships. That way, despite the fact that the Confederation has fewer worlds than the Alliance by orders of magnitude, they'll come closer to parity in shipbuilding resources."

"Which sounds," Jag interrupted, "as though they have

a pretty clear military plan in place. I wonder why they need a supreme military commander if they're already cooperating so well."

"That cooperation won't last without a commander they all agree on," Leia said. "Now back to Alema?"

Wedge smiled. "Sorry."

Jaina turned her tabletop display so everyone could see it. On it was the triangular plan of one entire Star Destroyer's deck level. "We've added the last several days' worth of *Errant Venture* security recordings to our sample, and Booster authorized the ship's computers to give their analysis top priority. And gave us a more complete set of deck plans to compare them with. We can confirm a pattern of Alema's movements." She began tapping the screen, and each time she did so, a different level was displayed. "Here, for example. Casinos and shopping. Thin traces, widely spread. She was searching. And not finding anything."

She tapped again. "A few casinos where she spent a lot of time. I don't think she's a gambler or attempting to build a new social life. Lavint shows up a lot in the holocam views during Alema's presence, so it's likely she's keeping tabs on her partner."

Another tap, and plans for small passenger staterooms came up. There was a bright spot in one area, suggesting frequent travel by Alema, and movement trails leading off from it in all directions. "Lavint's compartment," Jaina said. "No surprise there. But here's one."

She switched the view to a diagram of ship's areas far away from the luxuries that the passengers enjoyed. "Just prior to the Bothan-Commenorian breaking of the Corellian blockade, she began venturing into the crew portions of the ship."

Mirax, silent until now, sprang up and moved to stand directly in front of the monitor. "Bridge, technical centers . . . my father's quarters. *My* quarters! She's been in my room?"

In his best CorSec investigator voice, Corran asked,

"Have you noticed anything suggesting that someone has been sampling your cosmetics, trying on your clothes?"

Mirax shot her husband an unamused look. "Other than you?"

"Ow." Corran raised his hands. "I give up."

"It's not funny, Corran." Mirax moved away from the display. She resumed her seat, clearly rattled.

Jaina caught Leia's eye. "Mom, you may have saved Booster's life by coming back when you did. When Alena stopped being able to sense you, she probably thought about getting to you through Dad, through the loose network of smugglers—and Booster's an obvious target."

"Well, let's make sure she doesn't get another crack at Booster," Leia said. "Or at any of us. We're going to hunt her down and eliminate her as a problem—the easy way, if she'll cooperate, or the hard way if she won't. And that means Jedi."

Han gave her an incredulous look. "I'm not going to stay while you—"

She shot him a look suggesting that this wasn't a matter for debate. "I think you'd better. Alema's a Jedi who thinks like an assassin. How much training have you done against a combination like that?"

"I don't need training, I have reflexes," he blustered.

Wedge touched his arm. "Actually, you and I can do them a lot more good by monitoring everything on the security holocams. We can anticipate traps and ambushes, warn them about confederates Alema has that we don't know about."

"Well . . ." Then Han heard what Jag was saying to Jaina: "—need about five minutes to get some equipment from my X-wing."

"Hey," Han said. "If I'm not going, he's not going."

Jag turned his attention to Han. His reply was calm, reasonable of tone. "I've been preparing for this for years. And it's my mission."

"Jag's right, Dad." Jaina moved up to Han, then leaned over and kissed his forehead. "Please."

Han uttered a little growl, then slumped, defeated.

Alema was thrilled. Only half an hour ago she had detected the Force presence—the one that said Leia was probably aboard again.

"You were right," she told Lavint. She donned her black hooded cloak and felt around with her one functioning hand to be sure that all her weapons and tools were readily available.

"I usually am," Lavint said. She got up from the bed, moved to the compartment's tiny closet, and selected a dress jacket that was all piratical purple synthsilk and big gold-toned buttons. "I think I'll get some gambling in while you're out killing people. Hey, the deal is still the deal, right? You set eyes on either of the Solos, and I've met the terms of our contract."

"Of course," Alema assured her.

The truth was more complex than that, naturally. If Alema set eyes on Han but failed to kill him, she might choose to kill Lavint to ensure that the captain would not be captured by the Solos. Lavint knew too much about Alema's movements. But if Han died, what Lavint knew would not be as critical, so she might let the captain live under those circumstances.

Surely Lavint *understood* that.

ZIOST

"Ben . . . save girl."

"Ben . . . protect girl."

"I have to get her offworld," Ben murmured in his sleep. "I need a ship."

"Ship!"

"Ben ship."

"Learn ship."

"Ben learn ship."

"I already know how to pilot a ship," Ben protested. He struggled against the hold sleep had on him, but something reminded him he mustn't move right now. If he moved, he would—what? Fall down.

"*Learn ship.*" The voice was unusually emphatic, and in Ben's mind a picture appeared—the image of a ball-shaped craft.

It was odd and organic, with a rough red surface texture. In the center of the sphere facing him was a transparent hatch or canopy.

Red spars stretched upward and downward from the craft. They seemed articulated, insectile. But this vehicle was no living thing, not like a Yuuzhan Vong craft; Ben sensed it was machinery, but machinery that was aware of him, waiting for him.

He woke up with sunlight, broken up by the branches above, streaming into his face, and he knew where the red ship was.

Or rather, he knew the direction to take to find it.

If it was real.

The TIE fighter did not find them at noon. That was because Ben snipped the long leg of the tracking device in his pouch, assuming that it was the unit's antenna. He must have been right. Starting an hour and a half beforehand and waiting until some time past noon, he, Kiara, and Shaker rested in a small ravine, a place where infrared traces would be harder to detect from any angle but straight up. He distantly felt the eye in the sky, but it did not come near him.

If he ever needed to, he could reattach the antenna.

That was one good result of the day. Other events were not so promising.

Their food was beginning to run short. They had two

cans of preserved rations, which would last as long as they chose to stretch them. Ben could happily have eaten both cans himself at a single sitting.

Water was in good supply. All they had to do was pack snow into Faskus's canteen and wear it against their bodies to melt—which was chilly and uncomfortable, but simple. Occasionally they wandered across a frozen stream; at those times, Ben used his lightsaber to cut through the ice and give them access to the water.

He wondered, though, about the snow and the water on this world. He'd now seen a few bird-like creatures—their wings were webbed rather than feathered—and they were often distorted, with one leg bigger than the other or possessing a misshapen beak. Was there something in the water causing high levels of mutation? For his sake and Kiara's, he hoped not.

Worst of all, he was sure that the neks were following them. They stayed out of sight, but he could sense them pacing him and Kiara to the right and left, following their trail.

He and Kiara were meat to the neks, he knew. He didn't much like being considered meat. He hoped he'd have enough strength to do something about it when the time came.

CORUSCANT SYSTEM
ERRANT VENTURE

In one of the ship's great lobbies, where lights were bright and visitors mingled well away from the expensive attractions of casinos and shops—but not far from the expensive attractions of several surrounding bars—Alema spent a few minutes in a data kiosk, downloading the last several lists of new arrivals.

Of course, not everyone who came to *Errant Venture* consented to be listed. But many did, so that an automated search code would detect their names and announce their arrival to friends.

She had scanned through several hundred names, recognizing none, when she felt a flicker in the Force.

Then it was more than a flicker. It was a light, a signal. She looked toward its source.

Entering the grand lobby was a human man—unusually tall, light-skinned, his long black hair tied back in a ponytail. He wore dressy civilian clothes—black slacks and boots, a dark blue tunic with yellow striping angled across the chest, a black vest and belt.

Alema knew him at once. He had once been a Joiner, had once belonged to a Killik nest. He was Zekk.

But his actions confused her. He moved slowly through the lobby, smiling and nodding at everyone he passed, speaking briefly to several, especially young females. As he passed, a few of them turned in his wake, moving to keep him in sight.

Alema thought she understood, but it made no more sense than before. Zekk was radiating vitality and power through the Force, in a fashion that would be appealing to just about everyone but the most Force-blind. And if there were any Force-sensitives in the crowd, they might be drawn especially strongly to him.

She gaped. He was using his Jedi abilities to *attract females.* It scarcely seemed possible. He had always been quiet and reserved—not to mention pathetically infatuated with Jaina Solo. Alema wondered what had caused the change.

She also wondered whether she should kill him. He had nothing to do with her current plans. But it was inevitable that when Alema killed Han, Jaina would vow vengeance—or at least seek it, pretending it was just a dispassionate desire for justice. And if Jaina came hunting, Zekk would come with her. If Alema eliminated him now, that was one less thing for her to worry about.

She, too, drifted toward Zekk.

She came to a stop twenty meters from him, fingering her blowgun and still undecided. Zekk and two new female friends had paused to watch a fire-breathing Devaronian juggler perform his act for the patrons in the lobby when she became aware of another presence, this one much closer.

She turned her head to see a thick-chested man with a trim, graying beard and startling green eyes. He stood two meters from her, staring at her, smiling. He wore Jedi robes.

"Horn," she said.

"I'll say this once," Corran said. "Give up now."

She raised her blowgun and fired.

Horn plucked the dart from the air. He opened a datapad, dropped the dart onto the screen, and snapped the device closed.

That gave Alema time to ignite her lightsaber. Corran drew and followed suit, his silver blade contrasting sharply with her blue-black blade.

Alema became aware of applause. Corran, too, glanced around, not moving his head.

Patrons of the *Errant Venture* were drawing back from their standoff, but not very far. Many were clapping. Some were putting down bets. Alema saw Corran silently offer a curse at their stupidity.

And now Zekk was moving toward the two of them, his lightsaber hilt in hand.

This was a trap, and Alema cursed her *own* stupidity.

And then she disarmed herself. She hurled her lightsaber high into the air, giving it a touch through the Force to direct its flight, to keep the blade ignited.

Corran and Zekk followed its progress in the second it took to reach the ceiling and shear through the struts holding a huge, elaborate chandelier in place. It dropped toward the crowd beneath, its glows starting to fade, to plunge the lobby into comparative darkness.

Alema turned and ran as fast as her crippled foot and damaged body could manage. She let her lightsaber turn itself off but continued to pull at it, and a moment later its hilt slapped into her outstretched hand.

She felt a massive surge in the Force behind her—Zekk reaching for the chandelier, checking its fall. She glanced over her shoulder, expecting to see Corran coming after her, but she was alone; he must have remained behind, yanking people to safety from beneath the falling fixture. She smiled. Her enemies weren't functioning as a team. Had they been, Corran would have attacked her while Zekk caught the light fixture. She had a chance after all.

Transparisteel shards from the damaged chandelier rained down on the crowd, and shrieks of surprise and pain joined the noisy confusion behind her. The last of the light died; now the lobby was lit only by glows from the surrounding bars. Alema reached the exit and whipped around the corner, pausing for a moment to retrieve her blowgun from under her left arm and reload it.

The broad corridor where she found herself was well lit, and the panic from inside the lobby had not yet infected the streams of pedestrian traffic here. So she was quick to notice the figure in the distance ahead of her, running toward her with unusual speed and purpose.

It was Leia. Leia Solo, looking straight at her. Alema could feel a flash of anger from her through the Force. It was echoed by a similar flash from behind, down the hallway in the other direction.

Alema grimaced. This wasn't right. Han should be here. Alema would kill Han, Leia would suffer, Alema would escape.

But now, with two Jedi behind her and one in either escape direction, Alema would have to be instantly, lethally efficient if she was to get away. Getting away was the most important thing at this moment. She would have to abandon justice in favor of practicality. She would have to kill Leia.

Alema raised her blowgun to her lips.

Leia raised one hand.

Alema felt the blowgun twitch—and the dart within it shot backward, straight into her mouth.

Alema froze there for one long, terrible moment.

But she wasn't dead. The poisoned tip had not come down on her tongue.

With infinite care, Alema turned her head to one side and spat the dart out.

Then, as cold fear clawed at her heart, she ran.

There were too many of them to deal with, and the suddenness of the trap they'd sprung unnerved her. She had to get to a safe place, to recover her bearings.

Fifty meters ahead of her, striding forward with confidence, radiating anger, came Jaina Solo.

Alema cried out, a wordless noise of frustration. She turned leftward, toward a bank of turbolifts, and the door into one opened. She ran through and it closed behind her.

A family of three Duros looked at her, their heads tilted at the same angle of curiosity. The child had a Kowakian monkey-lizard on its shoulder, and the appalling little creature pointed at Alema and cackled.

"Deck, please?" the lift's automated voice asked.

"Down," Alema hissed.

But nothing happened. A second passed, and the sense of menace surrounding Alema increased.

She knew what was happening. Her enemies were all around her, had seized control of the *Errant Venture,* could use even doors and turbolifts to harry and delay her.

She reactivated her lightsaber and plunged it into the floor. The Duros drew back, suddenly afraid.

She took only moments to cut a hole in the floor, then dropped through it into the turbolift shaft.

* * *

Minutes later, she was in a cargo hold, hurtling between tall, lashed-together stacks of plasteel containers, continuing to move as fast as she could, certain that the pursuing Jedi were just an instant behind her.

They had to be using the ship's holocam system. Alema didn't understand. She thought that her techniques would defeat it.

The enemy must have new techniques.

A door in the bulkhead ahead of her hissed open, and a man stepped through. He wore a full-coverage garment of glistening blue material and a helmet, narrower and closer than a pilot's. Its faceplate was transparent, and through it she recognized the features of Jagged Fel.

He extended an empty hand. "Alema, surrender. I guarantee—"

She raised her blowgun and shot him.

He pitched forward.

No—he knelt forward. He was drawing his holstered blaster before she'd realized he wasn't dead, wasn't dying. Armor, he had to be wearing armor.

He raised his blaster and shot her.

The blast struck her in the left shoulder, spinning her around, throwing her to the ground. Pain lanced through her—pain, and a realization that he'd broken her clavicle, that he'd further mutilated her.

She rolled to one side as he shot again. The blast missed her. She lashed out at him through the Force, sweeping him aside, hurling him deep into a mass of cargo crates. The wall of crates, held together by tough webbing, folded in on itself as if devouring Jag.

She got up and ran, staggering worse than ever, through the doorway by which Jag had entered.

"She's entering the bow hangar bay for long-term vehicle storage," Wedge said.

Han, sitting at another viewing station, nodded. He switched from the view of the storage bay to one of the hangar bay; they could both see Alema running, looking between vehicles as if seeking one in which she could escape. "She's not messing with the holocams anymore," he said. "I bet it costs too much energy or concentration."

Wedge focused on his own view, which showed the folded wall of crates into which Jag had disappeared. "Jag, do you read me?"

His response was a series of words Wedge didn't understand, but they sounded like they were designed to peel rust off durasteel.

"Sounds like Chiss," Han said. He activated his comlink again. "Target is now entering the hangar bay for stateroom patrons."

Leia was the first of the pursuers to reach the hangar bay used by the *Errant Venture* customers who had rented compartments for more than a day. The main doors in the floor were open, and a shabby YV-666 light freighter was sinking through them into space.

Alema Rar was in the cockpit. Leia exchanged looks promising mayhem or death with her for a second, and then the transport was out of sight. "Han, why didn't you seal those doors?"

Han's voice was anguished. "I tried. I *couldn't.* The GA military has a program override that prevents *Errant Venture* or other facilities from locking in military spacecraft. If there's one lousy Tee-sixteen skyhopper aboard that belongs to the armed forces, those doors stay open."

Leia could hear Wedge's voice in the background: "How did she slice the access codes to a transport so fast?"

"She stole my ship!" Lavint clamped her head between her hands as if trying to prevent an explosion. She spun around as if seeking some corner of her small stateroom where she could find refuge from the truth. "*My ship.*"

Han glanced at Leia and shrugged. "Actually, she's taking it better than I expected."

Leia awkwardly patted the captain's shoulder. "I know you must have loved your ship—"

Lavint was abruptly still. "Actually, I hated her. But she was still worth something." She shrugged. "Oh, well. I have another one coming."

"Speaking of what you have coming . . ." Han produced a data card and held it before her.

She reached for it, but he kept it out of her grasp, and now she eyed him suspiciously. "What is it?"

"The location of the Confederation meeting you told me about," Han said. "Place and time."

Lavint's eyes gleamed. "So give it over. I met the terms of our contract."

Leia shook her head, smiling with just a little bit of malice. "That was no contract. You made requests, remember?"

"True." Lavint didn't look too disappointed. "But you obtained and brought the information. So it must be on the table."

"It is," Han said. "But among other things, we want to know what it's for. It cost me a lot of favors to get."

"Oh." Lavint considered, and looked between them. "I'm going to give it to a man. For a ship, and to clear me out of his life. Out of his consideration."

"Is he likely to turn it over to the Galactic Alliance government?" Leia asked.

Lavint nodded instantly. "I'd put the likelihood at about one hundred percent."

Leia said, "I don't think we can—"

But Han handed Lavint the card.

Leia finished smoothly, "—protest too much, after all the

help you gave us." She shot Han a bewildered look. "Are we done here?"

"I think so." Han gave Lavint a professional, pleasant smile and led Leia to the door. "Try to stay out of trouble."

"Soon, soon," Lavint said. "Nice meeting you at last."

Out in the corridor Leia said, "All right, I'm completely confused. As much as you've supported the Corellian cause—"

"—why have I suddenly turned traitor?" Han finished. "Sweetheart, I didn't have as much trouble as I should have in getting that information. Which means one of two things. Either security's not what it should be for that meeting, meaning the Galactic Alliance will have it soon anyway, meaning all I've done is to give her a couple of days' head start in getting the information to them, or there's a lot of disinformation out there. Meaning that everybody who gets deep enough is getting a different wrong answer. If it's the first one, then Lavint gets her reward from her government contact. No loss to me or to Corellia. If it's the second one, Lavint and her government contact will wander into a trap, probably a Dur Gejjen trap set up for *us*."

Leia nodded. "You know, if you could apply that smuggler's brain to *real* politics, you'd be my equal."

"Meaning I wouldn't be able to just draw my blaster and fire at the politicians? What kind of a deal is that?"

chapter nineteen

ZIOST

This set of ruins was no heap of rubble.

Which was good, since Ben wasn't sure he could reach the next place on the map.

He had been three days without food, Kiara one. Shaker was down to draining energy from the various batteries Ben had brought from Faskus's camp; of them, he retained only a partial charge in the primary blaster pistol. The datapads didn't count—their batteries didn't contain enough energy to permit an R2 unit to walk four steps.

But this set of ruins—

It clustered high on a mountain ridge, built just below a cliffside hundreds of meters tall. The cliff looked like a portion of the mountain had been sliced away by a giant lightsaber millions of years in the past, leaving the stone to weather until some species decided to build a citadel here.

Not *some* species. The original Sith species.

The citadel was made of black and mottled gray stone and looked large enough to house a thousand people. But no one lived there now, Ben thought. Not that he could be sure. He detected little flickers of life through the Force, but those impressions were always washed away by the flow of dark side energy that emanated from the place. Like the planet itself, the citadel was suffused in such energy, but more so.

Still, the voices were pleased that he was here. He heard them even when he was awake now. And when he dreamed, they taught him how to fly the eye-shaped craft they had shown him.

Desire, focused the right way, would cause the craft to lift off, to fly. Anger would direct its weaponry—weapons he didn't understand and could not quite visualize. And he could reach out through it, make contact with his ships, direct them on their missions of—

"Ben . . . Ben . . ."

He was tired of the voices, and didn't know why they even bothered to speak his name, since they had his attention all the time now.

Then he realized it *wasn't* the voices. It was Kiara.

He looked down at her and frowned. "What?"

She took an involuntary step away. "You're that way again."

"What way?"

"Scary."

He considered his answer. *I have to be this way sometimes. It's how I'm learning.* He imagined Jacen saying it to him, back when he was just learning the ways of the Force, back when the Force had frightened him.

Wait a minute. How can she tell? And what is she feeling? He tried to clear his thoughts—something that he hadn't really been able to do well since he had gotten hungry and stayed that way.

Because she walked behind him, she had to be sensing something in the change of his body language—either that, or she was sensing something through the Force. Perhaps she was Force-sensitive.

And if that was the case, then she was probably being spooked by manifestations of the dark side. In him.

Again, he shoved away notions of dark side and light side. It was all in what one did with the power.

And yet, since he'd been here, he'd been surrounded by an insinuating malevolence that didn't come from anything alive. It was energy that had been shaped and left here by hundreds of generations of Sith and followers. And if the energy had definite shape, even when not being generated by the living, was that not the dark side?

He took a deep breath and tried to push the voices away, to cleanse his thoughts. Gradually he did so, and felt a lightening of spirit. Silence came to his ears, broken only by the occasional rustle of wind through the dead branches behind them, by Kiara's breathing, by the tiny whine of servos within Shaker.

Finally he looked at Kiara again. "Better?"

She nodded, pleased. "Better."

CORUSCANT
SENATE BUILDING,
ADMIRAL NIATHAL'S OFFICE

Niathal answered the beep with a gravelly command: "Come in."

Jacen Solo entered, dressed in his immaculate black Guard uniform and a flowing black cloak. He gave her a crisp salute. "Admiral."

Niathal returned it. "Sit. Hurry. I have a meeting in thirty minutes."

Jacen sat. "Gilatter."

"I don't understand."

"Probably because I hurried. Gilatter Eight is where the Confederation meeting is going to take place. The election of your counterpart, their supreme military commander. And the launch point of their next fleet action."

Niathal sat up straighter. "Intelligence has been working

on this all this time, and *you* come up with an answer first?"

"I have sources distinct from Intelligence's."

"Such as your parents?"

Niathal didn't miss the slight frown that crossed Jacen's features. "My parents had nothing to do with obtaining this information. It's from another smuggling resource I've been cultivating for months."

"Interesting. Especially in light of the fact that Intelligence has offered independent verification of the information about the election being followed by a raid. A shipyard raid."

Jacen nodded. "That's what my source says, too."

"Promising. When?"

"Two weeks. Actually, thirteen standard days, nearly exactly."

Niathal made an exasperated noise. "It will take that long at least to put together a coordinated response. We're going to rush into our counterplan and get good people killed as a consequence."

"If I may." Jacen drew a data card from a pocket and set it on the desk before Niathal. "I've taken the liberty of putting together a proposal. For a response you would probably consider uncoordinated. But it would get forces there fast and possibly undetected . . . and I doubt our equally uncoordinated enemy will anticipate it."

Niathal gave him a dubious look and inserted the card in her desk slot.

Jacen's plan was simple and unconventional.

Gilatter was an undistinguished Mid Rim star not far from Ansion. Not one of its worlds was habitable for most of the galaxy's sapient species.

The planet Gilatter VIII was a gas giant, a world whose surface was a beautiful, glowing swirl of mottled reds, oranges, and yellows. At one point in the distant past, it had been a favorite vacation spot for the Old Republic, circled by a ring of resort satellites, from which patrons could marvel at its natural beauty.

But tastes changed, and the brief era in which planetary artistic appreciation could serve as the be-all and end-all of a wealthy family's vacation ended—and with it the years of usefulness of the Gilatter system. The last resort satellite had gone out of business a century and a half ago, and Jacen's estimation was that the resort would probably be the site of the meeting to come.

Step One of his plan was to send Jedi-piloted StealthX snubfighters into the system, giving the Alliance military information about the Confederation forces already there—particularly sensor platforms.

Step Two involved bringing in forces selected from fleets and task forces already in that area of the galaxy, choosing them carefully to keep any one unit from losing too much strength, and defeating the ability of spies and analysts to determine where those reassigned craft were going.

Step Three had the Jedi observers directing Alliance forces into the system, avoiding sensor observation or scouting patrols, and setting them up *within the atmosphere* of Gilatter VIII. The glowing, radiant atmosphere was so thin at its upper reaches—barely denser than empty space in a standard solar system—that vehicles and vessels of all varieties could be stationed there. Such a world tended to emit higher levels of electromagnetic radiation, making communication between vehicles more difficult—but also making detection more difficult. Step Three would continue until the mission commander concluded that it was no longer possible to sneak forces into the atmosphere of Gilatter VIII—and even then, larger capital ships could muster at a point outside the system and be ready to jump in.

In Step Four, the StealthX observers would signal when the meeting had begun . . . and all the Alliance forces would move in against the Confederation forces.

Niathal and her analysts evaluated Jacen's plan and, over the span of a day, considered and discarded several others. Eventually they settled on Jacen's. It would have to be modified and detailed, but it would serve as a template.

At their next meeting, Niathal informed Jacen of her decision, and said, "I will lead this mission myself."

He nodded, apparently pleased. "I also want to be there."

"With the *Anakin Solo*?"

"Yes."

"Good. Consider it authorized."

"My opinion doesn't count much with my uncle these days," Jacen admitted. "To get Jedi involvement, you probably ought not to mention my role in this."

"I'll have Jedi involvement. All it takes is issuing an order."

Jacen smiled. "I meant, to get wholehearted Jedi involvement."

"Yes, of course."

As he emerged from the Senate Building, Jacen felt a familiar presence. He did not react visibly as the tall woman wrapped in anonymous garments, her lower face shrouded by a scarf, fell into step beside him. "How are you?" he asked.

"Well," Lumiya answered. "Fully healed."

"Interested in going on an expedition?"

"I sensed that you were moving into a troubled period. Into much danger. That's why I came."

"I'll take that as a yes." Jacen changed the subject. "Any news of Ben?"

"No. His monitors have temporarily lost track of him." A note of worry entered her voice. "He may not have survived."

"I think I would have felt it if he had died."

"Perhaps not, where he is."

Jacen didn't ask. "I have faith in him."

"Clearly so," she said.

ZIOST

The last kilometer of the climb up to the citadel was comparatively easy. The roadway, made of dressed black stone slabs that were cracked here and there but otherwise seemed little worn by the passage of time, wheels, or feet, allowed Shaker comparatively quick passage. But the little droid began to slow again two hundred meters from the tumble of rock that apparently marked the citadel's main entrance, and came to a complete stop a hundred meters from it.

Ben felt like stopping, too. He shook from cold and hunger. He returned slowly to Shaker's side, noting that the droid's lights were still functioning. He pulled out his datapad. "What's wrong, little guy?"

I LACK SUFFICIENT POWER TO MOVE FARTHER.

Ben thought about sighing but didn't want to expend the energy. Shaker was running on a charge absorbed from the last blaster's power pack. If Ben wanted to give the droid more time, he'd have to sacrifice the power pack from his lightsaber. "How long can you stay awake on the charge you have, if you don't move?"

PERHAPS TWELVE HOURS.

"All right. Shut down now. I'll wake you up when I've found a power source."

The droid gave an obliging beep sequence, and its lights went off.

Ben turned back toward Kiara, swaying from sudden dizziness—and the gray-furred nek leapt at him.

The rampway leading to the citadel was raised, and the creature must have been paralleling their path from just past the drop-off. Ben's reflexes, dulled by lack of food and sleep, would have let him down, would have allowed him to become the nek's next meal, but he wasn't standing in the open; he pushed away from Shaker, staggering back into Kiara and tripping over her, and the nek missed.

It landed gracefully and turned. Ben rose on shaky legs and ignited his lightsaber.

The nek regarded him, head down, obviously considering whether to attack, then charged away, disappearing over the far lip of the walkway.

"They're going to eat us," Kiara said.

Ben switched off his lightsaber. "No, they're not."

"I'm not scared anymore."

It was clear to him that she was. But he knew she had said it to reassure him that it wouldn't be so bad. That he wouldn't be failing her.

"If one swallows you, I'll jump down his throat and we'll cut our way out together," he promised her.

"What if it chews?"

This time he did sigh. "You're too logical."

It took them the better part of four hours to climb to the top of the rubble heap that blocked the main entrance into the citadel. From the top, Ben could see the trench-like gap between portions of outer wall that had not fallen and the high, more intact inner wall of the citadel itself. He could see gray-blue skies and whitecapped forests stretching to the horizon. It was all so beautiful that he wanted to stay forever.

And it occurred to him that if he killed and ate the little girl, he'd recover his strength swiftly. Maybe he'd even cook her first.

But she was looking at him when the thought came, and the way she slowly drew away from him reminded him that the thought was not his own. He forced it away and gave her a little smile, a genuine Ben smile.

The stone doors beyond the rock pile were down, and it took far less time to descend into the outermost great chamber of the citadel.

The only lights available to him were little streaks of sunlight entering by windows near the ceiling. They let him see that there were no furnishings left in this chamber—not even moldy, tattered remnants. It had been stripped of goods long ago. All that remained were entryways into black hallways and curved stone staircases going up or down.

He desperately wanted to descend. He knew the eyeball-shaped ship was somewhere below, hidden, waiting for him. Calling to him.

But he had no strength, and he knew that if he were to become the ship's master, he would have to conquer it.

"We'll camp here," he told Kiara.

She looked around dubiously, but said nothing.

Ben slept and dreamed that, in the darkest hour of the night, something detached itself from the ceiling far above.

It looked like three giant balls, the center one slightly larger and attached to the other two by pivots. A cluster of five legs emerged from each end ball, and they worked together to allow the thing to walk slowly down the wall.

In his dream, he said, "Go away."

no

this is my home now

your kind is gone

I shall eat you

"I'll kill you."

It paused halfway down the wall.

give me the little piece of meat

I will leave you alone

"I'll kill you."

It began its descent again.

"Outside," Ben said, "there are neks. Hunting me. I couldn't bring myself to eat the first one. Now I wish I had. But you can. Go outside and hunt the neks. They'll be close."

The thing stopped again and waited a full minute. Then it changed course, moving toward the top of the rock pile.

Rocks tumbled down the pile as it squeezed through the opening.

In his dream, Ben thought he heard neks howling.

"Eat girl."

"Grow strong."

The voices faded as Ben awoke. Hurriedly he glanced around.

Kiara, looking pale, her features sharpening from strain and starvation, was still asleep next to him.

The ceiling was better illuminated. Around its edges there were many odd shapes—curved balconies, broken statuary, other forms he couldn't identify. He wondered if any of them might become the thing he had seen in his dream.

He prodded Kiara awake. "Come on. We have work to do."

"Are we going to wake Shaker up?"

"I hope so."

As his last act of preparation, Ben reconnected the tracer's severed antenna-leg to its main body, then hung the pouch loop around the dummy he'd constructed.

It wasn't much of a dummy—just a carefully built pile of stone with red blankets draped around it. But perhaps it would do. It was situated at a spot where the outer walls still stood and the base of the inner wall was littered with stones that had fallen from the high reaches. The pouch hung from its neck.

Kiara following, Ben retreated past the shriveled, frozen nek body they had discovered upon emerging that morning. They found a spot concealed between two courses of dressed stone, and they waited. Ben was as alert as his starvation-induced lack of focus would allow him to be.

Time passed. In the stillness Ben began to hear the voices again.

"Eat girl."

"Grow strong."

"You used to want me to protect her."

Ben had thought his words inaudible, but Kiara spoke up. "Who are you talking to?"

"No one."

"Eat girl."

Why were the voices different now? That was a puzzle, and Jacen had always said that puzzles should always be solved, because then they became information that could be used.

He tried to look at the voices' suggestion rationally. It made sense on a purely logical level. If he killed, cooked, and ate Kiara, he would have several days' worth of food. His mind tried to veer away from that line of thought—cannibalism had almost always been discussed in his presence in cautionary tales of stranded crash survivors and people driven mad—but he forced himself to consider the matter.

"Eat girl."

"Grow strong."

If he did kill and eat her, he'd never be caught, never be punished. Even if he confessed to Jacen, his mentor would analyze the data and determine that it was the correct survival choice.

In fact, just about every logical argument Ben could come up with suggested that eating Kiara was the most appropriate action. The plan Ben had just set into motion might not work. It might take days to complete. He could be dead before then.

Every *logical* argument—

Ben frowned. But not all arguments had to be logical. Kiara was a little girl, and one who had just lost her father. Her daddy. Never mind that her daddy seemed to have been a small-time criminal and the odds, supported by files of data Ben had seen on the Guard computers, were that Kiara would grow up to be a small-time criminal or another type of drain on society. She *might* grow up to invent a medicine better than bacta, or to write songs or act in holodramas that made things better for people. Or she might have children who did these things, or teach children to do these things.

But not if she died now.

He wasn't even sure he liked her; they hadn't had energy enough to talk very often on their long walk. But he felt bad for her, he felt protective of her—

He *felt*.

And it seemed to him that neither thinking nor feeling needed to be the boss of the other. In a Jedi, they should be mixed, partners. He wondered if that was the case with Guards as well.

None of that answered the question of why the voices had started by suggesting that he protect Kiara and now insisted that he eat her. But the answer—a possible answer, anyway—came to him.

They had told him to protect her because that's what he had decided to do, and he hadn't known how. In suggesting that they could get Ben and Kiara off this planet alive, they had made Ben listen to them. He had begun to understand them . . . and then had begun to think the way they thought. And now they could suggest different things. They could suggest what they'd wanted all along.

He felt a burst of anger, but clamped down on it. He didn't have the energy to be angry right now.

He noticed that the voices had grown quiet.

And in that quietness, Ben told Kiara the story of a young Force-sensitive slave boy who won a Podrace on Tatooine and earned his freedom.

"Did they feed him when he won?" Kiara asked.

"All he could eat, and even more," Ben assured her.

Not long afterward, Ben sensed the eye in the sky. He looked up into the clouds and pulled his all-weather cloak even tighter around them.

"Is he there?"

"Yes, he is."

This pilot was not subtle. He sent the TIE fighter into a screaming dive that ended up with the vehicle a mere twenty meters above the ground. Then he had to slow and circle, because Ben's dummy was not visible from the open spaces around the citadel. He had to climb and then drop into the gap between outer and inner wall . . . and then he lined his lasers up on Ben's dummy.

Now. Through the Force, Ben exerted himself against the stones at the top of the inner wall, all along the course of wall above the starfighter.

It was hard going. He felt so tired, and it was almost impossible to focus. But an understanding that this might be the difference between life and death—from cold, or starvation, or mummification—drove him, and he saw the stones high above begin to rock and then fall free.

The TIE fighter fired, and Ben's dummy fell over, the blankets catching on fire.

The TIE fighter glided forward slowly on repulsors. Ben knew why. The bolt from a laser cannon hitting a human being wouldn't necessarily destroy his body completely, but it would turn so much of the body to steam that the victim would seem to explode. It wouldn't simply fall over. The pilot had to be curious about what had just happened.

The TIE fighter was a mere five meters from the burning dummy when the first stone, no larger than a human head, hit its hull. To his credit, the pilot reacted instantly, veering away and climbing—

Straight into the thickest portion of falling stone.

The rocks had fallen more than a hundred meters. Some weighed a quarter ton or more. All had sharp right-angled edges, and some of them hit edge-first.

The TIE fighter spun wildly out of control, hit the citadel's inner wall, and bounced off again. The twin ion engines were still firing, but the starfighter was spinning so fast that they merely added to the energy of its spiral.

It landed beyond the outer wall, its hull collapsing on impact, and continued to roll, shearing off its solar array wings as it did.

It rolled half a kilometer before coming to a stop against a natural rock abutment.

Ben rose and immediately felt light-headed, but drew on the Force to strengthen and stabilize himself. He helped Kiara up. "We have to hurry," he said. "More fighters may be coming."

Ben told Kiara to climb a tree while he examined the wreckage. When he saw what was left of the pilot, a pale-skinned Chev in a bronze uniform, he was glad he had.

It didn't take him long to pry open the hatch into the starfighter's small cargo bay. Its contents had broken free of the cloth webbing that had restrained them, but were otherwise intact: two days' worth of rations for a grown man, a medical kit, power packs, a long-range comlink, a self-inflating raft, water purification tablets . . . He took it all, and scavenged other goods from the Chev's body. Then, as fast as they could manage, he and Kiara ran from the site of the crash and back toward the dubious safety of the citadel.

It didn't occur to Ben to be sorry about the being whose life he had just taken.

CORUSCANT
ERRANT VENTURE

"Alema Rar just commed me."

Leia stared incredulously into her display. But Lavint seemed earnest enough. "What did she want?"

"You two, of course."

"And what did you tell her?"

"I said you were going to be at Gilatter Eight in a few days. The way I figure it, she'll go there and get herself blown to pieces. A shame about the why-vee six-six-six, I guess."

"Well, you didn't lie," Leia said. "That's exactly where we're going to be."

"We are?" said Han.

"You are?" On the display, Lavint's jaw skewed to one side, an exaggerated expression of dismay. "I'm sorry. I didn't know."

"Not to worry," Leia said. "I didn't decide until just now. It's not enough to be told that someone like Alema Rar has been blown to bits. I really need to see it myself."

"Or even pull the trigger," Han muttered.

GILATTER SYSTEM
RESORT STATION ORBITING GILATTER VIII

From the distance of several hundred kilometers, Luke watched the activity at the station. He employed passive sensors only, including a holocam utilizing high-grade visual amplification hardware, and knew that Mara, floating less than a hundred meters away in her own StealthX, was doing the same.

Half a dozen vehicles were docked at the station. The crews inside were presumably effecting repairs and making the antiquated station ready for the ceremony that would soon take place.

Luke, Mara, and their fellow pilots—including Corran, Kyp, Jaina, and Zekk, plus Jag, finally getting some shift time in Jaina's StealthX—had scouted out the system pretty thoroughly. There were indeed droid sensor satellites along the standard approaches into the system, but none situated elsewhere, and there were routes to which the sensor array was blind from outside the system to the far side of Gilatter VIII. The Jedi had already led several ships from the Ninth Fleet to orbits within the outer atmosphere of Gilatter VIII. Another vessel they had guided into place was Admiral Niathal's temporary flagship, the aged but still-mighty Mon Calamari cruiser *Galactic Voyager*.

Luke shook his head over that choice. Was Niathal simply making use of an available resource? Or, recalling that the *Voyager* had once been the flagship of Admiral Ackbar, was she trading on the revered strategist's name to promote herself? Luke didn't know.

But thinking about that was much better than wondering about Ben.

ZIOST

Ben and Kiara rested the remainder of the day, and from the top of the rock pile, just inside the citadel entrance, they watched the shuttle.

It descended from the clouds less than fifteen minutes after Ben, Kiara, and the revitalized Shaker reached the entrance. It was an old shuttle with fold-up wings and a bronze paint job, and it did not land. It circled the crash site endlessly, then took off for the skies once more.

Ben was curious about that. Were the crew members afraid to touch down on Ziost? That actually made sense.

Hungry as they were, Ben insisted that they eat no more than half the rations they had scavenged from the TIE fighter. The rest they could eat over the next three or four days. Perhaps by then they'd be able to find more food, or find their way offplanet.

They slept well that night, with Shaker keeping its sensors alert for nocturnal movement. But there was none.

In the morning, glow rods attached to new power packs, they went searching.

It didn't take long. All Ben had to do was open himself up to the voices. They led him down several levels, to where the corridor floors were coated in ancient muck, to a long side shaft that carried them well away from the citadel proper. It led them to an unlit circular chamber. Its walls were decorated with eighteen niches, each large enough to hold a life-sized statue of an average human, but all empty.

"It's gone," Kiara said.

Ben shook his head. The images in his head were clear. The ship was here. "Come out," he said.

He heard laughter.

Kiara seemed to sense it, too. She drew back to stand next to Shaker and stared all around, looking for the source.

Ben frowned. His instincts, and what the voices had whispered to him when he only half understood their words, told him that emotion was the key. Nor would kind, soft, welcoming emotion do.

He deepened his voice, put some anger into it. "Come out!"

Had he tried it the day before, when he'd been at his weakest from lack of food, he doubtless would have failed. But now there was a rumble in the ground, and a crack appeared in the half-dried muck of the floor—a crack as straight as a laser beam, bisecting the room.

Shaker, whose legs straddled the crack, gave a tweetle of alarm and quickly moved to one side. Kiara joined him.

The gap widened more quickly at the room's center than toward the edges. There it became circular, and up from it, inadequately illuminated by Ben's glow rod, came a segmented metal arm several meters long . . . and then the top portions of a vehicle's spherical main body. Its circular central viewport, lit from behind and glowing an unhealthy yellow, seemed to be an eye regarding them. The sphere was some ten meters in diameter, half of it protruding above floor level; a gap of three meters separated the edge of the floor from the nearest portion of vehicle hull.

Ben swayed, both from weakness and relief. The vehicle was here, it was real . . . and if the presence he felt within it, a malevolent set of emotions detectable through the Force, was any indication, it was functional, even after centuries in the ground.

"Open," he commanded.

After a moment, a vertical line appeared beneath the viewport and lowered as a hatch, its near end just reaching the edge of the floor.

Ben bounded across and up into the vehicle.

But if he'd anticipated finding a control couch, a pilot's yoke, hyperspace and weapons controls, he was disappointed. The interior, which could have occupied only a fraction of the vehicle's volume, was a single disk-shaped chamber, four meters across and two and a half high. The corridor channel leading to the ramp was the only exit. The walls looked like orange pumice, glowing as though they were thin sheets over molten lava, and the vehicle's interior was very warm.

When he got to the center of the disk-shaped chamber, Ben turned around and around, looking for the controls. But he found nothing.

And now even the voices were gone. In their place was a powerful expectation, a sense of waiting.

Ben closed his eyes and tried to get a sense of this place, this vehicle . . . and he did. For a moment he saw a red-skinned woman in robes of volcanic hues kneeling, her golden polearm on the floor beside her.

That was it, then. The pilot had to communicate with the vehicle through the Force. Quickly he knelt where the woman in his vision had been.

Command. The voice, male, rich in expectant malice, spoke directly into his mind.

Ben looked down the ramp and beckoned for Kiara and Shaker. "Time to go."

The little girl shook her head. The astromech tweetled at her.

"Kiara, we *have* to leave."

"I don't want to go in that thing," she wailed. "It's going to eat me."

Ben shot her a reassuring grin. "And if it does?"

She took a moment to answer. "You'll jump down its throat and we'll cut our way out together."

"That's right."

Still reluctant, she came forward, tentatively took her first step onto the ramp, and ran up into the room. She flopped down to sit beside him. A moment later, Shaker rolled into place on his other side and locked its wheels.

"Close," Ben commanded, and the ramp lifted.

Now was the part he wasn't sure of. "Launch," he said.

For long moments nothing happened, and Ben wondered how many words he would have to go through before he found the correct command. But apparently intent was enough—intent, and visualizing what he wanted to happen.

The light outside the vehicle brightened. Suddenly, blinding white, it reached all the way to the niches in the walls. Ben looked up, seeing only the ceiling above him. Then he closed his eyes again and attempted to see as the vehicle saw.

And he did. The ceiling above the vehicle had drawn aside in two pieces, and sunlight shone down into the chamber. The vehicle began to tremble like a wild animal preparing to spring.

"Get ready," Ben said, "I think it's going to—"

The vessel accelerated straight upward, its movement pressing Ben and Kiara down onto the floor.

chapter twenty

GILATTER SYSTEM
APPROACHING GILATTER VIII ORBIT

The greatest reward came from the greatest risks, Jacen had said, and Lumiya had agreed with him. "So long as you accurately assess the reward and the risks," she'd added.

And then she had volunteered to accompany him on this expedition to infiltrate the Confederation election ceremony.

Setting it up had been easy enough. It had been Galactic Alliance Intelligence that had discovered there would be representatives of the Hapes Consortium Heritage Council—the conspiracy that had collaborated with Corellia to kill Tenel Ka—at the meeting. And Admiral Niathal had been the first to propose that authenticated independence groups, even from worlds most devoted to the Galactic Alliance, might find admission.

It hadn't been too much work for Jacen to persuade Niathal that he be the Galactic Alliance agent assigned to attend the meeting—his status as the Jedi with the closest ties to the military ensured him that right. Manipulating things so that Lumiya could accompany him had been trickier, but she admitted to maintaining a number of fully detailed false identities that would withstand scrutiny from either side's intelligence division, and one of them, that of smuggler Silfinia Ell, had a registered world of birth that would fit the profile GA Intelligence needed. So Jacen had arranged for documents for himself and "Silfinia" from the Ession government, and now, his features heavily disguised under dark spray-on skin color and a beard, he carried an identicard showing him to be a member of Ession's most violent revolutionary party. Working through Captain Lavint and her mysterious contacts, he had been able to wrangle an admission to the ceremony . . . but not a vote.

That was fine. He wasn't there to vote. He was there to note faces, identify traitors, and distract everyone present—perhaps by killing them all—when the battle began.

And Lumiya was beside him, acting as backup in case of trouble. Her scarred features concealed under her expertly applied makeup, she now had dark skin and hair like his.

Jacen guided the ugly disk-shaped shuttle, of Corellian make, into the approach vector the stern voice on the comm board had assigned to him. "Quite a force," he said. Through the viewport and on the main sensor display, he could see Bothan Assault Cruisers, Corellian cruisers and frigates, an *Imperial*-class Star Destroyer, numerous other capital ships, and shuttles. There was a lot of shuttle traffic to the station, which resembled a dome-shaped manual fruit juicer resting on a plate—but a kilometer across.

"And it's ready for action," Lumiya said. "Can you feel it in the Force, the readiness of the crews and officers? They want blood. That suggests they'll be going after the closest of the likely targets."

"Coruscant herself. Though Kuat's not that much farther." The shuttle shook as if fired upon. "Hey." He'd had no advance warning through the Force of an imminent attack. "Tractor beam," he said.

"Their security people obviously like to be in complete control," Lumiya answered.

In minutes, the shuttle was drawn to an external docking station, and Lumiya was proved correct. When the station-side hatch opened, personnel in CorSec uniforms boarded, with their commander stating, "Give your vehicle access codes to Sergeant Mezer. He'll take your craft to the designated retrieval zone."

Her voice low and amused, Lumiya asked, "Will he expect a tip?"

The officer blinked. "Regulations of the meeting prohibit any vehicle from remaining within ten kilometers of the station," he answered, then he realized he hadn't addressed her question. "No tip is necessary. He couldn't accept one if you offered it."

"Pity." She swept out through the open hatch.

Jacen gave his code to the temporary pilot, then followed Lumiya. He found her being greeted by a white-furred Bothan of decidedly friendlier disposition than the CorSec agents. "Silfinia Ell," she said, as she allowed the Bothan to squeeze her hand. "Ession Freedom Front. And my nephew, Najack Ell."

The Bothan blinked, clearly never having heard of either the Front or the Ell family. "Delighted," he answered. He reluctantly shook Jacen's hand in turn. "Breyf T'dawlish. One of your hosts."

"When does the voting begin?" Jacen asked. "We haven't received a schedule of events."

"Very funny." The Bothan waved to the far door out of the antiseptically white and clean room they had entered. "This was once a decontamination chamber. It is, sadly, almost immune to decoration. But beyond that door you'll find far more congenial surroundings. Food, drink, good company. Like-minded company."

"I could use some of that," Jacen said, and heard Lumiya stifle a laugh.

* * *

From this shallow depth within the atmosphere of Gilatter VIII, the crews of the Alliance force had a decent view of the distant space station and the stars beyond. The atmosphere made the stars twinkle just a little and made their view slightly hazy; that was all.

"Tight-beam transmission from Stealth One," Niathal's aide told her on the bridge of the *Galactic Voyager.* "A Hutt light cruiser arriving. But that's the only capital ship in the last half hour. The rate of major arrivals has dropped nearly to zero."

Niathal, sitting in her multiply articulated swivel command chair, grimaced. The odds were now just the wrong side of even, which would be problematic in a straight-up fight. Fortunately, the Alliance had the advantage of surprise. "Very well," she said, her words merely acknowledging that she'd heard her aide's report. "Any major players still missing?"

"No, ma'am."

Niathal raised her voice so that it could be heard across the entire bridge. "Issue the order to the fleet. All ahead slow. The outlying vessels are not to jump until they receive a direct command."

Jacen and Lumiya separated once inside, the better to acquire information across a broader area.

The main chamber of the resort, the dome above recently cleaned to provide an unobstructed view of Gilatter VIII, was laid out with long tables full of food and drink. Delegates wandered from one to the next, or from one small standing group to the next. There was no urgency or animosity to be seen among them.

That was . . . curious. As critical as the election of a supreme war commander should be, Jacen had anticipated more anxiety.

And more notoriety among the attendees. So far, he hadn't recognized a single face.

Jacen accepted a drink from a server, a tall, fair-haired woman in a white gown that looked like it dated to the late Old Republic but was probably just an in-vogue dress on some backwater world. "So where's the coordinator?" he asked, making the question sound innocuous.

"I don't know, sir."

"Any idea when opening arguments are supposed to begin?"

The server reached up to tug at her earlobe, just a nervous gesture—except Jacen could feel the lie in the casual nature of her movement. "I don't know that, either. Perhaps they've broadcast the schedule to everyone's datapad?"

"What did you just do?" Jacen asked.

The woman's nervousness increased by a factor of ten or more. "I answered your ques—"

"No." He leaned in close, intimidating. "When you touched your ear. Tell me. Or I'll be forced to kill you."

She looked right and left as if seeking an avenue of escape . . . or an observer. "Please," she said, "we're supposed to. If anyone asks questions."

"You sent a signal."

"Yes."

Jacen wheeled and walked quickly back toward the door by which they'd entered the big chamber. Through the Force, he reached out to Lumiya, a warning.

"Gentlebeings!" The voice was so loud, broadcast from on high, that Jacen was compelled to look.

Toward the center of the great chamber, a hologram was forming. Six meters high, it showed a male human in a white admiral's uniform, the cut and styling more suited to the Palpatine-era Empire than to modern military forces. The man was trim, with high cheekbones and fair hair cut into a military style. A scar, livid even in the hologram, started on his upper left lip and crossed straight down to the lower lip. To Jacen, he looked rather a lot like General Tycho Celchu, but lacked that officer's warmth.

"If you'll turn your attention to the sky," the admiral continued, "you'll witness the forces of the Galactic Alliance emerging from the planet's atmosphere. This will be visible as a series of bright flashes as they begin to hit our mine grid. Closer to us, I'd like to introduce you to a distinguished visitor."

A spotlight from high above blared right into Jacen's eyes. He twisted away, knowing he was framed by its glow, and turned to glare at the hologram.

The hologram continued, "If our specialists are worth what we're paying them, you may raise a glass to Colonel Jacen Solo, Galactic Alliance Guard. Some of you Corellians may have lost relatives and friends to this man's many recent activities."

Jacen heard a murmur of anger from some in the crowd, but most reacted only with curiosity. A few moved away from him a few steps. Others sipped their drinks, unconcerned.

"We haven't been introduced," Jacen said, projecting his voice.

The giant hologram nodded. "General Turr Phennir. Supreme Commander of the Confederation military. At your service."

"I thought—"

"That today would be the day that office was elected." Phennir shook his head as if saddened by Jacen's credulity. "A deception I thought would be useful in drawing your forces in. And your presence here is another benefit, an unexpected one. I know you're going to attempt to fight your way out, but I must ask, please don't kill the delegates. They're only actors."

Behind Jacen came the sound of running feet—the security agents. They, he was sure, were real.

Yes, he'd fight his way out. But he had something to do

first. He gestured upward, toward Gilatter VIII, and put his whole heart into two thoughts: *It's a trap! Mines!*

"It's a trap," Luke shouted into his comlink. "He's visualizing mines. I say again, mines."

"Acknowledged, Stealth One," came the voice of the *Voyager*'s comm officer. "Be advised, with that transmission, your position is compromised."

"No kidding. Stealth One out." Luke switched his comm board over to squadron frequency.

"What now?" Mara asked.

"We go in," Luke said. He could hear the reluctance in his own voice. "And rescue Jacen."

Over the X-wing's intercom, R2-D2, directly behind Luke, offered a melancholy trill.

Every officer on the *Galactic Voyager* bridge waited for the order to come—the order to take a new heading, to circumnavigate the mine grid ahead of them.

That's not what they got. "Continue all ahead slow," Niathal ordered. "All forward gun positions of all lead vessels, open up in a sweep pattern directly forward. Second-tier capital ships and starfighters still in formation, drop in behind the capital ships. The order is given for *Anakin Solo* and all outlying vessels to jump."

There was the briefest delay, and then the bridge crew turned to its new tasks.

Galactic Voyager's commander, a Quarren named Squinn, edged toward Niathal. His face-tentacles were motionless with forced calm, but a question burned in his eyes.

Niathal answered it. She had to speak more loudly as *Voyager*'s weapons batteries began firing. "If we hadn't gotten Solo's warning, Captain, what would have happened?"

"We would have advanced into the minefield."

"Until?"

"Until our forward ships began hitting the mines."

"And then?"

Understanding dawned in the Quarren's expression. "We would have set a new course, a lateral course. Into more mines that have been maneuvered into place while we were waiting here."

Niathal nodded. "Mines we couldn't detect because of the thicker atmosphere around and below us. Mines that would continue to close on us. This way, we're going to be hammered, but with the fewest number of hammers they currently have to swing against us."

"Understood." Captain Squinn edged away again.

"It's a trap," Leia said. Though Jacen's Force-based warning had not been intended for her, she could not have missed it—not a panicky emotion from her own son.

She leaned forward in the copilot's seat of the *Falcon*, but the only thing visible from the Gilatter system was its yellow star, straight ahead, distant and tiny. "Han, did you hear me?"

"I did." Han's face was, for once, a mask of indecision.

"We have to go in and get him," she said. The words hurt. Her anger at Jacen's actions had not abated. She didn't trust him.

But he was her son. She had to save him.

"We're waiting for news about Alema," Han said. But there was pain in his voice, too. His protest sounded weak.

"Go, Han."

"Yeah." He hit the thrusters. The *Falcon* was already oriented straight toward Gilatter VIII. All they had to do was engage the hyperdrive.

Lando rose from the navigator's seat behind them. "Not that I'm part of this conversation, but I suspect I should operate one of the laser turrets. Right?" Receiving no answer, he sighed and headed back to the turret access tubes, his cloak swirling behind him.

The Turr Phennir hologram had appeared so close to Alema that she was, initially, partly within his right leg. She edged away, disappearing into the crowd.

Getting to this meeting had been easier for her than for any other infiltrator, she thought. After all, memories of her presence faded from the minds of those she encountered mere minutes after she departed. That, and her Jedi skills, made it child's play for her to bypass guards, eavesdrop on conversations, and never stain the memories of those whose resources they used.

Unless she wanted them to remember, like Captain Lavint.

Now she hoped she would not be noticed as she made her way from the main hall. She didn't think she would be. Jacen Solo was doing too good a job of attracting everyone's attention.

He stood alone, a semicircle of security guards from several different forces blocking his path, and as she watched they opened fire. He leapt above the torrent of blaster shots, igniting his lightsaber as he rose, and came down behind his enemies. He spun, and two of them were suddenly headless. The rest fell back from him, firing as they turned.

All Alema had to do was flee from this disaster, join the throngs of actors now moving in panicky retreat toward the shuttle access chambers—

Then she felt her quarry. Leia was nearby, sending reassurance through the Force.

To Jacen. It had to be to Jacen. That message certainly wasn't meant for *her.*

But now she couldn't leave. She had to wait to see if Han was with Leia.

Veering from her escape path, she made her way to a wall and merged with the shadows there.

ZIOST

Hirrtu, the Rodian, jabbered at Dyur aboard the *Boneyard Rendezvous,* this time clearly surprised.

"Launch condition?" Dyur brought up the sensor display.

It showed an incoming spacecraft, its point of origin just a few hundred meters from where the Chev, Ovvit, had died. "He found a way off," he said. "Smart kid. By the way . . . battle stations."

Everything was so alien. Through the vehicle's skin, Ben could see the ground and stars—he could even recognize some of the stars.

And he could see a blocky, awkward-looking freighter change its orbit to approach the point toward which he was rising.

His heart sank. He couldn't possibly win an engagement in a vehicle he barely knew how to fly, one with either no weapons systems or systems older than most modern planetary governments.

"What are my weapons?" he asked.

They appeared in his mind's eye. The arm at the vehicle's bottom could curl around into a landing base, or could stay extended and direct a laser attack. The arm atop the vehicle could line up on opponents and fire metal balls at them.

"Cannon." He all but spat the word out. "Physical cannon."

To his surprise, the vehicle responded with indignation to his words. His mental view zoomed in on the top-mounted weapon. He watched as a metal ball the size of his head rolled, propelled by magnetics, from a hopper into the base of the articulated arm.

And then it was gone, emerging from the far end of the

arm as a blur, with no sound of propellants accompanying the action.

He peered more closely and the sequence ran again, more slowly, in his mind. The ball was there . . . and the same magnetism that had rolled it into place accelerated it along the arm, building up speed with every centimeter it traveled until it left the end of the weapon.

Magnetic accelerator. Ben had heard of such a thing—a Verpine weapon, he thought, though that was a much smaller device. He'd never heard of one being built on a starfighter scale.

And maybe his enemies hadn't, either.

His mental query told him he had less than a minute until he was close enough for those enemies to fire reliably upon him. A minute to practice.

"Dodge," he said. And the vehicle began a forward-and-back, left-and-right shimmy that nearly hurled Ben from his kneeling position. Kiara slid around on the floor, rough as it was, until she grabbed one of Shaker's legs to stabilize herself.

It was frustrating not to have direct control of the vehicle, but also exhilarating just to issue orders and have them carried out.

"Ready top weapon," he said.

As if it were part of his body, he could feel a metal ball maneuvered into place at the base of the weapon. He could also sense a growing impatience within the vehicle. It occurred to him, whether the thought originated with him or his craft, that he didn't need to say things out loud.

The freighter opened fire. Ben could see flashes of light around him—then pain crackled across his shoulders as one of those shots connected with the vehicle's upper hull. The shock of it almost caused him to lose concentration, but anger was his friend, anger helped him keep his focus.

Fire top weapon. The ball left the weapon, hurtling

toward the freighter . . . and grazed its shields and hull, ricocheting harmlessly away.

Too late, Ben realized that the ball was still an extension of the vehicle, an extension of himself. Even now, he could steer it a little, deflect its course. But he instinctively knew that turning it around and sending it back against the freighter would take too much of his energy.

Ben's vehicle flashed past the freighter, and it turned to follow. It began turning well before they were past, in fact, keeping its bow and starboard side toward the Ziost vehicle, and Ben thought he saw something twisting and changing on the freighter's port side.

He sensed his vehicle's desire to fire with its bottom weapon, to splash laserfire across the enemy, but Ben was focused more on what he'd seen. *Turn around,* he thought. *Dive toward Ziost. Come around the other side of the freighter.*

His vehicle inverted with the speed and turning radius of a modern starfighter and angled down to come up on the freighter's port side. The enemy commander sensed his intent, tried to turn to keep his bow and starboard side facing him, but the Ziost craft's speed and maneuverability were too great. When the angle was right, he could see that a large panel on the port side was locked open, with another TIE fighter there, ready to launch.

Anger roared up inside Ben, anger remembered from being strafed, anger at what the other TIE had done to Kiara and her life—and a second ball left his top weapon before he realized he had launched it.

The freighter was rolling now, trying to bring its bottom hull into line to take or deflect the shot. But Ben applied himself through the Force and saw the ball change its arc, rising to avoid the freighter's bottom—all but ignoring the shields, hurtling straight into the open hold, angling toward the stern.

The ball emerged through the starboard side, carrying

with it a debris cloud that had once been atmosphere and thruster components.

The freighter's course and speed were unchecked. In punching through it, the ball had imparted little of its own kinetic energy to the target and seemed at first to have done no damage of consequence. But then the freighter rolled and began an immediate descent toward the atmosphere.

Now Ben let his craft open fire with the laser. Red beams jittered their way across the freighter's top hull, putting just enough energy through the shields to scorch the paint and sever a comm antenna.

Ben shook his head, ordering his craft to cease fire, and oriented himself toward space. He relaxed, sitting instead of kneeling.

"What happened?" Kiara asked.

"We won." Now all he had to do was find his way home—use a spacecraft that had no navigational computer, might not have a hyperdrive, to reach the nearest civilized star system, probably Almania again. Coruscant was too much to hope for . . .

In his mind's eye, Coruscant grew large, and he could simultaneously see it as a distant gleam in the sea of stars.

Can you take us there?

He knew the vehicle could.

Before we grow old and die?

The vehicle didn't have a precise understanding of human time, but Ben could feel that the trip would take hours or days, not lifetimes.

So he sent the command.

GILATTER SYSTEM
RESORT SATELLITE

In the shadow where she was hiding, Alema saw two figures force their way in through the streams of actors trying to escape.

They were Luke Skywalker and Mara Jade Skywalker, dressed in black jumpsuits with X-wing pilots' accoutrements, and Alema nearly passed out from happiness. Luke was here and would see Mara die, Leia was still coming . . . the universe was about to experience some much-needed Balance.

She stopped bouncing up and down long enough to find her comlink. She spoke into it: "Activate and execute approach two."

On the *Duracrud,* now floating with all the other arrival craft steered to the holding area by resort security personnel, the nav computer would be loading and implementing a set of simple maneuvers. The *Duracrud* would move to a position directly above the resort's dome, a few kilometers away, and then begin accelerating.

"What are you doing, dancer?" The voice was cold, amused, familiar, and it froze Alema's guts.

She tore her attention away from the fight, where Jacen was coping with an ever-growing number of security agents, and looked to the right. The dark-skinned woman who had addressed her did not look familiar . . . except for her build and her green eyes. "Lumiya," she said.

"I asked you a question."

Alema gave her a one-shouldered shrug. "We are here to kill Mara Jade Skywalker, who is here, and Han Solo, who is coming. And you?"

"I was about to dive in and help Jacen."

"Do not do that." Alema shook her head vehemently. "If you rescue him, Luke and Mara will leave, and Leia and Han will not come. They must be here."

Lumiya considered. "Then let's jump in together. Our being here will keep the Skywalkers and Solos from leaving. Don't you think?"

"We do."

Lumiya reached down and tore a long gap in her gown, freeing her legs to maneuver. She unwrapped the decorative scarf she wore as a belt, revealing the lightwhip beneath it, and rewrapped the scarf around her lower face and scalp, giving her the aspect of Lumiya so familiar to Alema and others. Then she drew her lightwhip. "Ready?"

Alema brought her lightsaber up. "We are."

She was happier than she had been in a long, long time.

Luke and Mara made their approach a merciful one. They landed in the midst of the thickest group of security officers. Luke's lightsaber flashed in a circle, severing five or six blaster barrels, and Mara gestured with the Force to sweep aside half a dozen agents.

Luke deflected a blaster shot from an opportunistic CorSec woman. "Let's go, Jacen. Your ride's waiting."

Jacen struck, cutting a Bothan shooter in two. "I don't need your help." Then he looked past Luke and his expression hardened still more. "Oh, no."

Luke glanced back that way. Han and Leia were entering the main hall at a dead run. "And your *other* ride is here."

Then he heard Mara's warning hiss—more through the Force than with his ears—and when he turned back again, Lumiya stood before him.

As Han and Leia approached, the nature of the battle before them changed in an instant. Abruptly Luke was drawing and igniting his second lightsaber, the half-length shoto, and using his primary lightsaber to deflect a weapon that looked oddly like Lumiya's lightwhip.

Han squinted. The wielder was Lumiya, though her skin was dark. He raised his blaster and fired, but Lumiya must have been aware of him; she simply twisted aside and the bolt caromed off the floor, then passed through the chest of the six-meter hologram of an admiral that dominated the center of the room.

Mara, nearly surrounded by security agents, was batting their blasterfire back at them with her own lightsaber. Leia angled away from her, toward Luke—and then let out a surprised cry as a low table slid into her path, too suddenly for her to vault or sidestep. She tripped but came up on her feet and lit her lightsaber.

She stopped abruptly and stared to the left. Han followed her gaze . . . to see Alema Rar emerging from wall-side shadows, an odd smile on her lips, her lit lightsaber in her hand.

"Mine," Leia said, and leapt forward.

Han ignored her. He fired at the Twi'lek, but Alema casually caught the bolt with her lightsaber, then began spinning her blade in a defensive pattern as Leia reached her.

"I guess this settles the question of whether you're dead or not," Luke said. He caught another crack of the lightwhip on his long blade, darted in close, slashed at Lumiya with the shoto. But with an exertion through the Force, she lifted a severed human head into the path of the blow, and Luke's attack sent the head spinning through the air. It landed on a table stacked with food.

"Of course," Lumiya said. "I thought you knew. I *am* dead. I have been for decades."

"Then lie down and let us throw dirt on top of you." With a similar telekinetic exertion, Luke whipped the tablecloth from beneath all the platters and hurled it at Lumiya. It swept upon her from behind, but she cracked her whip backward, cutting the tablecloth in two, then continued the maneuver into a forward stroke. Luke deflected separate lightwhip tendrils with his two blades.

"You really do hate me, don't you?" Lumiya asked.

"You've given me plenty of reasons to. But no. I don't reciprocate your hate." Luke leapt over another sweep of tendrils, coming down atop a chair and leaping free of it as Lumiya's follow-up attack disintegrated it. He landed lightly, poised.

"I don't hate." She lowered her whip. "I'm sorry you

think that of me. I haven't hated for . . . a very long time. Yes, I've tried to kill you—but that was professional. Not personal."

Luke held up his own weapon long enough to deflect a stray blaster bolt, a security agent attack that merely strayed too near him, then lowered the lightsaber, matching Lumiya's action. "You *don't* hate. Somehow I don't believe that."

"We belong to rival schools, Luke. That's all. Shall I prove it?"

"Sure."

Lumiya deactivated her lightwhip and wrapped it around her waist. She gestured, palms up. "Kill me now, if you want."

He took a step forward. "I don't want. But you're a never-ending threat to me and my family."

"Then take your shot. But first, for old times' sake, take my hand." She extended her right hand, palm still upward, a gesture of peace.

Luke gave her an exasperated look. "I can't believe you'd stoop to such a childish tactic."

"No tactic, Luke. Listen to my voice. Listen to my feelings. I'm not offering you poisoned fingers or Force lightning, just a touch." Her voice became more sad. "If I'd wanted to hurt you tonight, I would have killed your nephew instead of letting him flee."

"Flee?" Careful to keep Lumiya in his peripheral vision, Luke scanned the chamber.

Most of the actors had disappeared. Mara was dealing with an ever-decreasing number of security agents. Leia was backing Alema up across the main hall, with Han following, taking potshots to provide support to his wife. The giant hologram was gone, and so was Jacen.

He left us.

"And I could have attacked you just now."

Luke returned his attention to Lumiya. He felt no danger

through the Force, none at all. From her there was only peaceful intent.

He extinguished his lightsabers and hung them from his belt, then reached out with his left hand, his flesh hand. His fingers grazed hers, and then her hand closed on his.

And nothing happened.

"Sweetheart?"

"Busy." Leia swung an almost ceaseless flurry of blows at Alema, but the Twi'lek Jedi continued backing away, fighting a defensive action, never trying to attack. It was unlike her.

"Jacen's run off."

Han's words created a tight knot in Leia's chest. She had risked her life, and Han his, to save their son, and Jacen had just left them behind.

But she couldn't dwell on that. Alema was still a dangerous foe. Leia had to win here.

"Sweetheart."

"Now what?"

"Incoming."

Leia backflipped away from her enemy, and in mid-rotation saw that the view of Gilatter VIII was partially blocked—the same ship she'd seen Alema disappear in only days before was headed straight for them.

As she landed, she saw that Alema had switched off her lightsaber and was donning a close-fitting, flexible helmet with a transparent faceplate—an emergency decompression helmet. Alema smiled at her.

Luke felt the danger coming, but it was not coming from Lumiya. He turned away and looked up just in time to see the YV-666 contact the top of the dome.

The dome, ancient transparisteel, did not shatter. It caved in, crumpling like a thin-walled metal can. The great mass of the ship hurtled to crash into the floor of the main hall, and a ripple like a tidal wave coursed through the floor.

Luke leapt toward the exit. Mara was ahead of him. He saw the ripple effect from the impact bounce bodies up off the flooring, and the cargo ship, its speed hardly checked, continued plowing into the floor, punching a ragged hole through the axis of the space station. Beyond it, he thought he saw the relit tendrils of Lumiya's whip lashing—against what? An enemy? A wall, to provide her with an escape path? Suddenly the whip was obscured by an expanding cloud of debris kicked up by the YV-666's impact.

The station's atmosphere, with two huge holes to choose from, began fleeing into space, tugging at Luke as it went.

Of those fleeing toward the exit, Leia was in the rear, Han just ahead of her. The ripple shock from the floor impact behind them took Han off his feet; nimble and determined, he was up again before Leia even reached him.

Up, but moving slowly. Increasingly, to Leia's eyes, Han's feet seemed not to want to find purchase as he ran.

Nor did hers. It wasn't from the atmosphere escaping. The station's artificial gravity had to have experienced a complete failure. As her ears popped and pain grew in her head and eyes, Leia knew that there was no way they could reach the exit—

No way they *both* could reach it—

She reached out through the Force and shoved Han's back, propelling him forward through the door Luke and Mara had just reached.

Leia took three more steps. But now, though her legs kept thrashing, she could make no headway at all. Her feet lifted clear of the floor. She had no forward momentum, no way to reach safety.

She closed her eyes, determined to be peaceful in her last moments.

Something wrapped around her ankle.

She looked down. Attached to her leg was a line with a tiny hook and grapnel—Luke's piece of stupid, preposterous, farmboy equipment, which he'd carried off and on since before she'd met him. He was at the far end of the line, braced against the door, hauling with all his strength, and as Leia watched Han joined him.

In moments they had dragged her through the door and into the shuttle access bay where they'd arrived minutes before. Han sealed the door. Dimly, in the reduced atmospheric pressure, she could hear a warning siren wailing. Leia lay on the floor, panting. "Thanks," she said.

"What's family for?" Luke asked. "Hey, can Mara and I get a lift around to the other side of this station? Our StealthXs are over there."

GILATTER SYSTEM

In the shuttle he'd seized, Jacen hurtled toward the *Anakin Solo,* broadcasting his identity as he went, demanding updates on the battle.

He could see how it was progressing. The Confederation ships had been ready for the Alliance task force. But they hadn't been ready for the Alliance vessels to muscle their way through the mine grid, throwing off time estimates and ruining carefully planned flanking maneuvers. What had resulted was a slugging match, and to his eyes, things were even.

He needed more than his eyes. Even when he got data from the *Anakin Solo,* it was only as good as the ship's instruments could provide, as good as harried, overburdened officers could analyze.

He saw a Bothan Assault Cruiser lose power to its portside batteries. Instantaneous response on the part of the Alliance starfighter squadrons could have exploited the situation, which could have resulted in the cruiser's destruction. It didn't happen.

He saw starfighter squadrons circling, looking for an enemy, wasting precious minutes until the *Galactic Voyager* could direct them to a worthwhile target.

He saw an Alliance frigate yield the field because its commander obviously felt the vessel was crippled, unaware that its Corellian corvette counterpart was even more badly damaged.

He cursed and pounded on the arms of his pilot's seat.

Finally he found an opportunity to board *Anakin Solo.*

Not long after, Lumiya reached him on his private comlink channel, reporting that she, too, had seized a vehicle—someone's private transport, little more than an airspeeder fitted with improved engines and an atmospheric containment hull—and needed landing authorization for the *Anakin Solo*. Grudgingly—for he knew she would talk to him, and he didn't wish to talk to anyone—he provided her the code she needed.

In the final analysis, the Battle of Gilatter VIII was a draw, with both sides retiring the field after suffering moderate losses.

The Confederation trumpeted it as a clear victory for Turr Phennir, its coolheaded new Supreme Commander.

The Alliance noted the fact that, even with superior odds and the advantage of a treacherous ambush, the Confederation had accomplished nothing.

EN ROUTE TO CORUSCANT
GALACTIC VOYAGER

Luke lay on the small sofa in the cramped quarters he and Mara had been assigned, looking at the ceiling. It was a neutral light blue, featureless but for glow rod banks around the edges, and the peaceful color helped soothe his thoughts.

They needed soothing.

"You're very quiet," Mara said. She occupied the chamber's one chair.

"Still nothing new abut Ben." Luke offered a slight frown. "And Jacen's actions worry me."

"Running out on Han and Leia, you mean?"

He nodded.

"They should. I think he's getting even worse." Mara returned her attention to her datapad.

Ben's continued absence and Jacen's actions *did* weigh heavily on Luke, but lying to Mara added to the burden he felt, and he hoped she would not detect those lies through their Force bond. Luke didn't consider Jacen's actions to represent cowardice, but Jacen clearly considered the danger his parents experienced to be of less importance than his need to get to the major scene of the GA–Confederation battle. And that was a coldhearted choice for Jacen to have made.

But it was not what weighed on Luke's mind right now. Luke also had to ponder the meaning of Lumiya's words to him, the gentleness with which she'd reached out to him. She hadn't been hostile or vengeful. His instincts about people, his skill with sifting truth from lies through use of the Force told him so.

Then he felt something new. He sat up and Mara gave him a close look. "What?"

He smiled for the first time since they'd left the Gilatter system. "I can feel Ben," he said.

ANAKIN SOLO

Jacen sat in his private office. The glow rods were dimmed, and the only illumination came from the corkscrewing streaks of hyperspace light outside his viewport.

Whisper-quiet, the hidden panel in the corner of his office retracted and opened. Lumiya entered, her face devoid of makeup but wrapped against prying eyes.

"I can feel your anger all the way to my quarters," she said.

"Are you admonishing or approving?"

"I approve of the anger, of course. It strengthens you, and you need strength. But if I can feel it . . ."

"There are no other Jedi aboard *Anakin Solo.*"

"Prove it. And, while you're at it, prove that there are no nascent Jedi, no Force-sensitives of any sort."

Jacen sighed. He did not relinquish his anger, but he did concentrate on diminishing his own presence in the Force.

"Good." Lumiya approached and seated herself opposite him. "Jacen, this was not a disaster."

"I was made to look like an idiot. I planned the mission. I bought into the trap."

"As did everyone, including Admiral Niathal, the mission commander. When the full report of the battle reaches the holonews, it will be cast as a dramatic Galactic Alliance success—the forces of good beating back a treacherous ambush, all with negligible losses—and you will probably find your popularity has grown. As for blame behind the closed doors of government—your information was independently verified, wasn't it?"

"Yes. All right, then, I was made to *feel* like an idiot."

"Ah. There I cannot reassure you."

He shot her a glare but said nothing.

"Would you like to avoid this in the future? To be matchless, undefeatable in strategic engagements?"

"No one is undefeatable."

"Perhaps not . . . but the commander who knows exactly where all the battlefield's forces are, who does not need to depend solely on limited sensors and fallible analysts, will be defeated much less often."

"You're talking about battle meditation. You've mentioned it before."

"No. Battle meditation is something many very accomplished Force-users, Jedi and Sith, can do. Consider battle meditation to be the learner. The technique I'm talking about is the master. It is the capacity to sense, to coordinate, just by the power of the mind and the will. This is the ability that comes with the assumption of the title of Master of the Sith."

He continued to stare at her. "You aren't the Master. So you can't teach it to me."

"I'm not, but I can. A blind woman who was once sighted can still experience colors in her memory. I learned everything there was to learn about this power . . . I can just never wield it." Lumiya stared down at her limbs. Her expression did not suggest that she felt betrayed by them, by their robotic nature—only that they were a bit disappointing.

Jacen considered it. "Am I ready?"

"In all other ways, yes. But you have to make the sacrifice of love. And then you must take your Sith name, to reforge yourself."

"Who must I sacrifice?" The question put a chill through him. If she were to say, *The one you love most,* he would be unable to do it. He would never sacrifice Allana. He would never sacrifice Tenel Ka.

"One you love. One who will leave a void in your heart."

"Anyone?"

"Anyone."

Jacen stared off into the distance. "Then it will be my father. Or mother. Or both."

"Or perhaps not."

Jacen stared at her, curious. "Do you have a sudden affection for them I should know about?"

Lumiya laughed. "No. I have forgiven Leia for what she has done to me, and Han was never that much of a nuisance. But it may be that you can't sacrifice your parents."

"Why?"

"You must sacrifice one you love. Are you certain you still love them? Search your feelings."

Jacen thought, and then reluctantly abandoned thinking to open himself to his emotions. He let images of Han and Leia float in his mind's eye.

He saw them as they had been when he was a toddler, as a teenager, as a man. He saw them in the ever-changing light of his own experiences, as he came to realize that they could not be ordinary parents, as he discovered that they were willing to abandon him and his siblings to surrogate parents for weeks or months at a time, as he learned that they *had* to. He felt again the wash of pain that all those separations had caused, that all those reunions had never healed.

All he could feel was pain and anger—pain they had caused, anger he bore against them.

But had the anger replaced the love, or did anger simply mask it? As hard as he sought an answer, he could not find one.

Lumiya whispered in his ear. "You don't know because you have trained yourself to feel too little, to analyze too much. That is not the Sith way. You must do both."

Jacen shook his head. "Emotion weakens you."

"Yet anger, an emotion, gives you strength. Emotion doesn't weaken you, Jacen. It *scares* you. You specifically."

He stared at her, suddenly furious. "Nothing scares me."

He could not see her face beneath her scarf, but he knew that she was smiling.

"Liar," she said. Before he could formulate an answer, she rose and returned to the secret passage. "I was wrong," she said. "You're not quite ready. You don't know yourself as well as you must. Find yourself, Jacen. Then make your sacrifice and take your Sith name. I'll be waiting." She departed, and the door slid closed behind her.

Jacen stared after her, feeling ill—ill that he had a weakness, that Lumiya had detected it, that he was confused.

And now he could not even begin the process of choosing his sacrifice until he knew where his heart lay.

Until he knew whether he loved his parents.

In one way, though, both answers to that question were similar. If he loved them, he should sacrifice one—and kill the other, to prevent retaliation. If he did not love them, he should consider eliminating them and the potential trouble they represented. Either way, both he and the galaxy would be better off without them.

"Good-bye, Mom," he said. "Good-bye, Dad."

Read on for a sneak preview of Karen Traviss's

SACRIFICE

The fifth novel in
the epic new *Star Wars* series!

SITH MEDITATION SPHERE: HEADING, CORUSCANT—ESTIMATED.

It was *odd* having to trust a ship.

Ben Skywalker was alone in the vessel he'd found on Ziost, trusting it to understand that he wanted it to take him home. No navigation array, no controls, no pilot's seat . . . nothing. Through the bulkheads he could see stars as points of light, and that meant it wasn't traveling at hyperspace velocity. He'd stopped finding the ship's transparency unsettling. The hull was *there*. He could both see it and not see it. He felt he was in the heart of a hollowed red gem making its sedate way back to the Core.

There was no yoke or physical control panel. He had to *think* his commands. The strange ship, more like a ball of rough red stone than a vessel made in a shipyard, responded to the Force.

Can't you go faster? I'll be an old man by the time I get back.

The ship felt instantly annoyed. Ben listened. In his mind, the ship spoke in a male voice that had no sound or real form, but it spoke: and it wasn't amused by his impatience. It showed him streaked white lights streaming from a central point in a black void, a pilot's view of hyperspace.

"Okay, so you're going as fast as you can . . ." Ben felt the ship's brief satisfaction that its idiot pilot had understood. He wondered who'd made it. It was hard not to think of it as alive, like the Yuuzhan Vong ships, but he settled for seeing it as a droid, an artifact with a personality and—yes, emotions. Like Shaker.

Sorry, Shaker. Sorry to leave you to sort it all out.

The astromech droid would be fine. Ben had dropped him off on Drew wa. That was where Shaker, like Kiara, came from, and so they were both home now. Astromechs were good, reliable, sensible units, and Shaker would hand her over to someone to take care of her, poor kid.

Her dad's dead and her whole life's upended. They were just used to lure me Ziost so someone could try to kill me. Why? Have I made that many enemies already?

The ship felt irritated again, leaving Ben with the impression that he was being whiny, but he said nothing. Ben didn't enjoy having his thoughts examined. He made a conscious effort to control his wandering mind. The ship knew his will, spoken or unspoken, and he still wasn't sure what the consequences of that might be. Right then, it made him feel invaded, and the relief at finding the ancient ship and managing to escape Ziost in it had given way to worry, anger, and resentment.

And impatience. He had a comlink, but he didn't want to advertise his presence in case there were other ships pursuing him. He'd destroyed one. That didn't mean there weren't others.

The Amulet wasn't that important, so why am I a target now?

The ship wouldn't have gone any faster if he'd had a seat and a yoke to occupy himself, but he wouldn't have felt so lost. He could almost hear Jacen reminding him that physical activity was frequently displacement, and that Ben needed to develop better mental discipline to rise above fidgeting restlessness. An unquiet mind wasn't receptive, he said.

Ben straightened his legs to rub a sore knee, then settled again cross-legged to try meditating. It was going to be a long journey.

The bulkheads and deck were amber pumice. From time to time, the surfaces seemed to burn with a fire embedded in the material. Whoever had made it had had a thing about flames. Ben tried not to think *flame,* in case the ship interpreted it as a command.

But it wasn't that stupid. It could almost think for him.

He reached inside his tunic and felt the Amulet, the stupid worthless thing that didn't seem to be an instrument of great Sith power after all, just a fancy bauble that Kiara's dad had been sent to deliver. Now the man was dead, all because of Ben, and the worst thing was that Ben didn't know why.

I need to find Jacen.

Jacen wasn't stupid either, and it was hard to believe he'd been duped about the Amulet. Maybe it was part of some plan; if it was, Ben hoped it was worth Fastus's life and Kiara's misery.

That's my mission: put the Amulet of Kalara in Jacen's hands. Nothing more, nothing less.

Jacen could be anywhere now: in his offices on Coruscant, on the front line of some battle, hunting subversives. Maybe this weird Force-controlled ship could tap in and locate him. He'd be on the holonews. He always was: Colonel Jacen Solo, head of the Galactic Alliance Guard, all-round public hero holding back the threats of a galaxy. *Okay, I'm feeling sorry for myself. Stop it.* He couldn't land this ship on a Coruscant strip and stroll away from it as if it were just a TIE fighter he'd salvaged. People would ask awkward questions. He wasn't even sure what it was. And that meant it was one for Jacen to sort out.

"Okay," Ben said aloud. "Can you find Jacen Solo? Have you got a way of scanning comlinks? Can you find him in the Force?"

The ship suggested he ought to be able to do that himself. Ben concentrated on Jacen's face in his mind, and then tried to visualize the *Anakin Solo,* which was harder than he thought.

The sphere ship seemed to be ignoring him. He couldn't feel its voice; even when it wasn't addressing him or reacting to him, there was a faint background noise in his mind that gave him the feeling the vessel was humming to itself like someone occupied with a repetitive task.

"Can you do it?" *If it can't, I'll try to land inside the GAG compound and hope for the best.* "You don't want Galactic Alliance engineers crawling all over you with hydrospanners, I bet."

The ship told him to be patient, and that it had nothing a hydrospanner could grip anyway.

Ben occupied himself with trying to pinpoint Jacen before the ship could. But Jacen's trick of hiding in the Force had become permanent; Ben found he was impossible to track unless he wanted to be found, and right then there was nothing of him, not a whisper or an echo. Ben thought he might have more luck persuading the ship to seek holonews channels—or maybe it was so old that it didn't have the technology to find those frequencies.

Hey, come on. *If it managed to destroy a freighter on the power of my thoughts alone, it can find a holonews signal.*

Ah, said the ship.

Ben's mind was suffused with a real sense of discovery. The ship dropped out of hyperspace for a moment and seemed to cast around, and then it felt as if it had found something. The star field—still visible somehow even though the fiery rocky bulkheads were still there—skewed as the ship changed course and jumped back into hyperpsace. It radiated a sense of happy satisfaction, seeming almost . . . excited

"Found him?"

The ship said it had found what it was seeking. Ben decided not to engage it in a discussion on how it could find a shut-down Jacen hiding in the Force.

"Well, let me know when we get within ten thousand klicks," Ben said. "I can risk using the comlink then."

The ship didn't answer. It hummed happily to itself, silent but filling Ben's head with ancient harmonies of a kind he'd never imagined sounds could create.

COLONEL JACEN SOLO'S CABIN, STAR DESTROYER **ANAKIN SOLO**, EXTENDED COURSE, HEADING 000—CORUSCANT, VIA THE BOGDEN SECTOR.

None of the crew of the *Anakin Solo* seemed to find it odd that the ship was taking an extraordinarily circuitous course back to Coruscant.

Jacen sensed the general resigned patience. It was what they expected from the head of the Galactic Alliance Guard, and they asked no questions. He also sensed Ben Skywalker, and it was taking every scrap of his concentration to focus on his apprentice and locate him.

He's okay. I know it. But something didn't go as planned.

Jacen homed in on a point of blue light on the bridge repeater set in the bulkhead. He felt Ben at the back of his mind the way he might smell a familiar but elusive scent, the kind that was so distinctive as to be unmistakable. Unharmed, alive, well—but something wasn't *right*. The disturbance in the Force—a faint prickling sharpness at the back of his throat that he'd never felt before—made Jacen anxious; these days he didn't like what he didn't know. It was a stark contrast to the days when he had wandered the galaxy in search of the esoteric and the mysterious for the sake of new Force knowledge. Of late, he wanted certainty. He wanted order, and order of his own making.

I wasn't ridding the galaxy of chaos then. Times have changed. I'm responsible for worlds now, not just myself.

Ben's mission would have taken him . . . where, exactly? Ziost. Finding a fourteen-year-old boy—not even a ship, just a small scrap of humanity—in a broad corridor coiling around the Perlemian Trade Route was a tall order even with help from the Force.

He's got a secure comlink. But he won't use it. I taught him to keep transmissions to a minimum. But Ben, if you're in trouble, you have *to break silence.*

Jacen waited, staring through the shifting displays and readouts that mirrored those on the operations consoles at the heart of the ship. He'd started to lose the habit of waiting for the Force to reveal things to him. It was easy to do after taking so much into his own hands and forcing destiny in the last few months.

Somewhere in the *Anakin Solo,* he felt Lumiya as a swirling eddy eating away at a riverbank. He let go and magnified his presence in the Force.

Ben . . . I'm here, Ben . . .

The more Jacen relaxed and let the Force sweep him up—and it was now hard to let go and be swept, much harder than harnessing its power—the more he had a sense of Ben being *accompanied.* Then . . . *then* he had a sense of Ben seeking him out, groping to find him.

He has something with him. Can't be the Amulet, of course. He'll be angry I sent him on an exercise in the middle of a war. I'll have to explain that very, very carefully . . .

It had just been a feint to get him free of Luke and Mara for a while, to give him some space to be himself. Ben wasn't the Skywalkers' little boy any longer. He would take on Jacen's mantle one day, and that wasn't a task for an overprotected child who'd never been allowed to test himself far from the overwhelmingly long shadow of his Jedi Grand Master father.

You're a lot tougher than they think. Aren't you, Ben?

Jacen felt the faint echo of Ben turn back on him and become an insistent pressure at the back of his throat. He took a breath. Now they both knew they were looking for each other. He snapped out of his meditation and headed for the bridge.

"All stop." The bridge was in semidarkness, lit by the haze of soft green and blue light spilling from status displays that drained the color from the faces of the handpicked, totally loyal crew. Jacen walked up to the main viewport and stared out at the stars as if he might see something. "Hold this station. We're waiting for . . . a ship, I believe."

Lieutenant Tebut, current officer of the watch, glanced up from the console without actually raising her head. It gave her an air of disapproval, but it was purely a habit. "If you could narrow that down, sir . . . "

"I don't know what kind of ship," Jacen said, "but I'll know it when I see it."

"Right you are, sir."

They waited. Jacen was conscious of Ben, much more focused and intense now, a general mood of business-as-usual in the ship, and the undercurrent of Lumiya's restlessness. Closing his eyes, he felt Ben's presence more strongly than ever.

Tebut put her fingertip to her ear as if she'd heard something in her bead-size earpiece. "Unidentified vessel on intercept course. Range ten thousand kilometers off the port beam."

A pinpoint of yellow light moved against a constellation of colored markers on the holomonitor. The trace was small, perhaps the size of a starfighter; but it *was* a ship, closing in at speed.

"I don't know exactly what it is, sir." The officer, sounded nervous. Jacen was briefly troubled to think he now inspired fear for no apparent reason. "It doesn't match any heat signature or drive profile we have. No indication if it's armed. No transponder signal, either."

It was one small vessel, and this was a Star Destroyer. It was a curiosity rather than a threat. But Jacen took nothing for granted; there were always traps. This didn't feel like one, but he still couldn't identify that *otherness* that he sensed. "It's decelerating, sir."

"Let me know when you have a visual." Jacen could almost taste where it was and considered bringing the *Anakin Solo* about so he could watch the craft become a point of the reflected light of Bogden's star, then expand into a recognizable shape. But he didn't need to; the tracking screen gave him a better view. "Ready cannons and don't open fire except on my order."

In Jacen's throat, on a line level with the base of his skull, there was the faint tingling of someone's anxiety. Ben knew the *Anakin Solo* was getting a firing solution on him.

Easy, Ben . . .

"Contact in visual range, sir." Tebut sounded relieved. The screen refreshed, changing from a schematic to a real image that only she and Jacen could see. She tapped her finger on the transparisteel. "Good grief, is that Yuuzhan Vong?"

It was a disembodied eye with double—well, *wings* on each side. There was no other word to describe them. Membranes stretched between jointed fingers of vanes like webbing. The dull amber surface seemed covered in a tracery of veins. For a brief moment Jacen thought it was precisely that, an organic ship—a living vessel and ecosystem in its own right, the kind that only the hated Yuuzhan Vong invaders had created. But it was somehow too regular, too constructed. Clustered spires of spiked projections rose from the hull like a compass, giving it a stylized crosslike appearance.

Somewhere in his mind, Lumiya had become very alert and still.

"I knew the Vong well," said Jacen. "And that's not quite their style."

The audio link made a fizzing sound and then popped into life.

"This is Ben Skywalker. *Anakin Solo*, this is Ben Skywalker of the Galactic Alliance Guard. Hold your fire . . . please."

There was a collective sigh of amused relief on the bridge. Jacen thought that the fewer personnel who saw the ship—and the sooner it docked in the hangar to be hidden from curious eyes with sheeting—the better.

"You're alone, Skywalker?" Technically, Ben was a junior lieutenant, but *Skywalker* would do: *Ben* wouldn't, not now that he had the duties of a grown man. "No passengers?"

"Only the ship . . . sir."

"Permission to dock." Jacen glanced around at the bridge crew and nodded to Tebut. "Kill the visual feed. Treat this craft as classified. Nobody discusses it, nobody saw it, and we never took it onboard. Understood?"

"Yes, sir. I'll clear all personnel from hangar deck area six. Just routine safety procedure." Tebut was just like Captain Shevu and Corporal Lekauf: utterly reliable.

"Good thinking," Jacen said. "I'll see Skywalker safely docked. Give me access to the bay hatches."

Jacen made his way down to the deck, resisting the urge to break into a run as he took the shortest route through passages and down durasteel ladders into the lower section of the hull, well away from the busy starfighter hangars. Droids and crew going about their duty seemed surprised to see him. When he reached area six, the speckled void of space was visible through the gaping hatch that normally admitted supply shuttles; and the reflection he caught sight of in the transparisteel airlock barrier was that of a man slightly disheveled from anxious haste. He needed a haircut.

He could also sense Lumiya.

"So what brings you down here?" he asked, and deactivated the deck security holocam. "Hero's homecoming?"

She emerged from the shadow of an engineering access shaft, face half-veiled. Her eyes betrayed a little fatigue: the faintest of blue circles ringed them. The fight with Luke must have taken it out of her.

"The ship," she said. "Look."

A veined sphere ten meters across filled the aperture of the hatch, its winglike panels folded back. It hovered silently for a moment and then settled gently in the center of the deck. The hatch doors closed behind it. It was a few moments before the hangar repressurized and an opening appeared in the sphere's casing to eject a ramp.

"Ben did very well to pilot it," Lumiya said.

"He did well to locate me."

She melted back into the shadow, but Jacen knew she was still there watching as he walked up to the ramp. Ben emerged from the opening in grubby civilian clothing. He didn't look pleased with himself: if anything, he looked wary and sullen, as if expecting trouble. He also looked suddenly *older.*

Jacen reached out and squeezed his cousin's shoulder, feeling suppressed energy in him. "Well, you certainly know how to make an entrance, Ben. Where did you get this?"

"Hi Jacen." Ben reached into his tunic and when he withdrew his hand, a silver chain dangled from his fist: the Amulet of Kalara. It exuded dark energy almost like a pungent perfume that clung and wouldn't go away. "You asked me to get this, and I did."

Jacen held out his hand. Ben placed the gem-inlaid Amulet in his palm, coiling the chain on top of it. Physically, it felt quite ordinary, a heavy and rather vulgar piece of jewelry, but it gave him a feeling like a heavy weight passing through his body and settling in the pit of his stomach. He slipped it inside his jacket.

"You did well, Ben."

"I found it on Ziost, in case you want to know. And that's where I got the ship, too. Someone tried to kill me, and I grabbed the first thing I could to escape."

The attempt on Ben's life didn't hit Jacen as hard as the mention of Ziost—the Sith homeworld. Jacen hadn't bargained on that. Ben wasn't ready to hear the truth about the Sith or that he was apprenticed—informally or not—to the man destined to be the Master of the order. Jacen felt no reaction from Lumiya whatsoever, but she had to be hearing this. She was still lurking.

"It was a dangerous mission, but I knew you could handle it." *Lumiya, you arranged this. What's your game?* "Who tried to kill you?"

"A Bothan set me up." Ben said. "Dyur. He paid a courier to take the Amulet to Ziost, framed him as the thief, and the guy ended up dead. I got even with the Bothan, though—I blew up the ship that was targeting me. I hope it was Dyur's."

"How?"

Ben gestured over his shoulder with his thumb. "It's armed. It seems to have whatever weapons you want."

"Well done." Jacen got the feeling that Ben was suspicious of the whole galaxy right then. His blue eyes had a gray cast, as if someone had switched off the enthusiastic light in him. *That* was what made him look older; a brush with a hostile world, another step away from his previous protected existence—and an essential part of his training. "Ben, treat this as top secret. The ship is now classified, like your mission. Not a word to anyone."

"Like I was going to write to Mom and Dad about it . . . what I did on my vacation, by Ben Skywalker, aged fourteen and two weeks." *Ouch*. Ben was no longer gung-ho and blindly eager to please . . . but that was a good thing in a Sith apprentice. Jacen changed tack; birthdays had a way of making you take stock if you spent them somewhere unpleasant. "How did you fly this? I've never seen anything like it."

Ben shrugged and folded his arms tight across his chest, his back to the vessel, but he kept looking around as if to check it was still there. "You think what you want it to do, and it does it. You can even talk to it. But it hasn't got any proper controls." He glanced over his shoulder again. "It talks to you through your thoughts. And it doesn't have a high opinion of me."

A Sith ship. Ben had flown *a Sith ship* back from Ziost. Jacen resisted the temptation to go inside and examine it. "You need to get back home. I told your parents I didn't know where you were, and hinted they might have made you run off by being overprotective."

Ben looked a little sullen. "Thanks."

"It's true, though. You know it is." Jacen realized he hadn't said what really mattered. "You did exceptionally well, Ben. I'm proud of you."

He sensed a faint glow of satisfaction in Ben that died down as soon as it began. "I'll file a full report if you want."

"As soon as you can." Jacen steered him toward the hangar exit. "Probably better that you don't arrive home in this ship. We'll shuttle you to the nearest safe planet and you can get a more conventional ride on a passenger flight."

"I need some credits for the fare. I'm fed up stealing to get by."

"Of course." Ben had done the job, and proved he could survive on his wits. Jacen realized the art of building a man was to push him hard enough to toughen him without alienating him. It was a line he explored carefully. He fished in his pocket for a mix of denominations in untraceable credit tokens. "Here you go. Now get something to eat, too."

With one last look at the sphere ship, Ben gave Jacen a casual salute before striding off in the direction of the stores turbolift. Jacen waited. The ship *watched* him: he felt it, not alive, but aware. Eventually he heard soft footsteps on the deck behind him and the ship somehow seemed to ignore him and look elsewhere.

"A Sith meditation sphere," said Lumiya.

"An attack craft. A fighter."

"It's ancient, absolutely *ancient.*" She walked up to it and placed her hand on the hull. It seemed to have melted down into a near-hemisphere, the vanes and—Jacen assumed—systems masts on its keel tucked beneath it. Right then it reminded him of a pet crouching before its master, seeking approval. It actually seemed to glow like a fanned ember.

"What a magnificent piece of engineering." Lumiya's brow lifted and her eyes creased at the corners; Jacen guessed that she was smiling, surprised. "It says it's found me."

It was an unguarded comment—rare for Lumiya—and almost an admission. Ben had been attacked on a test that Lumiya had set up; the ship came from Ziost. Circumstantially, it wasn't looking good. "It was searching for *you*?"

She paused again, listening to a voice he couldn't hear. "It says that Ben needed to find you, and when it found you, it also recognized me as Sith and came to me for instructions."

"*How* did it find me? I can't be sensed in the Force if I don't want to be, and I didn't let myself be detected until—"

A pause. Lumiya's eyes were remarkably expressive. She seemed very touched by the ship's attention. Jacen imagined that nobody—nothing—had shown any interest in her well-being for a long, long time.

"It says you created a Force disturbance in the Gilatter system, and that a combination of your . . . *wake* and the fact you were looking for the . . . *red-headed child* . . . and the impression that the crew of your ship left in the Force made you trackable before you magnified your presence."

"My, it's got a lot to say for itself."

"You can have it if you wish."

"Quaint, but I'm not a collector." Jacen heard himself talking simply to fill the empty air, because his mind was racing. *I can be tracked. I can be tracked by the way those around me react, even though I'm concealed.* Yes, a "wake" was the precise word. "It seems made for you."

Lumiya took a little audible breath, and the silky dark blue fabric across her face sucked in for a moment to reveal the outline of her mouth.

"The woman who's more machine, and the machine that's more creature." She put one boot on the ramp. "Very well, I'll find a use for this. I'll take it off your hands, and nobody need ever see it."

These days Jacen was more interested by what Lumiya didn't say than what she did. There was no discussion of the test she'd set Ben and why it had taken him to Ziost and into a trap. He teetered on the edge of asking her outright, but he didn't think he could listen to either the truth or a lie; both would rankle. He turned to go. Inside a day, the *Anakin Solo* would be back on Coruscant and he would have both a war and a personal battle to fight.

"Ask me," she called to his retreating back. "You know you want to."

Jacen turned. "What, whether you intended Ben to be killed, or who I have to kill to achieve full Sith mastery?"

"I know the answer to one but not to the other."

Jacen decided there was a fine line between a realistically demanding test of Ben's combat skills and deliberately trying to kill him. He wasn't sure if Lumiya's answer would tell him what he needed to know anyway.

"There's another question," he said. "And that's how long I have before I face my own test."

The Sith sphere ticked and creaked, flexing the upper section of its webbed wings. Lumiya stood on the edge of the hatch and then looked around for a moment as if she was nervous about entering the hull.

"If I knew *when,* I might also know *who,*" she said. "But all I feel is *soon,* and *close.*" Something seemed to reassure her and she paused as if listening again. Perhaps the ship was offering its own opinion. "And you know that, too. Your impatience is burning you."

Of course it was: Jacen wanted an end to it all—to the fighting, the uncertainty, the chaos. The war beyond mirrored the struggle within.

Lumiya was telling the truth: *soon.*

AUDIOBOOKS THAT ARE OUT OF THIS WORLD!

Featuring original Star Wars® music and sound effects.

Get the thrill and excitement of the critically acclaimed *Star Wars* series – on audio! For *Star Wars* fans eager to hear more about their favorite characters and dig deeper into the compelling storylines, these audiobooks are a "must have." *Star Wars* audiobooks are a cinematic experience for your ears!

For information about *Star Wars* audiobooks or other audiobooks available from Random House, visit www.randomhouse.com/audio.

Please visit the official *Star Wars* website at www.starwars.com.